Advance Praise for *Gigi, Listening*

"One woman's misguided quest for love takes us on an adventure through the English countryside. With delightful characters and gorgeous scenery, it's a sweet romance you'll want to cozy up with. Completely charming!"
—Carley Fortune, *New York Times* bestselling author of *Every Summer After*

"A vacation in book form—and I loved every minute of it. From a charming and relatable protagonist to a quirky supporting cast (plus two male leads to swoon over), this is a story to fall for from one of my favorite writers."
—Marissa Stapley, *New York Times* bestselling author of *Lucky*

"The rom-com read I needed with just enough tingly love goose bumps to make me want to plan my next trip to England. A beautifully written story exploring love and a life filled with taking chances."
—Sonya Singh, bestselling author of *Sari Not Sari*

"For the hopeless romantics in all of us. Endearing, uplifting, and with a vivid cast, it serves as a beautiful reminder to embrace the unexpected. I didn't want this ride to end!"
—Amy Lea, author of *Set on You*

"Curl up with the heartfelt and funny *Gigi, Listening* and prepare to be charmed by its unforgettable cast of characters. Chantel Guertin's utterly delightful love story will make you want to book the next flight to London!"
—Liz Fenton and Lisa Ste̶̶̶̶̶̶̶̶̶̶̶ ̶̶̶̶̶̶̶of
Forever Hold You̶̶̶̶

ALSO BY CHANTEL GUERTIN

FOR ADULTS
Instamom
Stuck in Downward Dog
Love Struck

FOR TEENS
The Rule of Thirds
Depth of Field
Leading Lines
Golden Hour

Gigi, Listening

CHANTEL GUERTIN

KENSINGTON
PUBLISHING CORP.

www.kensingtonbooks.com

KENSINGTON BOOKS are published by

Kensington Publishing Corp.

119 West 40th Street

New York, NY 10018

All Kensington titles, imprints, and distributed lines are available at special quantity discounts for bulk purchases for sales promotion, premiums, fund-raising, educational, or institutional use.

This book is a work of fiction. Names, characters, businesses, organizations, places, events, and incidents either are the product of the author's imagination or are used fictitiously. Any resemblance to actual persons, living or dead, events, or locales is entirely coincidental.

To the extent that the image or images on the cover of this book depict a person or persons, such person or persons are merely models, and are not intended to portray any character or characters featured in the book.

Special book excerpts or customized printings can also be created to fit specific needs. For details, write or phone the office of the Kensington Sales Manager: Kensington Publishing Corp., 119 West 40th Street, New York, NY 10018. Attn. Sales Department. Phone: 1-800-221-2647.

The K with book logo Reg US Pat. & TM Off.

Published simultaneously in Canada by Doubleday Canada.

Maps courtesy of Emma Dolan.

ISBN: 978-1-4967-3538-6 (ebook)

ISBN: 978-1-4967-3537-9

First Kensington Trade Paperback Printing: April 2023

10 9 8 7 6 5 4 3 2 1

Printed in the United States of America

For Chris,
who proposed to me in England,
thus making it the most romantic country in the world.

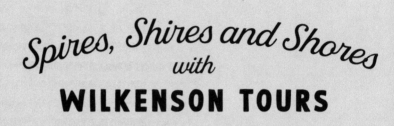

Spires, Shires and Shores
with
WILKENSON TOURS

Bristol

Bath

Glastonbury

Kingley
Vale

West Bay

Lyme
Regis

Isle of
Wight

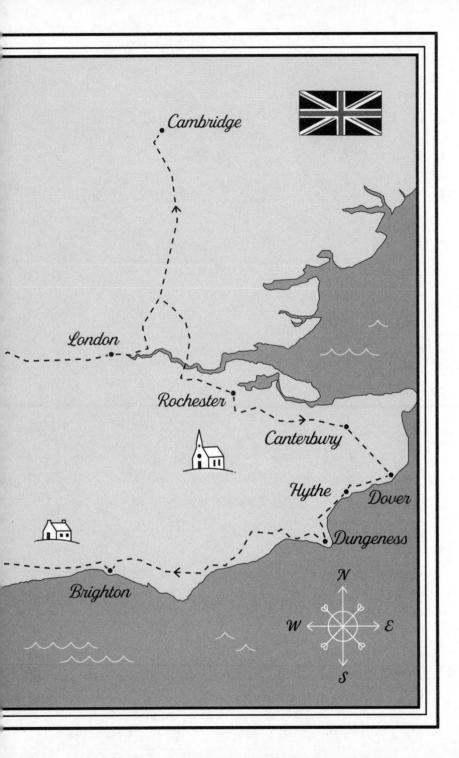

Chapter One

Ann Arbor, Michigan

I just want to read my book. But it's too dark in Knight's, the steakhouse on Liberty where I'm perched on a white pleather chair at a table by the window. Not even the glow of the lights on the marquee at the Michigan Theater across the street is bright enough to illuminate the space in front of me.

Plus, I'm on a date with Kevan. Ke-*van*. Rhymes with se-*dan*.

He's at the bar, checking the scores of the games currently showing on one of the flatscreens.

Maybe I could use the flashlight on my phone to read just a few lines of the Julia Quinn novel I started earlier today. The romance was just starting to heat up.

I reach into my black leather bag, slung over the seat, my fingers touching the soft paper as Kevan returns. As he slides into the seat, I drop the book.

"Tigers are up, Pistons are down. You wanna share the shrimp cocktail?"

"I'm good. I ate earlier."

"It's just a shrimp cocktail," he says. "They comp it for me. Part of being a member of the best customer club"—he thumbs to his black-and-white photo on the wall behind him, where dozens of other best customers are framed, including his father, who is also a prof at the University of Michigan. "There's calamari in it, too. You've gotta try it. Best thing on the menu." A guy at the bar cheers, his arms raised above his head, hands in fists, as he bounces up and down on his stool. Kevan lifts a finger to me. "BRB. Order the shrimp cocktail if the waitress comes by while I'm gone."

I'm going to kill Dory. It's the third time Kevan's gotten up to check the scores. If he can do that, why can't I pull my book out and read it? Because I promised Dory that I would give this date my best shot. Unlike the date with Roman a few weeks ago, and the guy before that. Aidan or maybe Adrian. The one with four cats.

Kevan returns—again—sits down and taps his fingers on the edge of the mahogany high-top, leaning back in his chair. "Do you wanna sit at the bar?" I say, because maybe if he's watching the game I could read my book and we'd both be happy?

But he shakes his head. "No way. This is a first date. I'm here to talk to you. Now, where were we? Oh, right, I was telling you about my band."

I don't think he ever mentioned a band, but I might have been daydreaming about being here with Zane instead. I look out the window. Across the street a lanky teen in baggy cargo pants has set up a metal ladder. Now, he's on the top step, holding a long pole with a metal claw on the end, changing the plastic rectangular letters on the sign that indicates the movies playing this weekend.

"We're called the Double As," Kevan says. "It works on a bunch of levels. All of us guys are profs in the Anatomy department, but also because we're here in Ann Arbor. We're playing at the Mash next week," he says. "You should come." He points a thin finger at me. "You could be my groupie."

"Sorry, I can't," I say.

"I didn't even tell you what day," he teases, the corner of his mouth turning up. He lifts his beer stein and clinks it against my half-full glass of wine, a move he's done every single time before taking a sip. I'm pretty sure there's beer in my sauvignon blanc.

I blink and try to be positive, like I promised Dory I'd be. Kevan isn't terrible looking. He has nice amber eyes and straight teeth and hydrated lips, though he also has a bit of a weird patch of hair under the bottom one that I didn't notice in his profile pic. And a row of earrings in his left ear, all amber studs—his mother's birthstone, he's told me.

As Kevan prattles on about something else, I go through what I'll tell Dory when she inevitably asks, with overwhelming optimism, how the date went.

I won't be going on a second date, I'll tell her. And she'll tell me to give her reasons why not. And I will. But the thing is, none of these little quirks are the dealbreakers. It has nothing to do with his earrings or the fact that he's a sports-score checker or in a band with other professors or is a little too enthusiastic about the shrimp cocktail at Knight's. It has nothing to do with Kevan at all, just like it had nothing to do with Roman or Aidan or Adrian or any other guy I've first-dated on the XO app. It has everything to do with the fact that Kevan is not Zane. Kevan and I will never have a romantic start to our story. That's the problem with dating apps, at least for me. The beginning is always the same: an algorithm. I want a *story*. If I can't have a story, I'd rather be reading my book.

•

Thankfully, a shrimp cocktail and a half hour later, we're out on the street, and since Kevan parked in the opposite direction to my apartment, I manage to convince him that I'd prefer the solo, seven-minute walk home.

The air is warm and smells like apricots, thanks to the tiny white flowers that blossom on the Osmanthus bushes under the canopied maples in Liberty Plaza. I turn up Washington, the mix of moon and sporadic streetlamp lighting my route back to Love Interest, my bookstore and my home. I unlock the shop's front door on Washington and pull it open, the bells clanging and the familiar smell of worn pages filling the air. I make my way down the Persian rug–covered hardwood floors that cough up a puff of dust with every step, tossing my purse on the scratched oak of the cash desk my grandfather built, where dozens of famous authors have etched their names over the fifty years the store's been around. I duck into the back storage closet to grab the broom, the metal cold in my warm hands. I pause. My black leather headphones sit on the shelf under the desk, beside a spray bottle I use to keep the air plants alive. I grab them and place the leather-cushioned cups over my ears. My phone is buried at the bottom of my purse and my fingers tingle with anticipation when they grasp it. The pad of my index finger flicks at the screen, and I hover over the title: *Their Finest Hour.* My heart swells, remembering the first time I saw the book appear in the audiobook app.

How I was reminded of my parents' own meet cute.

How I dismissed it, then finally listened to it.

How I heard Zane's voice for the very first time.

Now, I press Play. As Zane's voice fills my ears, reality slips away.

"Looks like a nor'easter's heading our way," Jack said, rubbing the stubble on his chin. Mirabelle looked over at him, wondering if he was speaking to her. Wondering if she should say something in return. She pulled her gauzy shawl tighter over her shoulders and looked out at the whitecaps in the darkening water.

Zane's smooth tone glides over every word, and I block out the story I know by heart and pretend he's talking to me, telling me about his day. While to any passerby on the street it might look like I'm just sweeping the floor, to me, Zane's here with me as I tidy up the shop.

Tonight, tidying the shop isn't the worst part of the day. It's the absolute best.

Zane's voice carries me through my chores. The floor goes from gritty to smooth. The bin of garbage under the cash desk, filled to the brim with paper coffee cups, plastic lids and cash register receipts, becomes empty. The worn rugs cough dust clouds onto the brick wall outside. The heavy wood counter goes from cluttered to neat. All of it happens as I'm alone with his voice.

An hour later, with Zane's voice still speaking to me through my headphones, I step outside, locking the door behind me before I nip around the corner to Fourth, to the first metal door. The stairs to my second-floor apartment creak underfoot, and the old oak door at the top catches, as it always does, on a raised floorboard. I give it a nudge and push it open to the room. The apartment is starting to show its aches and pains—many more than when Mom and Dad lived here with Lars and me. Dory's always suggesting I hire a handyman to fix the sticky lock, the dripping tap, the nail in the floorboard by my bed, which always snags my socks. What she really wants is for me to hire a handyman for more than his ability to fix my faucet—and then tell her all about it. "He might be cute, he might be single," she's said more than once, but let's be real: he's never going to end up being like Dominic, the handyman and single father that Emma falls in love with in Jane Green's *Falling*. They never are. And they're never going to have the same soulmate quality as Zane.

Turns out, it's not *that* hard to fix a leaking kitchen faucet, and doing so myself reminds me I don't need a man to complete me—even if it means the faucet ends up leaking again a few weeks later because I haven't actually fixed it properly. Dad always struggled with repairs, and Mom always put up with it because she knew it meant a lot to him to do it himself, too.

I kick off my soft blue leather flats, bend over and place them neatly on the small tasseled mat, then make my way through the apartment, passing the small room where years ago Lars and I used to sleep in bunk beds. It's now an office and a spot I go to on nights I can't sleep, to curl up on the blue velvet chaise lounge and read.

The back wall of the apartment is exposed brick, and overhead wooden beams span the entire width of the apartment, where I've attached so many twinkle lights I don't have to turn on any of the harsh overhead lighting. While the apartment was cramped for a family of four, it's plenty of space for just me.

The tile floor in the kitchen is cold on the soles of my bare feet. From the fridge I pull out a Tupperware of tomato soup and pour it into a pot. While I'm waiting for the soup to warm on the stove, I arrange a few crackers and cheese on a cutting board, then pour myself the remains of an open bottle of white wine. My headphones are still on and Zane is still whispering in my ear as I eat my dinner cross-legged on the mustard love seat in the living room. When I'm finished, I move the dishes to the sink, turn off the twinkly lights and make my way into my bedroom, where I change out of my long, flowy dress and pull on cotton shorts and a tank that takes a bit of maneuvering to slide over the headphones. I wash my face, brush my teeth, then crawl into bed. Under the heft of my duvet, I let myself sink into my mattress, realizing how many nights I've fallen asleep listening to Zane's voice. Tonight, the part *after* the date, was like any other day, but it's the kind of day I like best. I don't care that I ate the simplest meal at home, or that I spent a good part of the evening cleaning the shop, just like every other night. I'm happier doing this—any of this—than spending yet another night out on a dud date with someone who isn't going to turn out to be the one.

I close my eyes and, with no other distractions, reward myself with the pure joy that comes from listening to Zane read *Their Finest Hour.*

"What are you doing standing out there in the rain?" Mirabelle asked. She pushed open the screen door. Jack stood on the porch, his hair slick on his face.
"If you want to stand in the rain, you've got to be outside. It's not raining indoors," Jack said with a laugh.
Mirabelle gave a half smile, then turned away. A moment later, she turned back. "Well? Are you coming in or not?"
Jack reached forward to grab the door and followed her inside.

His voice is like poured chocolate, the kind you buy at a fancy shop, not Walgreens. In the funny passages, his voice belly-laughs. And in the sad parts, his voice hugs me. In the intimate parts, it's like he's right there beside me, whispering in my ear. I know he's just a voice, but whenever I hear his voice, I feel this connection to him. Like I already *know* him.

Listening to him read gives me all the feels. The way I first felt with David. When I couldn't wait to see him, and couldn't stop thinking about him when I wasn't with him. That's how I feel hearing Zane's voice. So much so that even when I'm on a date with one of the guys I've matched with on the XO app, I can't wait to get home to Zane. And it's not just his voice—it's everything that voice holds, everything it represents. It feels like more than just a coincidence that he's narrating the very book that brought my parents together.

I close my eyes.

Later that evening, by the snap and crackle of the dwindling fire, Jack wrapped his arms around Mirabelle as they lay on the couch. He smoothed her hair out of the way and nuzzled her neck. "Are you awake?" he said, but now, it's Zane whispering in my ear, to me, not Jack. I sigh and relax. My free hand touches my face, then slides down my neck, tracing the edge of my body to the top of my shorts. His breath is hot on my face, his whispers making my whole body tingle. My fingers slip under the elastic band of my shorts, dancing over my skin, warming it with every touch. My free hand reaches for the other pillow and I hug it into my body. My back arches. I moan softly, then cry out. Then sink into the mattress.

Eventually, I press Pause on my phone, then pull off my headphones, and toss both onto the rug beside my bed. The notched switch of the lamp is just barely in reach, and I twist it once, then roll onto my side, sighing with contentment.

I'm not delusional. I know Zane isn't my boyfriend—but when I'm lost in my own world with him, everything feels right. I wish I could find a real person who gives me the same feeling, but frankly, I don't think I ever will.

Chapter Two

Dory bursts through the bookshop doors on Thursday evening, a whoosh of color, chatter and infectious energy, just like she's been doing since we were kids. "Gigi, you wouldn't believe what just happened," she puffs, her arms laden with tote bags, a bunch of rose-gold helium-filled balloons tied to one of them. "Oh, wait, forget I said anything. Just pretend I'm not here!"

"You're early," I say, looking up at the clock on the wall behind the cash. It's quarter to six, and the romance book club doesn't meet until 7:15, once the shop has closed. And judging by the balloons, my best friend has other things planned.

"Don't ask questions," she says, and the curls touching her eyebrows float upward, then settle back on her dark skin again. "Just pretend you didn't see me. The side door was locked even though I specifically *unlocked* it earlier today so that I could sneak in that way." She scuttles past me toward the back of the store, under the glass atrium that juts into the sky, high enough to house the Millennium Falcon model that Lars built when he was a kid and a pair of sombreros my parents brought us back from a vacation in the Mayan Riviera. I've already set up chairs, with a copy of next month's book pick—*Rosh Hash-Anna*, a modern rom-com retelling of *Anna Karenina* set in an Orthodox Jewish community in New Jersey—on each of the five chairs. When the group first formed, we met once a month to discuss a romance novel. Now, we still discuss a book once a month, but we meet every week to chat about everything else.

"I was wondering why that door was unlocked!"

"Mystery solved, Finlay Donovan," she calls. "You're really *Killing It*." She disappears behind the bookshelf of LGBTQ2S+ romances.

"I told you I just wanted my birthday to be low-key," I say. "That's why we're still having book club."

"No comment!" she hollers from the back of the store. If she's got a plan, it's bound to be a late night, so I check the fridge to make sure there's plenty of chilled wine, then pull out the wine glasses from the low teak cabinet, as well as the box of chocolate chip cookies I picked up at the bakery down the street earlier today.

An hour later, the rest of the book club has arrived—also early—through the side door, which Dory has clearly unlocked again, failing to be quiet enough for me not to notice. At seven I flip the Open sign to Closed, cash out the till and turn off the front lights, before making my way down the dark aisle between the western romances to the long velvet curtains that separate the back room from the rest of the shop.

Years ago the cozy space used to be the children's section—back when the bookstore was a general interest one—where Mom used to host Saturday morning storytime. Now it acts as an event space for visiting romance novelists, as well as the gathering spot for the book club every Thursday night. I pause before the velvet drapes, listening to the not-so-hushed chatter of my best friends, and stifle a giggle. Even though I said I didn't want to make a big deal out of my thirtieth birthday, I'm secretly glad they planned something.

"Honey, I'm home," I call out, and the whispering decreases in volume and increases in urgency.

The drapes part and Dory appears, grinning. She's taken off her jean jacket and is wearing a gorgeous bright wrap dress that cuts into a V, revealing a silver necklace decorated with beautiful gemstones. She presses a champagne flute into one of my hands and a paper noisemaker into the other, and everyone else shouts Happy Birthday in a very *Something Borrowed* surprise-party moment. Like Rachel, the heroine of one of my favorite rom-coms, I'm not surprised, but I fake it just the same.

Beautiful floral buntings drape from wall to wall, tiny paper lanterns in various shades of blue hang from the ceiling, and in the corner, a white poster board is taped to the bookshelf and features a dozen pictures of me with my closest friends—the women in our romance-novel-loving book club.

"You guys," I say, wiping away a tear.

"Someone put the music on," Cleo says. At six-foot-one, she towers above everyone else, and we're all used to listening to her because we can't hide from her. Emily lifts the glass cover on the vintage record player, pops a record on and lowers the needle. Not surprisingly, Dolly Parton's *Jolene* album starts playing. Cleo and Jacynthe groan.

"What can I say? I love Dolly," Emily says. "You want to pick the music, you put the record on." She tucks her black bob behind her left ear. "Can we give her the gift?" Emily says.

"Already?" Dory says, looking around the room at the other three women. They're all nodding.

"You're going to love it," Emily says to me. "It's completely one of a kind."

"What she means is no one else would want this gift," Cleo laughs, taking long strides in her black Converse high-tops to pick up a tray of oysters from the top of a short bookshelf on the right side of the room. There's also a tray of sushi, a bowl of chips and guac, and a small cooler stocked with various drinks in cans and bottles.

"Here, everyone take an oyster and then let's just give her the gift," she says, holding out the dish.

"Are you ready?" Dory says excitedly. Her brown eyes are shining.

"I'm not sure whether to be excited or afraid," I say, taking an oyster and adding mignonette to it before popping it in my mouth. "But I'm loving that all of you did this for me."

Dory puts down her glass and claps her hands. "OK, who has Part One again?"

Jacynthe, my roommate from my first year in Kappa Kappa Gamma, who speaks fluent French and only wears black, pulls a slim envelope from between two books to her right, and then hands it to me.

I hand my glass to Dory, place the empty oyster shell back on the tray, then take the envelope, prepared to read a card filled with thoughtful sentiments from these women I love, the women I've spent every Thursday night with for the past several years. Sometimes it crosses my mind that the group means more to me than everyone else because I'm single. Jacynthe's divorced with a toddler, and Emily had a baby two months ago. Dory's been married for nearly a decade and has two kids, and Cleo's been with her girlfriend for several years, too. They're all busy with work and families. So it means even more that they planned this.

I slip a finger under the seal and open the envelope and pull out a homemade folded card, the creamy textured paper rough to the touch. The room is quiet except for Dolly quietly singing "When Someone Wants to Leave," and all eyes are on me. On the cover is an illustration of a woman sitting on a bus, looking out the window. She has long, wavy dark-brown hair like me, big sunglasses resting on her lightly freckled nose. Jacynthe's the artist of the group, and I suspect she drew it. "Is this me?" The skin around Jacynthe's eyes crinkles as she smiles and nods.

"Just open it," Dory says.

I do as I'm told, and read aloud:

You've listened for months. We can't let it be years.
If he's the one, it'll bring us to tears.
You have to find out, so don't make a fuss
Just pack your bags to get on the bus.

It feels like the temperature in the room's suddenly increased fifty degrees. The back of my neck starts to sweat and my heart pounds in my throat as I re-read the poem. Have my eyes betrayed me? When I get to the end, will I realize I completely misread the entire poem?

No one knows about the bus except Dory.

No one knows about Zane except Dory.

I take a deep breath and try to act cool. "Is this an XO singles bus tour?" I joke, staring at Dory. A few months ago I agreed to an XO singles boat tour, so I wouldn't put it past her to surprise me with a bus tour. Except . . . would she really do that when she knows all about *the* bus tour?

Dory waves a finger at me. "No, but a singles bus tour is a *great* idea. You're not *that* far off." A smile slowly spreads across her face.

My throat constricts. Talking is no longer possible.

"Who has Part Two?" Dory looks to Emily, who musses the roots of her black hair and pulls a slip of paper from the back pocket of her jeans. It's been folded in thirds, and as I unfold it, I can see that it's a confirmation email that's been sent to Dory.

The confirmation is in my name, for a ten-day bus tour, leaving next Saturday, from Victoria Coach Station. "We don't have a Victoria Coach Station," I say slowly, my heart pounding. But I know what city does.

London, England. The setting of some of my favorite romances: *Bridget Jones's Diary*, *One Day in December* and the *Bridgerton* series.

More importantly, I know which tour company departs from this bus station: Wilkenson Tours.

.

For a long time after first listening to Zane read *Their Finest Hour*—OK, six days, total—I resisted looking him up online. If he turned out to be ninety years old or worse—dead—what would that say about my intuition?

Then I broke the seal. After I'd binged all twelve hours of the book—twice. After another doomed XO date where I put in zero effort. After a few too many glasses of wine. After doom-scrolling through David's photos on Instagram of him and the woman who appeared in the last seven of nine pics. After all of that, I typed Zane's name into the Instagram search bar.

It turned out, based on Zane's Instagram account (updated three days earlier), that he was neither ninety nor dead. And that sexy, gravelly voice that wrapped every word in an embrace was attached to quite possibly one of the most good-looking men I'd ever set eyes upon: shiny, perfectly styled hair—short on the sides, just slightly longer on top—clean-shaven, impeccable skin, broad shoulders; green, almond-shaped eyes; thick lashes; good teeth; full lips . . .

Not that looks matter. But of course they do. It's the whole reason nobody wanted to marry poor Mr. Collins in *Pride and Prejudice*. Or Albion Finch in the *Bridgerton* books.

Still, what really made my heart feel like it was filling my entire chest was discovering Zane's story. His bio linked to the Wilkenson Tours website, and when I clicked over there, I discovered that his job wasn't reading audiobooks at all. In fact, *Their Finest Hour* was the only audiobook he'd ever narrated, which made the whole coincidence even more incredible because what were the odds that the one book he'd narrated was *the* book that brought my parents together?

Zane's real story was published in fine detail on the About page of his parents' British tour company website: years ago, when his father, Graham, was just a teenager, he booked a seat on a bus tour to get himself from Cornwall to Manchester because it was cheaper than booking a train ticket. Zane's mother, Anne, was the tour guide on that bus, working for the summer between years at university because her parents owned the tour company. A few days later they were in love. A few months after that Graham started working at the tour company, too. And a few years after that they were married, they bought the company from Anne's parents, who were looking to retire, and renamed it Wilkenson Tours. A year later, Zane was born. He grew up on the tour buses and now, having worked alongside his parents for years, he's pretty much taken over the business himself.

I read all this sitting on the edge of my yellow sofa, light-headed.

Swap buses for books and Zane's origin story is almost identical to mine; his parents' love story is really similar to my parents' own. There has to be something to that. But, now that I know who Zane really is, and now that I know his story, anyone else I meet, by coincidence or on dating apps, doesn't even come close to him. He's like finding a first edition among a stack of mass-market paperbacks—and he happens to live 3,777 miles away from me. And even though, more than once while listening to him read, I'd pictured myself in England, with him, I never indulged the thought of making a concrete plan to meet him.

And now . . .

My ears are ringing and there are black spots in front of my eyes. *I'm actually going to meet Zane.*

I reach behind me to grab the closest chair and plunk myself in it.

"Are you OK?" Emily rushes over and lowers herself beside me. I nod.

"I think it's safe to say she's figured it out," Cleo laughs. "Are you surprised?"

"I thought you'd get me a pair of earrings or something," I say as I try processing what's happening. I can feel my heart beating in my ears.

"It's your *thirtieth*," Dory says. "Anthropologie was not going to cut it."

I'm going to be on a bus with Zane. I picture myself sitting beside him on the bus, our legs touching, sending electric shocks through my core.

"The look on your face is priceless," Dory says, pulling out her phone. "I wish I'd videoed it."

"She doesn't even have the itinerary yet," Cleo says, leaning over. "Where's the itinerary, Dory?"

"Who was on the itinerary? That was Part Three, right?"

"You!" Cleo laughs. Dory nods and holds up a finger.

"Right." She looks around, then walks over to her red leather bag and pulls out a red folder thick with papers.

I take the folder, juggling it with the other papers in my hands and open the top flap and read:

Spires, Shires and Shores
Sit back, relax, and come along for ten unforgettable days in
the most charming country in the world. Visit some of the old-
est churches in England, step back in time while taking in the
sights in storybook towns and feel the wind on your face as you
look out into the English Channel. Our cozy luxury coaches
offer a maximum of ten guests the benefits of group travel with-
out the crowds. Overnight accommodations in first-class hotels,
all-inclusive meals and the opportunity to experience a holiday
you'll remember forever.
Your host: Zane Wilkenson

I mouth his name, and the familiarity of his voice, of Zane saying his own name at the start of *Their Finest Hour*, fills my ears: "Read by Zane Wilkenson."

It's like all the air's been sucked out of the room. The words in front of me blur as I blink away tears.

This isn't the first time I've read this itinerary. And it definitely isn't the first time I've fantasized about going on this trip—even if there *are* churches involved. I take a deep breath as that familiar feeling of anxiety creeps into my chest.

"So?" Dory says, grinning. I refocus on the present.

The papers drop to the floor, and I hold out my arms and instantly, my best friends throw their arms around me and each other, champagne flutes clinking, our heads close together, all of us laughing and hugging and sharing what feels like the best moment of my life.

When we untangle ourselves, Jacynthe smiles at me. "I hope you're not mad that Dory told us about Zane," she says, twisting her caramel-colored hair up onto the top of her head and securing it with a chopstick from the platter of sushi.

I shake my head and laugh. "You guys, how could I be mad? Embarrassed, maybe, that you all know I have a crush on a guy I've never met, but mad? Nope." My long hair swings in my face as I shake my head. "But I can't believe *you* did this, Dor." I lock eyes with Dory. "You don't believe in soulmates."

She shrugs. "So? It's not my story, it's yours. Plus, when I told the girls the whole story, there was no way they were letting us *not* get you this gift."

"I can't believe you didn't tell us *that* was the reason you've been going on and on about that audiobook," Emily says, her blue eyes wide as she sits down in the chair closest to me. She crosses her legs, the rip in the knee of her jeans spreading to reveal her brown skin. "It's *so* romantic. And we want the full story— from you. So your mom *heard* your dad reading the same book?"

I nod. Even though the girls know I inherited the shop from my parents, that they met here, I've never told them the full, *full* story.

"I know it sounds odd—who reads a book aloud in a bookstore, right? But my dad was always a read-aloud kind of guy. He thought you heard stories in a different way when you read them aloud." I laugh. "I remember back when I was just learning to read and my parents would insist that we sit around reading after dinner. Lars and my dad would get in fights because Lars couldn't focus with my dad reading his own book out loud. But I think it's what's trained me to be able to read no matter what. Now nothing distracts me."

"OK, OK," Emily interjects, waving a hand around. "But tell us about how they met."

"Right. So my mom's working at the shop, she was twenty-one, and one day she's reading *Their Finest Hour*. She said she'd never even heard of it, but someone had brought it in, traded it in with a whole stack of books, and she'd picked it up and started reading. And couldn't stop. So she's probably a third of the way through the book, reading it for hours that day, when my dad comes in. She doesn't see him, but while she's reading she hears someone talking and she realizes the words sound familiar. She listens, and realizes that whoever it is is reading *Their Finest Hour*, too. She remembers the opening of the book because she only started reading it a few hours earlier. So for a few minutes she just listens, kind of freaked out about the coincidence, but she likes the sound of the man's voice, so she ends up flipping back to the front and finding the spot where he's reading and following along as he reads it."

"This is so weird," Cleo says. She takes a last sip of champagne and then puts the glass under her chair on the hardwood floor. "And yet, I have chills."

So do I. Just like every time I think about this story. I clear my throat and continue. "So eventually he stops reading, and she's helping someone else check out and she's kicking herself that she didn't go over and find the guy. He doesn't come to the counter, so she assumes he's left. And then, this guy comes up to the cash desk. And she looks at him, and she just knows it's him, even though she hasn't seen the book. He puts a few books on the counter, and she starts ringing them in. And right when she gets to the final book, she sees the cover. It's *Their Finest Hour*. The same book she was reading."

"No," Emily says, her hands covering her mouth. I nod and smile.

"Yep. My mom is so nervous, because she thinks it must mean something, that it actually takes her a minute to tell him. But then he sees the book—her book, at the edge of the counter. The cover's flipped over, but he stops and turns and asks her what she's reading. She flips the book over, and he sees. And they lock eyes, and it's like that's it. The way they would tell it was that they were inseparable from that moment on."

All four sets of eyes are on me. My friends are total mush. Even Dory, who heard this story just a few weeks ago.

"Wow," Emily says eventually. "I can't believe you've never told us this story before."

I think of all the times I begged my mom to tell me the story, how each time was as good as the last. Then I snap back to life and jump out of my chair as it hits me. I give an involuntary hop, squeal and clap. "Guys, I'm going to England!"

Everyone starts talking at once. Cleo refills everyone's champagne flutes. Dory changes the record on the player and turns up the volume. "It's like your very own live version of *The Road Trip*," she says. "Except you'll be on a bus. In England. And you won't hate each other. It's perfect."

"I think that the minute he sees you he's going to know that you're the one, too," Dory says.

Chapter Three

I wake up with a massive champagne-induced headache, but it's dulled almost instantly as the details of last night come rushing back. The party. The gift. And the fact that I'm going to England to meet Zane. For a flash I'm reminded that there will be churches—a lot of them—but then I remember what Dory said after the other girls had left last night, when it was just the two of us cleaning up and then sitting on the cash desk, finishing the champagne off straight from the bottle. "You don't have to do anything you don't want to do—it's a *vacation*. Not a prison sentence."

I hope she's right, and that it'll be easy enough to grab a coffee or poke around the gardens of a church rather than actually going inside. I haven't gone into a church since Mom and Dad's funeral, and I don't want to start now.

I slide my headphones on and press Play to hear Zane's voice, skipping ahead to the part where Mirabelle and Jack meet in the town one afternoon.

"I thought we could walk and talk," Jack says. I close my eyes and picture Zane and I walking along a cobblestone street, tucking into bookshops or sitting on the grass by a river, eating scones and

drinking Pimm's—with a side order of random strangers from the bus tour, of course.

"What do you want to talk about?" Mirabelle challenges him.
"Oh you know," he teases. "The state of the railroad industry."
Jack chuckles.
"The what?" Mirabelle says, which only makes Jack laugh harder.

My eyes flick open as I remember there's one important factor to all of this: Lars. I press Pause and call Lars.

My call goes straight through to voicemail, in which Lars says he's living life to the fullest and will check his messages when he's done. The only way I can leave the store for ten days is if Lars takes over. The girls suggested closing the shop, but I don't want to do that. I never close the shop. Mom and Dad never closed the shop. But that means I'm going to need Lars to say yes.

I send him a text telling him to call me.

Thankfully, three hours later, he FaceTimes me.

"Finally," I joke.

"It's ten o'clock, G. A totally respectable time to phone a friend, or in this case, a sister. You might take note. Most normal people are sleeping at 7 a.m."

"Lars, it's a Friday. Most people are up at 7 a.m. Because they have to work."

Looking at Lars is like looking in a mirror—we have the same green eyes that turn up a bit at the outer corners, the same small nose, the same long brown hair our mother would always say was the exact color of maple syrup, though Lars's is matted and shoots in every direction like the kind on a troll doll—adding to his perfected laissez-faire look. The key difference at the moment is the scruffy beard he's grown since I last saw him.

"I need a favor," I say, leaning over the cash desk and holding the phone in both hands. And again, my chest feels tight. "I know you're trying to get the meditation studio open—"

"Mmm, that didn't really pan out."

"Oh no. What happened?"

"Long story. Anyway, on to the next. Which happens to be spreading the love for a new brand of loungewear." He flips his phone to show me a computer screen. I lean forward to figure out what I'm looking at.

"You love women's yoga pants?"

He flips the phone around again so his face comes back into view. "Loungewear," he corrects me. "You *can* do yoga in them, but you don't have to. And they'd be super flattering on you—they come in three different colors. The sage would match your eyes. And if you like them, all you have to do is tell a friend, and send them my way to buy their own pair."

"Lars, that sounds like a pyramid scheme."

"It's not a pyramid scheme." He dismisses me with a wave of his hand. "I'm just sharing my love of loungewear with women who I think would also love loungewear. And if *they* start loving the brand and sharing it with their friends, well then I make money. It's win-win-win for everyone involved."

"That's *how* pyramid schemes work," I whisper-laugh as the bells clang at the shop's door. I wave to the gray-haired woman entering the store. "Are you sure this is a good idea?" The thing is, Lars doesn't need me to give him advice on good or bad business ideas. And if it's a bad idea, he'll just move on to the next idea, like he always does.

"Gigi, you sound worried. Don't be worried. I'm not worried. Anyway, you were about to ask me for a favor." I see him push his hair off his face.

I exhale. "Well, I was going to ask you if you could watch the shop." My hands shake. If Lars says no, I'm not sure how I can go.

"Sure," he says. "What do you have, like, a doctor's appointment?"

"Dory and everybody got me a vacation for my birthday."

"Oh, that's nice," he says. There's a pause. "Wait—how long of a vacation?"

I take a breath.

"G—how long is this vacation?"

"Ten days," I say.

"Ten days?" He laughs. "In a row?" He stops laughing. "Where?"

"England."

"Couldn't you start taking time off with, like, a weekend in Chicago or something?"

"It's kind of a long story, and I'll tell you everything, but first I need to know if you can do it. You know I can't close the shop—"

"You don't *want* to close the shop," he says over me, but I keep talking.

"And you're the only one I can ask for such a big favor—"

"I'm the only one you know won't say no to you." Lars holds a finger up. "One question: Can I stay at your place?"

My fingers tingle with excitement, and I nearly drop the phone. "Yes, of course, for sure. That's actually easier than you having to trek back and forth to Ypsi." I'm rambling, trying to catch my breath. "So you mean you'll do it?"

He shrugs. "Sure," he says simply.

I exhale loudly, and the feeling of a massive stack of books on my chest gets reshelved properly. "Lars, this is huge. Thank you."

"Consider it my birthday gift. Even though I already got you a gift. It's sage and made of 70 percent spandex." He laughs. "So when do you leave?"

Chapter Four

Eight days later, as I'm waiting for Lars to meet me at Fleetwood Diner, I pull the yellow pad out of my purse and add a line about how the front door sticks when it rains and you have to slam your hip against it to shut it after every customer comes in otherwise the rain seeps in and gets under the floorboards and then you can't get the door shut at the end of the night. I have five pages of notes for Lars—about the shop and my apartment, our childhood home.

The door to the diner swings open, and Lars steps inside, dropping his worn navy duffle bag on the black-and-white-checkered floor and grinning at me. I get up, the black vinyl of the seat sticking to the backs of my knees. It's only eight in the morning, but the air is already thick. He throws his arms around me, his metal rings digging into my shoulders.

His jacket smells like a mix of stale weed and soap. When we pull apart, he picks up his bag and shoves it in the spot between his chair and the wall of the restaurant, then pulls out the chair opposite me and sits down, looking around. "Ahh, I love this place." A teen, his hair pulled back in a low ponytail, shuffles over to the side of our table with a carafe and two cups, pours coffee into both and clunks them on the table. Lars and I order the same thing, our usual, the Hippie Hash, eggs over easy. "I can't remember the last time I was eating breakfast this early," he says.

"We've got a full day ahead of us. Maybe you should've come yesterday so we'd have two days together before I left." How is he going to learn everything there is to know about running Love Interest in the seven hours the shop is open today, before I leave for the airport tonight at eight o'clock?

"Relax, it's a bookstore, not open-heart surgery. And I *have* worked there, remember? I doubt *that* much has changed. Anyway, I'm here now." He crosses his tattooed arms across his chest. "So, spill it."

"What? You sound suspicious," I say, but I can't stop the smile from spreading across my face, which has been my default reaction this past week every single time I think about the trip I'm leaving for *tonight*.

"I *am* suspicious. I've asked you like a bajillion times for details, and you've ignored every text and DM."

"I wanted to tell you in person," I say.

He closes his eyes and shakes his head. "Oh no. Don't tell me you're going somewhere with Dickhead." His eyelids flick open and he squints at me.

At the mention of David, my hands shake, and I spill hot coffee on myself. For months after David left, my entire body ached when I thought of him. Dory reminded me—like every old swoony love song says—that time heals. Eventually, it hurt less to think of him. And now, almost a year later, 99 percent of my attention is focused on Zane, and when I think of David, it's mostly only out of curiosity, in the same way I'm curious about what happened to my sixth-grade boyfriend or the hairbrush I misplaced last month.

I try a sip of the coffee. Still hot. "I'm not holding a grudge against him, I don't know why you are."

"He broke your heart, and my loyalty is one of my best qualities." My chest swells at Lars's words. As much as he and I are different, he's right—he *is* loyal, and I'm lucky he said yes to watching the shop so I could even go on this trip.

"Well, thank you for being loyal, and thank you for saying yes to this."

The waiter returns with our plates, and Lars leans back in his chair to make space. I unroll the paper napkin and place it on my lap, then stab a potato with my fork.

"Yeah, yeah—so now can you tell me who you're going with and why you're being so secretive?"

"No one. At least, no one I know," I say. Then I tell Lars everything, starting with discovering the audiobook version of *Their Finest Hour* all those months ago. His eyes widen at the mention of the book and he leans in closer—he knows all about the book's role in our parents' story. I tell Lars in full detail how I found out who Zane really is. By the time I get to the party details and the gift from my friends, Lars is finished his breakfast. He slaps down his fork, the metal tines clanging on his empty plate.

"You're going to meet him." His voice is an octave higher than usual.

I groan. "Go ahead, make fun of me. Tell me you think this idea is insane. My bags are packed, and there's no turning back now anyway."

"Nope." He shakes his head as I cut into my egg, the yolk running onto the hash and toast. "I think it's amazing. You're following your heart. You're being spontaneous. You're taking a chance. Gigi, I love you and I love that you're doing this. Everything you do is totally predictable, responsible and calculated. Here's a time you're listening to your heart instead of your head." He puts a hand to his chest. "I couldn't be more proud of you."

I was expecting him to mock me, but now I feel overwhelmed with emotion. I look away to blink back tears.

"So you don't think it sounds insane?" I say when I turn back to him. Lars is so much more free-spirited than me, and yet if he told me he was going to do something like this, I might think *he* was going a bit nuts, so I'm surprised that he seems so open-minded about the whole thing.

Lars wipes his mouth and tosses his paper napkin on top of his plate. "Oh, I think it sounds completely insane." He reaches across the table, putting a hand over mine. "For you, I mean." I look up at him, and his eyes meet mine. "Feels like something I'd do," he says with a grin. "Makes me feel like we're actually related. Also, it's something you *should* do. It's fun and romantic and a *great* story."

The pressure that's been squeezing my head dissipates. "Thank you."

"You're welcome. I wish I could say that's why I agreed to watch the store, but of course, I had no idea. And also, I needed a place to stay. I found a new place, but it's not ready 'til the first of the month."

"Oh no," I say, wiping my mouth with the paper napkin on my lap, then folding it up and tucking it under my plate. "You and Amber . . . ?"

I've been so caught up in my own plans, I realize, I know nothing about what's been happening with Lars in the past few weeks.

"Things were fun with Amber while she was still in vacation mode. But you know the saying, you can meet a banker on vacation and think you'll open a meditation studio together, but get back to Ypsi and . . ." He shrugs.

"The banker wanted to go back to the bank?"

"Six weeks' paid vacation, 401K . . . the entrepreneur life wasn't for her."

"I'm sorry," I say.

He shrugs. "You know me—nothing's the end, just a stop on the road trip. But there's miles to go before I die, you know?" He holds up a hand to the waiter, who nods and makes his way over with the bill, which Lars takes and hands to me.

"I was going to buy you breakfast, for the record," I say, laughing.

"Just making sure." He downs the rest of his coffee as I pay and then we make our way out of the diner into the warm sun. "So what do you want to do now?" he asks, and I punch him in the shoulder.

"What do you *mean*?" My voice is an octave higher than normal. "We're spending the day at the shop so you can learn how to run it."

"I know, I know, I just like bugging you."

I try to whack him on the shoulder again, but he ducks out of the way, laughing.

We cross the street and head up Ashley Street toward Love Interest.

"Listen, you have nothing to worry about." Lars rubs his hands together. "Frankly, I can't wait to get home to the mothership. It's gonna be a blast."

Back at the store, Lars and I work side by side for the day except for his many breaks—to get us coffees, meet up with an old friend for lunch, take what he calls an "afternoon sunshine break"—all of which I gently remind him won't be possible when I'm away. "You've got to pack something to eat and have it here while the store's empty. I really don't want you to close the shop—even for five minutes," I say, because I know that's going to be his rebuttal. I know I sound frantic, but I feel frantic. It's really registering—this time tomorrow I'll be in England. Every minute of the day will be entirely different than it is right now.

"Ahh, got it," he says, banging away at the old Olympia typewriter on the cash desk.

"I didn't realize you were attempting to convince people you're not human," he says, then taps me on the head. I sigh and go back to inputting the box of new releases into the computer database. "New releases go on sale on Tuesdays, so you have to put them out *after the shop closes* on Monday," I explain to him. "That's really important. And you can't sell one of them on Monday, even if someone asks. They have to come back on Tuesday."

"Mm-hmm," he says.

I'm not sure he's really registered all the information I've given him about how to run the store, and the knot in my stomach feels like it's getting bigger the closer I get to leaving for England tonight. And yet, there's not much more I can do except write everything on the yellow pads and hope he actually looks at them.

I'm not usually in a rush to close the shop, but at five o'clock sharp, because there's no one in the store, I lock the front door and then grab the broom and dustpan, to show Lars how to start the cleaning process. "I don't see why you sweep the floor every night. The whole point of a musty old bookstore is for it to look worn in. The dust adds charm," he complains, but still sweeps as I wipe down the counter. With both of us working we're done in twenty minutes and head out the front door. Lars hoists his bag over his shoulder, following me to the door that leads up to my apartment. I unlock it and push it open, letting Lars go first. He lumbers up the steep, narrow stairs.

When he reaches the top, I mean to toss him the keys so he can unlock the door to the apartment but I'm so nervous I fumble them and they land on the step in front of me. I hold my breath as I pick up the keys and push them into his hand. "You've got to give the door a shove as you're turning the key," I say. "It's sticky now." He bangs the door with his hip—twice—and it finally budges, then he passes the keys back to me.

He steps inside and drops his bag, kicking off his beat-up Converse, then begins humming the opening to the Barenaked Ladies' "The Old Apartment." I follow him in, watching him to see his reaction. Lars came over shortly after I moved back into the apartment last year. Then he moved to Peru, another long story, and he hasn't been back since I really made it my own. He shuffles into the living room, puts his hands on his hips, then spins around and I busy myself, bending over to pull off my shoes, placing them neatly on the mat, lining Lars's up beside mine, my hands shaking as I wait to hear what he thinks. It's my place now, technically, but for so long it still felt like Mom and Dad's. I think it'd be weird if the roles were reversed, and I was seeing the apartment totally overhauled by Lars. I've changed so much, from the recovered couches to the oil-on-canvas painting of a sunset over an autumn cornfield that I couldn't afford but splurged on anyway.

He lets out a low whistle. "You've really changed it," he says, looking around. He sounds impressed, and my stomach fills up with a tall glass of relief. He runs a hand along the top of the white wainscoting that separates the paneling from the illustrated owl wallpaper covering the top half of the wall. "Seriously, if this were listed on Airbnb, I don't think I'd recognize it as Mom and Dad's place. That's a good thing."

"Thanks." I feel overcome, for a moment—I know I don't need his approval, but it means a lot to have it. My fingers, which had been clenched, relax.

He sits down on the mustard-colored velvet couch and bounces up and down a few times on the cushions. "Ahh, this couch was always so comfortable. Remember us scheming to have 'sleepovers' together? You'd handwrite an invitation to invite me to your sleepover on the couch. Pretty hilarious given every night was already a sleepover in our tiny room."

"You loved it," I remind him.

"Did not," he says, but I know he did. He stands and walks over to the window on the far wall. He pushes back the paisley tapestry to look out onto the street. "Heart's still there," he says. I join him at the window and look out at the white heart painted onto the brick of the building a few feet away.

When Lars and I were little, the neighbors painted a white heart on the side of their brick building. It turned the nondescript wall into a work of art, and it was our family who benefited as it's right outside our window. A gift from them to us.

"Do you want something to drink?" I ask him. "Water, a soda—"

"I'd love a beer, thanks." He grins.

I make my way over to the fridge and pull open the door, then grab a green bottle from the six-pack I picked up last night with the groceries I bought for Lars.

He twists off the cap, flipping it onto the coffee table as he continues making his way around the room. He runs a hand along the piano that fills the wall between the couch and my bedroom door, one of the only original pieces left from our childhood, a piano both Lars and I begrudgingly played for years growing up. When our parents were downstairs at the shop, we'd often half-heartedly play with one hand while holding a book with the other—he, a comic book, me, a romance novel. I sit down in the emerald wingback chair and pull my legs up under me.

He takes a swig of beer then looks over his shoulder at me. "You ever play?"

I shake my head, smoothing my dress over my legs, which are jittery. It's starting to sink in: I'm leaving in two hours.

Lars places the bottle on the wooden window sill, a mix of chipped white paint and tan wood, then surveys the dozen plants I've assembled by the window—an asparagus fern, a trailing vine, a Chinese evergreen, a large jade plant, a tall yucca and a spattering of air plants. "That's a lot of plants. Any of them weed, by chance?" When I make a face, he laughs. "Kidding. I'll bring my own plants tomorrow." He returns to the couch, puts his beer on the table and sits down, stretching his arms behind his head.

I shake my head, then pop up and grab the yellow pad off the speckled counter. "Everything for the apartment is in here," I say. Even though Lars grew up here, he moved out when he was seventeen and certainly won't remember the old quirks or know about the new ones, like the trick to turning off the hot tap on the kitchen faucet and the way you have to pull on the left side of the window in the bedroom to open it.

"I color-coded the plants," I say, pointing out the dot system. "Yellow means you need to keep the soil moist. Red means let the soil run dry before you water—"

"Won't I be busy taking care of the shop?" He raises his eyebrows, teasing me.

"I don't want the plants to die," I say as I plop down on the couch beside him.

He exhales. "So you're getting outta Dodge. Never thought I'd see the day you'd leave this town. Do you even know *how* to leave Ann Arbor?"

I know he's kidding—*technically*, I leave Ann Arbor all the time, just not for more than a few hours, or on the rare occasion, overnight. Maybe a weekend if there's a holiday and the store would've been closed anyway.

"It's not that I don't know *how* to leave Ann Arbor, it's that I've never really had a good *reason* to close the store and leave," I say. "Now I do." This is true, but it's not the whole truth. What I leave unsaid is how many times I've *wanted* to go on a trip. After high school, I thought about taking the summer to travel with Dory, like Sydney and Leela in *I See London, I See France*. Instead, Dory went alone while I worked at the shop to save for college. For a few months I toyed with going to an out-of-state college, maybe California or New York—but in the end I went to U of M. In my last year of college I fantasized about getting my own apartment in Paris. But then, well—anyway, in every case there was always a more sensible reason to stay.

So Lars isn't wrong: aside from a weekend getaway to Napa with David a few years ago or Jacynthe's wedding in Nantucket, I've never been away for more than two nights in a row.

"Yeah, well, you deserve it." He slaps my knee. "I mean it. Have a blast. Don't worry about the store or this place. Really, what's the worst that could happen?"

I exhale, look around at the apartment, a dreamlike, rare sense of calm coming over me. Everything is in place. There's nothing left to do now but find out if Zane is really the one.

Chapter Five

Day 1, Sunday, 9:52 a.m.

London, England

The sidewalk on Buckingham Palace Road is packed with people walking in both directions, and I try my best to avoid running over anyone's toes with my bright-orange hardshell rolling suitcase. I'm walking from Victoria Station to Victoria *Coach* Station—which are, worryingly, two very different places—and my hands are shaking so badly I can barely hold on to the handle. The tour bus is leaving in eight minutes, which might be fine if I were suitcase-free and running in sneakers, but I'm wearing new suede flats without socks that are rubbing against the backs of my heels. Result: blisters. My feet are swollen from the plane ride so instead of my shoes completing my cute outfit of light-washed cuffed jeans and white linen/cotton V-neck with a handful of bracelets, it looks like I've shoved two balls of pizza dough into baby shoes. The wheels of the suitcase clatter along the cobblestone as I hobble as fast as I can. Why didn't I consider how massive Heathrow Airport would be and walk a little faster instead of taking in the sights, the sounds, the smells? Why didn't I think about how long it would take for me to pick up my luggage and pack a sensible carry-on bag instead of half my closet?

Why didn't I remember from the seventeen thousand books I've read set in London that the tube is notoriously delayed? Why didn't I take a cab rather than trying to save a few pounds by taking transit?

Seven minutes.

The five-story cream and glass art deco building comes into view up ahead, a centipede-line of passengers queued up to get through the sliding glass doors under a sign that says *Departures* in white writing on blue.

Six minutes.

A blast of cold air hits me in the face, throwing my hair back. Inside the doors, the station opens into an atrium, with a dozen overhead screens indicating trains and platforms.

The words and numbers are a confusing jumble, and the station is a blender of sounds: bus engines idling, the staticky crackle of the loudspeaker announcing departures and arrivals, the click of heels, the rumble of suitcases, the chatter of people all around. I give up on the screens and look around, then follow the steady stream of people deeper into the station, down a tiled hallway past fast-food stations and vending machines, pillars with pay phones and rows of metal seating.

Five minutes.

It smells a lot like sweaty feet. I blink, pushing away the overwhelming exhaustion that's come from getting no more than seventeen minutes of sleep on the overnight flight. I don't know where to go. I spin around looking for any clue, but there's too much information.

Four minutes.

"Keep moving! People are trying to get places!" someone barks behind me and jostles the bag on my shoulder as they pass. I pull my suitcase closer and hurry to the left, down a long hallway.

Three minutes.

Pain sears through my shoulder from the weight of my large, overstuffed tote bag. There's a long line in front of a series of ticket booths. The problem isn't getting a ticket, because I have one; it's what to do with it.

I look around, panic taking a front row seat in my chest, and then back down at the stack of papers I've been clutching for a good hour now, the edge where I'm death-gripping them moist with sweat from my palm, but nowhere on any of these papers does it say where to actually find the bus despite the hundreds of times I've studied it. All it says is Victoria Coach Terminal.

I've had nightmares about situations like these.

I turn around and start running in the direction from which I just came, back down the same hall, past a bank of floor-to-ceiling windows where a row of large white buses, *national express* written on the side in lowercase letters, are pulled into docks.

On my right is a booth selling totes, I ❤ London sweatshirts, ball caps, postcards and other touristy things that blur together as I rush past, dodging a woman wearing a coral-colored trench coat, her hair frizzy, her eyes wide. I'm sure I don't look much better. The pillars are now blue, the numbers in white, starting at *1* and counting chronologically up to *10*, maybe more, extending to the far end of the room. The convenience shop to the right is blasting Katy Perry. I weave through the people to the second pillar, around to the third, detour through the wire seats to four, and so on, straight to the end, wildly looking for any sign that will tell me where to find the gate for the tour. Past the tenth pillar is a set of sliding doors out into the coach area, which is useless to me because I still don't know which gate to go to, which bus to board. And then, seconds later, through another set of sliding doors, is a booth, the green sign reading *Information*, like a flashing beacon in the middle of a storm.

I can't even bring myself to look at my phone to see what time it is. My only hope is that all of these buses, still parked in their bays, are also supposed to leave at ten and are running late. That England time is like island time, and the bus will leave when the bus leaves. With me on it.

I press myself up so close to the linoleum counter that the sharp edge feels like it's going to cut through my middle, but I ignore it, let go of the handles of my suitcase and drop my tote bag to the ground, then wave a hand to get the attention of the kiosk clerk staring into the distance. He's in his mid-twenties and wearing an ill-fitting gray polyester shirt that's buttoned up the front, the collar splayed, a name tag over the left breast pocket that reads Chuck. His fingers ruffle the edges of a skateboarding magazine. Tattoos on three fingers of his left hand spell GET. I tilt my head to see what's on the other hand. The word LOST.

I refocus. "Hi!" I say brightly. "I'm signed up for the Spires, Shires and Shores trip with Wilkenson Tours?"

"That a question?" His tone is bored.

Obviously, I don't say.

"Oh, no." I let out a nervous laugh. "It's a fact. I just don't know where to go and I'm in a huge hurry and—" I wave my hands around.

"Ticket."

I shove the now-crumpled, sweaty wad of papers toward him, the sheet with the highlighted ticket confirmation on top. Chuck peers at the papers for way too long, flipping them backward and forward. I swallow the lump in my throat. Eventually he looks up, the whites of his eyes dull. "Gate 20."

I stare at him. "Twenty?" Why couldn't it be gate 10, which is only a few steps behind me, from the direction in which I came? I turn. "But the numbers only went up to ten."

He shoves the papers back toward me. "Twenty. That way." He tilts his head to the right.

I shove the papers in my mouth, sling my tote bag over my shoulder, grab the handles of the suitcase and pivot. I head down the hall, passing more kiosks, more coffee shops, more people, more more more—to gate 11. To the right, in the open area, the buses line up, no empty spots. I can do this, I can make it there on time. I rumble my suitcase across the pavement, back through the other sliding doors, past pole 11, around a group of people camped out in the middle of the floor, past pole 12. Around pole 13 and through a row of seats, someone stretched out, their arm across their eyes. Back through to the right of pole 14, weaving, bobbing; one of the wheels on the smaller suitcase is stuck, so now I'm just dragging it along with me. Lifting my massive suitcase into the air, I step over a group of kids sprawled across the terrazzo, using their suitcases as pillows. "Hey!" one of them protests as my suitcase drags across his midsection on its way up. Sweat drips down my back, pooling above the waist of my jeans, under my nose, in my scalp.

"Sorry!" I holler, wheels back on the tile, racing toward pole 20. Left turn toward the sliding door. A small poppy-red bus sits in the bay—a third of the size of the other buses—more like an oversized minivan. Cozy for sure. With the tour this small, my odds of sitting *very* close to Zane are *very* good, I realize with excitement. But first, I've got to get on the bus. There's no lineup of people, in fact there are no passengers at all, just the bottom half of someone bent over, rearranging the suitcases in the storage compartment under the bus.

Home stretch. I can do this. I'm going to make it.

"I'm here, I'm here, I'm here," I call out four thousand times or so with the little breath I have left, racing toward the person. Maybe I'm racing toward Zane himself. I manage to stop just short of the person, realizing it's a man and that his butt looks very good in his khakis, and let go of my suitcase, which tips over and falls on his leg. He backs out and stands up too quickly, knocking his head on the sharp edge of the door to the storage compartment.

"Fuck."

He grabs at the top of his head with one hand and trains his dark-chocolate eyes on me. His brow is furrowed, his dark hair falls in waves to his chin. Two-day stubble. A squiggle of indistinguishable lines on his toned, tanned forearm. As he stands, he stretches so that my head is in line with his chest—which is clad in a forest-green polo shirt, the words WILKENSON TOURS over his right breast, and a white name tag that reads TAJ over his left. Not Zane. Obviously it's not Zane—Zane has light hair, light eyes—but I'm still relieved for the confirmation that I'm in the right place. And I'll get a second chance to make a good first impression—maybe even one where I'm not out of breath and haven't just caused him a concussion.

"Are you alright?" I ask, but he squints at me, still rubbing his head.

"I'll live," he grumbles.

"Great. OK. Well, I'm here," I say breathlessly. When he stares at me blankly, I flail an arm at the bus, and repeat: "I'm here."

"Oh, thank god," he says drily. Then he turns to no one in particular and shouts, "She's here!" He turns back to me and raises a thick eyebrow. I swallow.

"Very funny," I say. "Is this the Wilkenson tour—Spires, Shires and Shores?"

He taps the crest on his shirt twice with his pen. OK, obvious question, but does he have to be *so* rude about it?

I shove the stack of papers in my hand at him, but he doesn't take them. "I know I'm a bit late but—"

He raises an eyebrow, pulls his phone from his pocket, looks at it, then holds it out to me.

I lean forward and squint at the screen. Blue sky, blue water, a lone sailboat on the horizon. "Yes, that," I say, feeling giddy with excitement. "That's what I'm here for." That, and Zane, but no sense mentioning that right now.

He glances at the screen and chuckles. "You're not going to find that on there." He thumbs to the bus. "That's Costa del Sol. Spain. But my intention was the time. It's quarter past ten. You're not a *bit* late. You're *really* late." He shoves his phone in his back pocket.

I reach out for the handle of my suitcase, which has started to roll away from me, as though it has a mind of its own and is opting for the Spanish sunshine coast instead. The handle's slippery in my hand, but I grip it tighter.

"Well, I'm here now. So I can just put my bag under there if you want." I point to the open storage compartment.

He holds his palm out to stop me, and I notice his bulging bicep. Focus, Gigi.

"I got it. That's my job."

"OK, so I should just"—I motion toward the front of the bus with my free hand and my suitcase starts to roll away again and I grab it again—"get on the bus, then?" I finish.

"Whoa, Nelly," he says. "First, let's make sure you're even on this coach before you go crashing it." He reaches into his back pocket again and pulls out a few sheets of paper. They're stapled together in the corner and folded in thirds, a pen clipped to the top. He grabs the pen, uses his teeth to pull the cap off and shakes out the papers.

"Name?" Taj mumbles, on account of the pen.

"Georgia," I say, snapping out of it. "Georgia Rutherford."

He runs the tip of the pen down the list, then shakes his head. "You sure?"

"Sure it's my name?" A bead of sweat somehow finds its way through my left eyebrow, pit-stopping on my lashes.

I lean toward him. "Can I see the list?"

He eyes me. "No." He holds the pages close to his chest. "It's confidential."

"I'm *on* this bus. I just checked with the guy down there in the information booth, and he said the Wilkenson tour left from gate 20."

"Oh . . . the guy down there in the information booth told you to come to gate 20, did he?" His voice is drenched in sarcasm but his dark eyes are twinkling. "Well then, alright, you *must* be on this list."

I press the back of the hand clutching the stack of papers to my forehead and exhale loudly. *Pull it together, Gigi.*

"Oh," I exhale. "They probably didn't put my full name. My friends, that is. They bought me this trip and . . ."

"Trying to get rid of you?" He raises an eyebrow.

"No," I say, my voice rising an octave. "They surprised me—for my birthday . . . never mind." Why am I telling this stranger my life story? "Gigi."

"What? Spell it, would you?"

I sound it out. "Gee-gee. Gee-eye-gee-eye. Gee-gee."

He drags the pen down the list again, then back up again to the top of the page. "Aha. There you are. Crisis averted. Now we just need a tour guide."

"What do you mean a tour guide?" The panic's back in full force.

"Guide didn't show so we're scrambling to sort it out. That's why we didn't leave on time—which was lucky for you, wasn't it?"

The guide hasn't shown up? I feel dizzy and grip the handle of my suitcase to steady myself, close my eyes and take a deep breath. What does he mean, there's no guide? Zane's the whole reason I flew thousands of miles. Zane's the reason I'm taking the first vacation I've had in years. Zane's the reason I'm trusting my lifeblood to my laissez-faire brother. This can't be happening. This was not the plan.

I snap my focus back on this guy. "You mean Zane?" Maybe he doesn't mean Zane.

Taj holds a hand out for my suitcase, but I grip the handle tighter. If Zane isn't on this bus, I'm not getting on this bus. Taj looks at me with curiosity—probably because I know the name of the guide but not my own.

"Where *is* Zane?" I ask, trying to keep my voice calm.

"Good question," he says. "I suppose that's for him to know and us to—actually, there's Angus now." He looks past me and I turn around, too, to come face-to-face with a happy grandpa. Like Taj, he's wearing a forest-green shirt with the patch above the left breast that reads *WILKENSON TOURS*.

"Any luck, Angus?" Taj says. Luck? Why do they need luck? Is Zane lost in the bus terminal? Is he hurt?

Angus puts a finger in the air and grins. "Found the guide." The skin around his eyes is crinkled and his gray hair sticks out in tufts over his ears from under his hat.

My entire body relaxes. *Thank god.* I touch my forehead with the back of my hand to see just *how* sweaty it is as Angus taps his chest. "Me. I'm your guide."

My ribcage feels like it's going to break through my skin. "What do you mean—you're the guide?"

He looks over at me. His eyes are kind and sympathetic. "We've had a bit of an issue," he says. "The original guide has been called away on an important . . . matter and isn't going to make the tour after all."

What? *What?*

My head feels like it's filled with helium and is detaching from the rest of my body, floating up toward the glass ceiling. I can't think properly.

"Is that . . . allowed?" I open my mouth to get in more air, hoping that'll help with the dizziness.

"It is," Taj says flatly. "Technically. Page six." He nods to the stack of papers I'm still clutching. "Small print. Guides and routes subject to change."

"But I—" I force my lips to form a tight smile and turn to Angus. "I'm sure you're great, but I'd sort of booked this trip specifically for the original guide." I avoid saying Zane's name so I don't sound like a complete whack-job.

"I thought your *friends* booked the trip," Taj says. I ignore him. Angus is clearly the one in charge—he's the one I need to convince to help me figure this out.

Angus scratches one woolly eyebrow. "I understand. Come with me. I'm about to explain the situation to everyone else on the bus. Unfortunately at this late juncture we wouldn't honor refunds, seeing as we're already late departing. But I believe under the circumstances, we'd allow any of those on the tour to rebook if they really prefer the original guide."

"I can't rebook," I whisper.

"Alright, then, why don't you just come up on the coach and—"

I shake my head. "I can't go on the bus. I can't just take this bus tour for ten days." This wasn't the plan. I never would've left the store for ten days for a vacation without any purpose. This was supposed to be something bigger. I'm still dizzy and reach out for something, anything other than my suitcase. Angus grabs my arm and steadies me.

"Here—have a seat." He takes my suitcase in one hand and leads me to the metal bench a few feet away between the buses. It takes all of my focus to put one foot in front of the next. "Give me two feathers on a pigeon. You wait here. You wait here, OK?"

Once I'm sitting, I swing my purse over onto my lap, my fingers scrabbling to feel the cold metal of my phone. I touch the first number in my Favorites list: the bookshop's voicemail. As it rings, that tight knot in my stomach starts to loosen.

I click the Pound button to listen to the messages, skipping to the saved ones. A moment later, Mom's soothing voice is in my ear.

Hi, Honey, it's Mom—

—And Dad!

We're just calling to check in, not because we're at all worried about how things are going. There's no one more capable than you to keep our shop running while we're away.

Your Mom's right. Seriously, Sweetheart, what would we do without you?

We're just calling to say hi, to tell you we're having a wonderful time and to thank you again for being the amazing daughter you are.

We love you!

The message ends.

I hold on to my phone for just a few moments longer, closing my eyes, and letting Mom and Dad's voices be the hug I need right now.

A scratchy voice on the PA system announces the departure of the coach at gate 19 in five minutes.

I shove my phone away and notice a pair of worn brown leather shoes close to mine. I look up. Taj looks down at me. "You gonna be OK?"

I have to squeeze my eyes shut for a second to prevent the escape of a tear. *Buck up, Gigi.* But the sound of diesel engines from the buses all around only reinforces the fact that I've made a huge mistake even leaving home. I never should've let the girls take charge of my life. It's so unlike me—and look where it got me. A dirty bus terminal and a failed plan.

Angus re-emerges from the bus and makes his way over to Taj and me, rubbing his hands together. "Alright, we're all set," he says to Taj. "Everyone else is happy to continue on, so now we've just got to figure out what you'd like to do, Gigi. I know a change of plans is never ideal, but I'm sure Zane will catch up to us tomorrow. And in the meantime you get me, Angus Brown. Longest-running tour guide in the company, I'll have you know. Started the same summer Graham Wilkenson started giving tours at his father-in-law's company. Got me a job and I never left. Anyway, enough about me. This is about you and Spires!" He pumps an arm into the air. "Shires!" Another fist pump. "And Shores!" I can't help smiling. "It's my favorite tour, and I'm happy to deliver it for as long as necessary, though, to be honest, I've come off a tour an hour or so ago, and I'm tired of hearing myself talk. I'm also quite tired and could really use a nap. But when duty calls, Angus answers, and when Graham calls, Angus also answers."

And so, here I am." He extends his arms. "So, what do you say, love? Will you get on board the coach and join us?"

Angus is so kind—and yet, it's not enough. I look over at the bus. The windows are dark. Who is on there? In all my fantasizing about the tour I really didn't give much thought to the other passengers. I was so focused on getting away, seeing England, hearing Zane talk . . . seeing if Zane might really be the one. Now, the reality of the situation sets in. I'm going to be stuck on a bus with a bunch of strangers—and what if Zane *doesn't* show up tomorrow?

I squeeze my eyes shut and try to focus. The way I see it I have three options. One: rebook the tour for the next time Zane's actually here from the start, which is impossible for way too many reasons. Two: turn around and go back to the airport, waste this gift and probably regret it forever. Or three: get on the bus and hope to see Zane soon.

Three. I have to do it. I open my eyes and nod.

That's all Angus needs. He claps his hands and grins, then holds out a hand to me. I take it and stand. Taj grabs the handle of my suitcase and rolls it over to the storage compartment, hoists it under the bus, and then slams the door shut. Angus heads toward the doors of the bus and then motions for me to go first. I sling my bag over my shoulder, look around the bus terminal behind me, cross my fingers and hope I'm making the right decision, and climb aboard.

Chapter Six

Day 1, Sunday, 11:30 a.m.

London ❭ Cambridge

The bus is bigger than it looks from the outside. Heads bob over the navy fabric-covered seats, the backs only coming up to most people's shoulders. The first set of seats has a stack of papers, a clipboard, a bunch of lanyards and a tattered paperback, the words *Well-Travelled England* in yellow font, the corner of the cover missing. An Indian couple bickers in the first pair of seats to my right. Behind them are two women in matching Patagonia fleece, hunched over something, their heads close together. Across the aisle from them is an older woman with buttery blond hair poking out from beneath a wide-brimmed pink hat. Behind her a skinny man with dark skin and a massive mop of black curls talks to himself, his voice scratchy. And finally, at the back of the bus, the only person younger than me is sitting, flipping her long, shiny black hair over one shoulder then the other, pursing her glossy lips and taking selfies on her phone.

"It's 11:32 and we're all sitting on the bus waiting to leave," the guy with the scratchy voice says. "The last passenger is a middle-aged woman who's taking a very long time to decide where to sit."

When I meet his eyes, he turns to look out the window.

"I've been standing here for, like, half a second," I say. "And I'm not *middle-aged*."

The woman with the pink hat tilts her head back; her eyes meet mine and she smiles, then pats the seat beside her.

"Sit, Darlin'." She stretches out the statement in a melodic Southern drawl as she moves her flamingo-patterned bag and white trench coat onto her lap.

I slide into the aisle seat, my head hitting the brim of her hat. She smells like talcum powder and freesia with a hint of pepper.

"Y'all know I've been wearing this hat since I left the hotel this morning. Can you *imagine* what my hair looks like underneath? It's gonna be a fright, but for you, I'm gonna take it off because there's no way we're gonna be able to chitchat with this between us." She removes the hat to reveal creamy skin, the wrinkles around her eyes and mouth like tiny ribbons on a gift. "I'm Charlotte," she says, smiling. Her lipstick—bright pink with just a hint of shine—looks freshly applied. She holds out a hand. Her fingers are soft, her nails slightly longer than her fingertips, rounded and painted pastel pink.

"Gigi." I lean back into the seat. It feels broken-in and comfortable even if there's no headrest.

My phone dings and I quickly pull it out of my purse.

So????? It's a text from Dory. It's got to be the middle of the night back home.

Hands trembling, I go to type back. *He's not here,* but I mess up the letters so that when I hit Send I see that it's autocorrected to *He's hot haha.* I shove my phone away.

"Travelling alone?" Charlotte asks with interest, not pity, and I nod.

"Me too." She sighs with contentment. "Oh, how I wish I'd thought to travel solo when I was your age. Are you enjoying yourself?" She doesn't wait for a reply, not that I have a solid one anyway. "But I was already married by then, and we just stuck together like butter on bread. Now where did I put my hand cream?" She passes me her hat then begins rummaging around in her flamingo bag. "My hands get *so* dry—I even put hand cream and then gloves on them when I was on the plane because I read something in *Good Housekeeping* that said that really helps seal in the humectants in the cream, and I do think it worked though how can you really ever know unless you were to only put cream and a glove on one hand and not the other, and well, I didn't do that, obviously." She pulls out a small white tube. "There we are. I never used to get dry hands. I think it must have all changed after menopause. Something for you to look forward to," she says with a chuckle as she rubs her hands together, then passes me the tube. I take it, squeeze a small amount into my hands and rub them together. At the front of the bus Angus appears, Taj behind him. Taj looks around, meets my eye, raises an eyebrow, then slides into the driver's seat, adjusting the mirrors. Angus takes off his paperboy cap and musses his hair.

"Isn't he a tall drink of sweet tea?" I follow Charlotte's gaze to Angus and then back to her. She puts a hand over her mouth. "Did I say that aloud? I'm not sure what's come over me." I smile. She's comforting to be around, like I've known her for much longer than five minutes.

"Hello, hello, hello, hello, hello!" Angus calls out, waving his hands in the air. The bus gets quiet. "I'm Angus—but you all know that because I just introduced myself to you three minutes ago. But if you weren't listening, there it is again. I'm Angus and

I am absolutely delighted to be your guide for the Spires, Shires and Shores tour. How is everybody doing?"

Cheers and claps reverberate throughout the bus, and I look around. Everyone is laughing, eyes bright, teeth bared behind huge grins. It all underscores how much everyone else wants to be here on this tour. No one else seems even remotely affected by the change in guide—because everyone else likely booked this tour for the right reasons: the tour itself, not for some fantastical ideal that the tour would be led by their soulmate.

"Well, I'm doing just great, too, thanks for asking," Angus chuckles. "Being a guide is my calling in life"—he cups his hands around his mouth and says: "Angus, Angus, time to tour!" Then chuckles to himself. "Alright, let's get to the rules. I only have one. Can anyone guess what it might be?"

"The tour guide is now on the bus, and he's asking us a question." I look across the aisle at the man beside me—the one with the scratchy voice. He runs a hand through his curls and they fluff up. "His name is Angus," he continues, "and he says there's only one rule. I wonder what it could be." Then he presses a button on a small black recorder, which makes a loud click.

Angus looks around. "Anyone? Anyone? Alright I'll tell you. No matter what happens—the good, the bad, the ugly—we've got to roll with it." He pauses for effect. "See why I like leading a *coach* tour? Roll with it?" He slaps his leg. There are a few chuckles throughout the bus, and Charlotte leans closer to me. "Isn't he charming?" she whispers in my ear. My laugh drowns in a pool of disappointment. I should be listening to Zane crack actual funny jokes, not Angus cracking eye-rolling groaners. The bus lurches forward, and I pull out my headphones and phone, then shove the bag as far under the seat in front of me as it will go.

"I can't promise that will be the last pun you hear from me," Angus continues. "Though I do promise you'll hear a lot more. I can also promise that each time I set foot on one of these coach tours I challenge myself to ensure each and every one of my guests has a wonderful time. I haven't failed yet. Of course, if we come to the end of the tour and you *haven't* had a wonderful time, please don't leave a bad review, it only breaks my perfect track record." He chuckles and looks around the bus as everyone laughs. When his eyes meet mine, he seems to give me an extra big smile, but I'm stuck on his words: *end of the tour*. Mere minutes ago he promised me he'd only be here for a day before Zane arrived. It was probably just out of habit—a spiel he's delivered for years and years.

"Oops, forgot the most important rule!" Angus says suddenly as the bus turns a corner, heading out onto a busy street, with cars, cyclists and pedestrians filling every inch of pavement. "I know I said there was only one rule, but I lied. Everyone must buckle up. Safety is sexy!"

I pull the tough seatbelt across my body as Angus makes his way down the aisle, prattling on about the tour and the itinerary and handing out little booklets that he explains contain all the important information we'll need on the trip. The stapled booklet is similar to the one Dory and my friends gave me. Flipping through the pages, I skim the town names, points of interest, hotel details and restaurant reservations. I close my eyes, remembering how I'd envisioned Zane explaining all these details in his sultry voice, standing a few feet away from me.

Is it possible to actually die of disappointment? Because I might.

"And there you are, your very first sight," Angus declares, pointing to his right. "The majestic Buckingham Palace."

I lean forward to see past Charlotte as we roll by the famous neoclassical limestone estate. Even though I've seen it dozens of times in photos and on TV, I'm blown away by seeing it now, in real life. I can't believe I'm here, thanks to my friends. I feel jitter-buggy with excitement, the way I'd feel lying in bed, waiting until it was 5 a.m. on Christmas morning as a kid, when Lars and I were allowed to wake up our parents. I'm in England, a country I've forever wanted to visit—how bad could this all be?

Angus claps his hands together and announces the first activity, an on-the-bus icebreaker to learn more about each other. My body tenses up again. This is another activity that I would've been game for had Zane been leading it, but it just feels overwhelming in the current situation. How can I share more about myself when all I can think about is the fact that I'm here to meet someone who isn't? "We're going to play the Name Game, which is always a good way for us to learn each other's names, yeah? So for example, if your name was Ben and you were six-feet-six inches tall, you could say, 'I'm Big Ben.' And it would be wonderfully British and coincidental if we were to pass Big Ben at that exact moment"—he points out the window as we pass the gothic-revival clock tower, which Angus explains is actually called the Elizabethan Tower.

The bus rumbles across Westminster Bridge. Down below, sunlight dances on the glassy surface of the water as a group of stand-up paddleboarders create a V-shape stream in the Thames. "I'm Animal-Adoring Angus. See what I did there, I used an allit-eration to give you a little bit more information about myself. This way, if you see me stopping to show you another herd of sheep or to listen to the call of a particularly interesting bird, you'll know why." I remember the summer Mom decided she was going to get into bird-watching. She'd wanted all of us to hike and bird-watch together, but after we went once, Dad and Lars and I complained how boring it was, and Mom decided she'd rather go alone than let our complaining ruin the experience. She ordered in a bird-watching book and bought binoculars, and early every morning she headed to Bird Hills, returning home at six, telling us how wonderful it was, how many interesting birds she'd seen. A few weeks into her morning ritual, Dad decided we'd surprise her one morning by joining her at Bird Hills. Shortly after she left, he got us out of bed, and we headed to the hiking area. There was a coffee shop near the entrance, so we stopped, thinking we'd get hot chocolates and coffees, then head onto the trail in the hopes of finding her. Instead, we found her inside the coffee shop, reading a book—not the bird-watching book—and drinking at a table for one in the corner. Turns out, she'd thought bird-watching was boring, too, but was too stubborn to admit it.

"How long were you going to keep this up?" Dad said, and I remember wondering if he was amused or angry.

"I wasn't sure," Mom said. "I'm glad you found out first."

After that we took our hot drinks and went for a short hike and laughed and played tag and completely ignored the birds. And that became a new family ritual, one we managed every few months.

Angus claps his hands again, and I refocus on the present. "Alright, Taj, you're up." Angus taps him on the shoulder. Taj looks into the rearview mirror, raising his eyebrows. "Tolerant Taj," he says drily. "I put up with all of Angus's jokes and *games.*"

Angus laughs and turns back to all of us. "Funny lad. Funny lad. Alright, who's next?" He points to the Indian couple in the first row. The man turns, smiling, and introduces himself as Really Excited Roshi.

"That's not technically an alliteration," the man with the recorder says, but Really Excited Roshi doesn't seem to hear him. He says that he loves travelling but for most of his career the travel was always tied to work. "It'll be nice to be on holiday for a full ten days with my lovely wife, Sindhi," he says with a big grin, turning to the woman beside him. She stares straight ahead, and Roshi's smile wavers. Sindhi looks around at everyone else and tells us she's *sensible,* and enjoys routine. "I would have never chosen a holiday where we'd be moving to a new hotel room every day," she says. "He's"—she throws a thumb Roshi's way—"going to lose his passport or a shoe within a day, I just know it," she says. "And then I'm going to lose my mind." Roshi laughs, but his face looks strained. Someone coughs. Charlotte squeezes my hand, and I shift in my seat uncomfortably at the awkwardness of the moment.

Vacation-loving Violet has streaks of purple in her graying hair, and loves to travel. Her partner introduces herself as Nervous Nelle, which she pronounces *Nell-ay.* "This is my first time to England," she says. "Violet was born here and I really wanted to see this part of her life, but I'll be honest, I don't love to travel and I'm quite nervous about getting sick or hurt or not having the right footwear or how it's all going to go." She bites her lip.

"Alright, then, we've got two people who like to travel and two who don't," Angus says jovially, making the peace sign with both hands. "What an *interesting* group," he jokes, then makes a face. "Just kidding, just kidding."

"Where are you from?" Roshi asks Nelle with interest, turning in his seat.

"Sweden, originally," she says, looking relieved at Roshi's kindness. Her face brightens. "Though we live in Connecticut now."

"Never been to Connecticut so I can't comment, but Sweden is lovely," Roshi says.

"Lovely?" Sindhi says. "It rained every bloody day we were there."

"That's statistically impossible," the man with the recorder says beside me, rubbing his nose, which is long and thin, a bump on the end. "On average, most of Sweden receives about twenty-five inches of precipitation a year, making it considerably drier than the global average." His skin is pockmarked and his fingers are long and skinny, and he interlaces them as he's talking. "Unless you were there in August, which is the wettest month, it's unlikely it could've rained every day you were there."

"Ooh, I just love Swedish berries," the girl at the back says. "Actually I think I have some in my bag." She disappears behind the seatback in front of her.

Charlotte is Charming Charlotte from Charlotte, North Carolina. "Easy to remember," she says with a smile, then quantifies the charming part by saying absolutely everyone in the South is charming. "It's the accent and the smile. We can be mad as heck but put a smile on it and it looks like we're paying a compliment."

Angus looks at me, and I suddenly realize I haven't thought of anything to say. "I'm, uh . . . Good? . . . Gigi." I say. A weird noise escapes my mouth. My face heats up. Charlotte pats my knee and chuckles sympathetically.

"Great!" Angus says, and I look up to see he's looking at me and clapping his hands. "Or should I say, Good?" I'm just relieved my turn is over. For someone who deals with strangers daily, I'm disappointed in myself for being so awkward and nervous.

"You're next," Angus says, nodding at the man across the aisle from me. He rubs his hands together. "I guess you could call me Factual Francis."

Francis explains that he's retired now but used to be a statistician. "I almost made the *Guinness Book of World Records* for being able to recite every fact in the book."

"There's a category for that?" the girl at the back asks. "That seems random."

He scratches his hair and it fluffs up. "No, that was part of the problem."

I look at Charlotte and we both laugh. When I look back at Francis, though, his brow is furrowed, and I feel bad for him.

"I entered a longest hair competition when I was seventeen," the girl at the back says. "But it turned out it had to be real hair." She pops a Swedish berry in her mouth then holds the bag up in the air. "Anyone want one?" She stands and moves into the aisle.

Angus makes a patting motion with his hand. "Sit down, seatbelt on, please." She sighs loudly and plops back down into her seat.

"The world's longest hair is recorded at over eighteen feet. A woman from China," Francis says. "I wonder if it's all the fish oil in their diet . . ."

"Are you implying I'm from China just because I *look* Chinese?" the girl at the back says. "That's racist."

"Whoa whoa whoa. No one's implying anything," Angus interrupts.

"I didn't mean anything by it." Francis's eyes are wide.

Angus nods. "Why don't you tell us more about yourself," he calls to the girl at the back, the final passenger on the bus.

"Fine," she says, standing, plucking an imaginary fluff off her white puff sleeve. "Anyway, I *am* Chinese. I was just messing with you," she says to Francis. "My parents adopted me when I was a baby."

"You really need to sit down," Angus says firmly. "It's not safe to stand while the bus is in motion."

"Alright alright," she says, flipping her long shiny hair over her shoulder, and introduces herself as Murder 'n' Makeup Jenny.

"That isn't an alliteration," Roshi says. "It's really not even close."

Jenny rolls her eyes. "It's not for the game. It's my YouTube channel. Murder 'n' Makeup Jenny. My agent says it's better if I always introduce myself this way, because I'm really trying to increase my subscribers. I'm already at 500K but my goal is to hit a million subscribers by the time I turn twenty-one. And that means reminding people about the channel whenever I meet any-one new."

"Murder and Makeup . . ." Angus says. "That's an interesting combination. Would you like to tell us a little more about it?"

The bus has stopped at a light or in traffic—it's hard to tell. Outside the window beside Charlotte, a little boy walks beside a woman wearing a floral trench coat. They're holding hands. In his other hand he's holding a red balloon, but lets go of it, then reaches up after it. The balloon drifts off toward a sycamore tree, the white string trailing behind, the balloon brushing the branches before shooting off up into the sky.

The little boy turns to the woman, his eyes showing his disap-pointment. The one that got away. *I know the feeling.*

"I tell true crime stories while doing my makeup," Jenny says. She waves a long gray coffin-shaped nail around. "I've been doing it for, like, five years now. I was ahead of the trend. There's a real art to it, because you have to know your story really well but you also have to time it to your makeup look. So *anyway*, I'm Jenny, obvs, and just so you know, this isn't really my kind of trip, but it's, like, a long story I don't want to get into." She pulls her hair into a high ponytail, then lets it go again, "but basically if you see me filming at the back of the bus you'll know why. I post twice a week and it's a schedule I can't mess with—YouTube is all about consistency."

"England is rich in tales of murder and mystery," Angus says. "I'm sure you'll get plenty of inspiration."

"Amazing," Jenny says, visibly perking up. She pops another Swedish berry in her mouth. "Anyway, if you wanna follow along, just look me up—Murder 'n' Makeup Jenny. Totally check me out, and don't forget to like and subscribe."

I stifle a laugh.

Charlotte leans close and whispers, "The last time I watched a YouTube video I ended up gluing false lashes to my finger. It wasn't for me."

"YouTube or false lashes?" I ask with a smile.

"Both," she says, and we both laugh.

"And where are you from, Jenny?" Angus asks.

"Murder 'n' Makeup Jenny," she corrects, waving her hands around. "The more you say it, the more it'll just automatically roll off your tongue. Anyway, I'm from New York"—her dark eyes dart to the right—"*basically*."

"So, *basically* you're from the Tri-state area?" Angus asks. "I've always wanted to say that."

"Basically. Anyway, what does it matter where I'm *from*? The internet is international. My home is on YouTube."

"Poor girl's embarrassed of her roots." Charlotte shakes her head. "You've got to be proud of your roots. Or spin your story so *you* make your roots, not the other way around," she says. "You think I'm actually from Charlotte?"

"You're not?" I ask, surprised.

"Of course I am. But I could've been from Tulsa, which is where I was born, or Phoenix, where I spent many years."

She pulls out a jar of Vaseline and opens the top, dabs her ring finger inside then swipes it across her face. Then holds out the jar to me. I shake my head.

"So then why Charlotte?"

"Charlotte's where my story really began. Where I became the Charlotte I am today. You must feel that different places have influenced your life in different ways, too."

I shrug. "There's just Ann Arbor. My whole life."

She tilts her head and studies me, then nods. "I can see that. You're safe. Steady. A sure thing. I like that about you already. Anyway, that gal"—she thumbs toward the back of the bus—"needs to figure out her story and stop being so defensive. But she's young. She'll figure it out one day."

Once all the introductions are complete, Angus tells us about our route east out of London and then north up to Cambridge, rattling off the names of towns we'll pass by on the way, and I feel myself getting excited. This trip is actually the perfect distraction from Zane and my obsession with his voice.

I look out the window, past Charlotte, as we pass the massive London Eye, the wheel turning slowly.

"You look pale," Charlotte says, looking at me. "Are you sure you're feeling OK?"

I put a hand to my forehead. "I think I'm just really tired."

"It's hard to get over the jet lag, isn't it? I think I went to bed at four yesterday and slept through until 8 a.m.," Charlotte says.

"That's what I should've done," I say. "I flew the red-eye," I say. "I think it was a mistake. Everything feels foggy."

Charlotte rummages in her purse. "It's lack of sleep," she says. "I have something that'll help." She pulls out something shiny and silver. "Ever had a peppermint puff?" When I shake my head, she continues. "They're practically a religion in the South, though I'm not one to talk about the Lord. It's not just a mint, it's a cure-all. Try it." She passes me a plastic-wrapped red-and-white-striped candy. The mint is soft and melts in my mouth.

"Why don't we change seats so you can lean against the window?"

"Are you sure?" I say, but only half-heartedly.

Sleep. Everything will be OK if I just sleep. I stand and let Charlotte into the aisle, then I slide across into the window seat and lean my head against the window, but I can't shut out the noise around me—Sindhi and Roshi are bickering again, Francis is talking to himself, Jenny sounds like she's recording a video. I flip through my phone, consider calling Dory, but it's still so early in the morning there and she's probably asleep. Instead, I put on my headphones and then hit the audiobook app and skim through the titles. My finger hovers over *Their Finest Hour*. I know I shouldn't do it—it isn't going to help. I should listen to something else, anything else. And yet, I can't help it. His voice is like rosé—I can't just have one glass. I touch the triangle in the center of the screen, then lean my head against the cool glass, the outside world turning to a blur as the bus picks up speed.

"I looked for you today," Zane whispers to me, sending shivers up and down my body. *"But you weren't home."*

I'm right here, I think. *You're the one who isn't here.*

Mirabelle arranged the black-eyed gerberas and baby's breath into a vase, not letting Jack get the best of her. But he always got the best of her. "I was right here," she said, her voice even.

"Well, no matter. I'm back again," Jack said, raising an eyebrow and curling his lip in a way Mirabelle could never refuse.

Come back, Zane.

I know he's not talking to me, and I know it's insane to pretend he is, and yet, I can't help myself from taking the conversation from here. Taking over Mirabelle's parts, letting Zane's gravelly, comforting voice fill my ears.

The bus chugs along, and it's as though Zane is right here with me. Maybe I can just shut everyone out for the next ten days and pretend it's just the two of us after all. Just him and me, together.

Chapter Seven

Day 1, Sunday, 1:30 p.m.

Cambridge

Pain sears through my neck. I open my eyes, blink a few times and pull off my headphones before I remember that I'm on the bus. But the bus isn't moving, and it's eerily quiet. I'm alone. Outside the window is a row of terraced Edwardian-style homes, ivy crawling up and around the front doors, extending to the second-story windows.

A clang makes me jump, and I look to the front of the bus. The doors open, and the top of Taj's head appears.

"You're awake," he says, taking off his square sunglasses.

"You scared me," I say.

"Boo." He waves his fingers in the air, then crosses his arms over his chest again, his tanned, toned biceps stretching the band on his polo shirt. "Come on. Up you get."

I blink a few times, stretch and tilt my head to the right. Pain shoots from the base of my skull down through my neck to my shoulder. "Sorry if you've been waiting. You could've just gone ahead. I think I'll just stay here, read my book, actually. Wait for everyone to return."

"Nope. Can't leave anyone on the bus. Insurance risk."

"Is that even true?"

He shrugs. "I wouldn't tell you if it wasn't. Come on, up you get." When I don't move, he claps his hands twice, like I'm a dog. He turns and disappears outside. I debate staying put because what does it matter to him if I see whatever town we're in, but unfortunately, defiance is not in my nature. Also, I have to pee.

My bag is poking out from beneath the aisle seat. I pull it up, sling it over my shoulder, then grab my book off the seat, just in case. As I step out the door and down onto a parking pad of fine-crushed gravel, sunshine warms my face. The sky is unbothered by clouds. I squint and shield my eyes with my hand. Sure, we're in a parking lot, but it's the most beautiful parking lot I've ever seen, surrounded by brick walls bathed in lavender pea-like blossoms. Off to the left, the narrow road sneaks between two-story Edwardian townhomes, their windowsills painted white, purple crocuses shooting up the glass. Taj is leaning against the bus, reading a book. *The Sweet Hereafter.*

"Dark choice," I comment, pointing to his book.

"Keeping it real." He tucks the book into the back of his pants, which I find both odd and impressive. "Let me guess, you're reading Austen. *Pride and Prejudice?*" He sounds bored.

"No," I say defensively. Totally thought about bringing it, though.

"Hmm," he says, appraising me. "Let's go. I'm *starving* and I've been waiting *forever* for you to wake up. Angus and the group are heading over to King's College Chapel—I'll catch you up." He starts walking toward the narrow road ahead, but I'm not budging.

Not a church.

Not yet.

I'm not ready.

He turns back, notices I haven't moved and lowers his sunglasses, his dark eyes on me. "You coming?" He nudges his sunglasses back into place.

"You know, I'm good. I'm—"

"Yeah, you mentioned that. In the name game." An eyebrow appears over the top of his sunglasses.

I squint up at him, wishing I'd thought to pack my sunglasses in my purse rather than in my suitcase. "What I mean is, I'm happy to just find somewhere to eat in town, read my book and meet everyone back on the bus."

I catch up to Taj, and he starts walking again. As we reach the end of the road, he turns left.

"Nope, not gonna happen," he says.

We make our way down a little easement between another stretch of row houses and a spontaneous patch of buttercups.

"Why not? I've got my phone for directions and time—" I reach into my bag only to realize I've actually left my phone on the bus. "Never mind—I don't even need a phone. Just tell me what time to be back on the bus and I'll be there. I'm sure there's a clock tower where I can check the time, right?"

Taj gives an exasperated sigh. "Unfortunately for both of us, Wilkenson Tours discourages its patrons from random roaming. It's called a *guided tour*. If you wanted to wander on your own, you should've taken a different holiday." His voice is cool, like he doesn't particularly care *why* I booked this tour. Not that I was about to share my soulmate story with him anyway.

"Trust me, the thought's already crossed my mind," I say instead.

"The thing is, you haven't got the best track record, have you? Last one to the coach this morning . . ." His tone is teasing.

"You can argue your point all you want, but part of me keeping my job is making sure that I don't lose any passengers."

"Alright, alright," I say, feeling too tired to argue.

"Great." He claps his hands together. "Then can you walk faster?"

A block or two down the way, the row houses are replaced with three-story buildings, the street level occupied by shops. To my right a black sign says *Tilda's Tea Room* in gold writing. A soft pink building the same shade as Charlotte's nails offers embossed stationery. A souvenir shop with large glass windows features pens, flags, T-shirts, socks, teacups and dozens of other tchotchkes, all emblazoned with the union jack. British accents fill the air. Everything feels totally different from home.

I skirt around a row of wrought-iron chairs facing outward into the street outside a pub and inhale the scent of greasy fries. "I don't see what the rush is," I say.

"This"—he waves a hand between us—"is the only time I get to myself. When I'm not driving the bus. And you've just eaten up two hours of it by sleeping."

"Wow, that's rude," I say, looking straight ahead. It's not like I want to be hanging out with him either.

He sighs and I look at him just as he looks at me. I can't help noticing how smooth his skin is. "Don't take it personally," he says a bit more gently. "It has nothing to do with you and everything with the fact that the stops on the tour are my chance to do what I want. And what I want is a roast beef sandwich."

"Well, I need a bathroom. I really have to pee." I look around for any signs of a public washroom. "Also, if you're always trying to get rid of the people you're in charge of, maybe you're in the wrong career."

"This isn't my career," he says without emotion.

"Whatever you say," I say under my breath.

We reach the town square. Set on the commons in the center are row upon row of stalls, all of them covered in striped awnings—blue and white followed by yellow and white, then green and white, then red and white. There's a flurry of activity and sounds of people laughing, chatting, and a faint sound of an acoustic guitar.

"Ah, it's your lucky day," Taj says.

"I think we both know that's not true," I grumble.

"Market's in town," he says, just as I glimpse a sign that says the farmer's market is open every day except Christmas and New Year's Day. Then he points: "And there's a portaloo for you."

I hurry in the direction Taj pointed. When I'm done, I walk back into the sunlight, passing a flower stand where tulips, hyacinth and narcissi create a rainbow of colors. I do love a farmer's market—not that I plan to admit that to Taj. The Ann Arbor one sets up downtown every Saturday and Wednesday, and I try to get there once a week to pick up fresh flowers before opening the store.

I find Taj a few stalls over, under a blue-and-white-striped awning. As I get closer, the air fills with the smell of sweet caramel.

"Here, try this," Taj says, holding out a long red-and-white wrapped piece of dough to me. "Churro."

"Is this British?" I say, feeling a twinge of excitement at trying my first British snack.

"Spanish, I think. Maybe Portuguese. When it tastes this good, who really cares?"

"Aren't you supposed to show me British things?" I ask, taking the churro from him.

"I'm not supposed to show you anything. I'm the coach driver, remember? Just take a bite."

The warm, sweet dulce de leche mixed with the fried dough is the best thing I've ever tasted. "Wow. Thank you." I hold the churro out to him, realizing how intimate it feels to be sharing this snack with a stranger, but he shakes his head.

"It's for you. You seemed hungry."

As if on cue, my stomach grumbles, and I realize I haven't had a thing to eat since the late-night snack on the plane at least twelve hours ago. I savor the pastry, feeling almost instantly better.

We cut through the market toward a stone-and-brick bridge with a wide sidewalk on one side, concrete balusters connecting to form a railing. At the end of the bridge, people are gathered on a terrace outside a white building with black letters that read *THE ANCHOR*. Bleeding heart flowers spill out of hanging baskets, their bright pink popping against the white of the building. It's the first of several buildings along the water. The concrete is rough on my skin as I lean over the bridge and out toward an island of green grass and canopy trees.

After the last bite of my churro, Taj points to my chin. "You have a little . . ." I quickly wipe, feeling embarrassed.

"What's that?" I point at the long thin wooden boat with flat platforms at either end that comes into view. In the middle a couple is seated, holding hands, their legs outstretched. At the back, a man stands on the wooden platform, holding a long pole that he uses to push against the river bottom, to propel the boat along.

"Ah," Taj says. "A punt. It's quintessential Cambridge. Great way to see the town. Goes along the College Backs—that is to say, it sails along the backs of the eight colleges that make up Cambridge. It's a bit touristy, if I can say that, but it's really not to be missed, in my opinion." He looks at me and smiles. "Hmm, guess I do know a thing or two about the town."

I wonder whether Taj actually wanted to be a guide but instead got stuck driving the bus and *that's* why he's such a grump. "When do we do *that*?" I ask.

"*We* don't," he says, looking amused.

"We don't? But if it's 'not to be missed'"—I air-quote—"why isn't it on the itinerary?"

"It *is*. On the itinerary. You slept through it. Right before the group had lunch there." He points to the Anchor. "Best sticky toffee pudding in town, which I missed because of you."

Punting looks relaxing. Romantic even. My thoughts go to Zane. I wonder what he's doing right now. Is there a chance he might join us before we leave Cambridge? England's tiny compared to America—maybe he'll get here sooner than he thought.

"Wait—" I say, registering what Taj has just said. "I thought you just finished telling me that you don't hang out with the group."

"I don't, typically."

"Then how do you know the Anchor has the best sticky toffee pudding?"

"Says so right on the sign." He laughs. "Come on." As we walk, the bridge narrows into a strip of sidewalk. People laugh outside a café on the corner, and we weave through the oncoming pedestrians, walking onto the road, then back onto the sidewalk.

"I feel like I missed the best part of this town"—I swerve to get out of the way of a guy hurtling toward me on a bike—"and I'll never be back. Can you give me the CliffsNotes?"

"The what?"

"A summary. The highlights." Maybe I can convince him to

give me a walking tour so we can skip the chapel altogether.

"Uh . . . no." He runs a hand through his hair, and I watch as it falls back into place on his shoulders, trying to figure him out. One minute he's an amateur comedian, the next he's a total grouch.

"Are you always like this on the tour?"

"When I'm starving, yes."

I wave an arm behind me. "Hello. You *just* got me a churro. Why didn't you get yourself one?"

He pats his stomach. "Holding out for the roast beef sandwich. Which I would've had two hours ago if it weren't for you."

For a whole minute we have blissful quiet. Then Taj claps his hands together and looks at me, pulling off his sunglasses. His eyes gleam.

"Cambridge's claim to fame is football," he says. "It's the birthplace of the sport. *Soccer* to you," he says, faking an American accent.

"Great. What else?" As we turn onto another street, a flicker of turquoise catches my eye, and I look up at the multicolored bunting fluttering back and forth in the breeze across the street from top of building to top of building. This town feels like it's straight out of a fairytale. I can't believe I forgot my phone. There are so many things I want to capture right now.

"Let's see . . . it's home to thirty-one-and-a-half colleges."

"Come on, there's no half a college," I say.

"Well, what would *you* call a college on wheels? Surely it doesn't get the same value as permanent ones."

"Are you kidding?" I turn to face him, and he stops so we're face to face. His lashes are really distracting—they're so long they nearly touch his eyebrows.

"Yeah." He gives a slow grin. "I stole that line from another guide. Good one, though, right?" We turn and we fall back into step together.

"What guide?" I say, wondering if it's Zane. Is Zane funny? Would his tour be peppered with quirky things like that? Would it be weird to ask Taj things about Zane?

Taj shoves his hands in his pockets, and keeps walking. "A driver never tells."

I roll my eyes.

"I saw that," he says.

"I wasn't trying to hide it," I say, but I laugh to cover my embarrassment.

As the street narrows, the buildings get closer and the sun disappears. I shiver, folding my arms across my chest as we pass a small storefront with peeling red paint and a large window filled with worn books, their edges frayed, their spines creased. Across the bottom of the window are a dozen brown paper bags, skinny and tall like the kind Mom would pack my lunches in when I was a teen. Their tops are folded, and £5 is written in red marker across the front of each. But that's not what has my fingers tingling.

A copy of *Love in the Time of Cholera* sits in the bottom left-hand corner of the bookshop window. It's an illustrated version—a salmon-colored cover with birds, flowers and fruit in grays and reds edging the four sides of the book, García Márquez's name in large gray uppercase at the top, the title in white cursive underneath. A sign.

"I have that same book in the window of my bookshop," I say, squeezing my hands into fists to get the blood moving. What are the odds that the first bookstore I see on this trip has the very same book that's in the window of my shop? It's got to be a sign.

Except—this is where I should be sharing this with *Zane*, not Taj. Although if Zane were here, he'd be leading the tour. But if Zane were here, I never would've let myself fall asleep!

"Fascinating," Taj interjects sarcastically, then immediately adds, "Sorry. I'm being an arse again." But it's too late—my entire upper body gets hot with embarrassment. I look away.

A red metal sign, *THE MYSTERIOUS BOOKSHOP* in white lettering, creaks as it swings ever so slightly over the entrance. Over the door is another sign that reads *Anna and William James's Bookshop*. The fact that there are two names to the store, and that *Love in the Time of Cholera* is in the window even though it doesn't fit with the mystery theme, both confuse and intrigue me.

I wonder what Anna and William's story is. How they met. Who *are* Anna and William? I close my eyes. Anna, in her twenties, studied English Literature at Cambridge. She did one of those haunted walking tours of the city. William was the guide who asked her out at the end of the tour. Her parents, both snobs, wouldn't approve of her relationship with a townie. When William realized she was keeping the relationship secret, he broke up with her. Years later, she realized he was *the one*. So she signed up for his tour, and when she arrived at the meeting place—an empty storefront on St. Edward's Passage—there was no group. She looked around, then saw him. William saw she had signed up, so he cancelled the group. There was only William. Still in love with her after all these years. It was this very spot—this empty storefront—that became their bookshop. A combination of their two loves: books and ghost stories.

"Hello"—a tap on the shoulder breaks me out of the story. "Anybody in there?"

I open my eyes to see Taj looking at me, one eyebrow raised.

"Just wondering how Anna and William met," I say.

"*Who?*"

I point to their names above the doorway. "Do you mind if I pop in there for a moment?"

"I do," he says, putting a hand to his chest as though I've just driven a spear into his chest with my request. "I really, really do. I'm starving. Why can't you just be a normal passenger and *want* to catch up to the group? I've never met someone who's decided she doesn't want to be on the tour *on the very first stop of the tour.*" He's flailing his arms around and nearly hits a woman passing by. She turns and glares at him. I laugh.

"Come on," I whisper, putting my hands on my hips. I'm practically begging but I'm so tired, it's like I *need* the comfort of the bookstore as a reset. "I'm just asking to pop in there for, like, five minutes. It's not going to kill you."

He shakes his head. "Five minutes here, five minutes there. It all contributes to a slow, painful death. I know your type."

My mouth hangs open. "I'm not a *type*. I'm a paying customer on this trip, and you're out of line." I'm done being polite or letting his rude attitude slide. I'm sure my face is red—I can feel the sweat pooling behind my ears.

For a second he looks stricken. "You're right. I'm—sorry. I really need to eat." His chocolate eyes narrow to half their size. "Five minutes," he says, sounding resigned. "I'll meet you back here."

Satisfied, I head through the small doorway into the homey store, a mix of the smells of cinnamon and worn paper hitting me instantly. I pause for a moment and close my eyes again, feeling the stress of the day fall away. The books are old but not dusty, carefully displayed rather than haphazardly stacked the way they are in some used bookshops. I run my hands gently over the spines, the cotton weave soft on the pads of my fingertips. A set of Sherlock Holmes books are lined up to create the famous silhouette on the spine. I make my way around the store, losing myself in the comfort of the books, the quiet murmurs of other shoppers creating a familiar lullaby. Despite the name, the shop is filled with a variety of genres, not only mysteries or horrors. There's something for everyone.

Out of the corner of my eye, I see Taj. He leans against a bookshelf, one leg crossed over the other, flipping through a novel. I hadn't realized he'd come in, too. I watch him read, wondering if he's confrontational with everyone else on the bus, or if there's something in particular about me that rubs him the wrong way. My eyes drift over the inside of his forearm, to the black lines of a tattoo, then I force myself to stop wasting my time in the shop looking at or thinking about Taj. I turn and head away from him toward the other side of the shop. I squeeze between two tables of books and down a row at the far side of the store.

At the end of an aisle, I turn around the corner of an oak bookshelf and come face to face with him. He's gazing down at the book in his hand and looks up, surprised, then clears his throat. "There you are," he says gruffly.

I smile. "You came, you saw, you found a book," I tease.

"It's a bookstore," he says drily. "It was bound to happen. And there's a wait for the sandwiches. Anyway, I was just looking." He shoves the book onto the top of a pile of books on a nearby cart.

"Oh, come on, you have to buy it," I say. "Anna and William want you to buy the book so they can pay their rent and feed their children."

"How do you know that?" His tone softens.

"I don't, I'm just—"

"Making shite up?" He shakes his head and brushes past me. "Right, well, it's been fifteen minutes. Sandwiches'll be ready. I'll meet you outside."

I turn away, and pick up the book Taj put down—a murder mystery by an author I don't know. I'm intrigued enough to tuck it under my arm, then walk over to the window to grab one of the mystery bags.

The woman at the cash pushes her glasses up on her nose and flips the book over. "I love a nice cozy mystery. Haven't read this one, though."

"It's actually . . . for someone else," I say, wondering if Taj comes in this bookshop every time they're in Cambridge, or if this was his first time. Did he buy *The Sweet Hereafter* in London, or from a favorite bookshop somewhere else along the tour? I rummage in my bag for my wallet then pull out my bank card. "Are you Anna?"

She raises her dark eyebrows. "I *am* Anna. And who are you?" She taps at the buttons on the cash register.

"Gigi. I was wondering about the sign out front. Or the *signs*, I guess you could say."

"Ah, yes, it's always so confusing to first-time visitors. My husband and I bought the shop some years ago. The previous owner made a request that we keep the original name, which is why we added our names to the sign. Now we're memorialized. When we pass the shop on to our kids, we're going to insist they keep our names up there." She winks at me.

"It will help them," I say, then stop, and Anna cocks her head and peers at me. I clear my throat. "It will help them get over the loss of you, if you let them put their stamp on it."

"Hmm," she says. "Hadn't thought of that."

A few minutes later, I'm back on the street. Taj sits on a bench a few feet away, in front of a large shop window that frames a cake plate piled high with baguette sandwiches. The door to the small lunch spot is open, and the smell of warm bread fills the air. His eyes flick to my hand, holding the brown mystery bag and the murder mystery. "No," he groans. "You fell for the grab bag?"

"I didn't *fall* for anything. I wanted to see what you get for five pounds."

"The books they can't sell," he says.

"That would be a bad business move," I inform him. "The best business comes from word of mouth. I'm sure it's going to be great." Taj points past me to the end of the alley, where a hundred feet away a Gothic spire shoots into the clear blue sky.

"That's where you're headed," Taj says. "King's College Chapel. You've got five minutes 'til they go in—just enough time to eat our sandwiches." He passes me one wrapped in paper.

"Thanks," I say, sitting down at the far end of the bench and putting my purse between us, then handing him the mystery he had considered in the shop. He stares at it, his brow furrowing. "Why did you get this?"

"I told you. Every sale makes a difference. I should know, I own a bookstore. This is the one you were looking at, right?"

"So you *do* own a bookshop," he says, as though I've just admitted that I dress up baby birds in tutus. He takes a bite of sandwich and shakes his head.

"Why is that weird?" I feel nervous, like I'm being interrogated.

"The first thing you did when you got here was go into a bookshop." His sunglasses are back on so it's impossible to read his expression, but his voice has an edge.

"I love books," I shrug. "It's not *that* weird." I unwrap the paper and take a bite. It's either the best sandwich I've ever tasted or I'm just *really* hungry.

"Come on, you're like, what, twenty-five? You don't own a bookshop," he challenges. His tone is teasing but I feel offended. At home, everyone knows I own Love Interest—and everyone knows *why* I own Love Interest. No one has ever thought of me as being too young to own the shop, even when I probably *was* too young to own the shop. I've always been older than my years, more responsible than my age.

"First of all, I'm thirty. Second of all, there's no age requirement for owning your own business, though if you must know, I took the shop over from my parents a little earlier than . . . I guess I'd planned."

"I'm not criticizing you. I'm sure there are a lot of perks to the family business. Like taking ten days off to come on holiday."

I feel myself getting angry. "You have no idea what you're talking about," I say, my voice shaking. "And it's none of your business anyway."

I don't bother waiting to see his reaction. I stand and turn, pushing the sandwich and mystery book into my bag and slinging it over my shoulder. We might be in the shade, but my entire body feels like it's on fire. Across the street in front of the chapel, a flash of pink catches my eye. Charlotte and the rest of the tour are gathering just a few steps away from the cathedral entrance. I weave my way through the crowd of pedestrians, cyclists and sightseers.

Charlotte beams as I hurry toward her. "There you are." She gives me a hug. "Are you alright? You look flushed."

I swallow. "I'm fine."

"Are you upset that we left you behind?" she whispers. "You were sleeping so soundly I didn't want to wake you."

"Gigi fell asleep and missed most of Cambridge, but she's just shown up," says Francis into his recorder.

"Has he been doing that the whole time?" I say, trying to forget my interaction with Taj. Why did I let him get to me?

Charlotte presses her lips together and nods. "It's a bit odd, isn't it?" She shrugs. "But he isn't hurting a fly."

"Alright, we're all here. Welcome back, Gigi," Angus calls out, giving me a wave. I smile, feeling glad to be part of the group. "Ouch, that hurts." He touches his left arm. "Might have to start waving with my right arm instead."

"Angus got a terrible cut on his arm earlier," Charlotte whispers. "Snagged it on a jagged piece of metal fence. I had to rush off to Boots for a bandage for him." She blushes.

"And now, we've reached the pièce de résistance, as the French say," Angus says as he stretches his arms out. "King's College Chapel is the largest chapel in the United Kingdom, second only in the world to the Vatican." He looks behind him. "It took nearly one hundred years to complete construction of this majestic piece of work. It's an example of late Perpendicular Gothic English architecture. Personally I think the outside looks a bit like a shoebox, but that's not the interesting thing. It's what's on the inside that is so fascinating," he says, and I reach out for Charlotte, feeling light-headed. She looks over at me, and smiles and squeezes my hand, which helps only slightly. In my rush to get away from Taj, I didn't fully think through my excuse not to actually go inside the chapel. "You're about to see the largest single span of vaulted roof anywhere in the world," Angus continues. As we walk toward the massive arched door, I lean over to

Charlotte. "I'm just going to sit out here and eat this sandwich," I say, producing the red-and-white waxed paper package.

"Oh, poor dear, are you sure? You've missed the whole town." But I nod and let go of her hand. As the group disappears into the narthex, I can't help turning around to see if Taj is joining them, but he's nowhere in sight. Thankfully. I think.

Chapter Eight

Day 1, Sunday, 3 p.m.

Cambridge ❯ Rochester

Taj's head is down, and he's reading the last few pages of *The Sweet Hereafter* as I board the bus. I consider thanking him for the sandwich, but I'm still angry with his comments and embarrassed by my own reaction and don't really want to deal with any of it or him. So instead I slip by him without saying anything. At my seat I find my phone wedged between the cushions. I touch the screen and see a barrage of texts, all from my book club group chat. Now that they think Zane is *so hot, haha*, they want all the details. Mostly, *how hot, haha* he is.

I type out a quick message, telling them they won't believe what's happened and setting up a time to FaceTime them from the hotel tonight before dinner, then punch in Lars's number. That call goes through to his voicemail. I hang up because I know he won't check his messages.

I feel like I've lost all control over my life.

Wake up! I type then hit Send.

When Lars doesn't reply, I call again.

"Gigi, *what*?" He sounds groggy.

"Why aren't you up?" I say, kicking off my shoes and pulling my feet up under me on the seat. Charlotte looks over and pats my hand. I must sound harsh, but I can't help it. Everything here is going wrong, and I was hoping to be reassured things were better at home.

"Because it's the middle of the night," Lars says.

For a split second I feel terrible, but then I hold my phone away from my ear and mentally double-check my time-difference math. "Lars, it's 9 a.m." I let out a frustrated sigh.

"Same same. Besides, aren't you supposed to be on England time by now?"

The bus roars to life and pulls out of the parking lot, past a copse of maples.

"Never mind what time *I'm* on. The point is that *you* should know it's nine o'clock and the store opens in an hour and you should be up so that you can get everything done that needs to be done before the first customer arrives." If he can't get up in time to open the shop by 10 a.m. on Sundays, how is he going to get it open by 9 a.m. on weekdays?

Lars groans. "Gigi, the shop is seriously ten steps away. Pretty sure I'm going to make it on time. Relax."

"You have to make the coffee before you open."

"I'll just grab one at that place on the corner. It's quicker."

"Not for you, Lars. For customers." I lean my head against the window as jet lag hits me for the millionth time today.

"You serve coffee? *Why?*"

Why can't Lars be the kind of brother who just makes things easy? Even though I'm used to him having an opinion about everything, right now it feels like too much to deal with. I sigh again.

"Because it's a nice thing to do. And you have to fill any online orders that came in overnight, before the store opens, otherwise you'll miss the delivery pickup and—"

"Didn't you write all this down on that massive notepad you left me?"

"Of course I did," I say. "But"—beside me, Charlotte pulls a ball of light-green wool from her flamingo-print tote. It's come unraveled, and she keeps pulling and pulling like a magician removing a scarf from a top hat.

"Then you don't need to tell me all of this. I'm really more of a visual learner anyway, so you telling me all of this, it doesn't play to my strengths. Relax, Gigi. I'm in charge now, remember?"

That's the problem. Even though Lars is completely capable of running the store, I'm not sure he's capable of running it the way I want it run. "Lars—"

"Gotta go. Later gator." He hangs up. I shove my phone back in my bag.

"Sounds like a tough call," Charlotte says, passing me the ball of yarn. I grasp it with two hands, digging my fingers through the soft threads.

"I left my little brother in charge of my shop," I say. "He's not that little, but . . ."

"He'll always be little to you?" She winks at me.

"Exactly." The yarn is soft and I have this urge to hold it to my cheek, but I don't. "What are you knitting?"

"I haven't yet decided," Charlotte says as the bus veers left and I lean into her. "A friend took one of these tours a few years ago and mentioned the long stretches of driving, and that it was best to have something to keep occupied, to pass the time," she continues. "So I figured I'd try my hand at knitting."

When I imagined these legs of the tour, between towns, between lulls in Zane's narration—even long before the girls gave me the gift—I'd pictured myself reading my book, head against the window, occasionally glancing out into the world as I passed it by. It felt incredibly romantic—and so different from home, where I spend my days reading inside the shop, waiting for the world to come through the doors. Now, though, I'm too distracted to read. Every time I think about Zane, I find myself wondering: What if he doesn't show up?

Charlotte reaches into her bag and retrieves two gray metal knitting needles.

"Trouble is," she says, and I remember she was telling me what she was knitting, "I don't have the faintest idea how to knit." I must look surprised because she exhales loudly. "See? Everyone thinks if you're a woman with wrinkles you know how to knit."

"No!" I say a little too quickly. "OK, maybe." I laugh and Charlotte leans into me as the bus veers to the right this time.

"I think I'm mostly doing this to prove to myself that I *can* do it."

"Of course you can do it," I say, even though I have no clue how difficult it is to knit.

"You sound so confident. You don't even know me."

"It has nothing to do with you," I say, pushing thoughts of Zane away. What I need right now is a distraction—and that's exactly what Charlotte's offering me. I swivel in my seat to face her. "It's like when someone comes into my shop and says they're not sure they'll be able to get through a literary romance like

Tess of the d'Urbervilles," I say. "I always tell them that of course they *can* do it. Read the words, turn the page. It's all about focus and that's all to do with whether they want to or not. Millions of people knit. It can't be *that* hard."

"Well, thank you. But that still isn't going to help me figure out how to start."

"I know just the person we can ask," I say, turning around in my seat. "Jenny!"

Jenny's hunched over, her head down, her big red headphones covering her ears.

Violet looks up, then turns and reaches behind her, touching Jenny on the head. Jenny looks up and lifts off her headphones. "What?" she says, making a face.

Violet points to me.

"Can you recommend an easy-to-follow knitting YouTuber?" I call back to Jenny.

Her eyes narrow. "No." She pops her headphones back on. I turn back to Charlotte, and bite my lip to stop from laughing.

"Pleasant, isn't she?" Charlotte says drily. "So now what?"

"Who needs her anyway?" I pull out my phone and type in *How to knit*, then hit Go.

A moment later, our heads are close together as we watch a pale-faced thirty-something guy in glasses and a striped T-shirt explain how to knit.

"Huh. Seems easy enough," Charlotte says, studying the video. "And if he can do it, I can do it." She ties the yarn in a slipknot and loops it over the end of one needle, slides the second needle in, loops the yarn over the point, and pulls it through in a repetitive motion.

"You're doing it."

"You were right. I *can* do it." For a few moments we're both silent as Charlotte knits and I look out the window. The scenery around us has transitioned from urban to rural. Pastures, a few cows grazing on the rolling terrain.

"Look at those moo-vie stars," Angus booms into his headset microphone suddenly, pointing out the left side of the bus. Multiple groans fill the air, but I smile. There's something about Angus that's definitely stress-relieving.

"Maybe we should have brought the kids," Sindhi says. "We never travel without them."

"That's exactly *why* we didn't bring the kids," Roshi says.

I turn back to Charlotte, who's managed three rows of stitches. "That looks great," I say, encouragingly, even though there's a huge hole in the middle of the second row. She gives me a look and I laugh.

"All my friends knit," Charlotte says. "Baby bonnets and baby booties and baby blankets. And they get together every Monday. I feel left out, which feels silly at my age, but there you go."

"I guess some human emotions never go away," I say, thinking about my friends, and how often I feel left out because I'm single and childless. "I know my friends do stuff without me—but I try to remind myself that it's not because they don't want me around; it's that they figure I won't want to come to the zoo or the playground or whatever. Maybe your friends feel the same way?"

Charlotte nods. "You're right. The funny thing is, I never felt this way when they were all having children and I wasn't—so I'm not sure why it bothers me so much now that we're at the grandparent stage."

The bus slows, and the back of a black horse comes into view on my left, a man in a navy-and-white-checked dress shirt, jeans and a black helmet on top. In front of him is a small girl with a pink helmet riding a smaller horse. Then another horse with its rider, and another and another, all in a straight line.

"Here's one for you Americans on the bus," Angus says. "What did the horse say when he fell over?" Angus waves out the window, then turns back to us. "I've fallen and I can't giddyup!" He leans over and slaps Taj's shoulder. Taj looks in the rearview and catches my eye, but I turn back to Charlotte.

"So you're not a grandmother," I say.

"Or a mother." She shakes her head. "I'm OK with it. I'm a very wherever-the-wind-blows kind of gal. Never bothered me not to do what others were doing, but ever since Harold died, I've been noticing how much harder—or lonelier it is, maybe—not to be like all my friends." She wraps the wool around the needle and holds it out to me. "Like this?"

I nod. "I think so."

"I'm not sure knitting's the answer, but . . ." she trails off.

"You've got ten days to find out?" I laugh and so does Charlotte.

"Exactly."

Ten days to find out about a lot of things, I think.

Chapter Nine

Day 1, Sunday, 5 p.m.

Rochester

"Charles Dickens adored Rochester," Angus says that afternoon as we walk down the bustling High Street toward the Rochester Cathedral. He explains that it's the second-oldest cathedral in England, after the one in Canterbury, which is on tomorrow's itinerary. "There are forty-two cathedrals in England," Angus says pretty much apropos of nothing, and my stomach tightens. There were definitely nowhere near forty-two churches listed on this tour, but what if the change in guide means change in itinerary? What if Angus not only adores animals, but also abbeys? But it's only the first day, and the tour hasn't been *all* churches—there was Upnor Castle, a miniature storybook fort tucked into the banks of the River Medway. And before dinner we'll be visiting Rochester Castle, which towers over the town farther down the river. The only church I've had to skip so far was King's College Chapel in Cambridge. And who knows— maybe seeing so many churches will help soothe my grief, but right now, I'm just hoping I can figure out an easy way to get out of the next stop.

We continue past the shops on High Street, a break between buildings on our left opening up onto a lush lawn, a stone path down the center leading to the gray stone cathedral, which looks foreboding against the darkening sky. The *Sleeping Beauty*–style spires of the cathedral disappear into the low clouds. There's nothing like this in Ann Arbor. "Dickens grew up here," Angus continues, "but he left and then returned, and he loved the place so much that he featured it in his work more than any other city, even London."

"Technically Rochester isn't a city," Francis interrupts. "Lost its status in 1998. Now it's a town."

"Boring," Jenny says, which makes Nelle shoot her a disapproving look and Roshi laugh out loud. I feel a bit like I'm in middle school again, on a school trip, with bickering classmates.

Angus points out a half-timbered house, a metal plaque affixed to the white stucco. "This is the house of Mr. Tope from *The Mystery of Edwin Drood*."

"Ooh, is it true crime?" Jenny shuffles closer to Angus. He relays the plot of Dickens's unfinished novel, and I only half listen, looking around. A small shop across the narrow street, books in the large bay window, catches my eye. I wander over to peer through the glass, which is mottled with dust and grime.

"Gigi bought a book in the last town, and she's looking like she's going to buy another book in this town," Francis says into his recorder. I turn around, feeling annoyed, but Francis looks so innocent that my emotions turn instead to embarrassment. Sindhi is standing beside him, hands on hips. "I thought I heard that you own a bookshop," she says to me. I blush. Another thing I never considered about this tour was that I'd be of any interest to anyone. I'd hoped to be interesting to Zane, but that's it.

"I wouldn't touch that topic," Taj says before I can respond, walking over with Roshi beside him. Seriously? Me looking in a window of a bookshop is more interesting than Angus talking about Dickens? Taj raises an eyebrow at me. "She really likes books. And she gets very defensive if you challenge her on it, for some reason."

I'm about to respond, but Sindhi interjects before I can. "Why in heavens would you purchase a book from another bookshop?" she asks. "That's a terrible idea. You're basically throwing money at your competition." She turns to look at the group for confirmation. At this point everyone is standing around, staring at me like they've just discovered a two-headed penguin on the streets of Rochester. The only one still listening to Angus is Jenny.

"Good point," Violet says, nodding.

"I didn't even go into the store." I throw my hands in the air. "And we're in a totally different country. If any one of you bought a book here," I say, pointing to the shop beside me, "it's not like I'd think you were taking business away from my shop. This shop's success is not my shop's failure." It's like the penguin is now tap-dancing for the crowd. I should shut up.

"My dad owns a Dunkin' Donuts," Jenny says, having appeared while I was performing. Angus is still across the street, now talking to strangers. "I've never had a donut from any other donut shop," she says. Her headphones are around her neck, and she fiddles with the cord. "Not even when donuts were trending. You've got to be loyal." She gives Violet a hard stare, even though Violet was the one who'd agreed with Sindhi's point.

Angus claps his hands and motions for us to follow him toward the church. "I thought I was getting away from the South, but it's just like home, isn't it?" Charlotte says, looping her arm through mine. "Everyone's business is everyone's business." She smiles, the pink lipstick bleeding into the tiny vertical lines around her mouth.

I nod, then whisper to her that I'm going to go into the bookshop. "Might as well fulfill the prophecy. I'll meet you when you get out of the church."

If Charlotte notices this is the second time I've skipped a church, she doesn't say anything, just nods and then untangles her arm from mine. But as I turn to go back to the bookshop, my phone pings.

Call me.

Lars's text immediately fills me with dread. What has he done? Flooded the store? Set it on fire? Forgotten to lock up and I've been robbed? It's only noon. The store's only been open for two hours. How could so much go so wrong already? I immediately call him, but the phone rings and rings. I hang up and try again as I walk away from the bookshop and make my way through the iron gate of the churchyard, down a few wide steps to a large concrete war monument. Engraved on the north side are the words *Lest we forget 1914–1918.* Underneath, a woman leans against the stone, reading a guidebook. I perch myself on the opposite side.

Finally, after countless rings, Lars answers.

"What's wrong?" I ask immediately.

"You don't have the new John Grisham." He sounds curious.

"*What?*" I relax. This is good news. Mentos in water, not Mentos in Coke. Weird, but not cause for a cleanup crew.

"You don't have the new John Grisham," Lars repeats, enunciating every word.

"No, of course not, Lars." I laugh as relief floods through me even though I'm going to have to go through some text etiquette with Lars if we're both going to make it through these ten days unscathed.

"Well I've had two customers come in asking for it. Apparently it just came out or something?"

"I don't sell John Grisham." Lars may not read as much as I do, but surely he knows John Grisham doesn't write romance.

"You know it's on the bestseller list, right?"

It's not just on *the bestseller list, it's number one on the bestseller list.*

"Lars, I only sell romance novels. Remember?"

"Yeah, but you're turning away sales. Give the people what they want!" he booms like a sports announcer. "People want John Grisham!"

I laugh, but my heart isn't in it. I feel homesick for the store, even though it's only been a day. I stand and follow the stone path around the cathedral. "People also want Helen Hoang and Elin Hilderbrand and Abby Jimenez and Emily Giffin." I'm sort of book-bragging, but I can't help it.

"I could pick up a few copies at Barnes & Noble, just to have on hand," Lars rambles on. "If it's on the bestseller list it's probably on sale, so you could just sell them for full price and at least turn a bit of profit."

My breath catches and I stop walking. One single tree dominates the lawn in front of the cathedral. The massive, thick trunk sprouts into a tangle of gangly branches, like a rollercoaster track winding its way through the clouds that are the billow of leaves. The entire tree takes up the span of an Olympic-sized swimming pool. I've never seen anything like it. It feels magical.

"Hello?" Lars says in my ear.

"Oh, right," I say, shaken back to the present, the magical effects of the tree dissipating. "If someone wants John Grisham, they can just go to Barnes & Noble and get it," I say. A wrought-iron fence surrounds the tree. I sit down and lean against it.

"Alright, but it's a missed opportunity for sales. Sales that are going to Barnes & Noble—or City Lit," he says, knowing the mention of my biggest competition—a popular new-and-used bookshop only a few streets away from Love Interest—will get under my skin. I think about what I just told the rest of the group about success and competition. Though City Lit isn't technically a direct competitor, people only buy so many books, and if they come into my shop before City Lit, there's always an opportunity to not only sell them the one book they're going to buy that day, but to change their mind about the romance genre, maybe forever.

Instead, I say to Lars, "I don't need you to challenge how I run the store. I just need you to run the store the way I asked." I don't mean to sound so irritated, but it's too late. Lars hangs up on me. I sigh and lean my head against the metal fence, letting my eyes close. It's hard to believe that less than twenty-four hours ago I was still at home, imagining how this trip was going to go. So far, it isn't like anything I imagined. I feel beaten down and exhausted and like I can't figure out how to just be here and *enjoy* being here.

"Tough call?"

My eyes flit open as Roshi approaches. I smile and muster up the energy to be friendly in a way that feels familiar, the way I do at the shop. The way Mom trained me when I was eleven, a skill I honed as a teen when I'd have rather been at the mall with friends. Or during a snowstorm when we'd only get one or two customers, just enough to interrupt a day immersed in a book. Or when David and I broke up and I would've done anything to hide from the world for even a day. In comparison, this—being here, on vacation—is easy, I remind myself. I motion to the grassy spot beside me, and Roshi sits down, removes his navy Breton cap and leans back against the fence, closing his eyes. "I'm imagining that we're leaning right up against that old catalpa trunk instead of this cold iron fence." He rests a crossword puzzle book on his thighs.

"Is it working?" I laugh, closing my eyes, too.

"Not really," he chuckles. "Wanna talk about it?" I look over at him. His eyes slope downward toward my phone. "I could use the distraction." His tone is light, but it makes me wonder what's going on with him and Sindhi. From what I've seen, they've barely had more than a few exchanges the whole day—Sindhi has spent most of her time off the bus with Violet and Nelle. I think about that saying, that people think being alone is lonely, but sometimes, being in the wrong relationship can feel lonelier. Are they in the wrong relationship, or is their relationship just going through a tough spell?

"Well," I begin. "As you probably heard, I own a bookshop. My brother's looking after it while I'm here. He should be able to handle it, but he's a . . . free spirit. Doesn't really love to follow the rules."

"And that stresses you out."

"Mm," I nod. "I like order. But who doesn't, when they're running a business?"

Roshi nods. "The thing is, when you're here and he's there, it doesn't much matter what you want. You've kind of got to bend to the situation." He thumbs toward the tree. "You know this tree nearly died? I remember reading about it years ago. It was so thick it split in two."

I twist to look at the tree, then turn back to him. "From a storm?"

He shakes his head. "Nope. No real reason at all, not that they could figure out. The town was in shock. *This* tree? They never thought anything would happen to *this* tree. But they rallied to save it. They pushed it back together. You wouldn't even be able to tell now, would you?" He gestures to the trunk again.

"That doesn't make sense. The splitting or the pushing back together."

He shrugs. "I don't know. Sometimes there's no explanation for why things happen, or don't happen, or work, or don't work."

Is this some sort of metaphor? But if it is, Roshi doesn't give me any further clues.

He pulls a pen out of his breast pocket and stares at the crossword puzzle on his lap. Then he writes the word *adaptable* into 18 Across and looks at me.

He belly-laughs at my stunned expression. "What? Total coincidence."

"Yeah, right." But I laugh, too.

"Here—" He turns the book toward me. "You can help me with 23 Down."

·

"She's here!" The side of Dory's face fills my phone screen.

I set the phone up on the shiny mahogany nightstand, then flop down onto the four-poster bed and exhale. This might be the most comfortable mattress I've ever lain on. It's definitely the nicest hotel I've ever been in—it's this massive Elizabethan townhouse with tall windows framed with long velvet curtains. Each of the spacious eight rooms is decorated in greens and golds, and my room looks out into a small vegetable garden bordered in topiaries, a gravel-lined maze of perfectly manicured hedges. We have the whole place to ourselves.

"Hang on, I'm connecting my iPad to the TV so we can all fit in front of it on the couch," Dory says. A second later, Cleo comes into view, sitting on the couch beside Emily and passing her a champagne flute. "You guys are all together?" I say, surprised.

"Dory insisted we come over for brunch so we could hear all about your first day," Jacynthe says, holding out her champagne flute to Cleo, who pours the bubbly into it, then Emily tops it with orange juice. Dory joins them at the end of the couch.

I feel a stab of loneliness, seeing them together, hanging out without me, but remind myself that I'm here *because* of their thoughtfulness, and I don't want to seem ungrateful. "Do you want to see the room?" I ask and Emily leans forward, nodding. I turn my phone around and give them a tour of the copper claw-foot soaker tub, the window seat, the wood-paneled walls, the pendant lights casting a soft glow over the room as the sun disappears into the horizon.

"Alright, alright, your room is great, but we came for the good stuff," Cleo says, sipping her mimosa. "Tell us everything that's happened so far. Don't skip anything." She settles back into the couch and crosses one thin, yoga-pant-clad leg over the other.

"It's been so beautiful," I say, describing Cambridge and making it seem like I was awake the whole time, missed none of the sites, and that the tour itself is every bit as incredible as I'd hoped. "I'm really so lucky to even be here," I say. "You guys are the best, you know?"

"Sounds dreamy," Emily interjects, "but what about Zane?"

My stomach clenches and I wish my phone would die so I wouldn't have to tell them the truth. But they're all staring at me expectantly.

"Zane isn't here," I say finally, biting my lip.

"Wait," Dory says, raising her eyebrows. "But you said he was hot."

I sigh. "Autocorrect. And there was too much going on to fix it. I had to figure out what to do. But Angus says he'll get here tomorrow," I say, though there's that little voice again that says, *What if he doesn't?*

"Oh no . . ." Emily says, her expression pained. "Are you *so* disappointed?"

"It's one day," Cleo says. "What's the big deal?"

"What if he doesn't show up?" Dory asks.

"*Please*," Jacynthe says, closing her eyes and putting a mani-cured hand to her forehead. "Gigi is not on the trip solely to meet this man."

"Jacynthe's right. Maybe it's a sign," Dory says. "Is there any-one else interesting on the bus?" Her hazel eyes sparkle.

"The bus driver has some pretty great forearms," I say, mostly for entertainment value.

"The bus driver?" Jacynthe turns up her nose. "Sheesh, pick-ings *are* slim."

I push the image of Taj and his arms out of my mind.

"It's mostly seniors, except me and this other girl who's a YouTuber." Then I'm about to tell them about Charlotte, but Dory holds up her phone with her free hand.

"I know just the fix," she says.

"What are you doing?" I say, my tone a warning, because I have a feeling I know exactly what she's doing. I shake my head. "No, no, no, no . . ."

"Where did you say you are again?"

"Rochester," Cleo says, then turns back to me. "See? I was lis-tening to every little detail."

Dory taps on her phone. "Hmm. OK, well, there's not much coming up." Her finger flicks the screen. "Ew. Nope." Dory leans closer to Cleo. Emily leans in on one side, Jacynthe on the other.

"I don't need a guy," I clarify. "I'm not the one who said I needed a guy."

"Right," Jacynthe says. "She's there to explore . . ."

"I know," Dory says, her head down. "I'm just finding someone for her to explore."

"Ewww," Emily says, making a sour face.

"Got him." Dory holds her phone out to Cleo, whose eyes widen. *Wow,* she mouths.

Emily leans over, then shakes her head and sighs, looking exasperated.

"What am I missing?" I say, my fingers numb.

"This guy." Dory stands and walks closer to the screen, then turns Cleo's phone toward me, and for the millionth time today, I'm at a loss for words.

Chin-length, wavy-brown hair. Unshaven. Strong jaw. Challenging look in his eye.

All of it staring back at me from a dating app.

Taj.

"Huh," I say, trying to cover my interest. "*He's* on XO?"

"The way you said that—*he*. What do you mean, *he*?" Dory says, looking at the phone. "You know him?"

"Yeah," I say slowly, feeling weirdly nervous. "That's the bus driver. With the forearms."

"*What* bus driver?" Dory says.

"The bus driver on *your* bus?" Emily says, standing beside Dory and grabbing the phone. She swipes at the screen with her thumb. I wonder how many pics he has on there—and what he looks like in them.

"*This* just got interesting," Cleo says in the background.

"So you *know* this guy?" Jacynthe asks, pushing Dory out of the way, and looking at me. Dory's face gets closer. They're all suddenly quiet, waiting for my answer.

"Sort of," I say. "But he's kind of a dick."

.

"Shall we take a post-meal dander, yah?" Angus asks after we've had a traditional British dinner of steak and kidney pie, and a beer tasting that included an ale from the oldest brewery in the country. I don't usually drink beer, but it seemed like the thing to do, and even though we were only sipping them, I feel a bit light-headed. A walk sounds good.

"I'll come along," Charlotte says, and Angus beams at her.

"I never say no to a walk," Nelle says. "Vi? Shall we walk?"

"Absolutely," Violet says, reaching for Nelle's hand. "Anyone who'd like to come with me," Angus says, "I think I'll lead us down to the river. It's quite spectacular at night, with the lights dancing off the surface of the water."

Sindhi says she wants to go back to the hotel, and Roshi says he'll join her. "I'm fine walking alone," she says.

"Anybody who'd like to head back to the hotel, it's straight away down High Street," he says, pointing to the three-story brown brick building at the end of the street.

Francis bends down to tie the lace on his shoe, then stands. "I think I'll head back. I'm going to call my daughter. It's her birthday," he says, which strikes me as surprising. For some reason I just assumed he was a lonely old man, never married, no kids. He tips his hat and looks around. "Good night, everyone," he says. I smile and wave and others murmur goodbyes. He follows Sindhi, and Roshi follows closely behind.

Jenny looks around. "I'm going on the haunted ghost walk that leaves from the cathedral. Which way is that again?" She twirls around, then looks down at her phone.

"That sounds fun," Violet says, looking to Nelle and then to Jenny. "Mind if we join you?"

"It's sold out. I bought my ticket earlier. Got the last one," she says bluntly.

"It's fine. The river walk sounds lovely," Violet says to Nelle, wrapping an arm around her.

Charlotte looks at me, her eyes wide. "What about you, Darlin'?"

"I'm going to go check out Restoration House," I say. "I'll see you in the morning?"

She waves her fingers at me and then walks over to Angus, who removes his checked hat and gives his head a scratch as he says something to her that makes her throw her head back with a laugh. I pull out my phone to find the way to the house that inspired the setting for the Satis House in *Great Expectations*. I've read that the gardens behind the mansion are the real sight to be seen: classically English with immaculate lawns, yew hedges and topiaries, statues and fountains inspired by Italian water gardens. They even have an entire area called the cutting garden, which supplies the fresh floral arrangements used in the house. The gardens won't be open, neither will the interior, but it's the outside I'm happy enough to see.

It's chillier than I expected as I start down High Street, and even though I'm wearing a jean jacket, it's not doing much to cut the wind. I wish I'd thought to wear a scarf. The shops are all closed on High Street, but within a minute I'm turning onto the first street on the right—Crow Lane—and a minute later I'm standing in front of the wrought-iron gates that surround the brown Tudor-style mansion.

As far as buildings go, it's not anything extraordinary, but for some reason my chest feels tight, my head heavy. It's probably jet lag, but I feel emotional seeing the house that played its own character in the novel.

"Let me guess, there's a bookstore in there."

I turn around. Taj is a few paces away in a crisp white shirt and dark jeans and leather sandals. His hair looks freshly washed. He looks good—but of course he does. He's probably meeting some girl from the XO app for drinks. I scowl at him. "That's not the only thing I'm interested in," I say. I turn back to face the building, though to be honest, it's not a lot to look at from a distance, behind the gates. But Taj doesn't need to know that.

"I thought you might be a bit friendlier once the jet lag wore off." I whip back around to face him, prepared to put him in his place, but he's grinning. "Listen, I owe you an apology." I must look as surprised as I feel because he starts laughing. "OK, I guess I wasn't the world's friendliest coach driver earlier today."

The new moon, low and yellow against the dark sky, creates a halo behind Taj that makes me stare a little too long at him. I refocus on our conversation.

"You were the world's *snarkiest* coach driver, actually, when you're paid to be nice to people," I say. He leans against the iron gates and folds his arms over his chest, his shirt tightening over his upper arms and distracting me from what I was saying.

"Actually, I'm paid to drive the bus, but that doesn't excuse my behavior. I wish I had a better excuse, but all I can say is that I was really hungry. And I get really cranky when I'm really hungry." He shrugs.

"You're not five. That's a terrible excuse," I retort, but then I smile. "But I get it. I was also really hungry and really tired." And really disappointed in the entire situation, I don't add.

"I was tired, too," he says and I laugh, because it feels like he's trying to one-up me. "I'd been to a stag night. Which was . . . a mistake." He scratches his chin, which I notice is now clean-shaven.

"So you were *hungover*."

"No, actually. Just tired and hungry. Truly. And you were a bit grumpy, too. Admit it."

"I got zero sleep on the flight." I throw my hands up. "I nearly missed the bus. I missed breakfast and *lunch*." I wave my arms around and hit the iron gate and groan, then grab my hand in pain. Taj presses his lips together, but it doesn't stop his whole body from shaking as he laughs. I glare at him. "You think this is funny?"

"I think you're interesting. And I did get you a sandwich."

"I know, and I didn't thank you. It was *really* good." I tilt my head and study him. By the light of the moon, his eyes seem to have a dozen different shades of brown—I stop myself from thinking about his eyes.

"Told you." He shoves his hands in his pockets, and my eyes move down his body, trailing over his broad shoulders.

"Tomorrow will be better," he says. "You've stayed up, so you'll sleep well tonight. That's the key to beating jet lag. And tomorrow's Canterbury. One of my favorite towns, even though I'd be burned at the stake for saying so," he adds, but before I get a chance to ask why, he keeps talking. "After that we hit the shore. You'll love it. Actually, I have no idea what you'll love—I don't even know you. But most people love the shore, especially if they're not into architecture and the stations of the cross."

But will Zane be here for all of this? I want to ask Taj—but it will be too obvious.

A middle-aged couple walks by. "Weren't you so disappointed?" the woman asks in an Australian accent.

"It is what it is," he says.

"Ten bucks!" I say automatically, slapping my leg. The man turns, obviously surprised. I hold up a hand. "Hi." He smiles, still looking confused, and turns around.

Taj stares at me like I've just thrown my clothes at the couple and am standing in the middle of the sidewalk, naked.

"What was *that* all about?" he says.

"It's a thing I have with my friends. If you hear someone say 'It is what it is' you have to yell 'Ten bucks!' and slap your leg— or something. A table, someone else, it really doesn't matter. Because—"

"It's nauseating?" he says.

I laugh. "Exactly. It means nothing. Like, have an opinion. *Care.*"

"Alright, so what happens after you slap something? Does the person have to pay ten *bucks*?" He says *bucks* with an American accent—sort of.

"Yes, usually."

"Off you go then. I'd like to see you get that bloke to pay." He folds his arms across his chest. The light of the lamppost hits them, turning them from 70 percent chocolate to milk chocolate.

"It doesn't work like that with strangers."

"Ah, changing the rules already," he teases, then nods toward the estate behind me. "The gardens here are really lovely, but you can't see them at night. Locked up."

"It's fine," I say. "Just wanted to see the house. *Great Expectations*."

"Ahh. Because you love books." He smiles, then thumbs behind him. "Don't stay up too late," he says, turning.

"I was going to go back to the hotel anyway," I say, falling into step with him.

"I'm actually on my way out to meet someone," he says as we cross the street. "But you can find your way back OK?"

My neck gets hot, though I don't know why I'm embarrassed that he thought I assumed he was going back to the hotel, too. Of course he's going out—this is his free time, off work. "Oh, right," I say. I give a weird wave like I'm a bird flapping a wing. He laughs, nods and turns right. A small paperback sticks out of the back of his pants, and I notice it's the cozy mystery I gave him. Is he going to read it while on a date? Is he going to give it to his date? And if he's bringing it with him, why did he make such a big deal about me buying it for him?

Chapter Ten

Day 2, Monday, 9 a.m.

Rochester ❭ Canterbury

Mom always said that style isn't about what you're wearing, it's about how you're feeling. But as I lie in bed, I do not feel like a million British pounds. I woke up at eight and have been trying to mentally manifest Zane into being in the hotel library, enjoying the full English breakfast that's being served. But now that I can picture him—dark jeans, crisp white shirt, swoopy hair, full lips on a cup of tea—I'm paralyzed with the question of what to wear to go down there myself. And when I take one look at myself in the bathroom mirror, I realize I have a bigger problem. I'm still wearing yesterday's eyeliner—I forgot to pack eye makeup remover—so now it's slid down a good inch from my lashline. I'm starving, but if Zane really *is* here today, as Angus said he might be, then I want to look good so I can feel good about myself, and I make the possibly terrible decision to risk hunger (did I learn nothing yesterday?) to take my time getting ready. If Zane's really here, what's one breakfast anyway? And because I don't have a tub at home and who knows if there'll be another soaker tub on this trip, I take an extra-long bubble bath, washing my hair and then blow-drying it straight, then sitting at the stool in the bathroom to apply fresh makeup in the mirror. When I'm finished, I feel really good about myself. And I *look* good, too. Not exactly well-rested, but the concealer I've padded under my eyes has done a lot. But I am hungry. I put on a pair of crop jeans, a striped sweater and a handful of bangles, look around the room one last time, then drag my suitcase out into the hall, closing the door behind me and taking a minute to breathe through my nose.

This is it.

I remind myself that Zane is just a guy. A normal guy who happens to lead tours and whose voice is tied to the most important book in my life . . . A normal guy who's also really good-looking and basically the reason I'm here.

No big deal, Gigi.

I take a breath and pull myself together, prepared to do my best to act breezy or at least normal, and head down two flights of carpeted stairs and into the dark, mahogany-paneled lobby—which is empty. The velvet-clad library around the corner is also empty, but the platter of pastries and a self-serve carafe of coffee on the sideboard catch my eye. I shove a pastry in my purse, then balance my coffee in my free hand and turn around as Jenny enters the room, her camera attached to a gimbal, which is swaying back and forth. "Did you know someone was murdered right here in the library?" she says.

"*Really?*"

"I'm talking to the camera," she hisses, then turns back to the camera and repeats the line. "I was sitting here last night having a cocktail, and the temperature dropped at least twenty degrees.

My lips looked like I was wearing frosted lipstick, and you all know how I feel about frosted lipstick," she says dramatically. "So I'm back now to see if I sense anything else suspicious."

I tiptoe out of the library, praying I'll casually bump into Zane, but the lobby remains empty. Out the front doors into the bright sunshine, I look around. Off to the right, most of the group stands in a semicircle chatting, their suitcases lined up in a neat row. To the left, Charlotte's mid-patter with Angus, and my stomach drops, because if Angus is here then does that mean Zane won't be? Charlotte waves and I walk over to them, my heart rate picking up speed with every step. Angus is flipping through the clipboard in his hand. "Good morning," I say brightly.

Angus grins. "Gigi, check! How'd you sleep?"

"Oh great," I say. "Maybe too well. Sorry to miss breakfast." I clear my throat. "I was actually hoping I'd still make it out to see you this morning before you left." My voice is an octave too high. So much for breezy.

He gives me a sympathetic smile. "Sadly, looks like you're stuck with me for another day. No word from Zane yet. Family emergencies. So unpredictable."

I bite the inside of my lip a little too hard, leaving a tender bump. "A family emergency?" It shouldn't matter that Zane isn't here, I reason with myself. But of course it does. It does, it does. Disappointment heaves my stomach. Darn it.

"Not to worry," Angus says. "His mum's had a bit of a health scare, and they're such a tight-knit family, that of course Zane needed to see her." He claps his hands. "But he promises to be here as soon as he can. Good thing, because I can't do back-to-back tours the way I could when I was thirty—last year." He winks at

Charlotte. "Anyway, enough about that. But guess what?" Angus looks from Charlotte to me. "I haven't told you the best part about being on one of my tours." I take a sip of coffee. It's lukewarm, but it's the first coffee I've had in two days, so I'm going to drink it anyway.

Off to the left, the red bus appears from behind a row of evenly spaced plane trees, the lower branches just brushing the top as Taj pulls it into the circular drive.

"OK, listen up, everyone," Angus says, clipboard under his arm, clapping loudly. The rest of the group shuffles closer, the gravel crunching underfoot. "Everyone has to choose someone new to sit beside. It's a great way for us to better get to know each other." He looks at Charlotte. "Mind if I join you?"

Charlotte takes a sip of water, then slowly smiles. "Fine by me," she sing-songs.

Roshi turns to me. "How about you and me?"

"Oh, sure," I say, then look to Sindhi. "As long as Sindhi's OK with it?" I wonder how she feels about coming on a trip with her husband, only to spend most of the trip sitting with strangers. Although, if Zane arrives later today—I can still hold out hope—or tomorrow, Angus won't be dictating our seating arrangements. Will Zane have the same rule? I imagine him being my seatmate . . .

Sindhi gives me a blank look. "I'm not going to stand in your way," she says drily.

The bus doors open and Taj descends. His hair is messy again, and he has a hint of stubble. He walks over to the pile of luggage a few feet away and, one by one, begins hauling our baggage into the storage compartment.

"I got a lot of the crossword done last night," Roshi says as he climbs the steps of the bus. "Want to try to finish it before we reach Canterbury?"

"You bet," I reply, trying to sound enthusiastic as I follow him onto the bus. I'm secretly disappointed not to sit beside Charlotte, who I already feel so close to, but maybe it's a good thing. I'd probably end up telling her all about the real reason I'm here, and at least this way I can maintain an ounce of dignity. Charlotte settles into the front seat beside Angus. Roshi slides into the second-row window seat, and I take the aisle. Sindhi's next on the bus and she glances at us, then brushes past, leaving the row behind us empty. Violet sits beside her. Nelle chooses the row behind us, and Francis sits beside her. Jenny heads straight to the back, as usual.

Roshi pulls out his crossword puzzle book and flips to the first page. "I actually bought this puzzle book thinking it would be something Sindhi and I could do together."

"She's not a fan of crosswords?" I say quietly.

Roshi shakes his head. "I think her exact words yesterday were: I don't want to ever do a crossword puzzle with you." He's looking down at the book, and I can't see his expression, but from his tone I don't think he's kidding.

I glance back behind me, feeling weird that we're talking about Sindhi when she's sitting only a few feet away. I hope she's deep in conversation with Violet and hasn't heard us.

"My mom and dad used to do crosswords together," I say, to change the subject. "It's a nice idea—something to do together."

"That's what I thought. So does that mean you've got the crossword gene?"

I laugh. "Not sure. They used to do the New York Times on Sunday. Those always seemed pretty tricky."

"That's what these are," he says, flipping the book closed to show me the cover. "A book of Sundays. But judging by how difficult the answers have been, I probably should've chosen Saturday, or maybe Friday." He smiles and flips the book back open to the second page.

Francis's head suddenly appears beside my elbow. "Actually," he says, and I swivel in my seat to face him. "The Sunday puzzle is easier than Saturday and Friday. It's on par with the Thursday puzzle, but larger and has a trick to it. More fun, and more prestigious."

He disappears and I smile at Roshi. "There you have it."

Roshi flips the book open again and angles it so I can see. "So your parents did the Sundays, too. In the paper or online?"

"Always paper," I say. "They ran a bookshop, but this was back when it was closed on Sundays, when I was little, so they had more free time."

Roshi nods, then writes the word *canteloupe* into the crossword. I take the pencil from him and change the middle "e" to an "a." He gives me a sheepish look. "Helps to spell properly."

"What else do you and Sindhi like to do together?" I ask, to change the subject, before Roshi can ask if my parents still do the crossword together today—or if I ever do it with them.

He lets out a disappointed laugh. "I'm still trying to figure that out."

I cock my head, trying to remember their introductions yesterday. I just assumed they'd been married for years—perhaps from Sindhi's comment about the other places they'd travelled.

"Turns out after so many years focused on work and our kids, we don't know what to do with each other," Roshi says sadly. "But I have eight more days to give it my best shot, right?"

Eight more days. A lot can happen—or nothing at all, I think, looking past Roshi as the bus rounds a bend in the road.

Chapter Eleven

Day 2, Monday, 11 a.m.

Canterbury

It's mid-morning when we roll into a narrow parking lot, our bus towering over the tiny European cars with the unfamiliar names: the Peugeot Rifter. The Vauxhall Viva. We disembark and I stretch my arms over my head. The air smells like honey and the pavement is covered in a light dusting of yellow leaves and gravel. On one side, past iron traffic bollards connected with chains, past a bus-lane road, is a line of low, nondescript residential housing. Over there it looks like the 1960s, maybe. And then, right smack up against the parking lot, is this huge stone wall looming over us, two stories high at least, speckled with purple bellflowers creating tufts of color in the otherwise gray stone.

"What's that?" I say in awe, to no one in particular, but Taj looks back.

"What?" he says.

I point to the wall.

"Oh, *that*," he says, grinning. "That, *Georgia*, is a wall. I would've thought you had those in America. Guess you learn something new every day."

114

"Come on. It's more than a *wall*. Is this a fortress or something? And those pretty little flowers," I say. "They're incredible. Do you think someone plants them into the wall, or do they just *grow* like that?"

"No idea," Taj says, but he looks up at them for a beat, then back to me. "I'm guessing they're just weeds. Who would plant flowers in a wall? I doubt someone's out here scaling the stone to add a splash of color. And they grow in walls everywhere—not just Canterbury." He looks over at me. "You would've noticed yesterday if you hadn't slept through half the tour," he teases.

"It wasn't *half* the tour," I say.

Moments later, Angus explains that Canterbury was once a walled city, with the first walls built by the Romans in 270.

"Told you it was a wall," Taj says to me, as we follow the wall to a turret, a small cross etched into it, halfway up.

"Isn't it the loveliest day?" Roshi is saying to Sindhi just ahead. "The weather is perfect for a jaunt about this town." He reaches out for her hand, but she shrugs out of her coat instead. "Much warmer than I would've expected for late June in England," he says. He seems like he's trying so hard with her—and she's so angry at him. I wonder if he's done something to upset her. If so, why agree to a vacation together?

"Actually, the average high temperature in Canterbury in June is 61.5 degrees Fahrenheit and it's 61 degrees exactly today, so really, it's right on par with where it should be," Francis interrupts.

"Well it's certainly sunnier than I thought it would be," Nelle says, pulling a pair of sunglasses out of her bag and popping them overtop of the glasses she's already wearing.

"Whoops," Angus chuckles, "you're doubling up there." He points to her face. "You might want to take one pair off before you put the other on."

But Nelle shakes her head. "Oh, no, this is the way I like it. I can see *and* I don't have to squint."

"You know that's why prescription sunglasses were invented, right?" Jenny says, walking past her.

"Oh, no," Nelle says. "I tried those, but they're absolutely senseless. You have to take them off every time you go into a store, and then you can't see anything. And if you keep them on you look like a weirdo, wearing sunglasses inside."

"Yeah, *that* would be weird," Taj whispers. Out of the corner of my eye, I see Violet grab Nelle's hand, which feels like the most supportive, sweetest gesture.

"This is not the most impressive entrance to Canterbury," Angus says, "but I've brought you this way for a very good reason."

"Yeah, it's the most convenient car park," Taj quips.

"Taj, you're giving away all my secrets," Angus says. He holds up a finger and then leads us inside the city walls and down the cobblestone Burgate Street toward something called the Christ-church Gate. This archway, a mix of Romanesque and Gothic styles, is an entrance to the Canterbury Cathedral, Angus tells us. I feel a sense of dread. I'd mentally tried to prepare for the four churches in Canterbury alone, but that was from the safety of the cozy bus.

I walk up to Angus and flip open my guidebook. "I think you know by now I'm a huge bookworm and there's this famous bookshop—"

"You needn't say more," Angus chuckles. "You can't come to Canterbury and miss the Crooked House. Of course, we do walk by it after the cathedral, but you can head out there now, if you'd like. You're sure you're alright missing the church tour, though?"

I nod. "I'd love time to poke around the shop." I try to sound calm even though my insides are churning.

"Alright, then, now's a great time as we're so close," Angus says, surprising me. He doesn't seem at all concerned that I won't be glued to the rest of the group, the way Taj seemed to imply yesterday. He points to his right. "It's easy as shepherd's pie to find. You just follow Sun Street here, and stay on as it turns into Palace and then you can't miss it. It'll be the crooked house," he grins.

"Great."

"Great. As long as you're back here within the hour we'll be fine. And if you aren't, well then I'll just give you a ring to find you. You have your phone?"

I nod.

"Well then, have a good time, Good Gigi." He turns back to the group. "Ah, everyone look up. Like a bird on a wire—or seventeen. That's where the starlings perch." Violet pulls out her phone to capture the burnt-orange bellies of the otherwise blue-black birds overhead. Charlotte flutters her fingers at me, and Francis lets his recorder know I'm going into the bookstore instead of the world-famous cathedral.

Take that, Taj. People *are* allowed to roam while on tour. I glance back at him and catch him watching me. I turn away quickly, feeling sweat pool at the back of my neck.

I head away from the group, past artsy cafés and moody gastro-pubs, a milliner with fascinators in the window and a Lululemon with University of Kent–branded athletic wear, which makes me think of Lars and whether he's been harassing my bookshop clients to buy his fake Lululemon athleisurewear. I should've reminded him *not* to do that yesterday, and it's too early to call him now. A few minutes later I'm standing in front of a black-and-white half-timbered house that juts into the street and leans to the right. Gold star for the accurate name: the Crooked House. The blue door is so slanted the bottom is cut at a forty-five-degree angle. Over the door, in cursive, reads: *A very old house bulging out over the road . . . leaning forward, trying to see who was passing on the narrow pavement below.* The sun is high in the sky, creating a halo effect over the peak of the shop as I duck through the door, the shop feeling even darker because of how bright it was outside. I pause to let my eyes adjust. The air is thick with dust, and ragged area rugs cover the floors and remind me of my own shop. The bookshelves are narrow and tall, and the books are stacked haphazardly on the shelves and piled high on the floor in front of the bookshelves and the wall, leaving only a narrow path to walk. It's a setup I both love and loathe. I adore the hunt, but I would never organize Love Interest in such an erratic way. I pick a middle aisle and walk slowly through, tilting my head to read the spines, running my finger along the dusty shelves. And then, at the end of the aisle, in a waist-high stack of books on the floor, I see it. A paperback copy of *Lady Susan* by Jane Austen. I run my hands over the cover—it's different from the copy I have at the shop. I keep an eye on the time and half an hour later, walk to the cash to pay for the book.

"The line over the door," I say to the clerk as he hands me my book after I've paid for it. "Is that Dickens?"

"Good guess," he says, looking like something out of a Dickens novel himself. "*David Copperfield*, in fact." I thank him, slip the book into my purse, and head outside. Taj is sitting on a wrought-iron bench just outside. I get this warm feeling rushing over me, but tell myself it's just a reaction to seeing anyone familiar in a strange place. Thankfully he doesn't notice if I'm blushing because he's engrossed in a book.

I clear my throat. "You didn't have to wait for me," I say as I approach him.

"I wasn't," he says, slapping the book shut. He meets my eye. "I just happened to choose this bench to read on."

"Oh." My cheeks burn.

"Oh—hey," Taj says. "It's called taking the piss."

I meet his eyes. "Taking the what?"

"Piss. Profoundly rude, of course. Sorry. Americans never get it."

"You *were* waiting for me."

"To clarify—yes."

"You said you weren't as a joke."

"Right—taking the piss."

Taj, I notice, has golden flecks in those dark eyes.

"No roaming, remember? And you're purposely avoiding churches," Taj declares. The statement digs into my stomach.

I attempt to force a laugh but it comes out as more of a snort. "Totally unrelated." I thumb toward the shop. "I love bookshops. That's it."

He watches me, but doesn't push back. Instead he stands. "You ready to go?" Rather than waiting for an answer, he turns and heads off to his left, my right. We start walking in silence, zigzagging through the streets, Taj leading the way, me following, my head flicking back and forth, taking in everything around me. We make our way back past the cathedral, which sits in the middle of a square—there's no getting around it. Scaffolding shields the better part of it, though, detracting from whatever Gothic majesty it should project. A small part of me knows I'm missing out on a huge part of history by avoiding any and all churches, but it doesn't matter. He doesn't stop at the church and continues walking. "Angus said to meet outside the cathedral," I say.

"Lunch is next, so we could head straight to the pub—I could use a drink."

"You're driving."

"I meant *water.*"

"Oh. Right. Me too." I could use a bucket of water to cool my burning skin.

We walk in silence for a moment, but then Taj nods to the copy of *Lady Susan* in my hand. "I would've figured you'd already read every Austen book." Then clucks his tongue. "Let me guess— you've read *all* the books—Austen or otherwise."

I look at him. "No one's read *all* the books."

"You say that as though you've looked into this. Like, if someone had read all the books, you'd be in competition with them."

"Is that taking the piss?" I ask. I spot a pink Winnebago parked in the middle of the cobblestone road, a chalkboard set up next to it listing a dozen varieties of ice cream. A long line of people forms at it.

"Not quite. That's just teasing."

"You enjoy teasing me?"

He nods. "I think I really do."

"I *have* read this book, but I don't have this particular edition of *Lady Susan,* and it's a truth universally acknowledged that anyone with a romance bookshop should have multiple copies of every Austen ever released—even *Lady Susan.*"

"Hold up." Taj raises his hands in protest. "What do you mean *romance* bookshop? Only romance?"

"Yes," I say, as a flock of pigeons whooshes past us and lands on the interlocking brick a few feet away.

Taj looks like he's just been hit with pigeon poop. "What about all the books that aren't romance?"

"What about them?"

"There are dozens, hundreds, thousands of excellent books that have absolutely nothing to do with romance."

"Right. I never said there weren't." I smile, enjoying his confusion.

"But what about general fiction?"

"Yes, if there's romance in them."

"Thrillers?"

"If there's romance." I dodge a confetti of breadcrumbs a woman to my right, sitting on a bench, directs at the pigeons. More pigeons dive-bomb the area.

"Westerns?" Taj says.

"If there's romance."

"Books about archbishops or bus drivers?" Taj says, sidestepping a kid who wobbles along the uneven stones in roller skates.

"Sure, if they have romance in them," I say, enjoying this banter. "It's a *romance* bookshop."

Taj looks pained.

I grin. I enjoy defending the store to those who challenge me on it—and I've had a lot of practice over the years. "So technically I do have some Westerns and thrillers and tons of historical fiction, too—but only the ones with some element of romance. Any kind of course—straight, gay, doesn't matter. Even love between friends." A busker juggles a bunch of brightly painted bowling pins while balancing one on his chin.

"But that's friendship, not love." Taj tosses a coin into the busker's hat, which surprises me for some reason.

"Friendship is simply a platonic romance between friends."

"Who said that?" Taj asks as we walk along a narrow, cobblestoned street lined with shops.

"Dickens," I say.

"I'm not sure it makes sense."

I shrug. "Tell that to Dickens." The road climbs up and over a bridge, and the buildings break for a river below. I lean over the low edge just as a narrow, flat-bottomed vessel pushed by a man standing at the back glides by. I recognize it instantly: a punt.

"Are we . . ." I press my hands together. "Going punting? Please?"

Taj shakes his head. "Sadly, we don't punt in Canterbury."

"Because we punted in Cambridge?" I say with disappointment, mad at myself again for missing it.

"Exactly." We continue walking until Taj stops in front of a Tudor-style timber-framed building. *The Old Weavers House, AD 1500* is written over the door in Old English lettering.

Taj pulls open the heavy wood door, and I follow him into a dark tavern. The older man at the maître d' stand seems to recognize Taj. "Nice to see you," he says, and turns to lead us under an arch, into another room where the walls are lined with framed photos and newspaper clippings, their headlines barely legible by the old kerosene lanterns on the oak tables, then out through another doorway to an ivy-covered patio that overlooks the water. A big table is set up at the back.

Taj sets his book on the table and says, "Guess you're stuck talking to me for a few more minutes." He pulls out a chair as the maître d' squeezes past him to fill the water glasses at the table from a jug he's retrieved from a nearby stand. I take the chair opposite Taj, which has a view of the river. A punting boat glides across the sunlit water. If Zane were here, would it be the two of us sitting across from each other at this moment? But of course not—he'd be with the group. And if he were with the group, *I'd* be with the group. I groan inwardly. Every time I think about Zane, how he was supposed to be here, how he's not here, I feel a stab of guilt and ungratefulness toward my friends and this amazing gift they've given me. I *need* to stop thinking about Zane. I turn back to Taj, who's downing his water in big gulps.

"So what are you reading?" I can see it isn't the mystery I bought for him yesterday.

Taj flips the cover over, and I recognize it as the latest John Grisham—the one Lars was trying to convince me to sell. I begin laughing.

"What?" He furrows his brow.

"My brother was trying to convince me I was an idiot not to sell that book. 'Everyone loves John Grisham! Give the people what they want!'" I'm still laughing.

He raises his eyebrows. "I thought you just finished telling me you only sell romances?"

"Tell that to my brother." I take a sip of water.

"So what was in the mystery bag?"

"I didn't open it," I say. "I might never open it."

"Weird," he says, but he's smiling, and the skin at the corners of his eyes crinkles. He grabs the water jug between us and refills his glass, then tops up my glass, too. "You bought that for no reason, then. There could be anything inside, or nothing at all. Basically you bought a paper bag."

"I don't want to be disappointed," I say with a shrug.

"You just don't want to find out that I was right and you were wrong," he challenges, but he's still smiling.

"Hey," I say. "I should tell you something."

"OK—"

"The platonic friendship and romance line—it wasn't Dickens who said that. It was me."

"Ah." Taj takes a sip of water. "That—*that's* taking the piss."

"Hmm!" I exclaim, delighted.

"But you shouldn't have told me you were doing it. You tell someone, you're not really taking the piss."

Before I can reply, a commotion behind me makes me turn to see the rest of the group arrive. I feel a twinge of disappointment but dismiss it. It's probably just hunger pangs.

.

Later that afternoon, I manage to dodge the tour of St. Martin's, the oldest church in England, by taking a call from Lars. (He couldn't figure out how to work the coffee maker.) After the church tour, we get a bit of time to explore and shop. Violet and Nelle emerge from the public bathrooms wearing matching T-shirts they bought at one of the souvenir shops that say "I'm Brit-*ish*."

Jenny walks past them and scowls, saying, "You're supposed to get those if you're like, a *bit* British. Like you have a great-grandfather who was British and you're suddenly adopting the British stuff. It's not funny otherwise."

"She seems personally offended by their choice of T-shirt," Sindhi says to me with a smile, and I stifle a laugh. We're on our way to the ruins of St. Augustine's Abbey by way of a quick tour of St. Thomas Church. I'm not sure how I'm going to get out of this one. I look over at Taj and notice Jenny chattering away to him.

She's been following him around all afternoon, talking his ear off, flirting with him and trying to convince him to help her film a video—though so far, she's had no luck. As we reach the Westgate Towers that act as an official entrance and exit to the town, Taj falls into step with me.

"Come on," Taj says with a wink. "If you've seen one church, you've seen them all."

"Well, technically, I haven't seen any," I remind him with a laugh. "Not that I'm complaining."

He looks down at his phone, taps it with his thumbs, then shoves it into his pocket. "Wait here." He doesn't wait for me to respond before jogging up to Angus and saying something that makes Angus nod and tip his hat to me. Taj returns, and says, "Come on, you've got to hurry."

He jogs away and I have to run to stay in step with him, weaving between people as we head back to King's Bridge, where the River Stour opens wide enough to accommodate a dock and a half dozen rowboats. At the top of the bridge, Taj looks out over the river and waves his arm as he shouts out, "Q!"

Below, in a punt, is a guy who looks like he's about to bust out of his khaki pants, light-blue button-down and green canvas vest. Mid-pole, he lifts his straw boater hat into the air and gives a hoot. "Taj Mahal! It must be Tuesday if Taj is in town!"

"It's Monday," Taj says.

"Po-tay-to, po-tah-to."

"You have room for two more?" Taj calls as he holds up two fingers.

Q replaces the hat on his head, lowers his sunglasses and gives Taj a look. "Go on, sweeten the deal."

"There's a pint in it for you," Taj calls back.

"What are you doing?" I ask, but he holds up a finger and gives me a sly grin, then turns his attention back to Q, which is a good thing because my body feels like it's on fire. Am I really going to go punting?

Q leans forward and says something to the family of four in the boat. Then he shouts up to us. "You're in luck. Meet us at the competition."

Taj weaves through the crowd of tourists crossing the bridge, and I hurry to keep up while trying to act cool. He leads us down a set of iron steps and along a narrow stone path to a wooden dock, then turns and holds out his hand to help me down a steep step. His grip is firm but his skin is surprisingly soft. "Excuse me," he says to a woman wearing a blue uniform who's guarding the dock. He's still holding my hand. I hope it doesn't start to sweat.

"We're full up right now for rowboats," she says, but Taj shakes his head. "Not here for a rowboat, just"—he points as the punting boat arrives beside us. "Grabbing ourselves a lift." Letting go of my hand, he bends down to grasp the bow of the punt. "Careful," he says as he helps me onto the wooden platform.

"Welcome aboard," Q says. A little boy wearing a polo shirt and khaki shorts stained with chocolate ice cream watches with curiosity as I take a spot immediately behind him, on a low wooden bench covered in a tufted pink-and-gold cushion. I smile and give him a wave. Taj steps onto the boat with ease and takes the only available spot—beside me. I wish I had a hat to cover my face, which I'm sure is red. I focus on the wood of the boat—oak? Who knows?—and the water—clear!—and the fact that I'm actually going to get to experience the punt ride. But that just loops my thoughts back to Taj again, and the fact that he would arrange this for me.

Q nods at the three people ahead of Taj and me. "This is the Walsh family of Wisconsin." The mom smiles broadly at us. I smile and say hello. As Q pushes us away from the dock, Taj turns to me, his knee accidentally brushing mine. "So?" He grins.

I wave an arm around me. "Come on—this? The sun's shining, the water's calm, this town is incredible. It's like . . ."

"Nothing at home?" he says. I nod because it's true, but also so much more than just simply the fact that this town isn't like Ann Arbor. "It's so beautiful. Thanks for arranging this," I say quietly, acutely aware that the others in the boat are likely hearing my every word.

Q digs his pole into the clear water, and the punt glides ahead. The surface of the water shimmers in the sunlight, and I can see long strands of green algae underwater. I watch as a little girl and her mother dangle their legs over the edge of a stone wall and toss pieces of bread to the mallard ducks milling about. As the river widens, willow trees on the bank lean into the water, creating a canopy overhead. It's all so perfectly, charmingly English. Within minutes of gliding through the narrow canal, I'm completely relaxed.

"This one missed out on punting in Cambridge," Taj tells everyone, elbowing me.

"Thank god for that," Q says sarcastically, then looks to me. "Never speak of punting anywhere else. There is no punting like punting in Canterbury."

"Oh, really?" I say, enjoying their repartee. What's Taj and Q's story?—they seem to know each other so well. Which somehow gets me to Taj on the XO app, which makes me wonder if this isn't the first time he's arranged for a girl to experience punting in Canterbury. Why does it bother me that he's on the dating app? He's not even the reason I'm here. He's not Zane.

Zane. At the thought of him, it feels like I'm being stabbed in the stomach with—what? A punting stick.

Taj leans toward me and I'm pulled back into the moment. "Q's very competitive when it comes to punting."

"Ahh . . ." I turn my head into the wind to get the hair out of my face, then turn back toward Taj, noticing, perhaps because he's so close, how good he smells. Fresh, like soap, but a hint of sandalwood.

"I earned the right," Q says, and I turn to look up at him. "Three-time national champion." He puffs out his chest, his vest bulging at the buttons, and I laugh.

Taj leans back and puts his hands behind his head. I can feel his body relax next to mine, and I sneak a peek at him. His face is tilted up toward the sky, his eyes closed. The sun is hitting it in a way that makes his tanned skin glow.

"Would you like me to take your picture together?" the woman across from me asks.

"Oh, um—" I start, because while I'd love a photo to remember this by, it feels intimate to have my picture taken with Taj.

Taj leans away from me. "Don't get me in that. She's the one on holiday, I'm just a local—sort of."

The woman looks disappointed. I am, too. She snaps a pic anyway and then leans forward. "I'll airdrop it to you." I accept the picture, and study it for a moment. It's nice to have a memory of this moment, but seeing myself alone reminds me of the fantasy I had of taking pictures with Zane. Maybe not on the second day of the trip—but at some point. *Oh, cry me a river, Gigi*, I say to myself, then send the pic to the book club group chat and tuck my phone away.

Q pushes us into a passage where two-story stone buildings

close in on either side of the water, colorful clay pots of flowers sitting along the narrow stone ledges. A woman pokes her head out of one of the windows, and I realize that these are probably people's homes. What would it be like to live on a canal like this—to open your window and look out into such a fairytale town? To smell the blossoms on the trees and hear the laughter and joy of tourists? How could you ever be upset living somewhere like this? When we pass a small park, Q points out the cherry and quince trees. Taj reaches up and, moments later, holds out his hand to me. On his palm rest two perfect cherries.

"Can I have one?" the little boy across from me says to his mother. She leans over and whispers something, and Q grabs a few cherries for everyone else. "Look what you started," he says to Taj, but he's grinning. I take the cherry Taj holds out to me and pop it into my mouth. It's surprisingly sweet. What would it be like to be able to pick these cherries anytime?

"Let me guess, you're imagining what it would be like to live here?" Taj teases, then puts the other cherry in his mouth.

I roll my eyes but I feel like he's just read my diary—though it's not exactly juicy material. "No I'm not."

"Yes you are. You're picturing what it would be like to open the windows and look out onto this field of cherry trees. Maybe even make a pie with them."

I freeze, afraid to turn and face him. Am I that predictable?

"Alright, time for a little history," Q interrupts, and I'm thankful. "In 1532 Henry VIII wrote a haunting love song for Anne Boleyn. Their relationship was very romantic."

"Henry VIII didn't actually write that haunting love song," Taj says. "And their relationship gets a little *divisive* near the end."

"Who's the guide here?" Q says, giving Taj the stink eye.

"I'm just helping with the facts," Taj says.

"Wait," I say. "Didn't he cut off her head?"

"The American knows her British history," Taj says.

"Let's just focus on the pleasant elements of his relationship to his second wife," Q says. He looks at Taj. "Ready, mate?"

Taj sits up tall, shaking his head. "Not this time."

"You owe me."

"I owe you a pint," Taj reminds him.

"I'd rather a wingman," Q shoots back.

"Take the pint," Taj says. Daylight gives way to dark under a mottled stone tunnel as Q crouches to fit under the bridge. When we're well into the darkness, Q starts softly: "*Alas, my love, you do me wrong.*"

Beside me, Taj joins in, his voice low: "*To cast me off discourteously.*" Then it's back to Q: "*And I have loved you oh so long.*"

And Taj: "*Delighting in your company.*"

I turn to face him. Taj is . . . singing? And more to the point—singing beautifully, with a smooth richness? His voice is like silk.

As Q and Taj sing the chorus together, Taj's baritone echoes off the walls of the tunnel as he harmonizes with Q. "*Greensleeves was my delight / Greensleeves my heart of gold / Greensleeves was my heart of joy / And who but my lady Greensleeves?*"

Everything, this moment—it's so unexpected, so surreal, so beautiful. I can feel Taj's voice running up my legs, past my heart and straight to my scalp. I shiver.

The punt emerges from the tunnel in the sunlight, and Taj and Q giggle, embarrassed, but I begin clapping, staring at Taj. As I bring my hands together over and over again, the Walsh family joins in. Q flips his hand over and takes an exaggerated bow.

"That was amazing," I whisper, leaning in to Taj. When he turns to me, his face has a pink hue, like he's blushing, but maybe it's just the sun on his usually creamy-brown skin. As we approach the dock, another guide holds onto the front of the boat. Taj leaps up first, stands on the platform, and extends his hand my way. He easily pulls me from my perch and onto the security of land. "If you liked my tour or my singing," Q says to me, "you can leave me a good review. And if you didn't, well then, off with your head." And he makes a grand sweeping gesture with his arm. I pull a few bills from my purse and offer them to him.

"It was my pleasure," Q says, smiling at me. "But . . . it's also my pleasure to accept this, and I'll think of you fondly when I'm drinking it away at the pub after my shift." He takes the bills and grins as he slips them into his back pocket. Taj pats him on the back and hands him a few bills, too. "Thanks, mate."

Back on the cobblestone street Taj and I walk past souvenir shops and pubs surrounded by outdoor beer gardens. We walk silently for a few minutes before I take Taj's arm. He looks at me with surprise in his eyes, and I give his elbow a squeeze. "Taj, that was so thoughtful. And beautiful. I don't know what to say."

He looks up the street. "It's sort of a long-running thing. Q's an old college friend, and he helped me out of a massive bind once, so when I'm around, I do that with him. Helps him with the tips. The ladies go crazy for it."

The ladies. I let go of his arm and put a step between us, thinking of his XO profile. "I'm sure they do," I say. "I'm sure they do."

Chapter Twelve

Day 2, Monday, 4:15 p.m.

Dover

That afternoon the bus heads south to the coast, toward the famed White Cliffs of Dover, the chalky limestone cliff-face streaked with black flint jutting out into the English Channel toward France and the island of Guernsey. I've been re-listening to *The Guernsey Literary and Potato Peel Pie Society* to get in the mood. As I'm about to wrap my headphones around my phone, a text pops up from Emily in our group chat: *So romantic. With Zane?*

It takes me a moment to realize she's responding to the pic of me on the punt.

Nope. Still not here, I text back, which starts a barrage of texts from the girls, and I skim them before hiding the still-buzzing phone in my purse.

Off the bus, Angus insists we pair up so that we've each got a buddy to prevent us from getting too close to the cliff edge. Nelle grabs his arm in fear, and Violet asks Jenny if she wants help shooting a video.

"Oh, I don't think that's a good idea," Angus interrupts. "I've seen it happen a million times, yah? One step backward so the photographer can get the perfect shot, and bam!"—he makes the "Action!" clapping symbol with his hands as though to indicate someone falling over. "And it's ta-ta forever." He chuckles, then turns to Charlotte and touches her hat, saying something quietly. She removes it and tucks her hair behind her ear, laughing.

Jenny hurries ahead to talk to Taj, and for a split second I think of Zane. Another opportunity to be in pairs. For the two of us to have had some time together. Where *is* he? What is he doing right now? Doesn't he know his destiny awaits? I snap back to the present and look around. Sindhi's walking alone, fiddling with the strap of her fanny pack, and I head over to her. "Want to be my partner?" I ask, suddenly feeling self-conscious.

"Sure," she says, still fiddling with her pack. "But I can't promise I'll be great company. I didn't wear the shoes for this and I'm getting unbearable blisters." She points at her sandals. For someone who introduced herself as "sensible," I'm surprised she isn't wearing sensible footwear. "Well you've got the fanny pack," I point out. "That was smart. I didn't think that part through."

"I like to call mine the *Franny* pack," Francis says, patting his own leather version as he passes us. Sindhi and I look at each other. Her eyes crinkle at the sides, and she looks happy for the first time since I've met her.

"OK. This is going to be great." Sindhi clenches her fists. "Just great."

"You sound like you're convincing yourself," I say, laughing.

"Oh I am." She gives me a sidelong look. "Remember, I wasn't exactly enthused about this trip."

I laugh. "Right. So was it a surprise?" I ask, stepping over a rock on the narrow path. On either side, lush green moss grows between weeds and wildflowers in yellows, whites and purples.

"Surprise," she repeats, shaking her head. "Yes. Roshi's full of surprises." She turns and glances behind her. I turn, too, and see that Roshi's a ways back. I wonder if that's who she was checking for, too. We walk in silence for a bit.

"My friends surprised me with this trip, too," I say, hoping it will make her feel better. "And they didn't even come along." I laugh.

Sindhi throws her head back and laughs. Not a joyful laugh, but cynical. "What terrible friends!" she exclaims. "If my friends did that, I would absolutely disown them." I'm so surprised by her reaction that I'm speechless for a moment.

"I guess you can say I don't like surprises. Not one bit. And Roshi knows that. Or he should by this point."

We crest a hill and I spy in the distance a white stone Victorian lighthouse—our pit stop for a view and a cup of tea.

"Well, we're here now. Might as well make the best of it, right?" Suddenly I've become Sally Sunshine. But I feel bad for Roshi, and I wonder if Sindhi will look back on this trip and regret being so grumpy the whole time.

"Plus, it probably came from a good place?" I offer. "Like, surely Roshi didn't surprise you with the trip together to make your life miserable, right?" I laugh. She doesn't.

"You wouldn't understand," she says. Then gives a half wave, hurrying ahead, seemingly oblivious to her blisters, catching up to Nelle instead.

.

An hour or so later we're back on the bus as it follows the coast-line, the road sometimes butting up against the break walls of the stone-and-sand beaches, other times disappearing into a marshy valley. Our destination is Hythe, which means "landing place," according to Angus. Hythe turns out to be a town of bridges and stone beaches with a cricket ground and a canal that Angus tells us was built to repel an invasion by Napoleon.

"How does a canal repel an invasion?" Violet asks Nelle behind me.

"This is my favorite spot to stay in England," Angus says as the bus slows to a stop on a residential street of hedges and stone walls and imposing Tudor-style homes. Everything seems impossibly green.

Off the bus, we gather our things and follow Angus through a wood gate onto a gravel path dotted with colorful circular stepping stones. He hands each of us an antique brass skeleton key. Mine reads *Homestead* in gothic type. "Any word from Zane?" I say casually. "Do you think he might make it here before we leave tomorrow morning?"

Angus's bushy eyebrows move closer together, and he pulls on the lapel of his tweed jacket. "I did give his father a ring earlier, just to check in, yah, but no answer. I wanted to see how Louisa's doing."

He seems distracted. Maybe Angus feels weird that he wasn't supposed to mention the family—is it bad for business to let guests know that the owners are ill? I picture Zane by his mother's side as she lies in bed. He's taken charge, fixing her toast and boiling water for tea, because he's the kind of guy who would drop everything for his family. I hope his mother isn't too ill. And then I wonder: Do I hope that because that's the right thing to wish? Or because I'm selfish, and that'll get him here faster?

Jenny brushes past me, dragging her suitcase behind her, and I step off the path, then maneuver my own bag in her wake.

Each cottage looks like a stand-in for Hansel and Gretel's cottage: curtained windows, stucco sides painted in various pastel shades. "Homestead" turns out to be fourth in the row. It's mint green. The front door is so tiny I have to duck to enter.

It's the house of a hobbit. Everything is tiny, everything is mint green: the oven, the sink, even the miniature washing machine beside the sink. On the tiny stove is a tiny platter with scones, a flowered ramekin of Devonshire cream, another with seedy red jam, a handful of strawberries and a tin of loose tea, all set beside a light-blue ceramic Victorian-style teapot, tall and only slightly bulbous in the middle, the edges worn white. A set of white and floral teacups is stacked against the mint-green tile backsplash. I twirl around and exhale, suddenly forgetting about Zane and feeling . . . happy.

From the kitchen, a series of narrow, steep steps climb up to the second floor, opening up into a cozy bedroom. I put my suitcase in the corner and walk across the short-pile mint-green carpet to the window, which overlooks a rectangle of freshly cut grass, the trimmings creating a thin veil overtop. The uneven slabs of wood that form a fence on all three sides support tufts of bright-orange gladiolas, pink tulips, deep-purple dahlia and blue hollyhock interspersed with wispy grasses. English ivy winds up the back fence over a shed, and lady's mantle covers the stepping stones of the path leading through the center of the grassy patch. Tiny lights string from one side of the fence to the other. Close to the cottage is a lounger with a blue-and-white cushion and a matching sun umbrella.

Whenever I visit Cleo or Emily—both of whom have somehow managed to afford beautifully landscaped homes off Washtenaw— I envy their gardens but quickly become overwhelmed once they start describing the yard work required to keep them up. Cleo makes the home renos she takes on with her partner, AJ, look easy. Emily loves to spend her weekends weeding the massive yard that leads from her A-frame house to the ravine behind. It feels like too much. But this? This little cottage with its perfect backyard? *This* I could definitely do.

The bed is springy, an old mattress under a thick, soft pink duvet covered in giant white lilies. It would be so easy to lie back right now, fall asleep and not get up until morning, but I resist the urge. Dinner is soon and I don't want to miss the pub in town that's known for its curry and rice. A shower will wake me up. Inside the bright white bathroom, I push the various buttons until the right combination results in hot water. Moments later I'm engulfed in steam.

I close my eyes and let the water run over my hair, not bothering with shampoo. My shoulders relax. And then I realize I'm humming "Greensleeves," the song Taj sang in Canterbury. "I have been ready at your hand," goes the line. "To grant whatever you would crave." How many other women have hummed the song in showers just like this one, after Taj sang to them?

I turn off the water and reach for a towel, holding the warm, soft terry cloth to my face for a minute. I wrap myself up and pad over to the window. As I'm closing the shutters, a flash of white catches the corner of my eye. Down below, in the garden to the right of mine is Taj. I slide to the side, out of sight, and watch him, in jeans and a T-shirt, kick a soccer ball into an old barrel he's turned on its side. He retrieves it, dribbles the ball, kicks it in again, does a bunch of push-ups and then jogs back to get the ball, kicks it back toward the cottage, turns, and repeats the process. After some more of this he stops, pulling his shirt up to wipe the sweat from his forehead and in the process revealing his taut, tanned stomach.

A knock at the front door startles me back to reality.

"Just a minute," I shout as I scramble to throw on a short sundress. I hurry down the narrow steps and open the door to Charlotte who's also changed and is wearing a beautiful silk maxi dress swirled with blues and oranges. Her feet are strapped into gold sandals, and she's wrapped a silk scarf in her blond hair like a headband.

"You alright, Darlin'?" she asks, concern creeping across her brow. "You look flushed." Her lips are freshly painted in bright coral.

"Oh," I say, thinking of the muscled knot in Taj's tricep on his final push-up. "Probably just the shower." I give my head a tiny shake and focus on Charlotte.

"Did you notice the cream tea? Isn't it absolutely adorable? Would you like to come over and sit in my place with me? Seems a shame to sit and have tea alone."

I tell Charlotte I'll be over to her cottage, Escape, as soon as I've finished getting ready. After closing the door, I head back upstairs to dry my hair and do my makeup. As I'm using a small brush to apply tinted moisturizer, I notice a few freckles on my nose that weren't there yesterday and smile. I look relaxed. Happy, even.

My phone dings as I'm adding a few bangles to my wrist. A text from Dory pops up.

So???? Update!! Gigi!!

There's been tons of texts in the group chat about other things, which I've mostly ignored, trying to focus on the trip instead, so now the girls have been adding my name to texts, presumably so I won't ignore them.

I type back a quick *Zane's still not here. But having a great day xoxo.* Then I toss my phone into my purse before any of them reply and head out the door. I have to pass Taj's cottage to get to Charlotte's, and I can't help but glance over as I pass by. (No sight of him.) Inside, Charlotte's cottage is the mirror opposite of mine, but decorated in soft pinks, circular white doilies on the top of every table. The kettle whistles and Charlotte pours the hot water into a chubby floral teapot, then places teacups, cream, sugar, spoons and the teapot onto a silver tray with handles twisted into hearts.

"So, go on . . ." she drawls once we're sitting in her tiny living room—me on the floral love seat, her on a wicker chair. I look around at the various abstract watercolor paintings on the walls, then back to her.

"What?" I'm confused.

"Where'd you disappear to when we were in Canterbury?" Charlotte says, her blue eyes sparkling.

My face heats up and I'm grateful we're inside, not in the back garden where Taj could hear every word of our conversation.

She shakes her head and points a finger at me. "I knew you got up to something good." She takes a sip of tea then puts her cup down on the white wicker table between us.

I take a breath and tell her about how Taj took me punting, about Q, and about their impromptu tunnel performance of "Greensleeves."

"I wonder why he would go to all that trouble to arrange a ride for you." She raises her eyebrows at me, her lips slightly turned up, the vertical lines under her nose disappearing.

I shrug. "I'm sure . . . Angus put him up to it, actually." I didn't even really consider that but now that I've said it aloud, I'm sure that's exactly what happened. Just like Angus put him up to tracking me down when I went into the Crooked House. "I'm sure he would've done the same for you if you'd slept through some of the tour."

"Well maybe so, but I'd rather stick with Angus," Charlotte says, then quickly throws a hand to her mouth, her eyes wide. "Did I just say that?" We both laugh.

"You like him," I tease. "I can tell."

She fans her face with her hand. "Oh, it's just silly. I really can't—I'm a widow. And I was supposed to come on this trip with Harold. For our anniversary." Her face falls.

"Oh, I'm sorry."

"Me, too," she says softly. "He was a good husband. Most of the time anyway. Still, it just—it wouldn't be right." She takes a sip of tea. "Anyway, what am I talking about? It's been two days and I'm going on and on about our tour guide. Shame on me . . . Anyway, Taj seems to like you. What are you going to do?"

I shake my head. "Taj isn't really my type," I say, running a hand over my hair. It's fuzzy from the humidity, even though we're sitting inside. "He's on a dating app and—"

Charlotte shrugs. "Isn't everyone your age on a dating app?"

I feel busted, because technically, until a week ago, I was also on the very same dating app. Until I deleted my profile after that horrible date with Kevan.

"Maybe, but . . ." I stand and walk over to the fireplace, leaning close to look at the tiny porcelain animals on the mantel.

"It's not the reason you came on the trip," she says, as I pick up a tiny porcelain sheep.

I turn around and look at Charlotte. She smiles. "Everyone's here for a reason."

I replace the sheep, then walk back and sit down on the couch, pulling the pink-and-cream herringbone wool throw over my legs.

"It's going to sound crazy," I warn her. I can't believe I'm about to tell someone—a stranger—my secret.

"Honey, the crazier the better."

"Well," I say, pulling the throw up to my chest. For a moment I feel like I'm talking to Mom—sitting in the main room of our apartment, telling her about boyfriend drama when I was a teen. "You know I own a romance bookshop," I start. "And I read a lot of romances. But I also listen to them—audiobooks. And a few months ago a book called *Their Finest Hour* popped up on my recommended listens."

"OK," Charlotte says, leaning forward in her chair. She puts her tea down on a coaster and clasps her hands together over her knee.

"It's a book I know well, because it's the book that my mom was reading when she met my dad. At her bookshop. She didn't know him, but he picked that very same book off the shelf and started reading it aloud."

"How bizarre," she says.

"It is weird, right? Like so random, and it's not like it was a super popular book either. Anyway, that weird coincidence caused my parents to meet, and fall in love."

"How lovely," Charlotte says, then frowns. "But how does that . . ." She's trying to figure out where all the pieces of the puzzle fit together.

"So I came across that book's audio version, and it turns out the person reading it has a great voice. Like, really great," I say. "So great that I—well, it's weird, but, I kind of became obsessed with that voice. Like, I sort of fell in love with it."

"OK," Charlotte says, still not understanding.

"Zane was the one reading the book," I say. "The audiobook," I clarify.

She looks surprised, but still confused. "Zane? The guide that you keep asking Angus about?"

I nod. "I didn't know who he was. To me I was just listening to this book that brought my parents together, so I knew I would have *feelings* about the book, but when I heard this voice reading it, I felt completely swept away. And I've heard hundreds of actors and *professionals* read some of my favorite romance novels over the years. I know that a voice can make or break your enjoyment of a book, and it's all subjective, but hearing this voice was like *nothing* else I've ever experienced. I've *never* felt the way I did hearing Zane read. His voice goes straight to my soul. I feel connected to him. There has to be something to that." I exhale, closing my eyes and remembering that first time. When I open my eyes, Charlotte's eyes are glued to me. She nods, urging me to go on. "It's like everything just made sense." I push the blanket away, suddenly hot. "His voice is so full of *passion*, Charlotte." I pause. "And then I found out about his family's business, and his life feels like it has all these parallels to mine. So when my friends gave me the tour as a gift, it felt like it was all a sign from the universe." I close my eyes. "That I could meet him. And maybe, just . . . see."

I open my eyes and look at Charlotte. She's holding her hands together in a prayer position, her fingers to her mouth. "Well that just dills my pickle," she says.

I laugh. "Is that a good thing?"

She nods. "You came on this tour because you fell in love with the tour guide's voice in an audiobook. It's nuts, Sugar, but, then, life is nuts."

"Would it be more nuts," I wonder, "if the tour guide never shows up at all?"

"Mishaps make memories, and Zane's voice got you here," Charlotte says, like she can read my mind. "But don't let the rest of the story pass you by or you might find an ending you don't like."

Chapter Thirteen

Day 3, Tuesday, 8:20 a.m.

Hythe

I wake up to pounding and sit up and look around at the mint-green stucco walls before remembering where I am. The noise comes from the front door, so I get up and carefully make my way down the steep steps, pressing my palms into the wall to keep my balance, through the tiny kitchen, the tile like ice on the soles of my bare feet. I flip the little eyehole on the door to the left and peer out.

Taj stares back at me, crossing his arms over his chest.

"One sec!" I call out, looking around the kitchen for the old-fashioned key needed to open the door. What if he's here to tell me that Zane's arrived?

"Bike tour leaves in five," Taj says once I get the door open. He wears blue cotton shorts and a white polo shirt. The shirt fits well and makes his tanned skin look creamy, like a latte. His eyes flick down and I follow them, realizing I'm wearing only a T-shirt and underwear. I yank at the hem of my shirt while pulling the heavy wood door closer in front of me.

"Five minutes? What time is it?"

"Eight-twenty," he says without looking at his watch.

"Wow," I say. "I never sleep in this late. Must still be the jet lag." I blink a few times, and try to wake up. "I haven't even had coffee yet," I say.

"Then you should've set an alarm." He tucks a bit of hair behind his ear, and I notice another tattoo—ever so tiny—on the inside of his ring finger, but I can't make out what it is.

"I think I'll just skip the biking," I say slowly. "See you when you get back." I'm about to shut the door, but Taj puts a hand out to stop it.

"Not an option. We have to be out of the cottages by ten so they can clean them. So you have to put everything on the coach now. So I can lock it up."

"Fine, I'll bring my things out and then poke around the town," I say. I know I sound frustrated. I am not the world's cheeriest person without coffee. "Is there a place close by to get coffee? And what time will you be back?"

"Do you always ask this many questions in the morning?" When I don't answer, he checks his watch. "Seriously, you've got, like, five minutes to get out of there. Come on, it's a fun ride, the exercise will make you feel great, and I promise we'll stop for coffee." He turns and heads down the walk. Since it doesn't sound like I'm getting out of it, I close the door and hurry upstairs. I pair an ankle-length flowy white cotton skirt with a U of M sweatshirt, since it felt a bit chilly, and a pair of high-top sneakers—possibly the only practical part of my outfit for this ride. I brush my teeth, pull my hair into a cute side braid, add two coats of mascara and a swipe of lip gloss, then check my reflection. Not bad. Seven minutes later I'm out on the narrow stone path with the rest of the group.

"There you are, Gigi!" Angus says with gusto and I feel a stab of disappointment that he's here, and Zane is not.

"You sleep well, yah?" Angus says and I nod. He's wearing a blue Oxford shirt beneath a tweed jacket and nice leather shoes that look like he's had them forever but polishes them every Sunday. He stands beside Charlotte, who's tying a blue-and-white-striped silk scarf over her smooth hair. Violet and Nelle wear matching hot-pink and black cycling outfits; Nelle fiddles with the pack of water bottles attached to her waist, and I wonder just how intense this bike ride is.

"Oh dear, you picked the wrong outfit," Nelle says, looking at me and shaking her head. "It's going to get caught in the gears. You'll get grease all over it, and wreck the bike while you're at it. You might even fall."

I look down at my long skirt. She's probably right, actually, and I feel a bit silly, even if ten minutes ago I thought this outfit was cute.

"Relax, it's not the Tour de France," Jenny says, squeezing her bike between us. She's wearing an oversized white dress shirt, white capris, white deck shoes with white-and-black ankle socks, big black sunglasses and a small black cross-body Chanel bag. Clearly she's not worried about a little bike grease.

"Jenny," Violet says warningly, but Jenny ignores her. Violet turns to me.

"Here." She reaches down and grasps the bottom of my skirt. "May I?"

I'm not sure what she's about to do, but I nod anyway as Taj rolls a dark-blue bike past us, passing it to Francis, who finishes whatever he's saying into his recorder, then pushes the red button and slides the small black device into the fanny pack around his waist.

"There you go," Violet says, standing back and putting her hands on her hips. She's gathered my skirt and tied a knot just above my right knee. "Now it won't get caught." So long as the knot holds, it seems like the arrangement should work on a bike. It even looks stylish.

Jenny turns back to me, passing me her camera. "Just hold it steady."

"What?" I hold the camera out to her and shake my head. "I don't think you want me filming you," I say.

"Everyone else is over forty. You're my last hope," she says, giving me a look.

I turn the camera over in my hands. It has several dozen knobs, and I'm not sure what any one of them does.

"Don't forget to leave a comment, like and subscribe," Taj says as he passes me. I stifle a laugh.

"Here, I'll do it, Gigi," Violet says, holding out a hand to me. "I used to take a lot of pictures." Jenny rolls her eyes, then throws a leg over the bike. Violet shoves the lens cap in her pocket, pushes her sunglasses up on her head and evaluates the scene. She crosses the street so the sun's at her back and uses the camera to follow Jenny back and forth as she rolls about ten feet in one direction, then ten feet in the other. Repeats several dozen times. Eventually Jenny leans the bike up against a car and takes the camera from Violet without even a thank you.

"Alright off we go," Angus says, swinging a leg over his bike. "The goal here is to avoid falling into the canal."

Nelle turns to Violet as she rides across the street. "Oh, Vi— maybe we should turn back?" she says nervously.

"What's he talking about? What's wrong with the water?" Violet asks.

"It's wet," Taj says drily. "Let's go."

I laugh as Taj finally hands me the last bike, a mint-green one with a white basket and matching bike helmet dangling from the handlebars. I look over to Charlotte's bike to see if hers also matches her cottage, but hers is black.

"Mine matches," I say to Taj, wondering if he saved this one specifically for me.

"Yeah," he says. "Not everyone has bike-colored eyes," he teases. My heart rate quickens, even though I haven't even started pedaling. He picked this bike to match my eyes?

The sycamore-lined road snakes back and forth past detached Georgian homes with large lawns and tall fences. We all ride in a line, following Angus. At the end of the hill, he takes a sharp right off the main road onto a paved cycling path. On one side is a green expanse between the path and the road. On the other is a canal, a little wider than the road, oak trees casting shadows over the surface of the water. My front tire hits a stone. I wobble and grip the handlebars tighter.

"Don't look down," Taj says as I pass him. "Always look ahead. You'll be steadier."

"I know how to ride a bike," I say. "I just haven't in a while."

"There you go, like riding a bike," Taj says from behind me.

"How often do you use that joke?"

"Let's see, we hit Hythe every two weeks so . . ."

"So I thought you didn't 'do tour stuff'"—I take a hand off my bike handle to air quote. My bike teeters and I grab the handlebar again. Probably I should keep two hands on the bars at all times.

"I'm a study in contradictions," Taj says. Up ahead Roshi catches up to Sindhi and they bike side by side.

"This is the Royal Military Canal," Angus calls back to the group as we pass a copse of lilac trees. One creates an arch that hangs so low I have to duck to go under the branches.

"We're bike riding along the Royal Military Canal in Hythe," Francis says into his recorder.

"Francis, you heard yourself. You're bike riding, not recording. Two hands on the handles there, yah?" Angus calls back. Francis stops, puts his feet on the ground and goes to tuck the recorder into his jacket pocket, but it slips to the ground instead, just as I'm rolling up to him. I stop and lean over to pick it up. "Thanks," he says. "He's probably right. No recording and riding, Francis," he jokes. "I should be in the moment. It's quite lovely, isn't it?"

I laugh, surprised to hear Francis take note of anyone else. He's usually just talking to himself.

"It is," I say, noticing how weathered Francis's skin is—thick with deep creases—but how bright his eyes are.

"I haven't ridden a bike in years. Maybe I should think about picking up an old beater when I get home," he says, then his eyes cloud. He shakes his head, tucks the recorder away, then starts to pedal. I wonder what came over him.

I start pedaling, too, now last in the group, but I don't mind the bit of space, to listen to the others' chatter at a distance. The path leads over a bridge and the incline, paired with the low branches of a willow, means we all have to duck.

Nelle asks if anyone needs water, which causes Jenny to remind her we've been biking for less than ten minutes. "No one's thirsty!" she says.

"I'm actually kind of thirsty," I say, feeling bad for thinking her multiple water packs were overkill back at the start.

"By the time you're thirsty you're already dehydrated," Nelle says. "Gigi, I'll wait for you in the next widening of the path."

"You'd be a fine nurse, Nelle!" Angus says.

"I am a nurse," Nelle says. "I told everyone that in the game on the bus."

"I thought you said you were nervous!" Angus bellows, echoing my own thoughts.

"Me too," I chime in.

"As did I," Francis says. Nelle's stopped and has turned around. "Did all of you think I said 'nervous'?"

"I wasn't really listening," Jenny says, riding past her. Francis stops beside Nelle and pulls out his recorder. "Nelle is a nurse. We all thought she was nervous."

Nelle looks at him with a worried expression, pulling a full mini bottle of water out of its pouch on her back and handing it to me. "I *am* nervous, now," she says to me, then looks around, I think, for Violet, who's continued cycling. "How much have I said that people have misunderstood?" she frets.

"I wouldn't worry," I say instinctively, then laugh and make a face. I take a sip of water, then hand the bottle back to her. "Thank you."

"I'll keep it right here if you'd like more," she pats the pouch on her left hip.

I ride quickly to catch up to the rest of the group. Taj is at the back again and he slows to ride beside me. My shoulders tense with nervousness for some reason. Sindhi is beside Francis now, in front of Taj. They seem deep in conversation.

"So what's with the yellow M?" Taj asks. I look down at my University of Michigan sweatshirt, the one I've had since before I was even a student.

"It's maize."

"If you're taking the piss, it's a terrible job. It's clearly the letter M," he says. "It's enormous on your chest."

"Yes of course, but you don't call the color *yellow*. It's maize, like the corn. It's from the University of Michigan, where I went to college. I'm sure you have a sweatshirt from—wherever you went to school." Oh, gosh, what if he didn't go to college? He probably didn't. A bus driver?

"I do not own a *sweatshirt* from Ox—"

I nearly fall off my bike. "Where'd you go to college?"

He mumbles something. But because I have to change gears to go up a slight hill, I don't hear him. My pedals falter for a second, then move smoothly again.

"What did you say?" I ask. "It started with "Ox . . .'" My mouth hangs open. I can't help it.

"Oxford."

"Oxford the university?"

"Oxford the university," he confirms.

"Let me get this straight. You went to *Oxford* and you're driving a *bus*?" I don't mean for it to sound quite as critical as it comes out, so I force out a laugh, as though I was just kidding.

His eyes narrow, and a frown appears between his eyebrows. "Sorry—I just mean, Oxford is a big deal." I'm sure he'd prefer to ditch me, but the path is so narrow that he can't get away from me even if he wants to. Alongside us mallards float down the canal, bobbing under the water, their tail feathers shooting straight up. Roshi's stopped to take a photo.

"Isn't this lovely?" Roshi says to Sindhi as she passes. "Why don't we ever ride bikes together at home?"

"We don't have bikes," she says simply, continuing on. She doesn't sound angry, just tired. I turn my attention back to Taj, hoping the whole minute that's passed is enough time for him to forgive my rude comment.

"What did you study there?" I ask Taj curiously.

"You don't *study* at Oxford," he says, staring straight ahead, "you read."

"Well, then, what did you *read*?"

But he doesn't answer because the group has stopped and is gathering around Angus, who has leaned his bike against a tree. He adjusts the lapels on his tweed jacket, then tells us that the canal stretches for twenty-eight miles. "It was built as a defense against invasion during the Napoleonic Wars with France back in the early 1800s," he explains. "About the time I was born," he cracks.

Violet puts up her hand. "How does a canal repel an invasion?"

"By being hard to cross," Angus says. "A bit like a castle moat."

But I'm not really listening. I'm thinking about why Taj went to Oxford and then decided to drive a bus. And why he told me in Cambridge that he doesn't like to do tour stuff but today seems very interested in the tour. He's standing a few feet away, next to Jenny, who even after a bike ride still looks YouTube–perfect, her hair straight and shiny. She laughs at something Taj says, then hands her camera to him. He shakes his head, declining to take it. Good for you, I cheer silently.

"We've got to almost be at the coffee shop," I say.

"Coffee? There's no coffee stop," Angus says, his eyebrows forming one line. "This is about putting wheel to pavement. Or gravel, rock and dirt, as it were."

No coffee? I turn around to catch Taj's eye, but he's still listening to whatever Jenny has to say.

Across a wide wooden bridge, Angus heads right, the rest of the group following behind. Off to the left is a squat stone pedestal, maybe ten-foot square, from which someone's carved out a circle. "Angus," I call, "what's that?" But Angus is too far ahead and doesn't turn back.

Taj slows to a stop alongside me. "Put your bike down for a sec," he says. He sets his in the grass verge and waves for me to follow him. I pull on my side braid nervously.

"It's a Sound Mirror," Taj says. And I run my hand over the rough edge of the concave circle, following the border up until it's out of reach. "They were built back in the First World War to detect the sound of approaching enemy aircraft. Stay here," he says. "I'll show you." Then he jogs across the bridge, disappearing behind the wild branches of buckbrush.

"What am I supposed to be doing?" I call out.

"Just listen," he calls back.

I close my eyes and take the moment to retie my skirt knot. Two sparrows call back and forth to each other, accompanied by the occasional blip of a duck dipping under the surface of the water.

And then I hear it. At first I'm not even sure it's real. But a moment later, the sound comes again, ghostly faint, then stronger.

Let's get you a coffee. The words reverberate through the concrete, even though Taj is across the bridge, out of sight.

I take a step back, staring at the Sound Mirror.

Taj re-emerges. "Hear anything?" His lip curls.

"Something about coffee," I say. "Were you *taking the piss*?"

"Well done. And no. I would never risk keeping an American from her morning coffee."

He picks up his bike where he left it.

I take mine and ride up to meet him. "But Angus says there isn't any."

The sun reflects in his eyes before he puts his sunglasses on. "On this matter," he says, "Angus is incorrect."

I stare at him. "Where?"

"Follow me, Gigi!" he calls, and leads us off the trail to a side street and a tiny tea shop, assuring me they also have coffee on the menu.

"You know," Taj says once I'm outside with a dark roast in hand. "If you liked the Sound Mirror, you should check out the Whispering Gallery when you get back to London." Then he sets off.

It's tricky to sip scalding-hot coffee while riding a strange bike. But several splashes on my white skirt later, I catch up to Taj just as he's nearing the rest of the group, who are waiting for the traffic light to change. When it does, Angus leads them across. "Stay to the left!" he calls out. "Just two minutes more until we're back at the cottages!"

"Aren't you going to ask me what the Whispering Gallery is?" Taj asks.

"Fine. What's the Whispering Gallery?" I finally say as we make our way up a slow incline.

"It's at St. Paul's Cathedral—you know, where Charles and Diana got married."

"And?" I say.

"It's a quirk of the design. If you stand on one side of the dome and whisper into the wall, it carries the sound to the other side.

Whoever's listening is said to be able to hear the deepest, darkest of secrets, confessions, even professions of love."

The hairs on my arms stand on end. "And does it really work?" I follow the group to the right, past a shiny red circular mailbox.

He nods. "Absolutely. Least it did when I went with my class as a kid."

"And? Did you hear secrets?" I slow down in front of the rounded gate to the cottages, putting a foot on the curb to steady myself. My fingers tingle.

Taj swings his leg over the bike, then begins wheeling toward the gate. He looks back, but I can't see his eyes through his sunglasses. "Nah," he says. "All I heard was a bunch of kids making fart noises."

Chapter Fourteen

Day 3, Tuesday, 11 a.m.

Hythe ❯ Dungeness

We stow our bikes back at the cottages and wait for Taj to bring the bus around. Angus suggests another seat change on this next leg of the trip.

"Do we have to?" Jenny whines, wrinkling her nose.

"I'll sit with you," Nelle offers.

"No thanks." Jenny grabs my arm. "You can sit with me, Gigi. You can watch me edit together the footage I got on the ride."

I look over at Charlotte, but she's talking to Angus, their heads close together. I realize that with all the rush to get to the bike ride I forgot to ask Angus what was happening with Zane—when he's coming, if ever. "Sure, Jenny," I say, but first I tap Angus on the shoulder. He turns and smiles.

"I was wondering—have you heard from Zane? Is everything alright?" I can feel Charlotte watching me, and now that she knows why I'm really on this tour, I feel self-conscious.

"Ah yes, thanks for the reminder," he says, looking sheepish. "I'll give him a ring once we've set off—see if there's a chance he'll join us later today."

A *chance?*

I nod and follow Jenny up the steps and to the back of the bus. She plops down in the window seat and clears a mound of stuff to make space for me.

"So what's *your* deal?" she asks once we're back on the coastal route and heading west toward the next stop. "Wait, don't tell me." She makes a square with her hands and holds them in front of my face. "I'm really good at reading people and I've got you figured out. This was supposed to be your honeymoon, but you called off the wedding and decided to come solo instead. Your ex is kind of a geography geek, which is why he chose a bus tour. He's pissed you got the trip in the breakup, but he got the dog, so . . ." She nods, convincing herself. "That's why you're here alone." Her analysis of me sounds very similar to *Float Plan* by Trish Doller, a book I loved.

"Not quite," I say, thinking of David, and how we'd flip through travel books, dreaming about honeymoon destinations. He always wanted somewhere cold and snowy: Breckenridge or Revelstoke. I wanted Bora Bora or Fiji, to stay in one of those overwater bungalows that jut out into the ocean. Who is Jenny to judge why I'm here alone, when she is, too? I'm about to ask her about *her* reason for coming on this trip, when it feels like she'd have been better off planning her true-crime tour, but she's still talking.

"Then this was someone *else's* honeymoon and you got the trip for free. Except, then there should be some guy on this tour that you don't like but are forced to hang out with. Wait, I think I read a book like that."

"*The Unhoneymooners?*" I say automatically. "You read that?"

"That's it! You sound shocked." Her eyes narrow. "I *do* read, you know. Otherwise how would I see all the comments from my fans?" She lets out a loud laugh then pulls out her laptop and hands her camera to me. "Here, can you plug that in on the side?"

"How did you learn how to do all of this?" I ask as I fit the cord into a small slat on the camera side.

"I've had to figure everything out myself," she says matter-of-factly. "I was adopted, but then my adopted parents abandoned me. So technically, I was abandoned twice. You learn not to rely on anyone."

"That's awful. I'm sorry, Jenny."

"I know. Clearly, I have issues," she says. "But it's really made me resilient. I'm probably going to become a therapist. Did you know that most therapists go into it because they're so fucked up themselves? And I'll be famous, because of the channel. So that'll help with clients. And I'll be able to charge more."

Francis, who's now sitting in front of me beside Roshi, turns around. "Statistically speaking, only 10 percent of psychotherapists are in mental distress themselves."

"No one asked you," Jenny says rudely. Francis faces forward. I slap Jenny lightly on the arm. She sticks out her tongue at Francis's seat.

"Jenny, the girl with the YouTube channel, wants to be a therapist," Francis says into his recorder. "She'd be better off continuing her YouTube channel. Though 63 percent of people who start a YouTube channel give up within a year. Those who make it longer than a year tend to stick with it, though only 5 percent of all channels provide the creator with an income above the poverty level." I turn back to Jenny. She's oblivious, staring at her laptop screen.

"So how did you start doing this?"

"Making videos or the whole murder and makeup thing?"

"All of it."

"Well, the makeup I've been doing forever. I started doing my own makeup when I was ten. I did all my friends' makeup at prom. Like, their moms paid me. I'm that good. And I'd had my YouTube channel, but like, the likes were lacking because you can't just do the expected thing. You've gotta be niche, you know?"

"Right," I say, thinking about the bookstore and my conversation with Lars. "My bookstore—"

"And I'm not the only one to do murder and makeup," she continues, ignoring me. "It's a whole genre now, but I'm really good at both. And some people, they're good at the stories but kind of shitty at the makeup, like, they're all one-trick glittery eye ponies, you know what I mean? I'm diverse. In my niche. Both niches."

.

"The air smells like fish," Francis says into his recorder. The road has ended in a barren landscape of small flint shingles that stretch to the horizon in all directions. There's no tree in sight. No hedges either—just scrubby grass and shingled stone and, in the distance, the English Channel. There's an abandoned railway carriage, a handful of rotten shipwrecks and, in the opposite direction from the Channel, a set of smokestacks spewing power station fumes for the power lines.

"Cosseted deep within this hidden quarter is the legendary Dungeness . . ." Angus pauses for effect. "Britain's only desert." He fans his arms out, and then motions for us to follow him. The area looks post-apocalyptic. The buildings are single-story weather-beaten shacks and look abandoned. Aside from us, there's not a single soul in any direction.

The shingles crunch underfoot as we make our way south, the line between water and sky barely distinguishable in the distance.

"It's very hard to walk on these shingles," Sindhi complains. "Isn't there a path or something?"

Angus pulls his tweed jacket tight and lowers his voice as though he's sharing a secret as he tells us the history of the area—that the shingles built up over centuries, and by the medieval period the area had jutted so far into the English Channel it had become a hazard to shipping boats.

"Did anyone die?" Jenny asks.

"Thousands," Angus says and Jenny perks up.

It feels like the edge of the earth. Whitecaps form atop the waves, the wind whips my hair and as I stare out into an endless void, I have a sinking feeling in my stomach. Angus leads us to a fish shack where we wait in line for sandwiches. "Should we get Taj one?" I say to Angus when it's my turn to order, and he nods. Taj had stayed on the bus. "Definitely, thanks for the reminder."

Minutes later, as I'm taking the last bite of my greasy battered fish sandwich, a small figure on the horizon gets bigger with every passing second. Taj is making his way to us across the stones in a way that reminds me of Luke Skywalker on Tatooine.

"Lucky for you, Gigi remembered to order you a sandwich," Angus says, handing Taj the foil wrap.

"You know how I get when I miss lunch," he says.

"I do. And I'm afraid to see that guy again. So it was more of a selfish act than you might have thought," I tease.

"You want to see something cool?" he asks me, nodding his head to the right and motioning for me to follow. I stand, crumple the foil from my sandwich into a ball and toss it in the nearby bin, then slip my bottle of water into my purse. "Most Brits think this place is creepy. A wasteland."

"Are they wrong?" He's led me off the path, far from the rest of the group. An old railway track leads through the shingles, low bushes like bunches of kale cropping up every few feet. A wooden boat, worn and cracked, molders on its side, the mast protesting diagonally into the air. A few feet farther, an anchor. In the distance, the remains of a rowboat.

"Fisherman's graveyard," he says. "In most places, they say the sea reclaims the land, but this is one of those rare places where the land's winning the battle. The sea deposits these stones on the coast, and over time it's built a headland that goes on for miles."

He bends down and picks up one of the shingles. "Did you feel one of these?"

I shake my head.

"It's called a hagstone," he says. "Or a holy stone, like"—he makes the sign of the cross over his upper body, "or holey, like a hole." He makes an O with his hand.

The white hagstone has a hole in its middle. My eyes flick to his wrist, to the thin leather rope where a smaller, similar stone is looped through the rope. "Is that what you're wearing?"

He nods and hands the stone to me—our fingers touching, sending an unexpected shiver up my arm. But instead of pulling away, we keep our fingers laced together so they touch just a second longer than necessary. My breath catches, but I keep my focus on the stone, taking it and then turning it over in my fingers. It's light, almost airy. Was that a moment?

"My sister is very into this sort of witchy stuff," Taj says, breaking the silence.

"Witchy stuff?"

"Moving water makes the hole," he tells me. "And witches, apparently, believe that no harm can come around running water. So the hagstone is said to ward off bad luck. You're supposed to wear it around your neck but"—he makes a face.

"What? You're too cool for that?"

He shrugs. "There's a certain kind of guy who wears a necklace his sister gave him—I love my sister, but I'm not sure I'm that guy. But I have had a string of pretty bad luck in the past year," he says, looking out to the water again. "So I'm not so sure it's working on my wrist. Then again, you never know what's good luck, or what's bad luck. Or what just is." His eyes meet mine. There's something so intense about his eyes. Suddenly he bends down, breaking our connection. He picks up another stone and throws it into the distance. It lands with a small clink.

What does he mean about luck? And what kind of bad luck has he had? And what's going on that he went to Oxford and drives a bus?

A phone buzzes. Taj reaches into his pocket, and looks at the screen. "Huh," he says, then answers it.

The wind has picked up and whips my hair into my face. I turn, pulling it behind my face. Francis walks toward me.

"Do you know which way to London?" Francis asks.

I look back to the water. "Well, the Channel is south, so . . ." I point away from the water. "That way? Generally?"

"Have we met?" he asks. "You seem familiar."

I laugh nervously. "Francis, it's me. Gigi."

He puts two fingers to the bridge of his nose and squeezes. When he looks up, he smiles. "Brain fart, as they say. Of course I know who you are. I *meant* to ask you . . ." He shakes his head and trails off, then looks at the silver watch on his wrist. "Time for lunch?"

"Francis, we just had lunch. At the fish shack."

"Of course," he says, and smiles. "Of course we did."

"This way, folks!" Taj calls out. "Time to go."

I study Francis a moment. He smiles, shrugs, and turns to walk toward Taj, leaving me to wonder what just happened.

Chapter Fifteen

Day 3, Tuesday, 6 p.m.

Brighton

"Brighton, we've got a problem," Angus says as we stand in the lobby of the Brighton Harbour Hotel: vaulted ceilings, elaborate crown molding, jade marble pillars and ornate, colorful rugs and runners. He clasps his hands together. "It seems we have *almost* enough rooms for everyone."

"Oh no," Nelle says.

"No room at the inn," Roshi says. "It's almost biblical."

"The average hotel overbooks by 15 percent to account for no-shows," Francis says, then pulls out his recorder. "There aren't enough rooms at this particular hotel in Brighton."

"Everyone calm down," Angus says, his voice going from friendly grandpa to annoyed dad. "The bad news is we're short two rooms."

"There's good news?" Sindhi asks. "I can't imagine what the good news is."

"Please don't say we have to get back on the bus," Jenny calls back. "This place is amazing." She points her camera up to the ceiling to photograph the chandelier with what must be hundreds of bulbs and crystals.

"I agree with Jenny," I say. "It's a big town. There had to have been a dozen hotels along this stretch of boardwalk alone. We'll just find another hotel. Split up if we have to."

"We're not getting back on the coach," Angus says. "And yes, there's good news. The good news is that they have two very special rooms with bunk beds. Sort of like being on a ship—one can look out to the water and imagine they're floating along."

"I always wanted to go on a cruise," Sindhi says wistfully, looking over to Roshi.

"Really?" He looks surprised. "I had no idea," he says.

"How would you?" she says, and I wonder if she means, *You never asked.* But if I learned one thing from my relationship with David, it was that you have to say what you're thinking. There's no benefit to hoping someone can read your mind—you'll only end up like we did, both of us wanting different things, different lives, assuming the other did, too.

"Taj and I will share one of the rooms." Angus looks to Taj, who nods his head reluctantly. "It's not the first time Taj and I have roomed together."

"Let's hope the fumes are better this time," Taj says. The group breaks up with laughter, and I wonder if Taj and Zane get along, too.

As if on cue, my phone pings.

So? Is he there yet? Dory texts.

If my life were a novel, this scene would get edited out. Too on-the-nose.

Nope. I text. *I'm starting to believe he's never coming.*

I tuck my phone away as Angus claps his hands together and announces they need two more volunteers to share a room. It's up to Charlotte, Jenny and me. Presumably, Francis is out of the running, and I don't want to share a room with Jenny. I catch Charlotte's eyes, which are wide. I'm guessing she feels the same way. Her hand flutters in the air. "Gigi and I will do it."

"Great," Angus says, passing the room keys to Taj to distribute.

"Sorry for your loss of half a room," Taj says as he passes me.

"Sorry for yours," I retort.

·

Charlotte wears one of those strips across her nose, which she promised was to stop her from snoring. But it doesn't work. I lie in the top bunk, staring at the ceiling.

It reminds me of sharing a room with Lars when we were kids, and how I'd smack him because he'd snore in his sleep, and then he'd smack me and tell me I was doing something annoying— talking or humming in *my* sleep, which was always a lie.

I try counting sheep—which makes me realize you're not actually counting *anything*, just counting. Doesn't work. I finish reading an old Colleen Hoover favorite, flip through *Lady Susan*, then grab my phone and open Instagram. At first I just scroll past friends and strangers. Then I type in Dory's name, then Cleo's and Emily's, tapping through their Stories to see what's going on in their lives. Dory and Emily took their kids to the community pool together yesterday afternoon, and Cleo's posted pictures of the floral arrangements she created in the class she's been taking.

And then—because is there ever good judgment this late at night?—I type in Zane's name and hold my breath as I hit the blue Search button. His feed comes up, but there's nothing new to see. The most recent picture is a few weeks old. Still no clue as to where he is. I swipe my way out of Instagram. My finger hovers over the audiobook app. I give in, slipping my headphones on and pressing Play.

"Let me fix you a drink," Jack said to Mirabelle. She gave him a slow smile, then shook her head. He nodded. "I'm quite good at opening bottles and pouring things into glasses, trust me."

I hit Stop and pull my headphones off. I know listening to Zane could help me fall back asleep, but something doesn't feel right. Maybe it's that I've just looked at his photos, or that I'm here now, well into this trip, and he isn't. I don't know what it is, but I'm not in the mood. So, as quietly as I can, I get out of bed, pull off my tank top and pj shorts, and pull on an easy floral sundress. I thread my toes into a pair of flip-flops, then head down the hall to the winding lobby staircase. A gray-haired man sits at the grand piano, his long fingers dancing across the keys. I consider getting a drink in the bar, which is packed with an older crowd, but instead, head outside.

The boardwalk is empty but for a few figures—some intoxicated with alcohol, a couple intoxicated with love. In the distance the Brighton Pier lights up the night sky and neon hues flash to the beat of dance music. Kept company only by the waves on the pebble beach, I trudge toward the pier. Is this trip a waste? How stupid was I to think that Zane and I would actually meet—that he might somehow find a connection to me the way I'm so sure I have a connection to him? Parapets fly union jacks on either side of the midway sign: *Brighton Palace Pier*. The scene feels appropriate to a century ago.

The pier is alive with activity. People drink, eat, laugh and dance to the disco music. Ice cream stands and souvenir shops line the pier by the beach. The main entrance beckons under those broad, lit-up letters. Past the doors is an arcade, a sensory explosion: music, jingling of coins, clanging bells informing players they've won.

As a kid, Mom and Dad would take Lars and me to Pinball Pete's until I started going with friends and then boyfriends. I haven't been to an arcade in years. At a cash machine, I enter my credit card to get a game card, then make my way over to Mortal Kombat in the corner. My favorite character is Sonya Blade, with her fishtailed hair, fingerless gloves and military cap. I slam at the joystick and punch the red and yellow buttons. For the moment I feel like a teenager again. When my character misses a blow to the face and the game's over, I tap the Start button for another match, and this time, I'm all focus.

"I wouldn't have guessed you'd be a Mortal Kombat kind of girl," a familiar voice says behind me. I chance a quick look: Taj, smiling. Is it the familiarity of seeing someone I know in an otherwise crowded room of strangers? Is it the way his white linen shirt hugs his torso in all the right places? Or does it have something to do with the way, under the flashing lights of the arcade machines, the whites of his eyes look whiter, the burnt firewood of his irises even more intense?

Whatever it is, my heart leaps. I brush it off as that old familiar feeling of seeing a friendly face. Like when I saw him on the bench in Canterbury. Nothing more.

"Don't distract me," I say, turning back to the screen. "This is serious business and I'm on a roll." I win the round, shake out my hands and then it's back onto the controls. Taj comes around to stand on the other side of me, and I smell soap and sandalwood—it distracts me just enough to miss a blow to the head. The round is over. "Impressive," he says, his voice husky next to me. "Not only do you like Mortal Kombat, you're pretty good at it, too."

"Pretty good?" I say, turning to face him. "You think you can do any better?"

He shrugs. "I remember being pretty good. When I was nine."

"Sounds like a challenge," I say, grabbing the same controls I was using before. I choose Sonya again and he chooses Johnny Cage, the character I always thought, with his mirrored aviators, looked like a cross between a young Tom Cruise and Johnny Knoxville. Arrogant, cocky yet good-looking. Also, the love interest of Sonya Blade. Not that I follow the romantic storylines of video game characters.

I win the first round.

Taj groans. "Rematch."

He wins the second round. I punch his arm and groan, but I'm secretly glad we have a reason to play again. "Tie break?" I suggest.

He turns to me. "Definitely. I'm just warming up. You're going down."

"Fat chance," I say. My body feels alive with excitement. This is fun.

"What's the wager?"

A siren wails and red lights flash from a nearby game. "Are you really supposed to be betting with the guests?" I ask skeptically.

"It's after hours. And it makes it more fun. Loser buys drinks?"

"Deal," I say, then turn back to the screen as the round begins. Every time my shoulder touches Taj's, sparks go through me, fueling my desire to win, to show him what I can do. Sonya whips her legs around to take Johnny out. He falls down and as he's getting up, I deliver the death blow. Knockout. "Yes!" I shout, and Taj slams his hand on the console. "Good game," he says, turning to me, holding out his hand. I take it. His hand is warm, slightly sweaty, his grip firm. The hairs on my right arm stand on end and I pull away, but not before our eyes meet, holding just a moment too long.

"Alright, Georgia," he says.

"Who said you could use my real name?" I say with a smile.

He punches my upper arm lightly. "Come on," he says. "We've played *your* go-to. Now let's play mine."

"Let me guess," I say, looking around. "Ms. Pac-Man?"

Taj raises his eyebrow. "You'll see." Confidently, he winds his way past Dance Dance Revolution and a motorcycle racing booth to the far end of the arcade. We approach a booth, and I look at Taj in disbelief. *This* is Taj's go-to game? The one with water guns, where you sit on a stool and squirt a stream at a tiny target at the other end, to make whatever plastic doohickey move across the board?

"I am so good at this game," I say, straddling the blue vinyl stool. "You're going down."

"I was the reigning champion three years in a row when I was in primary school," he informs me. He takes the seat next to mine, and our knees brush. Bare skin to bare skin, and I can't focus on anything else.

"You ready?" Taj interrupts. The butt of the water gun is surprisingly heavy, the metal trigger cold in my hands. I reposition myself to better aim the gun and lean forward. I have to focus my shot and get the plastic dolphin to leap through the water to the other side. Taj cannot win. The carnival music starts and I pull the gun toward me, the trigger making a clicking sound. I focus on the bull's-eye and keep aiming until the bell rings and I realize I've won. I whoop and nearly fall off my stool, but in a split second Taj's arms are around my waist, pulling me back onto the vinyl seat. I turn to him, our faces inches from each other, his eyes on mine. His lips look so . . .

I shimmy away and he takes the hint and immediately lets go of my waist.

"Well, I can't believe it. My reign is over." His tone is teasing, but it sounds a bit forced.

"Told you I was going to beat you," I say, just to fill the air. My heart is racing, and I can still feel Taj's touch.

You were going to fall off the stool. Don't read into it, Gigi.

"You wanna get out of here?" he asks. But then he makes a face. "That came out wrong. I'm not trying to get with you," he adds with disdain. "I just meant, I could use a break from the lights."

Right. Obviously. And even though I'm not interested in him, I somehow feel embarrassed and rejected. "Yeah. Sure."

We wind our way through the people and flashing lights to the nearest door.

"So." Taj clears his throat and looks around the pier. "What are you doing here?" He doesn't meet my eye. "I would've thought you had a strict sleep regime. Sleep seems really important to you." His lip curls up on one side. He walks to the right, back toward the beach.

I roll my eyes and bite back a smile, then glance over at him. Now he meets my eye. "That's only because you're always waking me up. Anyway, Charlotte snores." I shrug. "I couldn't sleep, so I thought I'd come out and explore a bit."

"Should've put Charlotte and Angus together. He claims he doesn't snore. But he's louder than a lorry."

I laugh. "Oh no. What are you going to do?"

He stretches out his arms, and I duck so he won't hit me. "I was doing it. Play video games until I'm so tired I've got no choice but to pass out when I get back to the room."

"Pretty sure playing video games is exactly the opposite thing you're supposed to do when you're trying to get to sleep. I bet Francis has a stat about that."

He laughs. "He probably does. Let me guess, *you* recommend reading a book."

"Yes. Though it didn't work for me tonight."

"I actually finished the book I was reading yesterday."

"The John Grisham?" I ask.

"Yeah," he says. "I usually have an extra just in case. I'll have to try to grab one tomorrow."

"What about the cozy mystery?"

He looks confused for a moment. "The one you got for me in Cambridge?" When I nod, so does he. "Ah, that wasn't . . ." He trails off. *That wasn't for me*, he was probably about to say.

"My ex snored," I say, not because I want to talk about David, but because the last thing I want to hear about is who the book was actually for—someone Taj met on XO, likely? Maybe the last time he was in Rochester. Maybe he sees her every time he's in town, knows enough about her to know the kind of books she likes, her favorite cocktail, how she takes her coffee.

"That was the dealbreaker, then?" he asks, interrupting my thoughts.

I groan inwardly. Why did I have to bring up David as the topic-changer?

"The snoring? That's not why we broke up. Not the *only* reason, I suppose."

"The longer you're together, the more complex the breakup."

"Spoken from experience?"

"Four years together. You?"

"Five," I say. "Almost."

Taj lets out a low whistle, but I'm stuck on his answer. So being on XO is his rebound. Or not. Maybe that relationship ended years and years ago. Maybe he's been on XO for years. Maybe polygamous dating is his long-term plan. I decide to just go for it. "So . . . no XO date tonight?"

His brow furrows. "What?"

"Never mind." I wave a hand. "I'm on the app, too," I admit. "And my best friend works there, so she's always playing matchmaker. She saw your profile on there when she was looking up hot guys in Rochester"—I clamp my lips together, realizing what I've just said. He looks amused.

"I went to see my mum," he says.

"Your mum lives in Rochester?"

He nods. "I try to visit her when I have a stop there. We had a falling out years ago, but I'm trying to make amends."

"Oh, I'm sorry," I say quietly. I imagine Mom and Dad still alive, like I have so many times in the past. How I wouldn't let a day go by without talking to them. I can't imagine letting anything be so big or important that I'd stop seeing them. But that's me thinking about my parents. I don't know anything about Taj's parents or his family life. I just know I'd give anything for even one more week, one more day, one more moment to hug them, to say goodbye. I never got that, and I don't think I'll ever get over that.

The entrance to the pier is quieter and prettier, illuminated by lights strung from the fence separating the boardwalk from the beach.

"Anyway, you weren't asking about my mum. And I don't want to talk about my dating life. At least, not without a drink," Taj says jokingly. "And I owe you one anyway. You wanna take a walk along the prom?" I'm not even totally sure what he means, yet I nod and we head west along the waterfront.

A few feet ahead, a white tent, like you might pitch in your backyard for an outdoor summer wedding, has a chalkboard sandwich board advertising a special deal on margaritas. I walk over and order two from the girl standing behind the makeshift bar.

"I was supposed to buy the drinks," he says, coming up behind me.

"I think it's nicer to have the winner buy." I stand up a little straighter and grin.

"Way to rub it in." I try to pass him a plastic cup, but he shakes his head. "I actually don't drink."

"Oh," I say. "Sorry, I should've asked."

Taj holds up a hand to get the bartender's attention and orders a Coke, pays, then turns around. "Don't be sorry. You didn't know."

"I thought you went to a stag party on the weekend."

"I did," he says. "And let me tell you—stag parties are not as much fun when you're not drunk. Anyway, cheers to Sonya Blade."

We clink plastic cups and then I take a sip from one of the cups and make a face. "Whoa, that's strong."

"Bad?"

I shake my head. "Delicious, just dangerous." I take a sip of the other. "Yep, just as strong."

"You got your money's worth." He takes a sip of his Coke and we walk along the rocky beach in silence for a few moments, the air a cavern of sounds—the wind, the waves, the ping of a sailboat halyard against the mast.

"You alright?"

I realize I was sighing. "Yeah, it's so nice out here."

"Much better at night than in the day," he says. "Usually guys who are here on stag weekends are passed out drunk by seven from drinking all day, so it's quieter," he laughs.

A couple of guys stumble toward us, leaning onto each other and trying to stay upright. One of them chortles as I move out of the way, margarita sloshing over my hands.

"I take it back," he scoffs. "You want me to hold one of those cups for you?"

I pass a sticky cup to him. "Thanks." I wipe my hand on my sundress.

"For someone who seems to dislike tourists you've chosen an interesting career," I say, then take a sip of my drink.

"Career is a pretty strong word. It's more like a pastime."

I raise an eyebrow. "Pastime? Most people take up knitting, like Charlotte, or crosswords, like Roshi or—"

"Talking into a recorder like Francis?" Taj grins.

"Don't think you can elude my question by talking about Francis. So what? Are you independently wealthy, and thought, Hmm, should I hang out in the hot tub, at my mansion"—I raise my left hand, which is empty—"or drive a bus?" I raise my hand with the cup. "And you decided driving the bus was the hands-down way to go?"

He pauses.

"No! Don't say it," I say. "Or say it and you'll owe me ten bucks. But no, don't say it. I won't be able to talk to you."

"Say *what*?" He looks at me like I'm crazy. Understandable, I guess.

"'It is what it is,'" I say. "You were about to say that, weren't you?"

"No, definitely not." He looks offended. "I thought we already established that it's—"

"Nauseating," I joke, remembering how he described it.

"Exactly."

"Alright, then, go on."

"Oh, I have permission now, do I?" He grins.

"Uh-huh," I say.

"I have my reasons," he says, unfortunately ending the banter. I wait for him to say more but that's it. Does this have something to do with the string of bad luck he mentioned in Dungeness?

The music from the pier fades into the night air, and the sky gets darker as we move away from the lights. The water of the English Channel is almost invisible, only evident from the sound of the waves crashing into the shore.

"So tell me about your bookshop," Taj says into the blackness of the night.

I get that easy feeling of floating in saltwater whenever anyone asks me to talk books. "Where should I start? What do you want to know?"

"I don't know what I don't know. Tell me what I don't know."

"Well," I start slowly. "It's in Ann Arbor, pretty much right downtown. It's called Love Interest, which I told you before," I say, meeting his eyes. "It wasn't only romance when my parents owned it—but people buy their books in different ways now. I wanted to set myself apart, and I love romance novels, so it was a pretty easy decision. For me, anyway. My brother, who's running the store while I'm here, feels differently."

"Your brother didn't want to run it?" Taj asks curiously.

"Nope. He was never into it the way I was, but when my parents died, he wanted to even less. He moved to Ypsi—that's a town nearby. I think he just needed . . . space."

"Everyone has their own way of coping."

"I guess," I say.

"So, romance," he laughs. "I was joking before about you having read all the books, but I might not have been far off. Have your read *all* the romance books?"

"Laugh all you want, but I believe in being passionate about my work." I take a sip of margarita. "And people laugh at romance, brush it off like it's unimportant, but everyone's been in love at some point. Or thought they were in love, or wished they were in love. Romance is universal." I stop walking and look at Taj. "You can get anything at Amazon, but at my store you get an experience. And who doesn't love a romance novel?"

"Did you know there are 5.8 million lonely women roaming the earth looking for a kind of love that doesn't exist, thanks to romance novels?" he replies, wiggling his eyebrows.

"Taking the piss?" I ask.

"But you have to agree," he says, his voice suddenly serious, "that romance novels aren't exactly *realistic*."

"I think the real problem is that people *expect* them to be realistic. Look at Vin Diesel. You don't watch a Vin Diesel movie and think, this doesn't feel totally realistic, so I think I'll stop watching."

"I'm not sure Vin Diesel is the best example of being true to life," Taj says with a laugh. "He's practically a cartoon character himself."

I finish off the last sip of my first margarita and wander over to a garbage bin to toss the cup. Taj follows me, tossing his empty cup into the bin, too, then holds out my second margarita cup. "Well." I take a sip. "Nicholas Sparks isn't writing stories that are realistic and depressing. He's writing stories that make you feel good about humanity." I look up at the night sky. "Love makes people happy. Alive." I raise my free arm in the air. "Love is good for your health."

"So are vegetables," Taj says.

"Come on," I say. "Vegetables? You think love is like a head of broccoli?"

"So, which came first—you turning the bookshop into romances-only, or your love of unrealistic romance?"

"Let me tell you a story," I say, ignoring his question. "A man walks into a—"

"I've heard that one before," Taj interrupts as we approach another pier. This one's smaller, and there's a tiki hut, a few people swaying to music on the makeshift dance floor out front. "Alright, so a bloke walks into a bar . . ." Taj says.

"Right. This guy, he's about twenty-three or twenty-four. Anyway, he walks into a bookshop. He's supposed to be writing an essay but he's procrastinating. He's at the University of Michigan, pre-law but he hates it. Tells himself he'll just pick up a book as a reward, something to read when he's done studying."

"Bloke's rewarding himself for reading by reading some more," Taj laughs. I slap him lightly on the shoulder, but leave my hand a beat longer, my entire arm heating up by touching him. I pull my hand away.

"He likes reading, what can I say?"

Taj reaches down to pick up a pebble, then tosses it out into the water. It skips a few times, then disappears.

"Alright. Go on." I down the second margarita quickly and toss the cup into a nearby bin.

"So he randomly chooses a book off the shelf. No reason at all. And he opens it. Starts reading it aloud."

"That's odd."

"It *is* odd, but it's a thing he likes to do. Thinks books are meant to be read aloud. To hear the characters come alive." I sidestep a small plastic bucket. "He's trying to lose himself in the book—to stop thinking about law school."

"Because he's so unhappy," Taj says, and there's something about his tone, that he gets it. I nod.

The sky is dark now, only a few stars dotting the black expanse. The sound of the waves crashing into the shore, and the crunch of stones beneath our feet, create a soundtrack to the story.

"So there's a woman standing at the cash. She's twenty, it's her parents' shop. He doesn't know it, but she can hear him reading."

"She thinks he's odd."

"A bit, but the thing that she realizes is that he's reading from the very book she's reading. She can't see him, but she can feel his presence, and it's like nothing she's ever felt before. It's a tingling in the back of her head, a rush through her chest, a warm blanket wrapped around her."

"All from a voice?" Taj sidesteps a pair of flip-flops in the shingles.

"All from a voice, but *more* than a voice. It's a connection," I say. "She's thinking about it, but helping other customers because the store is busy and she keeps thinking he'll come to the desk with the book but he never does. At one point she helps a guy her age. He doesn't have the book, but she figures maybe he put it back on the shelf. She chats to him, to get him to speak, but when he does the voice is all wrong. She assumes he's left the store without buying the book—and she'll never know who he was."

Up ahead, a group of guys is throwing a glow-in-the-dark Frisbee. Taj slows and turns to me. "Let's turn around before one of us gets bonked in the head."

The gentle breeze is now at our backs, and my hair whips at my face. I tuck it behind both ears as we retrace our steps.

"Don't tell me—it's been her mission ever since to find the guy."

"No," I laugh, feeling light, from the story, from the tequila. "I'm not done. Eventually he comes to the desk. She doesn't know it's him, at first, though she thinks he's cute. He's got a stack of books, so that makes her like him even more. He's pleasant and easy to talk to, and she's pretty sure he's the voice, but by now she's actually not sure, because she's been chatting to so many other people and so much time has passed."

"OK," Taj says, scratching the back of his head.

"So they're just sort of chatting and laughing and it's just *easy.* Like they already know each other. And then she gets to the final book on the stack and it's the book. The one she was reading. And so she knows that it's him."

"So what happens when she tells him that she's reading the same book?" Taj is hooked, I can tell. I started the story to prove a point. To prove *my* point. About the power of sound, and the beginning of a story. To prove that soulmates exist outside romance novels. That true love finds its way to you if it's really meant to be. But now, I'm just telling a good story.

"She doesn't," I say. "She freezes. She wants to, but she's too nervous."

"This is a terrible story." He bumps shoulders with me, and I shake my head.

"You're really irritating, you know that?" But I'm teasing, too. "She can't tell him, because she knows."

"Knows what?"

"That he's the one." I sigh, thinking of Mom and Dad. How happy and in love they always seemed, despite spending every single day together—at the shop and at home. Sure they got in silly spats from time to time, like when Dad left his dirty socks on the kitchen table. But they'd always end up laughing it off a few hours later. And if they got in bigger fights, it always seemed like it was truly out of love, of wanting what was best for each other or for Lars and me. That's the kind of relationship I want.

"So she doesn't tell him?" Taj asks. "They never get together?"

"Of course they do. I'm standing here, aren't I?"

"What do you mean?" he asks, not getting it. Then he raises his eyebrows. "Oh." His voice drops. "You're the one—at the shop? *You* heard the guy's voice and . . ." he trails off. I think of Zane—the reason I'm here. Maybe I should tell Taj the truth— maybe he's the missing piece to this puzzle, to help me get Zane here. But right now, I don't want to ruin this moment by talking about Zane.

"Not me," I say, his interest sending a tremor up my spine. "My mom worked at the shop. My dad was the one reading the book. The couple became my parents."

He lets out a low whistle. He hides his hands in his pockets, his arm brushing mine in the process, sending shivers straight to my head.

"Yep. My dad gave up law—and he and my mom took over the shop from her parents. My dad would read stories aloud to little kids on Saturday mornings. The shop was such a happy place, always music playing, always people talking." I swallow back the lump in my throat.

I love this story so much, and I love telling it, and I never tire of it. Every time I do, I get that familiar, bittersweet feeling about my parents. I feel so happy that this was their story—and then, of course, so unbelievably sad.

It's so dark but I can still make out Taj's face, his chiseled jaw, his smooth skin. I don't know if it's that this story is my ultimate fantasy, what I want for myself, or the margaritas, or being here, on the beach, the waves, the salty air, and finally feeling like I'm on vacation, but I'm standing so close to Taj it feels like . . . we're alone in the universe. His fingers graze mine and when I turn to look up at him, he's looking at me. He stops walking and turns to face me. "That's a *pretty* good story," he says, his voice low. "And now I can see why you'd be a hopeless romantic."

"I'm not hopeless," I protest. "*Hopeful.* Their story proves that the kind of romance in romance novels really exists in real life. That when you least expect it, someone can walk through the door of your bookshop and trigger the start of your story—and your lives—together."

The wind pushes my hair across my face and he reaches out and, ever so gently, tucks it behind my ear, his fingers caressing my earlobe. "I like the way you think about stuff," he says, taking a step toward me. Our bodies are now only inches apart.

His breath is hot on my forehead. His fingers brush mine, this time intentionally, and he loops his pinkie around mine. I take a step closer, tilting my head up, as he bends down to me. I close my eyes, anticipating the feel of his lips on mine.

But they don't come. The air stings my face and my eyes flick open. Taj has taken a step back.

"I don't think—I don't think this is a good idea," he says, and back in his pockets go his hands. He looks down at his feet, kicking the stones with the toe of his shoe.

It's like the wind is no longer whipping my hair in my face—it's completely knocking me over. When his eyes finally meet mine, I look immediately away. "Right," I say, trying to keep my voice steady.

"I just got out of a relationship—" Taj stammers and I turn back to him. His brow is furrowed. "I'm not looking for anything—and you're a guest on the tour and—"

I cut him off. "I get it. You don't have to say anything else." I turn and walk down the beach, the stones digging into my soles through my thin flip-flops. It's painful, but I walk faster anyway. I just want to run into the water and swim far, far away. Or drown.

"Gigi," Taj calls after me, but I don't look back.

Chapter Sixteen

Day 4, Wednesday, 7:43 a.m.

Brighton ❯ Kingley Vale

The sun streams into my small room through the slit in the drapes, hitting me smack in the face. I roll over, into the bar preventing me from falling off the top bunk, and remember where I am.

"Charlotte?"

No answer.

Pain sears through my head.

Charlotte's bed is empty. My phone on the nightstand says it's 7:43. Exactly seventeen minutes to get downstairs before the bus leaves. Three steps to the bathroom and I'm in front of the wall-to-wall mirror, which confirms: I look like a raccoon. Or maybe, like I'm a raccoon that's been attacked by a raccoon. Not taking off my makeup or running a brush through my windswept hair before bed was clearly a bad decision. But then, the entire night was a bad decision.

For the first time since the tour started I pray that today's *not* the day Zane shows up.

I run the water, catching it in my cupped hands, then splash it onto my face. Instant regret. Leaning over the sink was a terrible idea. I stand up again. Also a bad idea. Turns out, any sudden movements make my head feel like it's being whacked with an Oxford Dictionary.

Maybe the bus will leave without me and I won't have to face Taj, I think hopefully. But then I feel annoyance. Except, *he's* the one who should be embarrassed, not me. He led me on. I pause. Wait, *did* he lead me on? Or did I totally misread the signals? Was he just being friendly? No, he definitely seemed interested. He was definitely the one who got close and touched me (with his *pinky!*) and made me think he was going to kiss me—and he *hadn't* had anything to drink.

I groan and reach for the soft marine-blue hand towel looped through the brass ring on the wall, hold it under the cold water, then press it to my face, but it doesn't help. I whip it onto the floor angrily. None of this would've happened if Zane were here. I would've been walking on the boardwalk *with Zane*. On the pier *with Zane*. On the beach *with Zane*.

Actually, scratch *missing* the bus. I need to get *on* that bus. Zane might show up today . . . Except, I'm in no condition to meet Zane.

I rest my head on the counter for a moment, the marble cold on my skin. Then I push myself up, splash more water on my face, grab another towel—and dry it. I try to erase the dark circles under my eyes with a thick layer of concealer, then add blush to my cheeks and a swipe of peach gloss on my lips. Moments later I stand before my suitcase, naked. I am too hungover for anything but cozy. No scratchy fabrics, no tight waistbands. Something that will feel like I'm being wrapped in a comforter. Sitting beside my suitcase, I dig around for the pair of Lululemons I know I packed, when I spot a pair of yoga pants I don't recognize: in sage. I laugh, which hurts my head, but pull on the pair of pants Lars must have snuck into my suitcase. They feel like butter. I grab a super soft and loose knitted gray sweater and pull it over my head. The sleeves are long and I roll them a bit, creating a thick cuff. Then I run my fingers through my hair, trying to get out the tangles without adding to the frizz. I twist it up into a knot on my head and check my reflection. Not amazing, but not bad. I still feel like my head's been pressed into a waffle maker, but at least I don't look like it.

I throw everything into my suitcase, haul the suitcase out the door into the hall, then hightail it over the ornate runner in the hallway to the winding staircase and into the majestic lobby. At the bottom of the stairs, Francis stands at a glossy mahogany sideboard, flipping through a newspaper. He turns and I give him a wave as I look around for any sign of coffee.

"Gigi is late for breakfast," he says into his recorder. "She only has three minutes to eat if we're going to leave on time today."

"Three minutes is plenty of time to grab coffee," I say, spotting a stack of white cups and a shiny metal carafe at a high-top table near the entrance to the library. Seconds later, cup in one hand, suitcase in the other, I'm through the doors. At the end of the red runner, right in front of the hotel, Taj leans up against the bus, covering the W of Wilkenson, one foot against the side. His head's down, and he's reading the John Grisham book. No one else is around. He looks up as I approach, tucks the book under his arm, then grabs my suitcase without a word. I want to say something to him, but I don't trust myself not to get emotional—and what kind of emotions would come out? Annoyance? Hurt? Embarrassment? Better to say nothing at all. While he's turned, I hurry toward the front of the bus. "Hey," he says, and

I turn back quickly. He's walking toward me, but what's he going to say when we have seconds to get on the bus? I turn and run up the steps and slide into the seat beside Charlotte. She pats my leg. "I tried to wake you when I left but you were dead to the world."

"I still might be."

Angus taps me on the shoulder. Is this the moment? Has Zane arrived? "You're beside Violet today," he says instead. "Up you get."

I'm in no mood to argue, so I slide out of the seat and into the one across the aisle beside Violet. Angus directs Roshi, who was sitting beside Sindhi, to move beside Charlotte. As he does, she leans forward to look past him. "Would you like a peppermint puff?" she asks me, holding one out.

"You have anything stronger?"

"Do Eastern milk snakes have stripes?" She chuckles, then passes me a small bottle of Advil along with the candy, her eyes full of sympathy. Last night, when I got back to the room, I woke her up as I was maneuvering into the top bunk and proceeded to tell her everything.

"Well he's only got one oar in the water if he didn't want to lock lips with you, then, Hon," she'd said before rolling over and resuming her snoring session. I didn't have any clue what that meant last night and I still don't, but I'm pretty sure she's on my side. Not that this is some kind of war. It's not . . . anything. It's just something I've got to forget about.

I take two pills and then down them with a gulp of coffee and hand the bottle back across the aisle.

"You feeling OK?" Violet asks. Her notebook has lavender asters pressed into the cover. I nod, then shake my head. Rub my eyes. I lean forward, pressing my head into the seat in front of me, but it's like pressing Play on the almost-kiss. But where's the Delete button?

I take deep breaths. I'm here to meet Zane. I want to kiss Zane. Not Taj. I need to stop thinking about the bus driver. I lean back in my seat and look up to the front just as Taj's head appears at the top of the steps. His sunglasses are on, so it's impossible to read his expression. He says something to Angus, then slides into the driver's seat. The bus rumbles to life.

A few moments later, the long stretch of coast whizzes by on our left, the hotels on the right replaced by rolling hills of green. The bus lurches as it heads up a slight hill.

"I'm looking forward to today," Violet says, and I try to remember what's on tap. "Do you like to cook?" she asks, and it comes back to me: pizza-making in stone ovens in the middle of a forest. I was looking forward to *that* with Zane, too.

"I used to cook more often," I say, thinking back to when I lived with David in his condo by the Big House, the University of Michigan football stadium. I'd get home after closing the shop, and David would pour me wine, and I'd sit on one of the leather stools at the island in the sleek, modern, all-white kitchen while he diced onions or crushed garlic using the side of a Wüsthof knife against a wooden chopping board.

"I don't do a lot anymore," I say, putting the coffee cup between my legs and pressing my fingers to my temples.

"Used to be in a relationship?" she asks, running her hands over the flowers on her notebook.

"How'd you know?"

I kick off my sneakers and pull my knees to my chest. These pants actually *are* so comfy, just like Lars insisted.

"Takes one to know. When I lived alone in New York, I didn't do much cooking either. Why bother when I could grab something at a bodega, or go out to eat with friends?"

"Exactly," I say. "Or read," I add with a laugh that doesn't make my head hurt as much as it did twenty minutes ago. "And now?"

"Nelle loves to cook." Violet smiles. "And she's an incredible cook. I'm lucky."

"How did you two meet?" I ask, picturing Nelle walking into a bodega one snowy February night, the wind so strong she had trouble closing the door behind her. Her glasses fogged and she took them off to let them adjust to the warmth of the small convenience store, unable to see anything. Violet was filling a small plastic container with spinach, and she looked up, seeing Nelle before Nelle saw her. She put her glasses back on and . . .

Violet reaches between the seats to touch Nelle on the shoulder. She's sitting in front of us, next to Francis. "I know you love to tell this story," she says when Nelle turns around. "How we met," she adds, and Nelle smiles and pushes her glasses up the bridge of her nose.

"I was married," Nelle says, "to a man. Violet was my neighbor. I say 'neighbor' but we live in the countryside, so her farmhouse was a good half a mile down the road."

Outside the bus, the road has narrowed and snakes through green meadows speckled with white sheep grazing.

"You moved to Connecticut before you met Nelle?" I ask.

Violet nods. Her finger traces the outline of the flowers on the front of her journal. "I actually moved with another woman—to try living together. She'd had some health issues, wanted to get out of New York. I wasn't that keen on the idea; I love New York, but it was either move or break up, and I figured I'd give it a shot. I kept my apartment in case it didn't work out. Anyway, my ex ended up hating life in the country so she moved back to the city and I ended up staying." Violet shifts in her seat. "So there I am, alone in the country, and I start walking. Partly for exercise and partly because there wasn't much else to do out there in the middle of nowhere and I was starting to think I might go a bit nuts, all by myself in that old house."

"Every morning I would see Violet out walking," Nelle says. "My kitchen faced out onto the road that passed by both our homes, and I started to notice that she had a pattern." She takes off her glasses, inspects them, swipes them with her sleeve, then puts them back on. "Every morning at eight o'clock she'd be out there, marching along. At first I was just curious about her, but I was also intrigued by her dedication to walking. I'd tried to get my husband to walk with me, so many times, but he had no interest. Why walk when you could just drive? he'd say." She looks up at the ceiling of the bus, then back to us. "He had a hard job and worked long hours in the city. By the time he got back to the house he just wanted to stay in, or putter in the barn."

The landscape of low grass has changed to thick brush, a mist hovering over the tips of the tall grasses, the sky gray.

"One day, I'm walking by Nelle's house, and she's sitting out on the porch, drinking a coffee and waving at me." Violet tucks her journal into the pocket of the seat in front of her and clasps her hands together.

"It took me a good week to work up the nerve to even go outside when she was walking by," Nelle says, pushing her glasses up her nose again.

"Aww," I say.

"She was very cute out there, watching me walk. This was before she started wearing sunglasses over her glasses," Violet teases. Nelle tries to swat at her but ends up smacking Francis on the side of the head. He turns, looking alarmed. She puts a hand to his shoulder and apologizes. She turns back to us.

"So—" she resumes.

"Violet and Nelle are telling a story about how they met," Francis says into his recorder. "Nearly a million same-sex couples live together in the US, and more than half of them are married." Nelle looks back at him. "I'm in the middle of a really good story, here, Francis. Cool it on the stats for a sec, OK?"

I laugh, then press a hand to my forehead. Francis looks offended, but nods, then turns away.

"This sounds like I was obsessed with her or something, but it wasn't that, it was more like—intrigued," Nelle says. "There was something comforting about seeing her walk past every morning. Finally, one day, I pull on a pair of joggers and a T-shirt and head outside at five to eight with my runners on. Like clockwork, she comes booting up the street and I just go straight up to her, and I say hi. And she looks at me, and says, 'Would you like to join me?' Like she knew." Nelle meets Violet's eye. "Did you know?"

"I was just being polite," Violet says. "But I regretted it almost immediately. I thought, what if I hate walking with her and then I'm stuck with this weirdo?" She gives me a knowing look that makes me laugh again. "There aren't many roads where we live, and if I had to start walking in the other direction to avoid her, it wouldn't be as nice a walk. Not to mention that it would be awkward."

"But it was fine," Nelle says. "Like we'd known each other forever."

"It's true," Violet says.

"We went for another walk a few days later. Before we knew it, we were walking together every day," Nelle says.

"I just thought she really liked walking," Violet says, reaching out to touch Nelle on the shoulder. She smiles.

"I hated walking," Nelle groans.

"I guess that should've been obvious. She was so nervous. 'Am I wearing the right shoes?'" Her voice gets an octave higher. "'What if it rains? Is that lightning? Should we be wearing brighter clothes so the cars see us? Maybe we should walk on the other side of the road, maybe we shouldn't walk on roads at all . . .'" I stifle a laugh, not wanting to make fun of Nelle, but she's grinning as she reaches over and swats at Violet, this time clearing Francis's head.

"I was so out of shape I would go home and take two Advil every day," Nelle says. "The thing was, I'd known for a long time that I was attracted to women, but I couldn't really bring myself to think about what that meant. I was married, I had a daughter. That was my life. Then one day, I threw out my back. It actually had nothing to do with walking at all—I'd been gardening. But I was in such pain. I was lying in bed for days." She looks at Violet and smiles. "I realized two things: the highlight of my day was walking with Violet. And it wasn't just her companionship or the walking." Her tone softens. "I realized I was in love with her. I also thought, what if I got sick, really sick, and I could never walk again? I'd never see Violet again. Walking with her was my window into another world, one where I accepted myself for who I really was, and where I was able to be with Violet. And if I got sick, I'd never see that life."

"It's possible. Nine-point-eight million people die every year from cancer," Francis says, then looks sheepish. "Sorry."

"I knew I was going to be fine," Nelle says, "but it was my *aha* moment, and I didn't want to imagine a world where Violet wasn't in it."

Violet beams. Nelle reaches for her hand, which is awkward over the seat, but Violet still grasps it. "You know all this. But I still love telling the story."

The bus rumbles over a rickety wooden bridge, and I crane my neck to catch a view of the narrow river. Pampas grass lines the water, swaying in the wind. I turn back to Nelle.

"So what happened to your marriage?" I ask, then regret it. That love story had an ending. All that's left now are the messy details.

"I sat my husband down, and told him," she says. "He thought I was making an excuse. He couldn't understand why I'd mess up everything we had—our family, our home, our life. He said, 'Why bother being true to who you are?'" Nelle says. "How sad is that?"

"Did that make you reconsider?" I ask, realizing just how much I suddenly admire Nelle.

Nelle shakes her head. "No, it just made me stronger. I had to be true to myself. And I wanted to show my daughter that it was important to be honest—no matter what other people thought. I would never want her to hide who she really was." She laughs sadly. "Not that I really needed to worry about that—she's so strong and self-assured. And really, I had to do it for myself."

I look from Nelle to Violet. They seem so happy, and maybe one version of Nelle's family is no longer the only version of her family; now she has another family, and so does her daughter, and so does Violet.

"I think that what you did was really brave," I say to Nelle.

"It's the bravest thing she's ever done," Violet says, meeting Nelle's eyes. "So when she frets about every other little thing in life, I let her be." Violet titters. "It's just part of who she is. And compared to what she did to be true to herself and find happiness, none of that other stuff even matters."

Chapter Seventeen

Day 4, Wednesday, 11 a.m.

Kingley Vale, South Downs National Park

The bus pulls to a stop in a gravel parking lot outside the gate to Kingley Vale, the oldest forest in England. The sky is gray. Tendrils of fog wisp around ancient oak trees. I wait until everyone is off the bus before pushing myself out of my seat in an effort to minimize the amount of time I have to stand.

As I step off the bus, Taj hands me a long, thin plastic bottle filled with an orange liquid.

"What's this?" I say.

"Energy drink. Replace the electrolytes you lost last night. You probably could've used this when you got on the bus. It was cold then, but you were in such a rush to get on the bus I didn't get a chance to give it to you."

"You could've passed it back," I say.

"You mean, thank you?"

My ears burn. "Yes, that's what I meant."

"You're welcome." He looks like he wants to say something else, but reconsiders.

The rest of the group is already through the wooden gate. Standing for thirty seconds has already made me feel woozy, but I quicken my pace, cracking the top of the bottle and taking a long swig. The label reads *Lucozade* in yellow font. The orange liquid drowns last night's drinks. I look back to see if Taj is behind us but he, and the bus, are out of sight.

"I hope everyone's wearing comfortable shoes," Angus says once we've started down the dirt path. Every step kicks up dust as we shuffle along.

"We're going into the forest?" Nelle asks.

"Well we can't forage in the parking lot, can we?" Angus jokes.

"Does everyone have long pants, socks, closed-toe shoes?" Nelle says. "You wouldn't want to step on poison ivy."

"Ah, no poison ivy in there," Angus says.

"How can you be sure?" Nelle stretches her neck as though she might spot the poison ivy from where we are.

"Well, simply because we're still in England and there's no poison ivy in England," Angus says.

"I can walk for miles," Sindhi says, turning to me. "Look!" She points at her clean sneakers. "I feel very proud of myself. I bought comfortable shoes yesterday in Brighton. They cost a *fortune*, but—"

"They're cute," I interrupt her. She beams.

Angus leads us into a grove of ancient yew trees, their trunks thick as houses, many of their thick limbs reclining on the ground, others barring our way at waist or chest level. It's like an obstacle course built by C. S. Lewis. "Some of these trees are two thousand years old," Angus calls back.

"I got lost in the forest as a child," Nelle says to Violet. "I was gone for three hours. I was crying and calling out for my mother.

Maybe I'll go back and wait on the bus."

Violet takes her hand. "You're going to be fine," she says, her voice soft with patience. "We're all going to be together." Nelle turns to her and gives her an appreciative look.

"Approximately two thousand people get lost in forests every year," Francis says. "When you account for how many forests there are around the world, that's actually not that many people. Of course, 47 percent of those who get lost actually die."

"What percentage get dragged into the forest and bludgeoned to death?" Jenny asks.

"It would be hard to say." Angus winks at Jenny. "Seeing as anyone who disappears into the forest disappears without a trace." When Jenny's mouth falls open, Angus throws his head back and laughs. "I'm kidding, of course. But Kingley Vale *is* a special place, rooted in five hundred years of history. Ahh." Angus waves to someone in the distance, who's walking toward us along the dirt trail. "There he is," Angus says. When he reaches us, he introduces himself to us as Kylar. His hair falls in dreads down to his shoulder blades. His cargo pants are baggy, his T-shirt loose. He gives the peace sign and a short history of his life—how a near-death experience while working as an investment banker in London was his sign to return home to Kingley Vale. Then he leads us off the dirt trail and into a copse of ash trees, sparse and ghostly in the thickening fog.

"Can you tell me about almost dying?" Jenny slides into step beside Kylar, flipping her long hair over her shoulder. "Were you almost murdered? I have a channel, you'd get a lot of publicity from it. It could help your business—"

Kylar puts his hands together in prayer position and gazes at Jenny. "If you can hold that thought, I'll be able to give it my full attention after I've finished preparing the others for their foraging experience." Jenny stops cold.

"Most people think cooking is simply the act of taking raw food and making it palatable," Kylar continues. The temperature's dropped so much that I pull my jean jacket from my purse and shrug it on.

"It's not?" Roshi says. "I was pretty sure that was exactly what cooking was."

Sindhi shakes her head. "Oh, Roshi." She sounds exasperated.

"How much farther?" Jenny moans. "I think I'm just going to hang out here. Can someone make my pizza for me?"

"I'll stay behind, too," Nelle says. "I really don't think this area looks safe." She ducks under a gnarled branch. "Was that a *bat*?"

"No bats in this forest, yah?" Angus says, taking Charlotte's hand to help her over a root.

"That sounds like a question, not any sort of reassurance," Nelle says.

"Actually, you can find Barbastelle bats in the South Downs," Francis says, then clicks on his recorder. "Nelle's afraid of the forest, and no one's sure when we're going to be making pizza."

"Can everyone just stop complaining and let us just do whatever we came here to do?" Sindhi says. All heads turn toward her. But no one says a word. "What?" she says.

"Sindhi just told us all to stop complaining," Francis says into his recorder. "Which is odd because she complains all the time."

"So how exactly are we making these pizzas?" Charlotte interrupts, trying to lighten the mood. "Will we be using an oven? I thought about putting an oven in my backyard. Had a salesman come to my door one day a few months ago, showed me this fancy oven that was on *Shark Tank*. But ultimately, I said to myself, 'Charlotte, are you the type of woman who's going to be cooking in her backyard?'"

"And what did Charlotte say to Charlotte?" Angus asks.

"She agreed wholeheartedly," Charlotte says.

"Can you explain how we're going to be making pizza when there doesn't seem to be any sort of contraption for making pizza, let alone the ingredients?" Sindhi says. Roshi sighs.

"Aaaaand Sindhi's back to her usual ways," Jenny says.

Sindhi gasps. Roshi puts an arm around her, and she turns to him and says something indistinguishable.

"Jenny," Nelle warns.

"Nelle," Violet says.

"What? We've been together four days now. Feels like forty, seriously. We can't be honest with each other?" Jenny retorts.

"I honestly didn't want to come on this trip and look what good that did me." She glares at Roshi, then turns to Jenny. "And I wasn't complaining, I was pointing out an obvious statement."

"No drama, no llama." Kylar clears his throat. "That's right. You might see a llama out there. So let's get to it, shall we?"

Angus gives us all the "simmer down" sign, flapping his hands at us and looking embarrassed.

"We're going to make pizza, but pizza doesn't just come from the sky, does it?" Kylar continues. "First, we must forage for ingredients." Kylar twirls a dreadlock, then tells us that everything from yeast for the crust to toppings for our pizzas all comes from the surrounding vegetation.

Up ahead, a clutch of branches forms something like a tepee. Kylar disappears through the triangular opening, then returns with an armful of woven baskets, like the ones they use to serve bread at the little French bistro a few doors down from

Love Interest. He hands them out. In the bottom of each is a sheet with pictures of weeds or flowers—it's hard to tell. The pictures are faded, as though they were photocopied in 1982. "The forest extends in every direction, but you have to pay attention to the markings on the trunks of the oak and ash trees. For one thing, we are only allowed to forage within our permitted area. And more importantly, you don't want to get lost, because mobile service is spotty in the area—so if you're gone, you're gone."

"I knew it. You've *got* to tell me about people who've died doing this," Jenny says, then looks up at the sky. "The lighting is actually perfect for filming. Should I bring my stuff with me in case there's somewhere to set up to do my makeup—or would it be better to leave everything here?" She points to the tepee as though we're at a five-star hotel.

Kylar scratches his head. "Uhh—"

"If we get lost can't we just eat the plants we find?" Roshi asks.

"Definitely not," Kylar says. "There's poisonous hemlock out there, so once you return, we'll carefully go through everyone's baskets to make sure that you've only picked edible plants and weeds. It's imperative you do not eat what you collect before it is inspected."

"Angus, you said there was nothing to be worried about," Nelle says, her eyes wide.

Angus takes off his hat and scratches his head through the curls. "Not quite, yah? I said there was no poison ivy. Other sorts of poisonous plants are aplenty!" he chuckles. "But it's all on the handout. To keep you safe."

"I don't feel safe," Nelle says.

"I'm still not pleased about the price of these shoes but I'm certainly glad I bought them," Sindhi says to me.

"And wore them," Francis says. "No use to you if they're packed away in your luggage."

I laugh. My head throbs.

"I think I'll forage, then come back here to film," Jenny decides, nodding. She tucks her head into the tepee, and then pops her bags inside.

My stomach grumbles. "When do you think we'll actually make the pizza?" I ask. "Ballpark?"

"We create the pizzas when the ingredients are ready to be included in the ritual," Kylar says breathily, then laughs. "Or two o'clock, whichever comes first."

Two o'clock? It's only eleven-thirty. It's suddenly clear to me how people die out here: Starvation.

"Now off you go!" Kylar calls.

Angus falls into step beside Charlotte. Violet and Nelle head off together, and I start off on my own. I consider pulling my earphones out and listening to Zane, for the company. The disappointment of this trip is settling on me. It was supposed to be such a great story! *There's Gigi*, they would have said. *She met her husband because of an audiobook. And then there's Taj.* Why did I allow him to thicken the plot? Now he's an ever-present reminder of rejection.

"Looks like you've really got the hang of this," Taj says, his voice low, and for a second I'm confused—why is *his* voice now in my head?—but then he's beside me, peering into my empty basket. I look around and realize that no one else is in sight. How long have I been lost in my own thoughts?

"I didn't ask for your opinion," I say, scowling. "Are you following me?"

"I thought I'd recycle the Lucozade," he says, nodding at the empty plastic bottle in my hand. "The fine for littering in here is horrendous."

"Right. I don't need help—with recycling or otherwise."

"No, of course not," he says. "You're clearly having a fabulous, very successful go of it."

I fix him with a stare. Is he just going to act like *nothing* happened last night? It was so awkward—or was it just me, because I was so drunk? Is he going to bring it up? I don't want to talk about it, and yet I don't want to *not* talk about it. "Yeah, looks like your pizza will be really good," he says. "Who doesn't love plain pizza, zero toppings? Minimalism at its best." He kisses his fingertips like he's Italian.

"Are you done? It's hard to know what I'm supposed to be looking for," I say. I study the little pictures on the paper, then look around. The fog has lifted but the sky is darker. It feels like dusk.

"I bet it is. You know you have to look down, right?" He bends down, picks up some sort of weed and drops it in my basket. "You're welcome."

I toss the weed back on the ground. "I didn't ask for your help."

"Fine, you're right. You need to be proud of your own pizza. Sorry, I'm obviously bugging you." Taj reaches down and picks up a branch, then pulls a penknife from his back pocket. He scrapes at the stick, flicking the flecks of wood away from himself.

"Do you always carry a blade?" I ask, but keep my voice detached. New strategy: act like nothing's weird, and turn Taj into a boring driver, nothing more. Remove all sexuality from his being. Maybe it'll help me get over the whole scene on the beach last night. Maybe that's what he's trying to do, too. We *do* have another six days together. Not *together,* but in which to endure each other's presence. I think I'm overthinking it.

"Yep. Where there's wood there's time to whittle," he says.

I roll my eyes. "Sometimes you say the strangest things."

One corner of his mouth turns up. I gulp. He's really sexy *even* when he's saying the strangest things. The thought of those lips *almost* touching mine flashes through my mind again. "I'll take that as a compliment. You know what I could really go for right now?"

My palms sweat and I take it back—I need him to get out of here. This whole 'Let's just chitchat like normal acquaintances' thing isn't working out for me.

"I guess you're stumped," he says when I don't answer. "A BFCS."

"A what?" I study the paper, then a bunch of flowers, and decide they're close enough to whatever the white one looks like and yank one out of the ground, then place it in my basket. If I can get this basket filled, I can turn back and join the others.

"A BFCS. Butter Fried Chicken Shawarma." He tilts his head back and closes his eyes for a moment. "I can almost taste it." He looks at me with a solemn face. "I get one every time I get home from one of these tours. It's a ritual: I head straight for the laundrette, pop my jumpers in the machine and then head across the street to the best little hole in the wall. It's just big enough for Gerry, the guy who owns it, his little counter and then one customer."

"That's nice," I say, trying to act like I'm totally disinterested in whatever he's talking about, but the truth is, I wish he were talking about last night, not chicken.

Taj reaches his arm out in front of him as though smoothing out an invisible tablecloth. "Gerry takes these thin slices of chicken and roasts them on a spit. Then he batters it, deep-fries it, coats it in butter chicken sauce and then wraps it into a pita and fills it with rice and peas, and it's like the best thing you've ever tasted in your life. And because of this job I have to go without the sweet, sweet (technically savory) goodness that is a BFCS for ten days every time I'm driving one of these tours. All the more reason I've got to make this a temporary gig."

"You're really into sandwiches, huh?" I say.

"A BFCS is not a sandwich," he clarifies. "Were you even listening?"

"But you got a sandwich in Cambridge. So you're not technically *against* sandwiches."

"You're focusing on the wrong part of this story," he scoffs.

"OK, so if chicken shawarmas are so great, why didn't you get a chicken shawarma in Cambridge then? You only buy girls roast beef sandwiches? You deny them chicken shawarma?"

We may be talking about chicken, but I'm fishing for more.

"To answer what you're really asking . . ." His mouth twitches. "I've actually *never* bought anyone else—female or otherwise— any sort of sandwich of any kind in Cambridge."

My entire body burns, as though I've walked through poison ivy. I dip my hair forward, wishing it would shield my face, but it's in a knot on top of my head, so no such luck. There's a cactus-looking thing at my feet, the bulb at the top dark purple and fuzzy, which is sort of how my head feels right now. I check my sheet, look back at the weed and yank at it. "I wasn't asking," I mumble, wishing I could shrivel up like dehydrated birdweed—or bindweed, it's hard to make out the name of the weed on the sheet.

"You know you're not supposed to yank the entire thing out of the ground, right?" I ignore him and toss the bindweed into the basket. "Actually, you're the first girl I've bothered to get to know on these tours." Taj stops and looks me in the eyes. "I told you, I can't get involved."

A small brown woodlark lands in my basket and attempts to grab a jagged nettle, but Taj waves it away.

"Don't be weird," Taj says, bending down and gently plucking a few sunny yellow dandelions. My eyes slide down to his butt, and I force myself to look away.

"I'm not being weird." I hold out the basket.

He drops the weeds in, then resumes whittling, scraping the knife against the branch. The end is beginning to take shape into a point. "Listen, about last night—"

"I don't want to talk about it." I quicken my pace, but he takes longer strides to keep up with me.

"I just didn't want something to happen and then have you wake up this morning regretting it." His voice is low. My heart pulses into my fingertips.

"Thanks for looking out for me," I say genuinely. "I didn't come here to get involved with anyone either," I say. Er, actually, I didn't come here to get involved with anyone who isn't Zane. And Taj is actually right—I would've regretted it this morning if I'd kissed him.

"The thing is, I'm sort of regretting . . ." he says, rubbing his chin, and stops walking.

"I'm glad that you stopped it," I say, pushing my shoulders back.

He raises his eyebrows. "Right. OK."

Now we're facing each other. A standoff.

Then comes a scream. I spin around, but it's just brush in every direction. Then I see it: there, near a large oak, there's movement. Jenny is crouching on the ground, her upper body rocking back and forth. She's clutching her left palm with her right hand. Her camera's on the ground, her bag beside it. She's moaning. Taj passes me, reaches her first and kneels down. Jenny's face is red and blotchy. She's fixated on her hands.

"What happened?" I ask her.

"May I?" Taj asks in a gentle tone, one I've never heard from him before. He reaches for her hands, gently prying her right hand off her left.

"My hand, I touched something," she says between sobs. "It stings. Is it hemlock?"

"Not hemlock," Taj says calmly. He unfolds her fingers, one at a time, and inspects her hand, then nods. "Stinging nettle," he says.

"Oh god, is that worse? Am I going to die?"

Taj's eyes meet mine, his eyebrows raised, his eyes wide, then refocuses on her hand. "You're not going to die," he says to Jenny.

"You don't know that. You're just a bus driver. Oh my god, I'm going to die and I've . . ." she whimpers. "I've been such a bitch to my mom." I kneel on the other side of her. "Please"—she draws the word out, and I squeeze my arms around her. "I want my mom," she says. Her words are muffled, but I know what she's saying. "Please, just get my mom."

"Sweetie, do you want me to call her?" I crane my neck for her bag. "Just tell me where your phone is."

"Nelle," she says impatiently. "Nelle's my mom."

Chapter Eighteen

Day 4, Wednesday, 4 p.m.

South Downs National Park ❯ Isle of Wight

"Who said bus tours were boring?" Roshi says on the way back to the bus. Nelle and Jenny take the back row, and Jenny reclines on the seats, her head on Nelle's lap. Apparently the nettles sting for a few hours.

Violet takes the seat next to me. "Poor girl," she says, and I get the sense she's talking about more than just stinging plants. Taj slides into his seat, flipping up the sun visor. He was so kind with Jenny, and knew exactly what to do. Do bus drivers get this kind of special training, or is Taj just instinctively caring and calm in emergency situations? I wonder.

I had no idea Jenny was Nelle's daughter—I don't think anyone did. I'm about to ask Violet why it was a secret when she turns to me. "She didn't want to come," she says simply, shaking her head. "Didn't want to be a kid on a trip with her parents. Or, rather, with her mom, and me. She's a ball of fire, that girl."

Violet looks out the window as we pull away from Kingley Vale, the ancient trees giving way to grassland. Ponies graze in the hills. "I don't have any kids of my own, and I've been gay since I could spell the word," Violet says. "But Nelle—it was all so much harder for her. Poor Jenny was blindsided," she whispers. "She was away at college when everything happened, and by the time she came home for summer, it was like"—Violet clasps her hands together—"her whole world had changed. Her mother was a lesbian, her parents were divorcing and she suddenly had to share her mother with the woman she thought was just some neighbor in the farmhouse down the road."

I try to imagine what that would be like, but even though I've read thousands of books, I've never read that storyline.

"It must be hard on you, too, though," I say. Jenny has been pretty rude, and if that's the way she's been since Violet and Nelle have been together, I can't imagine it's been very pleasant to be around.

Violet raises an eyebrow. "I'm tough. I can take it." She looks out the window, and I twist in my seat to look at Nelle. Her head is down, and she's whispering to Jenny. From the outside it's an idyllic mother-daughter moment. How different would the rest of this trip have been if Jenny hadn't touched the nettle? Would she have given her mother the silent treatment for the entire trip?

I pull my headphones out of my bag and jab at my phone. But not to hear Zane—instead, an instrumental playlist fills my ears. What I wouldn't give to have Mom and Dad back—to take a trip with them. Either one of them. Because they're gone, I have this do-no-wrong idea of them. I don't really remember their disagreements, and I don't really consider their relationship with each other at all, only my relationship with each of them. What if they had fallen out of love with each other, or one of them had cheated, or one of them realized they were gay? Would I have acted the same way as Jenny?

The bus slows. The window is cold against my face. An image of Taj from last night appears in my mind. And then, before we found Jenny in the park, he was about to tell me something. What did he regret? I rattle through the possibilities, but only one comes to mind.

My phone buzzes.

"I've been calling for hours," Lars says, sounding irritated when I answer.

"Why? What's wrong?"

"Five copies of the same book just arrived in a box, something *By the Sea*, and first of all I don't understand how you can be a used bookstore but you're buying new books and second, there's no room on the shelf for all five. I've just spent the last hour rearranging things and there's no way they're fitting unless I move all of Nora Roberts to her own section because you also said not to split authors onto different shelves." He sounds really stressed out.

"It's fine," I say. "And, Lars, this doesn't really sound like an emergency."

"I guess you're rubbing off on me," he says, and for a moment I feel guilty for how controlling I've been.

"I'm sure you're doing a good job."

"OK. But what was the thing about the stacks?"

"I just hate when there are piles of books lying around," I say, but then I think about the Crooked House. It was chaos, and impossible to find anything, but then I *did* find that rare copy of *Lady Susan*, a book I never would've come across because I rarely spend time in the Austen section—because I long ago assumed I had accumulated all the various printings of her novels.

"What I meant was you should put the books people take out during the day back on the shelves so there aren't stacks lying around," I say. "But if there's a few lying about, I think that's OK, actually."

"But what about the five books?"

I cradle the phone in my ear. "Are you sure it's something by the sea? Not *The Weather in the Streets*? We're reading it for book club," I say. I was looking forward to reading the 1930s classic by Rosamond Lehmann with the girls.

There's shuffling and then Lars says, "Oh, right. The sea thing was something else."

"I think it's all on the yellow pad," I say calmly.

"I can't find the yellow pad, OK?" he admits.

I sigh. "Oh, Lars." The bus is suddenly dark, and I lean to my right to look through the front window at the narrow road ahead. Trees have created a canopy over the road, blocking the sun.

"And what book club?" He groans. "And what did I do with that pad?"

"My book club. They meet every Thursday, but they're not meeting at the shop while I'm away, so don't worry about it."

"OK." Lars exhales loudly. "But what about the *pad*?"

"It's fine," I say calmly. "I'm sure I can just text you the important stuff. It's not a big deal."

I replay those words. *Not a big deal.* I've never heard myself say that before.

Lars groans. "OK, thanks, Geeg."

I hang up the phone as we roll into Portsmouth Harbour, which is marked by the massive modern spindly tower in the center of the harbor. Angus tells us it's the Spinnaker Tower, made to look like a sail, shooting high into the sky. The harbor is littered with ferries shuttling tourists and commuters between the UK and various ports in France. But our trip is to the Isle of Wight, a small island less than an hour away.

The bus pulls onto the white ferry and, once parked, we're able to get off and make our way up the steps to the top of the ship.

The air is thick with fuel but within minutes of pushing off from the shore, the wind makes it all a faint memory. I stand by the stern railing, watching the coast recede. Jenny walks over to me.

"Hey," she says, her face reddening. Her hair is in a long fishtail that reaches the middle of her back, and I wonder if Nelle braided it on the bus.

"Hi," I say, giving her a tentative smile. "How are you feeling?"

She shrugs. "Embarrassed that I made such a big deal." She holds out her hand, which is bandaged. "It's fine. Just my pride."

"How are things with your mom?" I say.

"Oh, that." She rolls her eyes. "Fine. I just—don't make a big deal about the whole mom thing, k?"

"Jenny," I start, not really sure what I even want to say, but she holds up her good hand.

"We're fine, OK?"

"You know, no one's family is perfect," I say quietly.

"Oh yeah?" she challenges. "Well I'm pretty sure no one else pretended not to know their own mother." She crosses her arms.

"You were hurt." I reach out to touch her arm, but she pulls it away. "You've still got the rest of the trip, Jenny. Don't let your embarrassment get in the way. You might never have another trip with your mom."

"Oh god, not you, too. I just endured a whole guilt trip on the ride," Jenny says, frustrated. "Honestly, I just wanted to say thanks for coming over when I was hurt. You didn't have to do that. But please don't make me feel like I have to be this perfect daughter with her two mommies now," she says.

"Jenny," I say. "I wasn't going to—"

"Forget it." She runs a finger under her eye, wiping a tear. "Must be the wind. Anyway, truly, I was just saying thanks for being nice." She turns away, then turns back. "Oh, and I like your yoga pants. They're a cool color." I watch as she heads toward the door into the interior of the ferry, then I pull out my phone to text Lars.

Thx for yoga pants. V. comfortable. Got compliment too.

He texts back a minute later. *Make a sale! 6 diff colors! Almost sold out of marine.*

How much loungewear selling has he done, I wonder, versus book selling? I tuck away my phone, and look out over the stern. The railing is cool, the white paint chipped and rough under my hands. The last few days have been intense. This isn't at all how I thought this trip would play out, and yet it's nearly half over.

As the ferry heads deeper into the middle of the Solent, the strait connecting the mainland and the island, my thoughts turn to Zane, and I can feel disappointment creeping into my thoughts. I begin wishing, for the hundredth time, that he were here.

I pop my headphones on and press Play on the app.

Jack couldn't wait to be finished at the docks, but he knew he still had a good two hours ahead of him before he'd be done. He wiped his sweaty brow and looked out at the rough water.

I hit Stop. This isn't helping. Hearing Zane's voice is keeping me from enjoying this trip. I'm exploring a fascinating country, I have great conversations and so many laughs, and I'm growing sort of attached to the cast of characters, who are proving to be deeper and more interesting with every day that passes.

What am I doing, mooning over a voice on an audiobook, simply because it was the plan? *Forget about him*, I resolve. *Live the life you've been gifted!* I think back to what Charlotte said in her little cottage in Hythe. About not letting this story—the one I'm in right now—pass me by.

I have to delete Zane. Or, at least, his audiobook. My phone is in my hand before I fully process what I'm about to do. One swipe of the finger will be all it takes delete *Their Finest Hour* from my library. My finger flicks to the left. "Delete?" pops up in the text box, and—oh, but wait. I swipe the other way, slip on my head-phones, press Play. Just one more time. His voice . . . it's that spot in chapter fourteen that gets me every time. With eyes closed, with the boat rocking starboard and port, with the seabirds calling over Zane's dulcet tones, and the occasional spray of salt water, I hear out the paragraph.

> *The waves splashed up onto the dock; the cold made him jump. What was he doing here, when he could be with Mirabelle? What was more important, right now, at this very minute? He had to be with her. He had to tell her how he felt. That he'd stayed for her all this time. That this job—this job was nothing if she wasn't here. He hadn't left, because of her. Now he had to stop her from leaving him.*

When the chapter's over, without letting myself think too much, I swipe a second time, and when the text box demands, Are you sure? I touch the spot that says, Yes. Yes, I am.

To punctuate this moment, I need to do . . . something. Something symbolic. A statement, something definitive. After all, no audiobook is ever truly gone. I could just download it again.

An impulse has me almost throw my phone into the ferry wash. But my phone has everything on it, and it was expensive, and I need to be available in case something goes wrong at the store. And also, throwing my phone away is not something I would ever do. It's not *me*.

Instead, I whip off my headphones, and throw them over the railing and into the murky water.

There.

Goodbye, Zane.

That's when I first hear it.

The sound is indistinguishable at first. It's just something familiar. Maybe it's an audio hallucination, the way I'll hear the bells of the Burton Tower in Ann Arbor. They chime every fifteen minutes, and sometimes, even when they don't chime, I think I can hear them anyway. Now, the sounds become syllables, and the syllables, words. Is the audiobook somehow still playing? Have the headphones materialized somewhere close by, like Zane's version of "The Monkey's Paw"? The ferry is speckled with island-goers leaning over the railings, looking out into the water, or chatting with one another. Families in so many different shapes and sizes, strangers who are now friends. Then, from behind an orange rescue dinghy, he steps into view.

He has the eyes of Alex Wheatley in *Safe Haven*, the lips of Gilbert Blythe in *Anne of Green Gables*, the mischievous grin of Jack Twist in *Brokeback Mountain*. His light-brown hair is shiny and swoopy, cut short against the sides of his head, slightly longer on top, not a strand out of place. His jaw is slightly rounded, his nose perfectly proportioned to his face. Even though I've seen dozens of photos of him, he looks a billion times better in person. Every feature is amplified. He's wearing the green Wilkenson

Tours shirt, and the name tag, as though I needed confirmation, reads exactly what it should.

Birds sing. Dolphins leap from the water. Clouds evaporate into thin air.

He's here. He's really here.

Also, Angus is with him—and he waves. "Gigi!" he shouts. "I'd like to introduce you to someone special!"

Understatement of the year. I release my grip on the railing and take a step forward. Everything continues in slow motion as I make my way toward him. It's like I'm in the real-life version of that moment in *Sleepless in Seattle* when Annie is on the top of the Empire State Building.

"Hello," I say. Zane looks at me. Cocks his head. Smiles.

"Hello," he says pleasantly, and then gives me the most unnecessary line ever: "I'm Zane."

"Hi," I say again, really wishing I'd thought to rehearse something in preparation for this meet cute.

And then he extends his arm toward me and grins. "So you're . . . Gigi?" The way he says it, the g-sound is as soft as warm caramel.

"Uh-huh." It's all I can manage. Then I reach out. Our fingertips touch. Our palms press into each other. Flames ignite. My hand burns and yet there's no way I'm going to pull it away. His soft skin is touching mine. I've never felt skin so smooth.

Zane smiles at me, and I get a flash of his perfect, straight white teeth.

Angus puts his hands on his hips. "Zane made the ferry just in time."

I blink, remembering it's not just the two of us.

"Wasn't sure I was going to make it, to be honest," Zane chuckles. "It's been quite a whirlwind few days." And that picture of him, by his mother's side, pops into my head. Maybe reading to her— maybe reading *Their Finest Hour* to her. My knees buckle at the thought, and I flex my legs.

"Angus has been leading me around the ship, introducing me to everyone," Zane says. I nod, mesmerized not only by his voice, but his eyes, his mouth, his hands that move when he talks. I know I should blink, but it's just not really possible. "You were the final piece of the puzzle," he says.

"You were the final piece of my puzzle," I whisper.

"Beg your pardon?" Zane asks. Mortified, I just smile.

"Have you seen any porpoises?" he asks. I shake my head. "Would you like to?"

I would watch ants walk across the deck of the ferry with him.

He walks over to the railing and I follow him. I turn to face the water, but all I really want to do is face him. *He's really here.* All the doubts and the long days and the churches and the mis-haps—it's all worth it. I would do it all over again in a heartbeat— well, maybe not the massive hangover—to end up right here, in this moment.

Zane turns to me and touches my arm. "Look." He points, and I turn, expecting to see a porpoise leaping out of the water, just because he asked if I'd like to see one, but instead, I follow his fin-ger, which is pointing at two enormous gray cranes soaring across the sky, their long necks extended, their foreheads blood-red. Not exactly porpoises, but better than ants.

"Sandhill cranes," he says. "Actually native to North America, like you, am I right? But we get rare sightings here. Majestic bird, isn't it?" His voice glides. There's no catching between the words. No scratchiness. It soars effortlessly. Like the cranes. Which Zane's still talking about.

"Sandhills mate for life," he says. His hands are on the railing and he's leaning forward. I think of the novel *Mating for Life.* The main character meets her soulmate and it changes *everything* for her. Is it a sign, now that Zane's here?

Zane is talking plumes and bristles, vanes and barbs. His voice is still smooth, like poured chocolate. But now, it's as though the audiobook version used a cheap chocolate bar for the fondue. Still smooth and sweet, but lacking dimension. And this voice, mere inches from me, is like the highest-quality chocolate. Handpicked cocoa beans, with hints of rose or lemon, fermented and roasted, then milled into the finest powder. Melted and poured like satin ribbons. Not just chocolate, but art.

"Gigi?" Zane says my name the way no one has ever said my name before. Soft g, drawing out the i's. Like a choir singing—altos, sopranos, tenors, baritones, bass.

"Sorry?" I say, shaking myself out of my trance. How can I zone out at a time like this? But how can I not, when he's no longer reading a book I've heard dozens of times, but actually talking *to* me?

He smiles. "I was just asking if you had a favorite bird?"

"A favorite bird?" I say, blinking. I've never really given any real thought to birds, except the pigeons that make a mess on the eaves of the bookshop. *Don't say lovebirds, Gigi.* "Chickens are pretty tasty," I say instead, thinking of the chicken sandwich conversation Taj and I had earlier today. I'm about to ask Zane if he's ever tried the chicken whatever that Taj was going on about, but he makes a face and says: "Oof, chicken. Wouldn't know. Vegetarian for life."

"Huh," I say, surprised. Not that I'd ever given much thought to his dietary preferences. I didn't fantasize about meals. More like, post-meal cocktails. And other things.

On the horizon the sun rests on the surface of the water. I inhale, trying to freeze-frame this moment so I can remember it forever.

"I've been coming to this island since I was a small child," he says, and the choir starts up again. "It never gets tiresome."

"I'm sure," I say. Like his voice. I will never tire of it.

Angus clears his throat and I start. I'd completely forgotten he was standing with us. "Zane, I should catch you up on a few matters before we dock."

Zane turns. "See you on the coach?"

I hang on every word. Nod. Then he's gone.

The ferry arrives in West Cowes a short while later, and I somehow wake myself up from my dreamlike state so I can jockey for position beside Zane on the bus. I lose out to Angus because they need to discuss logistics. What logistics? Zane is here, the end. Everything is *perfect*. I slide into the seat behind them and Charlotte sits beside me. She squeezes my hand and leans close. "I'm so excited for you," she whispers. I squeeze her hand but don't say anything because I don't trust myself not to squeal. Plus, I want to hear every single word that comes out of Zane's mouth. I'm close enough to do so, but he's having a pretty boring conversation about the shoulders of roads—still, when Zane speaks, I feel like I'm listening to a world-class orchestra play Beethoven's Symphony No. 5.

The short drive to Newport, the market town where we'll be spending the night, is a straight shot south on a two-lane paved road through fields of beetroot and potatoes. Not that I can tell— it's all just bushy greenery, but that's what Zane tells us. Then he and Angus go back to working out how Angus will get home to Oxford.

"We're going there anyway, why don't we just give Angus a ride?" Charlotte says. She leans forward into the aisle, poking her head around the side of Angus's seat.

"I'm fine with that," Angus says. "I've always wanted to be a backseat guide."

The conversation turns to room assignments. What if Zane and I share a room? Not tonight, obviously, but maybe tomorrow? A girl can dream.

I keep my suggestion to myself, and Angus and Zane decide that Angus and Taj will share a room. "We're used to each other, aren't we?" Angus calls to Taj. I look to Taj for his reaction, thinking about Angus's snoring. He looks at me, then rolls his eyes. I laugh, then feel a stab of something. Sadness that Taj and I won't have these little inside jokes anymore? Guilt that I have them at all?

"What's so funny?" Charlotte whispers.

"You and Angus have a lot in common," I tease, and she gives me a quizzical look. "You think?" she says, having no idea, obviously, that I'm talking about their snoring habits.

A few minutes later the bus pulls into a small square in the center of Newport, with a tall monument enclosed by a black wrought-iron fence. Off to the right is Newport Minster, a church dating back to the twelfth century, and to the left is the Rye, a traditional two-story inn-and-pub building with a thatched roof. The surrounding buildings feature painted metal gables over the front doors, bay windows jutting into the cobblestone streets, and window boxes bursting with brightly colored blooms. The town has a nostalgic feel that's only slightly tarnished by the modern signs for Primark and Barclays.

"Welcome to your home away from home," Zane says as we get off the bus. I know he's talking about the hotel, but the word "home" takes on a bigger meaning. Like I'm here for a reason, that this all wasn't for nothing. That I'm not crazy for wanting to meet Zane. All of it—being here, Zane here, it all feels right. Like this was supposed to happen. As we wait for Zane to hand us our room keys, I pull out my phone and send a group text to my friends.

He's here.

A second later a gif of Allie and Noah from the movie version of *The Notebook* pops up on my screen. There's no sound but I know this scene: it's when Noah is standing in the rain facing Allie. The words read: *It wasn't over. It still isn't over.*

Chapter Nineteen

Day 5, Thursday, 9 a.m.

Isle of Wight

The sheets are so soft and that dream was *so* good. I flip onto my side and attempt to get back to it, then realize: it was not a dream. Zane is here.

I close my eyes and replay last night.

Dinner was at a pub just off St. Thomas's Square, at a big table so the whole group could eat together. Everyone else, too, seemed very happy about Zane's arrival, about Zane himself. Maybe it's just that he's fresh blood, or maybe it's that everyone wants to see what they missed out on, having Angus instead of Zane as a guide for the first half of the tour. What would it have been like to get him all to myself? Unrealistic? Maybe. At least I was able to dropkick Francis to score the seat next to Zane, but he seemed to think I'd just lost my balance.

And oh, how he talked.

And oh, how I listened.

I replay the many stories he told—everything from the history of Newport and the Isle of Wight to other tours with his parents, stuff about his brother, celebs who have taken the tour (like Meghan Markle), though as the night went on and the wine bottles accumulated on the table, actual details got a bit fuzzy. Except the Meghan Markle bits—that was fascinating. But the rest—well, he could've been talking about kale. I think he *did* talk about kale, actually, at one point. Not that it mattered. I was busy imagining it was just the two of us, on a date, alone.

Sitting so close to him made every word, every syllable dance over my skin, sending shivers of excitement up and down my arms and legs. It's like I'd discovered another title by Zane. Or better—an ongoing podcast with more than a thousand episodes to date. But better, because he's right here. And I know he was talking to everyone at the table, but I'm sure his eyes met mine at least twice as often as everyone else's. He kept glancing over at me, smiling, nodding, winking. And that was no easy feat, since I was right beside him. Surely it would've been easier to make eye contact with Roshi or Violet or Jenny, who were across from him.

After dinner we strolled back along the cobblestone to the hotel. The air was cool, but I was warm with happiness. Back at the hotel, I eyed the worn couch by the Victrola in the cozy lounge, picturing the two of us on it, reading and listening to old 45s. But before I worked up the courage to ask him if he wanted to grab a drink, Zane had to head off, to take care of a few administrative details. Of course he did. He's responsible. He's in charge. This isn't only his job—it's his entire life. Just like I'd be at the shop. Of course I understood.

"See you in the morning," he'd said to me. I'd held on to those words as I floated up the carpeted stairs to my room.

Sure, it might have been nice to have some sort of intimate exchange with him—even just a bit of time alone without the others around. But it was the first night, and he had to spend time chatting with everyone. I would've thought less of him if he hadn't.

And so I'd FaceTimed the girls to catch them up to speed. It was a bit disappointing not to have anything dramatic to share with them, but as Emily pointed out, "All you want to do is lay the groundwork. Think of it like *The Bachelor*. The first night is just about getting to know him. No getting plastered, no embarrassing stories, no weird hang-up reveals, and you're fine."

Now, I close my eyes, conjuring up a picture of the real Zane. If his voice is in surround sound, the real Zane's like watching a movie in 4K. Everything about him is more intense than his photos.

He's so expressive when he talks, his eyebrows budging, the cleft in his chin deepening, his arms moving up and down and around, his entire body part of the story. This is the kind of soulmate connection I dreamed about—where you can't take your eyes off the person. Where everything they say goes straight to your heart, where everything they do feels like turning the page on a book you never want to end. This is what I hoped for when I fantasized about this trip with Zane—and yet, it's even better than I could've imagined because it's real.

I can't even really remember most of the details of anything he told us on the bus or during dinner. Which felt comforting. I'm so used to tuning out the actual story when listening to *Their Finest Hour*, listening to his voice but not the story, that it felt as though he picked up right where I left off when I threw my headphones away.

Now, I spring out of bed to get ready.

I pull item after item out of my suitcase like a magician pulling scarves out of a hat, but nothing seems right. If I debated my daily outfit before Zane arrived, now that he's here I'm agonizing over it in a way that borders on unhealthy. But, just like most mornings on this trip, I haven't actually left myself that much time to get ready. I'm going to have to set my alarm earlier if I plan to relive the previous evening every morning in bed. I eventually decide on a black sundress that hits above the knee, black sandals, a black cross-body bag. Classic, and will hide any unfortunate sweating.

When I arrive in the lobby of the hotel, which is dark and cozy with low, wood-paneled ceilings and kerosene lamp–style wall sconces, Zane's already there, chatting with Charlotte. He nods and smiles when he sees me. His face is smooth and glossy, like he might have applied moisturizer. His lips are full. He's wearing a red tour shirt and khakis, and his hair is perfectly styled—it doesn't move. Taj brushes past, coming from the opposite direction, through the bar, and catches my eye. His lip turns up. "Where's the funeral?" he jokes. I give him a dirty look. He laughs, then brushes past, but I look away, feeling as though I've been caught. But there's nothing to feel weird about, I remind myself. I haven't done anything wrong. Unless meeting your soulmate is wrong.

I walk over to Zane and he smiles at me again, then turns away from Charlotte.

"Sleep well?" If only he knew what I dreamed about.

"Uh-huh," I say, swallowing.

"Excellent. We've got a great day ahead of us so no dozing off on the bus. I saw you with your eyes closed, head against the window yesterday," he says.

I want to die. Thankfully, I'm dressed for it.

"I—it wasn't, you're not boring," I stammer. *I love to listen to you with my eyes closed. Old habits die hard.*

"I know I'm not boring." He grins. He extends an arm toward the bar. "Help yourself to pastries, coffee, and then I'll see you outside in about fifteen minutes to get started on the day."

I savor every word.

Fifteen minutes later, right on schedule, Zane gathers us outside the war memorial in St. Thomas's Square. The area is alive with people. A café has set up outdoor seating, and white tents have been pitched at the side of the church, tables selling homemade sweets and handmade tchotchkes. Angus stands beside Zane and claps his hands. "I have good news and good news. The good news is that as you can see, this is your first full day with Zane, your original guide, back on the tour. The other bit of good news is that you've just got yourself another passenger on the tour."

Charlotte looks pleased with this information, and I get a fluttery feeling in my stomach for her. Charlotte mouths something to me: "Phew." I wonder if she was worried he'd just disappear for the day now that he was free of obligations.

There's chatter but overall happiness at this news—mostly that we're not saying goodbye to Angus, whom we've all grown to love, bad jokes and all.

Angus meets Charlotte's eye, then walks over to her and says something. She laughs.

"Who's ready to explore this island on e-bikes?" Zane motions for us to follow him a few feet away to a stand of e-bikes outside a rental shop.

"More biking?" Sindhi complains.

"Didn't you read the itinerary?" Nelle says, looking at Sindhi's dress and sandals. I notice that Nelle and Violet aren't wearing their cycling outfits this time, maybe because e-bikes aren't as intense. Thankfully, since I'm wearing a dress and sandals, too.

"Oh, it's such a nice day," Roshi says, putting an arm around his wife. "It'll be nice to get some exercise." Taj rolls the bikes out, one at a time. When he passes one to me, he rings the bell.

"No yellow M this time?" he says, and it takes me a second. He passes Nelle a bike.

"*Maize*," I correct, as he hands Nelle her bike.

"May's you come with me today?" He raises an eyebrow. "Hmm. Not sure that joke landed."

"What?"

He scratches the back of his neck. "I'm going to head down to Compton. Go surfing for an hour or so. My buddy runs a surf shop. He'd set you up with everything you need, give you a lesson. We'd be back in plenty of time. If you're—up for it?" He hands Violet her bike. That's the last bike.

Surfing? He's asking me to go surfing? Surfing sounds fun. But that's not why I'm here now. I wanted this—for Zane to be here, and he is, and I have the whole day ahead of me, with him, now. Maybe it's good Taj is going surfing instead. No distractions while I'm getting to know Zane. "Oh, I really want to see the whole island," I say feebly.

"You know the bike tour starts at that church, right?" Taj nods behind me.

I turn around but instead of looking at the large stone church, it's Zane, talking to Jenny, that catches my eye. I watch them for a beat longer than necessary, then turn back to Taj. He's followed my gaze. His eyes meet mine. His jaw hardens.

"Right. I get it."

My ears burn, but I turn away, rolling my bike to catch up to Zane and the rest of the group. Who cares if Taj knows I like Zane? I *do* like Zane.

"Hey," Zane says when I'm next to him. He's straddling his bike. There's a large soft-sided cooler strapped to the back. "Everything OK?"

"Perfect."

He grins, then waves to the group. "Let's go."

Zane leads us down the cobblestone, back past the Rye and Newport Minster. I feel my stomach tightening, but happily for me, the church is closed for a special function, so instead Zane gives us a detailed history of the church as we continue riding our bikes. A very detailed history. Which Jenny interrupts multiple times with questions about a supposed séance that happened in the 1800s, laughs loudly and flips her hair back and forth unnecessarily.

As the town disappears behind us, Zane continues to chatter, explaining the itinerary, the highlight of which includes a visit to Osborne House on the northern coast of the island. It's the one-time summer palace of Queen Victoria that's now open to the public.

The sun is shining; we're on a shady dirt path through a fruit orchard. There's only a gentle breeze and I'm bike-riding with Zane, listening to his intonation, the highs and lows, the way his accent clips vowels and stretches consonants. What life is this?

"Remember when we went to Nantucket?" Roshi says to Sindhi behind me.

"That was before the children." Sindhi sounds wistful. "Things were different."

"Of course they were different," Roshi says. "It would be weird if they weren't."

"Mmm," she says.

"We had fun together then. We can have fun again, my love."

"We were together then, *Roshi*," she says, and I wonder what she means by that. Are they separated? Are they trying to repair their marriage on this trip? I don't hear the rest of their conversation because Zane interrupts to tell us about our next destination: Appuldurcombe House, an eighteenth-century estate. I shrug to myself. Other people's problems are not my problems.

Eventually the dirt road leads to a large mansion atop a sloping hill and surrounded by lush, manicured lawns. I brace myself for the climb, but the e-bike kicks into high gear and I just coast along, not a bit out of breath, not a bead of sweat anywhere on my body. It's like e-bikes were invented for first dates.

Zane tells us that this was once the grandest estate in the entire island, and I imagine myself as the heroine of some historical romance, living in this house, getting ready to go to a ball, hoping Zane's name will be on my dance card. But as we move past the near-pristine front, to the sides, the walls are broken down, offering a clear view of the barren interior. "Not much left after World War Two," he explains.

"The perfect example of looks being deceiving," Sindhi says, looking at Roshi. I notice her tone is sad. Roshi doesn't say anything, just lets go of his handlebars, straddles his bike and crosses his arms over his chest.

"Or all of us trying to put our best faces on," I suggest, trying to cut the tension.

"Or our best lips," Charlotte adds.

Francis rattles off a few facts about the war, including the fact that seventy people on the island died during the air raids. He's popped his recorder into the front pocket of his short-sleeve button-down checked shirt.

"How awful," Charlotte says, turning to Angus beside her. He nods, then dips his head to say something else only to her. She nods and smiles at him.

"Imagine losing the person you love the most," Violet says wistfully. "Or worse, never having told them?" She looks at Nelle, who smiles, but it looks forced.

Zane turns to me. "You ready to keep going?" I notice how mossy green his eyes are, like the moors in *Wuthering Heights*, and his nose is slightly crooked. A wisp of his hair sticks up. I reach out to fix it, then pull my hand back.

"Mm-hmm," I say.

We pedal along the path. Large trees drop light purple flowers. The air smells like syrup.

My phone pings, but I ignore it. It's nearly noon, and I'm sure that it's Cleo, catching up on my conversation with Dory while on her Peloton.

It pings again.

And again.

"Somebody's popular," Zane says.

"It's my friends. They're dying to know how the tour is going."

"How *is* the tour going?" he asks.

"A lot better now," I say. "Angus was great, too. But I like a plan—and I signed up because you were leading the tour." It's bold and it's not exactly true, and the words just spill out.

"I get that a lot. I *do* know my stuff." I want to know more. How many other women have been on this tour, hanging on Zane's every word? And yet, the truth is, I actually don't want to know.

"You must have to read so much," I say instead. Stick to the facts.

"Mmm, not really," he says, then taps his head. "It's all up here. Heard my parents give the same information over and over again for sixteen years before I even started handling some of the stops. Osmosis. No need to read."

No need to read? I know he means tour guides, not reading in general, yet it still startles me. There's never a *need* to read, there's just a desire. At least for me. I assumed he'd feel the same way.

But what about when we're lying on the couch by the fire? Maybe I'm reading aloud to Zane while he gives me a foot massage. Maybe if he doesn't enjoy reading, he'll enjoy listening to me read. We don't *both* have to love reading.

But I can't let it go. "So do you like to read just for pleasure?" I say. The path curves beside the water. The waves crash into the rocky shore.

"Read for pleasure?" he says, as though I've just mentioned cleaning toilets for fun. "A bit, I guess. Usually non-fiction. War stuff. Facts I'm not sure of, if I have to. How about you?"

I titter. "Yes, I love to read. I get most of my facts from fiction, though." He cocks his head. "Historical romances, that sort of thing. I do love ones set during war times. *The Rose Code* and *Our Darkest Night* are two of my favorites." He gives me a blank stare, but his green eyes make me lose my train of thought. Whoever said opposites attract really knew what they were talking about.

Francis interrupts us, asking a question about the collection inside the castle, and Zane turns his attention to him.

I fall back beside Charlotte. "How's *that* going?" she whispers. I know I'm blushing.

"What?" I say innocently, then remind myself of the big picture. Five days ago, if someone had told me I'd be riding my bike beside Zane, chatting easily about anything and everything, I would have told them to hit me over the head with a book to make sure I wasn't crazy. This is everything I've dreamed of.

The path along the water leads us to a harbor dotted with racing yachts and dinghies, edged with brightly colored beach huts. We park our bikes and Zane unhooks the cooler bag strapped to the back of his bike. A group of people paddle by in kayaks. "It'll just take a few minutes to set this up, so feel free to roam for a bit. At the word *roam* I laugh, remembering Taj on the first day, adamant that there would be *no* roaming. Zane turns and raises an eyebrow; it feels odd to explain to Zane why I'm laughing, and I push the thought away. "Need help?" I say instead.

"Sure," he says as Violet approaches.

"Nelle and I are just going to take a little stroll down the beach," Violet says. Zane nods and gives them a wave.

"Nelle and Violet like to walk. They usually walk every day," Francis says into his recorder. "It reminds them of how they met." I watch as they hold hands and walk closer to the water's edge, their laughter carrying in the wind. Maybe Nelle wishes Jenny were around, but maybe it's also nice for her to have time with Violet. Francis walks over to us. "I used to take my daughter for a picnic on the last day of school," he says, hands on his hips.

I melt at the thought of Francis and his daughter, the two of them on a pink-and-white-checkered blanket, eating miniature sandwiches. "She'd bring those bubbles to blow. She'd make me run around the beach popping them. She said if the bubble didn't pop, her wish wouldn't come true. I'd be racing around like a madman," he chuckles. "But oh, how I loved it."

"Francis, that's so sweet," I say, so touched that I feel a bit teary.

But his expression changes in an instant. "Sorry, I'm going on and on about me. What can I do to help?" he says to Zane.

Zane points to the cooler. "Want to give me a hand with this?" he asks, and Francis nods, taking a handle on the end of the cooler. Together they carry it to a shaded spot under a large cotoneaster bush, and Zane pulls out several beautiful blue-and-white-checked picnic blankets. Francis and Roshi clear all the debris from the area, making a pile out of the way, under a tree.

"Come with me," Angus says to Charlotte. "I want to show you something I think you'll love."

"Oh?" Charlotte says, then blushes. Her hair is in a tiny ponytail, her lips bare. She looks healthy and youthful.

Sindhi passes me the box of sandwiches, and I imagine I'm having a picnic for two. It's not that weird. Francis was remembering his time with his daughter. Surely I can block everyone else out and pretend it's just Zane and me.

After everything's set, we all sit. Nelle and Violet return, shoes in hand, Nelle brushing off her feet before sitting down on the blanket. Roshi pulls out his crossword. Sindhi shifts a bit closer to him and points at the page. "Fireworks," she says. Roshi looks like he might explode with joy.

Everyone else is having their own conversations, so it doesn't seem odd to turn slightly toward Zane. "So you grew up on these tours—what's your favorite stop?" I ask him.

"Ahh, they're all great. Just sort of second nature to me, you know, I don't even really consider them objectively anymore." He passes around a jug of water and reusable cups. "Sometimes Dad and I will cross paths on the tour in this very spot," Zane says to me. "We try to time the groups to have picnics here together. It's nice to make sure we see each other without more than a few days passing. Family's everything to me." He pauses. "What about you?" he asks. "What's been your favorite spot?"

An image of the clear, flat water, the bridge up ahead, gliding along in the punting boat comes to mind. "This island is really cool." *This island is really cool?*

Charlotte leans toward me and asks me to pass her a napkin. When she goes back to her conversation, Zane nods. "That your mum?"

"Charlotte?" I shake my head. "No. My uh—my parents passed away." Really, Geeg? Way to kill the conversation. "Oh, wow," he says. "I'm so sorry. I can't even imagine. Family is *so* important to me," he says again. He takes a bite of sandwich. I swallow his words. Family is so important to me, too, I want to say. It's not like I chose for Mom and Dad to die.

"Mum and Dad are the life of this company. I don't know what I'll do if anything happens to them." The way he says *if* strikes me as odd. Like, obviously something *will* happen to them at some point. Is he in denial?

"How *is* your mom?" I ask, trying to alter the course of this conversation.

"Mum's OK," he says, his eyes meeting mine. "She had a really bad cold and the doctors were worried about pneumonia. But she really gave us a scare. Thanks for asking."

"It's nice you stayed."

"Of course, I could never leave Mum in such a state. I still live with them, and I haven't gone more than a few days without seeing them, probably my entire life."

"Oh, come on," I laugh, because I think he's joking.

When he gives me a quizzical look, I press my lips together. "Well, obviously you don't see them when you're on the tour. That's ten days right there."

"I often do the tour with either Mum or Dad. We're all able to drive and guide, so we can swap roles. And if we're not together, our tours cross paths a few times."

"Oh," I say, realizing that instead of Taj I might have gotten to meet his Mum or Dad on this tour. Even though, strategically, they'd be better off making sure there was a Wilkenson on every tour rather than two on one, the romantic in me thinks it's sweet he's so close to his parents.

"So tell me something about you, Gigi," Zane asks, looking at me intently and smiling.

"Well I . . . own a bookshop," I say. "It was my parents', but I took it over." I stop myself from going into the full story of the shop, the way I already did with Taj. I want this to feel different from that night in Brighton with Taj.

The rest of the group are completely engaged in their own conversations, and it really is like I have Zane all to myself. A romantic picnic on the beach, like something Jack and Mirabelle would do, in *Their Finest Hour*. I can hardly believe it.

"When they died?" he says softly. I turn back to him. Nod.

"That's part of the reason why books are my thing. The thing I love most. It's safe to say I love reading. But I also love listening to audiobooks," I say pointedly. I can't help myself. This is what I want to talk about. How he came to narrate *Their Finest Hour*. Why it's the only book he's ever narrated.

Zane nods. "Audiobooks, huh? I've listened to a few. And podcasts," he says. "You ever listen to *How I Built This?*"

"Um, yeah, a few times." I don't want to talk about podcasts. I want to talk about audiobooks. *The* audiobook.

I remind myself of what Emily said. Just lay the groundwork. That's all I'm doing. And in that case, things are going pretty great.

Chapter Twenty

Day 5, Thursday, 2 p.m.

West Bay

My skin feels windburned, my body's tired and my heart is full when we step back on the ferry to leave the Isle of Wight and head back to the mainland. On the bus, after the ferry's docked in Southampton, Zane slides into the seat beside me like it's *no big deal* at all, and I want to turn and take in this moment—this very moment that I've plotted out and played out in my mind so many times—but I have zero control over my body. I feel like one of those inflatable stick figures you see blowing in the wind at car dealerships. Totally unpredictable. And then he turns to me, and his knee brushes my bare leg and it's like a gust of wind bustles right through me. I'm filled with life, floating high into the sky, and it's the best feeling in the world.

"You weren't saving this for someone else, were you?" he says, and I manage to gain enough control over my body to eke out a weird sound that's half laugh, half cough. "Erm, no."

His leg is still touching mine.

I want to reach out and touch his knee, to run my fingers up his leg, to shimmy close into the crook of his arm. And because

I don't trust myself *not* to do that, I shove my hands between my legs instead and hold my breath, not wanting to do anything to make him shift farther away.

"Great," he says, giving me a slow smile.

The sun is high in the sky when we arrive in West Bay, turning the sandy cliffs into mounds of gold. Taj lets us off the bus near a gathering of shops. We pass a fishmonger. The smell is overpowering but not unpleasant.

"Ten years ago," Zane says, as we make our way toward the beach, "that cliff was a landmark, but now, some of you may recognize it as a prominent setting if you've ever watched—"

"*Broadchurch*," Jenny interrupts. "This place is Murder 'n' Makeup gold." Her hand is still wrapped in gauze, but she waves her free hand around. "I'm off to do the tour." She spins around. "Mom, do you want to come?"

Nelle puts a hand to her chest. She looks like she's going to burst with happiness. "I'd love to come with you, Hon."

"Go where? No one's going anywhere," Zane says. Jenny looks at him.

"We'll see you back at the bus. C'mon." She grabs Nelle's hand. Zane looks to me.

"She sort of does this a lot. It's probably better to just go with it," I say with a shrug.

"Oh yeah?" he says. "So I should trust you?" His voice goes straight to my core.

I nod. "Yes," I say.

"Alright." His eyes are on mine and I'm unable to look away. Eventually, he winks, then turns back to the group. "Alright, let's keep going."

"You have to give Jenny credit," Sindhi says to no one in

particular. "For someone who didn't want to come on this trip, she's certainly done a lot of extra planning."

"Would you like to do that tour?" Roshi asks. "You watched that show, too, didn't you?"

Sindhi looks surprised. "Yes. Remember I tried to get you to watch it? But you didn't have any interest."

Roshi nods. "I actually did watch it, a few months ago."

They slow. I slow. They may only be talking about a show, but this feels important.

"You did?" she says. "But, why?"

"When I booked the trip," he says. "I knew about this stop on the trip. I thought it might give us something to talk about when we were here."

Sindhi's lips are in a hard, straight line. She looks angry. And then I realize, she's holding something in—her lips the steadfast guard at the gates of her emotions.

"I don't know." She shakes her head. "It's been so long, Roshi."

"I know that I was busy with work," he says sadly. "That I left you with the girls."

"*All* the time, Roshi. In strange countries. I had no one. I was so lonely. I was so alone."

"I'm trying to make it up to you," Roshi says. "Not just the trip. This won't end with the trip. This is just the beginning."

The start of their story.

Sindhi shakes her head. Then nods. "OK," she says. "OK."

My phone pings and I move away from Sindhi and Roshi. I updated the group on the bus about the day so far, but now that they're all caught up, they want even more details.

About to catch crabs.

Jacynthe texts back: *Have we taught you nothing about using protection?*

Zane clasps his hands together. "Alright, so our tour starts right here." He waves an arm out toward the harbor, which is stacked with fishing boats and jet boats. "We're about to engage in one of the longest-standing pastimes in the country—one unique to West Bay."

"And the reason I asked you to pass along your leftover bacon at breakfast this morning," Angus says. He reaches into his pocket and pulls out a plastic bag of bacon and waves it around.

Sindhi wrinkles her nose. "That's a terrific example of why I'm a vegetarian."

"I understand completely," Zane says with a wink. "You and I can use these." He pulls a small container out of his pocket and hands her what looks like a plastic Lifesaver. And for the first time in my life I consider joining Team Vegetarian.

"You can take the tour guide off the tour . . ." Taj says as he passes by, trailing off.

"But you can't take the tour guiding out of the tour guide?" I finish. But if Taj heard me, he doesn't let on; he just looks both ways then crosses the street to a set of blue-and-white huts selling quick bites like fried fish sticks, ice cream and chocolate fudge. I look away before he reaches the other side.

"The people of West Bay are mad about crabbing," Zane says. He leads us over to the cement ledge by the harbor's edge, and I lean over to peer down at the black water at least fifteen feet below. Zane walks over to a wooden hut decorated in union jack flags, hanging baskets dangling from the eaves, and grabs a stack of clear plastic buckets from the pile out front. He hands them out to the group.

"I can almost see myself, a young lad, coming here after church with my folks," Roshi says.

"What are you talking about?" Sindhi asks, shaking her head. "You never went crabbing or to church." But her tone is kinder than usual.

"How do you know what I did when I was five?" he teases.

"Because I know everything about you, Roshi," Sindhi says.

"Ahh, well, I suppose that's true." He smiles, then touches the top of her hand.

Angus demonstrates how to tie a small piece of bacon to the end of the string. "Now you toss that into the water and wait for the crabs to come."

"Why wouldn't you just use a net?" Sindhi asks.

"That's part of the art," Angus says.

"Crabbing is practically a national pastime in these parts," Francis says into his recorder.

"It's just for fun, my love," Roshi says, giving her a kiss on the cheek. She doesn't pull away.

"This isn't just about catching crabs, it's about passing the time," Angus says. "Enjoying life. Taking things slow. Tradition. Doing." He ties another piece of bacon to a string then hands it to Charlotte.

"Have you been doing this since you were their size?" I say, nodding to a trio of little kids sitting on the edge between their parents.

"Yep," Angus says, handing me a string with bacon. I walk over to the edge, where Violet and Charlotte are already seated. Zane sits beside me.

"Does crabbing ever get boring?" Violet says, turning around to Angus, and I think about the bookshop—those days when it's not busy, when I sink into the slow pace. Seems to me crabbing is like that.

"It is what it is," Zane answers instead.

"Ten bucks!" I shout and slap my knee, then look around for Taj, but remember he's not here. Zane stares at me, open-mouthed.

"Cripes, Gigi! You shouldn't scare people like that, when we're all teetering on a ledge," he chides. "This is a calm pastime, remember?" My neck feels hot. I grip the string and swallow.

"Sorry," I say.

"It's fine. So what was that all about?"

"Habit." I briefly explain the game, but Zane only shrugs, tying his plastic lifesaver to his string, then lowering it into the water. "Why get riled up, though? Why not just accept things as the way they are?"

I consider this. Then shake my head. "Don't try to argue your way out of it. It's my game and I take it very seriously. You owe me ten bucks, or whatever that is in pounds." I bump shoulders with him, and Zane looks alarmed.

"The ledge, Gigi." He smiles, but I still feel reprimanded.

I pull out my phone to text the group that another ten dollars has been added to the pot, even if it doesn't seem like Zane's game to play, then text Lars to tell him to take a ten out of the register, make a note on the yellow pad and put the ten in the box under the counter that's marked *IIWII*.

He texts back. *What's that box 4? I used $ to buy fairy lights 4 front.*

Tell me you're kidding, I write, trying to envision where exactly he would've put the fairy lights. Not that I have anything against fairy lights. But he didn't even ask. I scroll back through our texts to make sure I didn't miss something.

A picture pops up on the screen. Tiny lights twinkle, draped from corner to corner of the front of the shop, in the window, creating a magical little nook. I love it.

"I'm not having any luck," Charlotte turns to me. I'm grateful for the distraction and stow my phone in my purse.

"Alright, let's see." I check my string to make sure the bacon's still attached, then dangle it over the edge until it reaches the surface of the water. If there's one thing I know from the shop, it's patience. It's why I don't close even when it's slow. Because that one customer who might come in, could be a customer for life.

The concrete wall is rough against my body as I lean over, hoping for something to snag the line. Angus taps my shoulder. "Funny thing about crabs," he says. "They only come when you're not looking."

"Deep thoughts," Charlotte teases.

Angus looks mock-offended. "I am full of deep thoughts. Shallow ones, too."

Charlotte suddenly squeals and pulls on her line. "Caught something!"

But as the line comes up, she sighs. There's a clump of seaweed at the end. "Keep trying, Charlotte," Angus says, his eyes crinkling at the corners.

"Do you mind getting that seaweed off my line?"

"Don't mind at all," he chuckles and pulls the seaweed off the line. She looks over at me, her eyes sparkling, and I feel like I've just read a swoon-worthy scene in one of my favorite romance novels. Now what can I do to ensure my exchanges with Zane give me the same kind of feels?

Chapter Twenty-One

Day 5, Thursday, 6 p.m.

Lyme Regis

From my vantage point on the bus, side by side with Zane in the front row, the seaside town of Lyme Regis, carved out of the hillside, looks like an acrylic hotel painting of a seaside summer scene, the buildings like white, orange, turquoise and yellow Lego stacked on top of each other from the water up the side of the cliff. The sidewalks look as though they were power-washed just this morning. Brightly colored pots hold sprays of narcissus and lilies. But it's the stone harbor wall jutting out into the water that takes my breath away. "Is that the wall . . ." I start to say, turning away from the window back to Zane.

"Not you and another wall," Taj interrupts from the driver's seat. Zane follows my gaze out the window, then interjects.

"The lady knows her romances," Zane says. "It's the spot where Charles first sees Sarah in *The French Lieutenant's Woman*." I can't believe he knows the reference.

"I love that movie," I sigh. "Actually, my mom loved that movie. She didn't watch a lot of TV or movies, but she loved that one. I would know that break wall anywhere."

The fact that Zane knows a movie that Mom loved—that has to mean something. The premise is actually a story within a story, in which two actors are playing the roles of the couple who fall in love—and then they fall in love themselves, too. The meet cute happens in a storm, the waves crashing over a massive stone wall. Right now, it's just too bad it isn't raining—that would make it perfect. But it's still pretty incredible.

"I met the actress's daughter once," Taj says. "She came back here for some award for that movie or something, from the town," he says.

I gasp. "You mean *Meryl Streep*? You met *Meryl Streep*'s daughter?"

Zane pats my knee. "There, there, Gigi. So excitable. Let's not discuss Taj's love life."

He's right: I definitely do *not* want to think about Taj's love life. Even thinking about not thinking about Taj's love life gives me butterflies that are too confusing to consider right now.

Taj gives me an amused look, then focuses back on the road in front of him. He pulls the bus up to the Rock Point Inn, a blue-and-white two-story building overlooking the waves.

"Shall we check in and let everyone freshen up or have a little free time?" Angus says.

"We're a bit behind schedule," Zane says, checking his watch. "Taj, you mind getting us checked in, and we'll get out to fossil before high tide?"

Taj nods but says nothing. If he's annoyed to do the grunt work he doesn't let on, but I notice how different his role is with Zane around, compared to when Angus was the guide—even though it would make sense, given Angus's age, that Taj would help out more. Maybe it's similar to the shop: I know I wouldn't be running it the same way Mom and Dad did if they were around. And it *is* nice that Taj is getting us checked in so we can spend time outside, when he's been in Lyme Regis probably countless times.

"Alright everyone, off we go," Zane says, clapping his hands. "Let's fossil."

We amble toward a black lamp pole, the top swirled in the shape of a snail fossil, and Zane points toward a set of steps. "The steps can be slippery from the tide," he warns me. "Do you want to take my arm?"

Yes, absolutely yes. As we start down the steps, though, I realize it would actually be easier to just grip the railing, but there's no way I am giving up his arm.

"This area's history dates back to the eighth century," Zane says as we step on the rocks, which, as he cautioned, are wet from the ebb tide. "It's rich in history and fossils and the birth of history's most important paleontologist," he says, then goes on to tell us the story of the famous Mary Anning. I don't know if it's the story of the young girl, struck by lightning as a baby, who survived and went on to make the first discovery in the area of fossils, or it's the view of the sun setting over the ripples of water, but I'm moved. Perhaps it's the feeling I get just hearing Zane's voice. Is this what everyday life would be like around him? Would chatting about the grocery list make me feel so alive and *in love*?

Zane explains exactly *how* to fossil, which is basically looking at rocks, picking up rocks, and turning rocks over to see if there's a fossil. Everyone disperses. Violet turns to Jenny and says, "Join us?"

Jenny looks reluctant. "I've already hogged Mom this morning," she says.

"Nonsense. There's more than enough of Nelle for all of us," Violet says.

Nelle reaches her arms out to both women, looping her arms through theirs.

"It's actually going to be a bit tricky to fossil like that," Angus chuckles.

"But I've got my two favorite ladies on my arms," Nelle says, looking from Jenny to Violet. "I'll take this over fossiling any day. At least for the next few minutes." They wander off and Zane and I pass Francis, who's perched himself on a large curved rock. He looks up. "Having any luck yet?" Francis asks. I shake my head.

"Lift that rock there"—Zane points out a rock, about the size of a baseball, by Francis's foot. He lifts it and peers underneath. A little farther on, Sindhi's staring out into the water. She's taken her shoes off, the water covering her feet.

"Realistically, how easy is it going to be to find a fossil out here?" I say to Zane beside me. "My friend has a son who's in that dinosaur phase right now." I think of Emily's three-year-old son, Cole, and how it would be nice to bring him back a fossil.

He tilts his head back and forth. "Easy and not easy. You can take them if they're loose along the beach, but not from the cliffs"—he points away from the water, to the precarious cliffs behind us. "Some days you'll find one almost instantly, other times you can go for hours and find nothing. The thrill is the chase anyway. Made me want to become a paleontologist, at least for a few years when I was kid," Zane says, looking into the wind, which is coming off the land. When he turns back, he tucks a loose strand of hair off his forehead, returning his appearance to its original perfection. How is it possible that he's *so* good looking? "Wasn't meant to be," he says, pouting dramatically.

"Because of the tour company?" I ask. "Did your parents give you an option, or was it just understood that you'd take over the business?"

"I don't think we ever really discussed it, but by the time I was old enough to get a job, I just knew this is what I'd do." Zane bends down to pick up a rock, turning it over. He looks around, then chucks it out into the water. "Doing the right thing. Three generations."

"A lot of people don't get it," I say softly. "Don't get the family business—how maybe it takes away the choice, but it can be an honor." I think about my own journey to owning the bookshop. Where would I be right now if Mom and Dad hadn't died?

"And your brother?" I ask. "Is he part of the business, too?"

Zane shakes his head. "Nope. Doctor in London. You've got a brother, too, right?"

I nod. "Yeah. He does his own thing. I could've, too—it's not like Mom and Dad *expected* me to carry on the business," I say. "They always supported all my dreams: to be a tap dancer. First female firefighter in Ann Arbor. Magician in Paris. I had the skill, of course," I joke. "Even as a teen I had a ton of other jobs—I was determined not to work for my parents, actually." I remember how rebellious I was. How I sweated through a summer in the kitchen of a greasy spoon with Dory, refusing to quit even though I was making less than Mom and Dad would've paid me at the shop.

"Really? I've never done anything else," he says. "Wouldn't think of it." Somehow the British accent makes his tone feel disapproving. But then he laughs. "I guess I'm loyal that way. Loyal in all ways, actually." And his eyes meet mine. Then he reaches out toward me. "Careful on this stretch. It's slippery." I reach for his arm and he takes my hand in his, closing his fingers around mine, pulses of electricity shimmying through my arm. My heart soars. A flock of gulls swoop down in front of us, landing at the edge of the water. Farther ahead, Angus must be saying something funny to the others because Nelle and Violet and Jenny and Charlotte are all laughing. This moment is perfect.

Or *almost* perfect. The only thing that could make it *more* perfect would be to talk about *Their Finest Hour*. But if he's keeping it a secret, it's *our* secret. Like he doesn't just randomly tell every other guest on his tours about his audiobook narrator persona.

"Nothing else?" I say, and he looks down at me and tilts his head. "I thought maybe . . . you would've wanted to be an actor or voice actor or . . . audiobook narrator?" I tease.

He runs a finger along a perfectly groomed, raised eyebrow. "Ahh, that. So you've listened to my book?" His surprise wraps my heart in a little blanket of happiness. Either he's a *really* good actor or I'm *really* not one of a million women who's taken this tour after hearing him read.

"Yes," I say, not telling him how many times I've listened—that isn't important.

Zane lets go of my hand, bends down, pointing to a group of rocks. "This is where you want to look for a fossil. Rocks hidden by others. Remove the top layers, see what's underneath."

How can he talk about fossils at a pivotal moment like this? This is where it all comes together—when I learn how Zane came to narrate the very book that became my parents' story. I can't wait to get the whole story. I pick up a rock, and hold it flat in my palm then lift it to smell it. I am with Zane, I'm fossiling. I've just asked him about the audiobook. I want to remember this moment.

"So tell me about it. It's not everyone that narrates an audio-book."

He nods. "I guess not. A friend worked at the audiobook company doing an edition of *Our Finest Hour* and he asked," he says simply. "So I said yes."

"*Their* Finest Hour," I say. Maybe I misheard him.

"Hmm?" he says. "Isn't that what I said?"

"No, you said *Our* Finest Hour."

"Oh. Right, whatever. Anyway, I don't know, it was just one of those things you do, but don't give much thought to, you know?"

He picks up a rock, turning it over in his palm, then tosses it back onto the other rocks. It lands with a *clunk*. This isn't going as well as I envisioned, but I'm not about to give up. I study Zane's face. His smooth skin, his long lashes. Does it really matter what the title is? It's still the same story.

"It's such a beautiful story, isn't it?" I say.

"Hmm?" he asks, looking up from a stone. "Sure, yeah. Well, to be honest, narrating is really tough, getting all the voice stuff right. There was a whole way to read it—I was mostly so focused on the words, it was hard to take in the whole story."

"Oh," I say, and a wave of something washes over me, like I'm one of the rocks on the shore. Disappointment, I guess.

He looks over. "But you loved it?" His tone softens.

I pick up a stone. "Loved is probably an understatement. The story was so beautiful. The perfect soulmate love story."

Zane laughs. "Soulmates? Oh, come on." I must be making a face, too—because his face falls. "Oh, geez, you're serious. You really believe in soulmates?"

"I love love stories, remember?" I say. I can't feel my fingers or toes.

He shakes his head. "Right. The bookstore thing."

I switch gears. "Anyway, your voice . . . well, it's so beautiful, too." My chest is tight and I suddenly feel overcome with emotion.

Something in his expression shifts. Almost like a realization. Like he gets it. "Wow, um, thank you." His eyes meet mine. "So you . . . knew I was leading the tour?"

I nod, not sure I can get any more words out.

"I'd heard there was maybe some chemistry between you and Taj?" he says, his tone light, questioning.

My heart pounds in my throat, squeezing the airway shut. Who would have said that? *Taj? Angus? Charlotte?* "Pffft."

Zane raises his eyebrows. I can't swallow. I can't breathe. But he looks like he needs more explanation than whatever *that* noise was that just escaped my lips. I say the first thing that comes to mind. "I'd never be into our bus driver." He chuckles and shakes his head, and my heartbeat slows. Zane walks ahead and I try to process what just happened. Who would've said anything about Taj and me? There is no 'Taj and me'—he made that very clear in Brighton. Forget about Brighton! Zane is asking about my love life. Why? Because he's interested? He seems interested. Is he interested?

A few moments later, I hurry to catch up with the rest of the group ahead. The wind picks up and I shiver, wishing I'd thought to bring a coat. As I reach everyone, Zane looks over at me and shrugs out of his jacket. "Here, take this." He puts it around my shoulders in a way I've always wanted someone to. David never shared his clothes—he hated scents of any kind and always complained that anything that touched me smelled like my hairspray or body wash—like that was a bad thing.

I wrap his coat tighter around me. "Your jacket smells like bonfire," I say. I imagine him at his parents' house, a moss-covered one-story homestead surrounded by fog and meadow, Zane stoking the fire for them, having chopped wood to leave them enough to keep the fire going while he's away here, on the tour. Although he doesn't really seem like the chopping-wood kind of guy. He's more of a sit-by-the-fire kind of guy. Maybe that's better.

"Does it?" He leans over. "It's actually Dad's."

His father gave him his coat to wear. Passing down of traditions—or at least, polyester. I feel swoony with excitement to wear the coat, even if it's not technically his coat, and is kind of scratchy.

A few feet away, Sindhi shouts and holds up a rock. "Found one!" she squeals, then throws her arms around Roshi. He hugs her. I feel happy for them. It feels symbolic—they have all this history, and she's found history, and found her way back to him.

"So you listened to that book, huh?" Zane says with interest. "How'd you even discover it?"

I exhale, because this is it, this is our real chance for him to see the importance of the book.

"The book was so important to my parents' story," I start, wondering if, by telling him the story, I'll reveal that he's the reason I'm on the trip. Will he think I'm weird? *Gigi, you can't worry about that right now.* This is my chance to tell him the story I've told a million people. I take my time and tell him about how my parents met as we walk slowly along the shore and toward the curve that marks the end of Lyme Regis and the start of Charmouth, the adjacent town. "To me, that book brought them together," I say at the end. "And they were together from that moment on—until they died." I hold my breath. I usually lose myself in the story, and others' reactions are merely accessories. But now, I wait to hear what he'll say.

"How sad that they died so young," he says. I'm puzzled. Of course it is, but he's focused on the wrong part of the story. And yet, I nod. "I would give anything to have more time with them, for sure."

He nods. "What happened?"

I wasn't planning to talk about their death, but now, I tell him that story, too.

"They were away, on vacation," I start. "They left me in charge of the store. I was twenty-two, just graduated from college. It was only for a few days. They drove up to Toronto, to visit some friends. Lars, my brother, he was supposed to help out at the shop, too, but he never showed up—he'd decided to go away with some friends for the weekend. I'd taken time off work—I was tutoring on the weekends and running an after-school reading club at the library. I'd sort of thought I might cobble together a business of my own." I know this is too much detail and that my part-time job has nothing to do with their death, and yet, it has everything to do with it, too. It's the part of the story I can never forget. Because if Lars had been there, if he'd been around to help out with the shop, I wouldn't have missed the call.

"Gigi?" Zane says softly, touching my shoulder. He's so kind. He's so *nice*. He *cares*. I refocus on the story, which, no matter how many times I've shared it, always feels raw, like peeling the top layer of skin off a sunburn, even after all these years.

"Anyway, my parents were out for dinner, and they were walking back from the restaurant to the hotel." I take a deep breath. "There was someone driving past. He lost control or fell asleep, they never really knew. He drove up on the sidewalk."

Zane pulls me toward him. His arms wrap around me. His hand presses the back of my head to him. The bonfire scent.

The sound of the sea. And Zane's sexy voice that reverberates in my core. "Oh, Gigi, I'm sorry."

.

My hotel room has a clawfoot tub by a window that looks out onto the moody sky. I take the opportunity for a long soak and a chat with Dory about my day.

"I have to say, I was skeptical," she says.

I laugh. "I know you were. You didn't hide it."

"But I was wrong—clearly. So he's just . . . great?"

"I think so," I say, brushing away the part where he can be a bit boring. Like the whole "it is what it is" thing, or when he was going on and on about road construction. But the fact that he was so kind when listening to my story about Mom and Dad makes up for all of it. He was there for me. He listened. He *cared*.

"He's either had a ton of experience with the ladies, or his parents taught him well for when he met *the one*," she observes.

"I'm choosing the latter." I take a sip of tea from the cup I've set by the side of the tub, lean back, and sink into the water, letting it rise up to my chest. "It really didn't seem like anyone has ever come on the tour because of his audiobook before. Like he is *not* capitalizing on that."

"No," Dory says, mock-shocked. I laugh. "And Taj—what's going on with that? Are things awkward with you two?"

At his name, my chest tightens. "Who knows?" I say dismissively. Taj had his chance to explain why he looked like he was going to kiss me, but then didn't, but he didn't finish whatever he was trying to say while we were foraging for flowers in South Downs, and hasn't tried again since, not that I've given him a lot of opportunity. So where that left off was him regretting Brighton and our drunken almost-kiss. "Who cares? It doesn't matter anymore—everything with Zane is so good. There hasn't been a thing that's rubbed me the wrong way, not once. Not like Taj, right from the get-go. And things are going better than I ever expected."

After we hang up, I take a long shower, and then, wrapped in a fluffy robe, I set up my makeup bag on the vanity. I've been re-reading an old Nora Roberts romance—*Sea Swept*, about a guy who returns home to Chesapeake Bay to care for his brother—which I turn on in my audiobook app and listen to as I straighten my hair until it's sleek and shiny. Then I sort through my suitcase, deciding on a pair of white jeans and a chiffon-like halter top that has sage leaves that match my eyes. After applying my makeup, I do a mirror check (I pass), grab a small bottle of wine from the mini-fridge and knock on Charlotte's door beside mine.

"Hi," I say, holding up the bottle as she opens the door, smiling in a pink silk robe. Her room has dark walls and a slanted roof, and wide windows looking out onto the water, a view similar to mine.

"I feel like we haven't had a chance to really chat today," I say, realizing how caught up in Zane I've been. "I miss you."

"Well, you were a bit distracted," she says, her eyes glinting. "Understandably so," she says. "And so was I."

She takes the bottle and two glasses from the top of her mini-fridge and, a moment later, hands me the glass. We sit by the window.

"So, how are things with Angus?" I say.

"What do you mean?" she says innocently, then titters. "Oh, I've never been good at lying. And why would I? Is it that obvious?"

I nod. "Takes one to know one," I tease.

"I'm just . . . that's not why I came on this tour. Romance, I mean. I was supposed to do this trip with my husband. And Harold—he was so good to me. How could I . . . ?" she trails off. "And yet, I've never met someone who makes me laugh the way Angus makes me laugh. Or maybe I have but they've annoyed me in countless other ways. But Angus . . ."

A knock at the door interrupts her. Charlotte raises her eyebrows, steps to the entrance, and opens the door, revealing Angus in a light-blue short-sleeve dress shirt and dark pants, his hat in hand, his tweed jacket draped over his arm.

"Angus," Charlotte says.

"Correct," Angus says. "Would've been a bit worried had you got that wrong." I wave and he grins. "Hope I'm not interrupting. Now that I'm not the official guide anymore," he says, "I'm free to do whatever I like for dinner, yah? And I've got a favorite place here in town, and I thought it would be nice to share that experience with someone." He cocks his head and smiles charmingly at her. "Correction: I'd like to share that experience with you."

Charlotte doesn't hesitate. "I would like nothing better than to have dinner with you." She holds up a finger. "I just need to put on my lips," she says. "I'll meet you downstairs in ten minutes."

She closes the door, and leans her back against it, then stamps her feet up and down like an excited schoolgirl. "You think he's asking me to dinner because he enjoys my company?" she asks me hopefully.

I laugh. "I think that's *exactly* why he's asking you out for dinner."

"Do you think I'm an awful widow?" She wrings her hands together.

I shake my head. "No. And I don't think you should think about what Harold would think. You and Harold had a life together. Don't you deserve to be happy now even though he's gone?"

She nods, hesitantly at first, but then more emphatically. "You're right, Gigi. You are right. How are you so smart?" She shakes her head as though trying to puzzle it out. "Now I better go put on my lips." She disappears into the bathroom.

.

The elevator opens at the top of the Rock Point Inn onto a canopied, open-air bar and restaurant that overlooks the channel. Tiny fairy lights dangle from the ceiling and votive candles illuminate each tabletop. Music pumps from the overhead speakers in each corner of the space.

Zane leans against the glossy bar. Just the sight of him makes the roots of my hair tingle as though I've put my hand on a Van de Graaff generator rather than the high-top table beside me. I touch the top of my hair to make sure it's not standing straight up. He's wearing a green Wilkenson Tours golf shirt with black jeans with black high-tops that look brand new. His hair is freshly styled, shiny with gel, and his five o'clock shadow has been erased. I muster all my confidence and give a breezy wave. Zane smiles then walks toward me. After our moment on the beach, things feel different. There's a real connection. He knows my history, I know his. What will tonight bring?

"You look lovely," he says, which I can't decipher. It feels both a bit *too* formal and exciting. He leans close. "I'm probably not supposed to say that," he whispers, and I want to lean even closer to him, to close the space, the days, the weeks I've waited for this moment. "We have a strict no-getting-intimate-with-guests policy that Dad implemented years ago."

I hope he's into rule-breaking, then, because not getting intimate's not in my game plan. "Then again, my dad was a guest on the tour and met my mom, so maybe I have a bit of leeway." He raises an eyebrow.

That's more like it. "Oh?" I say. There's no need to let Zane know I know all about *that* story, too.

"Would you like something?" he asks.

Besides you? I might need an intervention. "Sure," I say instead. "A sauvignon blanc would be great." When he walks away, I slip my hands in my back pockets. How am I supposed to hold a glass of wine when my hands are shaking and my mind is behaving as though I've already had seven glasses?

At that moment, Sindhi and Roshi walk in together, followed by Jenny, then Taj. His eyes meet mine and he holds my gaze as he walks toward me. He's dressed all in black, which makes him look toned and tan and—

Something touches my arm and I turn. Zane holds out the glass of wine.

"Thanks," I say. My fingers jitter as I take it from him, so I wrap my other hand around the bowl to steady it, hoping two hands are better than one.

"You'll warm your wine doing that," Zane says disapprovingly.

"Maybe I like it lukewarm." If it's between warm wine that makes it to my mouth or cold wine all over my shirt, I'll take the former.

"You're one of a kind, Gigi," Zane says.

The shakes get worse.

"Sorry to interrupt," Taj says, when he reaches us, his eyes on me. He breaks our gaze and turns to Zane. "Just wanted to let you know that the inn needs the parking lot cleared for construction, so I'm going to move the coach over to another lot. I'll bring it round the front in the morning at nine, though."

"Sounds good," Zane says. "You staying for dinner with us?"

Us.

Taj shakes his head. "Big Liverpool-Chelsea game tonight—heading over to the Malt to watch it on the big screen." Disappointment and relief face off inside me.

"'Course you are," Zane jokes.

"'Course you're not," Taj retorts before he walks back toward the elevator.

Violet and Nelle get off the elevator, and Taj catches the doors before they shut.

I turn back to Zane. "Not a sports fan?" *Neither am I.* I think of Kevan, watching sports during our date. Is Taj watching the game while on a date? Not that I care.

He shrugs. "Not really. More of a musical kind of guy. Live theater, that sort of thing. Culture." He puts a hand to his chest. "One of our tours goes through Cornwall, and we see a performance at the Minack Theatre. It's this centuries-old open-air theater, the stage and seats carved right into the clifftop. You're up on a slope, watching the actors down below. And in the background"—he spreads his arms wide, knocking my glass but I manage to catch it—"the cerulean sea." He sighs. "Nothing like it."

"Sounds amazing."

"It is. Ah, looks like our table is ready," Zane says, walking to the far end of the room, to the glass barricade close to the water. He turns back, motioning for me to catch up, and my heart leaps five paces ahead. I hurry to catch up. The sun is setting, a rainbow of colors reflecting off the waves. Colorful pashminas cover the backs of each chair. Zane pulls out a chair for me, then slides into the one next to it. Could this be any more perfect?

"You've got to get the fish 'n' chips," Zane says, leaning over, and I catch a strong whiff of musk and vetiver. It stings my eyes and I blink. "They catch the cod fresh every morning." The soft breeze sends any lingering cologne into the night air.

"Done," I say, closing my menu and taking a sip of my wine, realizing that my hands are steady. Calm, even.

"You won't be disappointed." He closes his menu and sips his beer.

"So which stop has been your favorite?" he asks.

Unbidden comes the image: the punting. The sun glistening on the clear water. Q. "Greensleeves" ringing through the air. And Taj. "Every town is my favorite," I lie. "'Til I get to the next one."

"I often feel the same way. It's what keeps me coming back, day after day, week after week, year after year."

The conversation just flows, and I'm not sure when I ordered another drink or our meals arrived, but before I know it, dinner's over and everyone's standing by the bar and making plans for the rest of the evening.

Roshi asks Sindhi if she'd like to play a game. She stares at him. "A game? We've never played a game in our lives."

He looks crestfallen. "We used to play games, when we were first dating."

"I don't remember that." Her brow furrows. "But I'll play a game anyway." He looks over at me and winks, and I give him a thumbs-up.

My phone pings and I pull it out. *Deets pls!* A text from the book club gals.

Zane leans in. "Would you like something else to drink?" I nod and get rid of my phone. Absolutely, positively, yes. "But not coffee," I add. He gives me a funny look, which makes sense because Zane and I don't have a coffee joke. Taj would say something quippy back, I think wistfully, then push the thought away.

"What'll you have—a gin and tonic?"

"Sure," I say, and he walks over to the bar.

Jenny asks Violet and Nelle to head off on a haunted ghost tour of the town, and Sindhi and Roshi move to another table to play backgammon. Francis stands. "Think I'll take a stroll."

"By yourself?" I ask.

"'Course," he says with a nod. I smile and he turns to walk away.

"Want to move to the lounge?" Zane holds two glasses. "I'm technically off-duty at ten, so I like to remove myself from the work environment." He unbuttons another button on his shirt and I laugh.

"What's so funny?" he says, and I stifle the next guffaw because I guess he didn't mean that gesture to be part of a joke.

"Oh, nothing." I wipe away a bead of sweat on my hairline.

"Great. It's dark and cozy down there." Dark? Cozy? Us, alone? Yes, yes, yes.

"Sure," I say breezily. I stand and take my glass, swiping at the condensation then sipping the cocktail on the way to the lounge, which is one floor down, accessed through a set of stairs behind the bar. The lounge is dark, with a row of leather-backed booths, a fireplace in the corner. I slide into a booth, and Zane slides in beside me. I finish the drink and order another when the waiter comes by a moment later. Zane orders a round of shots. I look at him in surprise.

"Not a shots kind of girl?" he says, and I feel challenged even though it doesn't seem like *he'd* be a shots kind of guy. But maybe shots are exactly what we need right now?

"Of course I do shots." Pretty sure I haven't had a shot since college.

"Great," he says, his eyes on mine. "Wow. You have the most beautiful eyes," he says, and I melt. For the first time ever I don't want Zane to say anything else. I want to live in this moment forever. No such luck. We're interrupted by the waitress delivering our shots. Zane clinks his glass to mine, and I throw back the drink, feeling like I'm swallowing needles, not tequila. Zane takes the glass from me, his fingertips grazing mine and clinks them together over his head, shouting to get the waitress's attention. He orders two more, and at some point those arrive and at some point I lose track of just how many shots we've done. We're laughing and singing and touching—accidentally, at first, a brush of shoulder here, a touch of knee there, and then intentionally, when he puts his arm around my shoulders.

"You're a very bad influence, Gee—" he slurs, not finishing my name. Or maybe he's giving me a nickname?

"Who, me?" I say.

"I'm not really supposed to drink on the job."

Not supposed to drink? He's not drinking, he's *drunking*.

"But you do such a good job of it," I tease. "We've almost drunk *all* the drinks." I messily point at the lineup of glasses of various sizes on our table, knocking a shot glass over in the process, and it rolls off the table, clanking on the floor.

"I'm not sure what came over me. Guess I just needed to let loose. And you're so fun," he says.

Me? Fun? I'm not *not* fun, but I wouldn't say I'm the most fun. Still, I'm not about to argue with him. I shimmy a little closer, so we're touching, and it feels like tiny little shocks all over my body. A bit like pin pricks. Is this what love feels like?

"I've been talking your ear off all night and you still seem interested."

I can't remember much of anything we've talked about. It's either the drinks or the fact I've been daydreaming while listening to his voice.

"I love listening to you talk," I say impulsively and he laughs.

"Well, I do like talking," he says with a grin. "Occupational hazard, I suppose. Would you like me to keep talking?" He picks up the small leather bar menu and starts reading: "Nibbles. Baker Tom's Rosemary & Sea Salt Focaccia. Chorizo Bites. Padron Peppers." He pauses and looks over at me. "Shall I go on?"

I'm laughing and nodding at the same time. "Yes, please, keep going."

"Small plates. Whipped Goat's Cheese and Beetroot Chips. Chicken Liver and Brandy Parfait . . ."

"OK, OK you can stop." I laugh.

"Can't stop me now. Maybe there's a need for menu narrators."

"I don't think that's a thing," I say, putting a hand on his arm to stop him. He puts his other hand on top of mine.

"So how many times, exactly, did you listen to my audiobook?" he asks. My face feels like I've just dunked it into a cup of steaming coffee. I should drink coffee, in fact, but instead, I take another sip of whatever it is I'm drinking now. Straight tequila?

"A lot," I admit.

"What's a lot?" he asks, his leg brushing mine.

"Like, ten times?" It's a tiny fraction of the truth.

"You really like my voice, don't you?" he whispers.

I take a sip of liquid courage, then add: "It's why I came on the trip."

"The book?" he says, though he must know what I mean. What else could we possibly be talking about?

"Your voice. You. I looked you up. I read all about you."

"Really." He puffs up. My entire body is on fire, and I hold my glass to my cheek. Honesty is the best policy, even if it's mortifying.

"So you must have been pretty upset that I wasn't here, that you had to listen to Angus talk instead of me," he says. "I'm surprised you didn't file a complaint." I can't tell if he's serious, but now is certainly not the time to get into Yelp review logistics.

"I was," I say. Zane nudges even closer. His lips are so close to my earlobe I'm sure they'll touch any minute. "Want me to say something else?"

I nod. "Yes," I say. Then change my mind. "Not really." Because I'd rather his lips be on mine.

"Something else," he says. And then: "Antarctica. Pickleberry. Log flume. Span of acreage. Muster point."

He's proving a point—it doesn't matter what he says; I'd still think it was beautiful.

As if reading my mind, he says, "I could say anything, couldn't I? And you'd like it?" His hand touches my chin, turning my face toward him.

I'm staring into his green eyes. I blink, to focus. Hours of listening to his voice, hours of sweeping the bookshop floor, closing up the shop together. All those nights in bed with his voice in my ears. Can we slow this moment down a notch? So I can remember it? And yet, I can't wait to get to the best part.

His fingertip traces my jaw. He closes the gap between us.

I can't resist. I lean in and our lips meet. His are parted, his breath hot. My pulse quickens. My hands move to his hips, my fingers loop through his belt hooks and I pull him closer as our tongues meet. And I wait for it to hit me. For all those feelings I've had for all these months to come together in this moment.

But there's nothing except overpowering vetiver.

I try harder. I'm working his tongue with the enthusiasm of a golden retriever with its first can of wet food. Saliva is everywhere. My jaw aches but I'm not giving up.

And yet.

Nothing. When we come up for air, I open my eyes and press back against the seat. Zane leans back, too. He lets out a low whistle, mimicking all the air being sucked out of me.

"Closing time," the bartender announces from the bar, his eyebrow raised.

Zane bumps my shoulder with his. "Do you want to . . . continue this downstairs?" he asks. I close my eyes. But instead of picturing Zane and me, our bodies intertwined, a flash of Mirabelle and Jack—or how I picture Mirabelle and Jack—floods my vision. Why are the main characters of *Their Finest Hour* stealing my steamy sex scene? I need to press Rewind and hear him ask me again.

Better yet, just say yes, Gigi, and then you won't have to imagine a steamy sex scene. You'll be *in* a steamy sex scene.

"Gigi?"

Zane's watching me with expectation in his eyes. What is *wrong* with me? Zane and I have just had the most unabashed makeout session. And now he's asking if I want to go back to his room? This is what I wanted. This is what I spent so many nights dreaming about. Except this wasn't anything like how I dreamed this night would play out.

"Gigi?" Zane says again. Now he's standing. He holds a hand out to me.

"I think we should take it slow," I say reluctantly. This is the sexual tension I live for in books, only here, right now, it feels sort of sloppy. I need to cut the scene short before I end up having sex I only sort-of remember.

His brow furrows.

"We still have five more days." Yes, this is the right thing to do. "See you tomorrow, Zane Wilkenson." I'm slurring my words, but at least I get them out.

"Tomorrow?" he says, his face fallen. I nod and stand, wobbling. I grab my purse and start toward the door. *Walk in a straight line, Gigi.* That's what I focus on. That's all I can focus on.

Chapter Twenty-Two

Day 6, Friday, 9 a.m.

Lyme Regis ❯ Glastonbury

Everything hurts. Not just my head, but my entire body. I stretch out on my bed, try to sit up, then fall back against the down-filled pillows, the ends flipping up to touch my ear. Just like Zane did last night.

I replay the whole moment in slow motion. He moved his lips from my ear, to my mouth. To the kiss, that warm kiss. That moment I'd been waiting for. What I'd always wanted to happen when I was listening to Zane's voice, before I could actually listen to Zane in real life. Now I have the real deal. So why do I feel so disappointed in the whole situation?

"It's the Christmas morning letdown," Dory said when I called late last night. She was getting ready for the rest of my friends to arrive at her place for book club, but they hadn't shown up yet, and I got her to myself for a few minutes. "It's a temporary feeling. I always tell myself that when the kids are being little shits about not having any more gifts to open. You give it a few hours, they have a nap, then they realize how fucking lucky they are, or at least how great their gifts are, and they're, like, This was the best

Christmas ever. Sorry, Benji just reminded me how many days until Christmas this morning so it's top of mind. But you know what I mean, right?"

"Yes," I mumbled into my pillow. "That's how I feel when I get to the end of a great book."

"Right, you get it. So the kiss was Christmas morning, and you're going to go to sleep and wake up and feel completely different about it all."

Then the rest of my friends arrived at Dory's, and she put me on speakerphone while I closed the cover and shelved my book of feelings and instead tried to play up just how *amazing* the past few hours with Zane had been. Emily and Cleo and Jacynthe didn't seem to have any idea that everything wasn't turning out exactly how I'd hoped. They swooned appropriately. To them, this was more than they could've hoped for me when they bought me the trip. To them, I got the Final Rose. The House Cup. The Oscar.

Now I roll out of bed. It was only three days ago I felt this awful, after my night on the Brighton beach with Taj, I think, then stop myself. Why am I thinking about Taj? This situation is completely different—except for the hangover: that part's the same. Right now, I'd give anything for a bottle of that orange drink. I scramble around the room, doing my best to look better than I feel, because it's good to have goals. I put on extra cream blush, to compensate for my pallid complexion.

Getting to the bus feels like I'm scaling Everest.

Taj takes one look at me and raises an eyebrow. "Late night?"

My face gets hot. Should've skipped the cream blush. Does he know about Zane and me? But how would he? And why do I care what he thinks?

He points at the coffee cup in my hand. "Have I taught you nothing, young Jedi?"

"You're just trying to take away my coffee," I mumble. "You're always trying to take away my coffee."

I hold it tight and shuffle to the back row.

"Wow, you look like a corpse," Jenny says, sliding into the seat beside me. "With a really mid makeup artist." She laughs and looks at her phone.

"Shush," I say, then take a sip of the coffee, but it feels like acid going down.

Zane's the last one to board the bus, and looks like someone sucked all the blood out of him while he was sleeping. He's gray, just like the Wilkenson Tours golf shirt he's wearing today. He looks around and musters a smile. My churning stomach settles for a moment.

Angus misinterprets Zane's appearance to mean that he got bad news about his mother, but he shakes his head. "No Mum's fine," he says. "Must be food poisoning." He slides into the first seat.

"Leafy vegetables are the most common culprit of vegetable poisoning," Francis says, noting that Zane's a vegetarian. If anyone suspects Zane is hungover, they don't say so. It's my secret.

Taj catches my eye in the rearview mirror, his expression thoughtful. Then he turns his head to look out his side window, starts up the bus and pulls away from the inn.

"Say goodbye to the coast," Angus says as the bus heads north on a two-lane road, thick green brush on one side, a low stone wall on the other. I lean my head against the window. The brush clears and I see a group of guys in soccer uniforms run back and forth across a pitch.

Charlotte passes me a peppermint puff from across the aisle and a note that says *I had the most wonderful night. I hope you did too?*

I fold the note up and look over at her. Her eyes are bright, her cheeks flushed.

I just smile, close my eyes and lean against the window. The cold glass feels good and slightly slows the spinning feeling.

•

Later that morning, Glastonbury Tor comes into view. It's a pyramidal hill carpeted in green sod, topped with a tall stone tower. In the hilly pastures around it are little white creampuffs of creatures. The sheep are completely oblivious to us, their heads hidden in the grass, their cloven hooves dirty with mud. The sun has disappeared behind layers of gray clouds, and the air is cool and damp, like it might rain any minute. Taj pulls up to a stone path, parks, and opens the doors. We amble off the bus and onto the sidewalk, and Zane turns to me. "How are you feeling?" I whisper.

"About as well as I look," he mumbles. "I'm not sure I can do this." Do what—talk to me? He turns to Angus. "Angus, do you mind if I sit this one out?" he asks.

"Zane, if I felt like you look, I'd sleep it off in the bus," Angus says jovially. Zane nods gratefully and seconds later the bus door folds shut behind him. I'm disappointed—this isn't how I wanted the morning to play out. I want us to be hangover-mellow together. I want to make sure he gets why I turned him down— that it's for the story, not anything to do with me not wanting him. But now that will all have to wait.

Angus turns his attention back to the group, digs his umbrella into the ground, and leads us along the path and away from the road.

We walk in silence for a few moments, me at the back of the group, when suddenly I hear the sound of approaching footsteps.

I turn around to see Taj. "You're coming?" I say, feeling confused. Zane's not coming. Taj is.

"Need to walk off that greasy food from last night," he says, rubbing his flat stomach. He jogs ahead of me. "You're about to see the best view in town," he says before shaking his hips in front of me, then turning and raising an eyebrow. I laugh even though it makes my head feel like it's being trampled by sheep. Is he flirting with me? I turn to make sure Zane is still safely on the bus.

We follow Angus through a gated area that leaves the gravel path behind, and feels like the real start of the climb up the massive hill to the tower, which sits atop a massive green expanse. Angus explains we're about to get one of the best views of the entire West Country. I exhale and try to focus on my surroundings instead of my feelings.

"Glastonbury is a city," Francis says. "It has an abbey. Cities have abbeys. Towns do not."

"The real question is, does anybody care?" Jenny rolls her eyes at Francis but she's smiling. "I'm kidding, Francis. Kind of."

"I guess my facts are a bit tiresome?" he says to no one in particular. I get a sinking feeling in the pit of my stomach.

"No, Francis, it's interesting," I say softly, reaching out to touch his arm.

"That's the thing about group tours," Sindhi says to Francis. Then looks around at all of us. "You're reminded that you're in a group. With very different personalities and temperaments. We'd all do well to think before speaking."

I hold my breath, praying no one's about to say anything to Sindhi about how she herself has been a bit difficult this whole trip, but she speaks up again before anyone else. "Should take my own advice."

Francis catches my eye, and we both laugh. I'm not the only one with complex feelings on this trip.

"Oh, love," Roshi says, but she looks away, her face reddening. Jenny groans loudly. "Alright, alright, let's not get all sappy now." She turns her attention back to Taj. "Taj, tell us about the Glastonbury music festival."

"It's a billion times better than any American festival," he says, catching my eye. Jenny looks offended. I stifle a laugh.

Yellowed grass turns to green as railway ties cut steps into the side of the hill. Angus digs the end of his umbrella into the dirt, Charlotte by his side. I stare out into the vast expanse of green and blue.

"How long does it take to get to the top of the hill?" Violet asks.

"Two hundred and twelve steps," Taj says without hesitation.

"It's actually three hundred and one, though I believe it technically depends from which side you're starting," Francis repeats into his recorder and then starts counting. "One. Two. Three."

"You can't count the whole way, Francis," Sindhi says.

"Why not?"

"Because it's annoying, and I want to have a pleasant conversation with my husband." She loops her arm through Roshi's. He looks surprised, then grins.

"How do you know how many steps it takes to get to the top of the hill?" Violet asks Taj. "Is there a sign?"

"He's counted, obviously," Roshi says. "You've counted, right Taj?"

"Nope," Taj says. "I made it up."

"Why would you do that?" Sindhi says with a frown.

"Who cares how many steps it takes and how long it'll take us? You have something better to be doing? It's the journey, not the destination that matters." Taj catches my eye. I laugh. I can't help it. He gives me a sexy smile, which makes me feel light-headed. Then he turns away.

"I thought the destination was the tower," Sindhi says.

"True," Taj says.

"Does someone die?" Jenny asks. "Fall from the top? Get pushed?"

"You'll have to find out, yah?" Angus says, then stops walking. "Actually, Taj, you mind taking this one? That bench looks like it could use a visitor." He points to an iron-and-wood bench poking out of the Queen Anne's lace a few feet away.

"You sure you're alright, mate?" Taj asks, backtracking toward Angus. We all stop walking. Taj puts a hand on Angus's tweed shoulder.

"I think two tours back to back is finally catching up with me." He adjusts his cap. "Just feeling a little fatigued. You're all in good hands with Taj," he declares to us, before stepping off the path, Charlotte following him.

"Y'all get that exercise for me and tell me all about it when we're back on the bus," Charlotte says, and flutters her fingers. I watch them walk away, then turn back to the path.

"Everyone ready?" Taj says, walking to the front of the group and motioning for us to follow. "So most people think the word 'tor' refers to the tower at the top." Taj walks sideways, stepping one foot over the other in a kind of grapevine fashion so that he can watch where he's going but also talk to us.

"That isn't the tor?" Nelle says. "But then where are we going?"

"The hill we're climbing is the tor." Taj spreads his arms. "It has seven levels of terraces, also known as lynchets. The tower at the top is St. Michael's, and it's hollowed out now, but it wasn't always that way." He gestures to the tower. "In fact, it was once a clock tower," he says, his voice low. I quicken my steps to move past Jenny and get closer to Taj, to hear the story. "Many hundreds of years ago, there was once a young chap who was trying to make a better life for himself. His parents abandoned him when he was young. He came to Glastonbury because he heard it was an enchanted town full of witchcraft and lore." Taj turns to us. "And it *is* an enchanted town. He found a job as the clock-tower keeper. From dawn until dusk, he had to ring the bell at the top of the hour. No exceptions. 'Miss it once,' the tower ogre told him, 'and you'll be banished from the town.'"

We've come to the second of the terrace walls. Taj pauses to let us catch our breath. Violet takes off her jacket and ties it around her waist.

"But how did he eat?" I ask Taj. Taj raises a finger.

"When the sun dipped below the horizon," Taj continues, "he was done for the night." His voice is quiet. "He was only required to ring the bell during *daylight* hours. So at nightfall he could venture into the town. And he did. For a bite to eat, a drink at the local pub, that sort of thing," he says. "But he was lonely and wished he would meet a woman." I imagine the clock-tower keeper sitting at the table alone, lonely. In my mind he looks like Taj. Then I imagine Taj on a date with a beautiful woman. Had Taj been on a date last night?

"Then, one day," Taj says, interrupting my thoughts, "he hears the pleasant call of a pheasant."

"A pheasant?" Francis says. "No, it couldn't be a pheasant. Pheasant calls are not pleasant."

Taj gives Francis a look, and clears his throat. "Then one day," he says, "he hears the unpleasant call of a pheasant."

"Are we listening to a Dr. Seuss story?" I joke. Taj gives me a mock-angry look, and I laugh again. He's just so easy to tease.

"He heard the voice of a bird. I forget what kind. It's not important."

"Of course it's important. A mourning dove would be a good choice," Francis says.

"Ooh, good one, Francis," Roshi says.

"Oh my god, let the dude get to the part where someone gets murdered," Jenny cries.

"He hears the call of a mourning dove," Taj says, holding his hands up to silence everyone. "He looks down and he sees a golden-haired young woman walking to the market with a basket of eggs. It's Wednesday morning—the market day. She sells eggs at one of the stands. So from that day forward, every Tuesday night, the clock-tower keeper could barely sleep, waiting for Wednesday morning when he would see this woman. And at 7:30 sharp, he'd watch her arrive to set up for the day. Then, by eleven, she would be gone."

We come to another step in the terrace. This time I offer my hand to Jenny and heave her up.

"How could the clock-tower keeper meet this fair lass?" Taj continues. "She was only ever around in the day, when he had to attend the bell. The only thing he could think of was to ring the bell on the hour and then immediately rush down the stairs. He'd have nearly sixty minutes before he had to be back up. He decides to catch her while she's setting up. There was a risk, of course.

He'd only seen this woman from afar. What if she was dreadful? Annoying? Had a really big nose?"

At the fourth terrace, Taj turns around to check that we haven't lost anyone. Satisfied, he turns and keeps walking.

"The clock-tower keeper knew he would have to be quick. Getting down to the market stalls would be no hurry at all. The return—that would be the issue. And so he started training. Jogging on the spot. Jumping jacks and squats. And most of all, he climbed the stairs in the tower. Every day he worked through his exercises. He grew lean. He grew hard."

Taj is walking slowly now, stretching out the story.

"Finally, the day came when the clock-tower keeper decided he was ready to make his move. The night before, he'd gone into the forest and picked a bouquet of wildflowers to give to the woman, keeping them in an old milk jar filled with water. The next morning, he woke up early, unable to sleep." I look up to the peak of the hill, trying to imagine the clock at the top of the tower. Taj continues, rubbing the back of his neck, his bicep flexing. "He ate a crust of bread, rang the seven o'clock bell, then made haste down the steps, bringing his flowers with him. But the stall where she always kept her egg cart was empty. Seven-thirty came and went, and she didn't arrive."

Taj turns back and takes my hand to help me up the fifth terrace. "The clock-tower keeper searched around, thinking maybe she'd set up somewhere else. People would need eggs," he continues. "Surely, she would still need to bring eggs. Had her chickens gone fallow? Had someone stolen the hens?"

"The things they concerned themselves with back then," Nelle whispers to me. I nod, but don't say anything, not wanting to interrupt the story.

"At ten minutes until eight, he knew he could wait no longer. He set off for the tower, running the same trail we're on right now. He reaped the benefits of his training, and he would have made it with time to spare—but when he was almost halfway up the tower steps, he missed a stair and tripped. He banged his chin. He saw the blood, and his right ankle seared with pain. He looked down and could tell that it was already swelling. But he had to get to the top of the stairs, or he'd lose the post."

"So he had to pull himself, even though he knew he didn't have enough time and that he wouldn't be able to ring the bell. He'd be fired and banished from the town." A flock of gulls squawk as they pass overhead, and Taj scales the sixth terrace before continuing. I hold my breath. Even the wind seems to have quietened. "And then, he heard it," Taj whispers. "At first, he couldn't believe his ears. But he heard it again. The clang of the bell in the clock tower." Taj leans down and strikes the stone path with the metal edge of his pocket knife. The ting makes us collectively gasp, and I'm reminded that Taj and I are not alone. "Twice, three times, four times." His voice increases in volume with each strike of metal on stone.

"He figured it must be the ogre, who'd somehow discovered what he was up to. The man considered turning around and fleeing." Taj pauses, and his eye meets mine. "But something told him not to run. To face his fear. So he kept going. At the stroke of eight he made it to the top." Taj first, then Jenny, then I crest the seventh and last terrace, so we're steps away from the tower. We're all out of breath—this hill is not for the out-of-shape or elderly. I look around. The view is 360 degrees, green expanse in every direction, Glastonbury tiny in the distance. Taj motions for the group to follow him to the tower, to stand under the arch. I'm so close to him that I can feel the heat from his body.

"He reached the top of the tower just as the bell stopped ringing."

"It was her," I whisper.

Taj's voice is low, just loud enough for the group to hear. "It was her," he says softly. "And she was standing right there." Taj points to the uppermost floor. "All those times, as he rang the bells, she'd been down below, looking up, wondering who he was. She'd climbed up the hill to meet him."

I feel light-headed. It's everything—Taj, this story, the view, the tower.

This moment.

"Wait. So she planned to climb up on the very same day that he decided to go down?" Roshi asks. Roshi and Sindhi are inches from Taj on one side, Violet and Nelle behind them. Jenny beside me, Francis leaning over her shoulder. But I block them out and turn back to Taj.

He nods, his eyes meeting mine even though Roshi asked the question. "The very same day. She figured if he had to ring the bell, he could never come down. So she decided to climb up."

"And saved him from losing his job," I whisper.

"And from being banished from the town," Taj says.

"So then what happened?" I ask, my voice barely above a whisper. His eyes are on mine. His chest is hard, his arms are strong. I'm lost in the story and all I can think about is how close we're standing. It doesn't make any sense, and yet, it makes perfect sense.

"Well. They stood right here, in this spot, and as the final chime echoed in the distance, they had their very first kiss."

We're all so quiet, you can hear us all breathing. Finally, Roshi breaks the silence. "You better watch it or you're going to get promoted to tour guide." He points a finger at Taj.

Not a chance," a familiar voice says. I turn and Zane stands under the arch. Color has returned to his face. So has a scowl. "Angus came back to the bus, and I figured I'd better get up here and do my job," he says. "Glad I did. Sorry to leave you all with the coach driver," he says, his eyes on Taj. "Why didn't you call and let me know?"

"Doesn't seem like the kind of experience to be making a phone call. Anyway, it was no big deal," Taj says, his voice even. "You said you weren't feeling up to it."

Zane walks closer to us, keeping his eyes on Taj. "Well, these people paid for a guide, and I don't want word getting back to Dad that they had two guides and neither of them performed their duties." He turns to us, looking stricken. "I really do apologize for this. Poor decision on my part." Does he mean staying on the bus, or the hangover? "I promise I'll make it up to everyone." I watch his lips, trying to muster up last night, but Taj's story is taking center stage. When I look over at him, though, he's nodding at something Sindhi is saying.

"Nothing to fret about." Roshi slaps Zane on the back. "Taj did a fantastic job. And we're all in this together, aren't we?" he says, defusing what feels like it's about to become a situation.

"Did Taj tell you all about the type of stones they used to build the tower?" Zane asks, hands on hips. He motions for us to follow him out of the tower, over to a patch of grass. When no one moves, he claps his hands together. Of course I want to hear him talk—who cares about the content? I walk out of the archway, but once everyone else is out, I turn back. Taj is under the arch, leaning against the stone.

"That was a good story," I say. The clouds have pushed to the west and the sky above is clear. "Was it true?" I ask as my hair whips across my face. His eyes are on mine, dark and intense.

He scratches the stubble on his chin, then grins. "Not a word."

My mouth hangs open. "It was so good."

"For someone who owns a bookshop full of made-up stories, you sound surprised." He runs a hand through his hair, his lips slightly turned up, his eyes still on mine. Beads of sweat dance above my upper lip.

"Gigi," Zane calls. He's standing a few feet away. "Come on, we're all waiting."

I look to Taj, but he's already headed back down the hill.

·

That afternoon, when we arrive at our hotel, the second floor of a two-story building over a stationery shop on High Street, Zane gives us the options for the next few hours of free time. Instead, I begin planning some time alone—maybe a shower, or a quiet walk.

"Gigi?" Startled, I realize that Zane has been calling my name. "I've got to take care of a few logistics for Bristol, but would you like to meet here before dinner? We could have a glass of Pimm's in the garden at the King Arthur. *A glass.*" He smiles. "Maybe attempt a do-over of last night? Get it right this time?" He whispers so close to me I'm sure I can feel his long lashes dancing on my cheek.

It's only after I've agreed to meet him at six—sharp—and then walked up the stairs to the hotel reception, that I realize I'm completely calm. No heart palpitations or clammy palms. That must be a good thing—isn't it?

I have every intention of checking in on the shop, then taking a long hot shower, and taking my time getting ready for my date, but after dropping my bag in my room—a quaint space with a cozy, shabby chic feel—I turn and head back down the stairs and out onto the street.

And I walk. I have no plan. The streets and shops and trees and clouds and other people pass me by, only slightly coming in and out of my consciousness, in the same way that my thoughts fade in and out, too. I've got a lovely afternoon to myself. Zane's asked me out for a drink. Everything has fallen into place. This is everything I've ever dreamed of.

And yet by the time I reach the edge of the town square a few minutes later, I realize I'm not thinking about Zane anymore. I try to redirect my thoughts to think of him, but it feels like too much effort. Instead, I let my mind wander. To Dory and Cleo, Dad, Mom, Lars, the shop, my life in general. What I love about it, what I want to change. Little things, big things. It doesn't feel scary, it feels exciting, calming, *new*.

Before I know it, the sun has set. The bells chime from the clocktower in the square, and I count them. Nine. I have missed dinner. I have missed Pimm's in the garden with Zane. I have missed what could have been the next chapter in the story.

And yet, I don't feel panic or disappointment or regret.

I feel free.

Chapter Twenty-Three

Day 7, Saturday, 12 p.m.

Bath

Bath is a town of two-story buildings made of parchment-paper-colored stone. The streets bustle with tourists and buskers, and the air smells like lavender as we step off the bus. Taj drives away and Zane leads us through the streets to a lush manicured lawn in the middle of the city, rattling off facts about everything from architecture to anthropology. I zone out, letting his voice fill my ears and my imagination run wild. Couples picnic on blankets, sipping wine and discussing the true nature of love . . . Because what else would you bother to talk about when you're in the very spot that spawned so many romances? A ways off, a row of Edwardian stone townhouses form a semicircle that I recognize instantly from the opening scene of the first season of *Bridgerton*.

I've read every Jane Austen novel so many times I can recite the lines, so when Zane turns to us and says, "'Who could ever be tired of Bath?'" I know instantly it's from *Northanger Abbey*, one of the two novels Austen set in Bath. But it's bittersweet, because while Zane's voice still gives me all the feels, I'm not sure where he and I stand. I ran into him on the way back to the hotel last night, with the rest of the group that was returning from dinner. I apologized for missing drinks, trying to find a balance between apologetic and breezy. I felt guilty for standing him up, but not regret for how my evening played out.

"Did you have a nice time in the town?" he asked, as way of response. When I'd nodded, he'd nodded, too. "Well that's all that really matters." He didn't sound annoyed or unfriendly, which almost made the whole situation worse. Then he went off to chat with someone in the lobby. And that was that. I went up to my room, and read until I couldn't keep my eyes open any longer, unsure how to feel.

Now, we make our way past the covered shops on the Pulteney Bridge. Angus shows us a spot where we can peek through a jeweler's shop window out to the water. Zane points out the Roman baths—and the wall where backpackers who don't want to pay the admission hoist themselves up for a glimpse. Where they want to be, rather than where they are. Ash and alder trees dapple the sunlight over the Gravel Walk behind the townhouses of Gay Street, the same path where Anne Elliot and Captain Wentworth shared an intimate moment in *Persuasion*. I close my eyes to be alone with Zane and his voice—and the rest of the group's chatter, of course. OK, so not alone at all. Zane seems exactly the same as he was last night, and the day that I met him, too: friendly, cordial, and perhaps a bit flat. Like, aside from our drunkfest, he only has one speed. He's steady. Dependable. Drama-free. That's a *good* thing, Gigi. And yet, it makes me feel out of sorts—and that unsettles me even further because even though he's the reason I came to England, I don't *want* him to be the focus of why I came to England. There's so much more here for me now, that putting all my focus on him doesn't feel right. And yet . . .

Be cool, Gigi.

As Zane points out the tower of Bath Abbey, and Jenny asks Violet if she's going to ask how many steps to the top, I think back to yesterday, to Taj's tale as we made our way up the hill to St. Michael's Tower. It was just a story—a fake story at that. Now, Zane's honeyed voice issues facts—there are 212 steps to the top of the Bath Abbey tower—and trivia with the earnestness of a math teacher.

He leads us into the courtyard of the majestic Bath Abbey. Zane describes the sculpture on the front tower that shows angels climbing Jacob's ladder to heaven and tells us that Bath Abbey has existed here in some form since the seventh century. I close my eyes. Not because what he's saying is boring, but because I know the connection will feel stronger, as though I'm lying in bed back home, listening to him. And I'm right. It feels right. But a second later Francis's own gruff voice interjects. "The Abbey is the last great medieval cathedral built in England," he says. He turns on his recorder and starts talking to himself. The moment, with Zane's voice, is gone.

The group moves toward the cathedral entrance, and my palms begin to sweat and my ears ring. I stop walking, as though the honey that coats his voice has spilled on the cobblestone, creating a sticky mess that secures me in place. I try to focus on Zane's voice, but even that doesn't help. I watch everyone else go through the door, but I'm stuck. "Coming, Gigi?" Zane calls from the doorway. "You definitely don't want to miss the Abbey."

"Zane," Taj says suddenly from behind me, and Zane and I both turn around. Where did he come from? He stands a few feet away, beside a sandwich board advertising *Bridgerton* tours.

"I've got an issue at the hotel, they need one of the guests to come back with a key card to be able to look into it." He shrugs. Then he turns to me. "Gigi, do you mind? Since everyone else is already up ahead?"

"Gigi won't want to miss the Abbey, right Gigi?" Zane says.

Gigi will very much want to miss this. "I'll go," I say. "I really don't mind." I turn toward Taj with relief.

"Are you sure?" Zane asks, but I'm already walking toward Taj. I give an emphatic nod and wave, then follow Taj, who's turned and is taking long strides in the opposite direction, away from the entrance to the cathedral.

Once we're around the corner, passing the entrance to the Roman baths on one side, the fluorescent lights of Primark a stark contrast across the street, Taj says, "The church thing, huh?"

My stomach tightens. "So there's no hotel emergency?" I turn to look at him and he raises an eyebrow.

"It felt like you needed an escape plan," he says simply. The Abbey Churchyard is bustling. "I'm gonna grab a coffee and sit and listen to that band." He points to a trio of guys in fluorescent plastic top hats. "If I go for more than a week without hearing someone play Spice Girls on a harmonica, I start to get the shakes."

I laugh. Oh, the relief of this escape.

"Coffee?"

"Please. With milk."

Taj ducks under a black awning and a moment later returns, handing me a cup before we head back down Stall Street, past a window filled with books. He catches my eye. "Go on," he says, "I know you can't resist."

I shake my head. "Can't bring the coffee in. I want the coffee."

"And I want to show you that not all the buskers in town play terrible nineties covers."

"Is that a criticism of the Spice Girls? Don't you get, like, put in jail for that over here?"

"I didn't say the Spice Girls are terrible. I said those dudes' rendition of Spice Girls is. And yet, strangely fascinating." Taj puts his arm out to stop me from walking as a cyclist zips past. Another step and he would've taken out my kneecaps. "Ooh," I say. "Thanks."

Purple and gold marigolds in hanging baskets decorate our path. In the distance I hear a saxophone playing. The sound gets louder with each step we take until we are standing before a bearded busker in front of an empty shop. Taj points to a row of wide steps a few feet from the musician. "Front-row seating."

The busker raises his sax into the air, then lowers it down again, the pitch fluctuating between sharp and soft. We take a seat on the steps and sip our coffee.

"Better than another spire?" he says, nudging me.

"Yeah. Churches aren't my thing."

"You don't say," he says sarcastically. "You know the company offers other tours of England—ones without churches, right?"

"But are there bookstores?" I joke, and he gives me a half smile.

"Avoiding the question with humor."

I'm not about to tell him I'm on this tour for Zane, so I give him the abridged version. "My friends booked the trip, remember?" I take another sip of coffee. "I knew there'd be churches, but I just thought it would be easier to avoid them."

"Well, you have a spotless track record, don't you?"

"Surprisingly, yes. When I put my mind to something . . ." I trail off.

Taj bumps my shoulder lightly. "If you want to talk about it, I'm a good listener."

I hold my breath, then exhale. "I haven't been in a church since my parents' funeral." What does it mean that I'm bringing up my parents' death for the second time in two days, and to Taj? He's a near-stranger. Except, he doesn't feel like a near-stranger. The song ends and claps from the impromptu audience echo throughout the makeshift amphitheater the audience has created.

"What happened to them?"

I tell the story. Taj puts his coffee cup down, leaning forward, his head in his hands while he listens. When I finish, he looks at me. "Weren't you so broken?" he asks in shock. "Did you just want to turn off the lights and make the world go the fuck away?"

"Yeah, pretty much." I fiddle with the lid on my cup. "I kept thinking, maybe if I hadn't gone to the funeral I wouldn't have had to say goodbye." I shake my head. "Because they died in an accident while they were away, I never saw them sick, or injured. One day I had parents, the next, I was an orphan. It was all so sudden, and we went straight to the church. Visitation. Funeral. And me sitting there zombie-like, pushing back any recognition that I would never again receive a hug from either parent. It makes no sense."

"It makes more sense than you think," he says, his voice low.

"But I didn't lock myself away. As much as I wanted to. I worried that if I did that, I might never be fine again. So I just figured it out," I said with a shrug. "My brother was at college, and I couldn't let the store just sit there. It was them—keeping that store open was keeping Mom and Dad's spirit alive." I put my empty cup down on the ground. "That isn't really what you asked, I guess. You asked about the churches. And I know I should separate churches in general from *that* church—these churches over here, they're hundreds of years older, they're beautiful works of art. But I just can't."

Taj rubs his hands together slowly. Then he turns to me. "Yeah, but you haven't missed everything. Just because a bunch of churches were on the plan doesn't mean it has to be *your* plan. Besides, how would you have squeezed in all those bookshops if you'd been stuck in those old churches?" A smile spreads across his face, then he slaps his knee. "They'll be done at the Abbey shortly, and while I don't necessarily think you need to do everything that every other person on the tour does, people come from all over the world to see the Roman baths. For what it's worth, I think they're worth seeing." He stands then holds out a hand. It's rough yet strong, and pulls me to my feet easily. And I don't want to let go, but I do. Maybe it's that I have zero expectations of Taj, but it feels so easy being around him. "You know what else is worth going to," he says, then points to a more modern building, gray slate, lots of glass. "The thermal baths on the top of that building. It's not on the tour—too much liability with heart problems, that sort of thing. But when it's a beautiful day like it is today? Nothing beats the view." His eyes meet mine. He doesn't look away. Neither do I.

Is that an invitation?

"Perfect timing," says a very familiar voice, and I turn. Zane is leading the tour toward us. I turn back to Taj, but he's already backing away.

"You're not coming?" I ask him. He shakes his head. *Why not?* Maybe it's that he just comforted me or I'm feeling vulnerable, but I don't want him to leave.

"I'm just the bus driver," Taj says. "I don't do the tour stuff, remember?" The corner of his lip twitches.

I nod. "Thanks for this," I say, holding up the coffee cup, though I mean more than the coffee. I wonder if he knows, but then he holds my gaze, which tells me that he does. Then he turns away.

"Come on, Gigi," Zane says. He leads us back along the cobblestone for a few minutes toward the grand entrance to the Roman baths. Inside, the marble floors are shiny, the air damp. We head down a narrow passageway and out into the courtyard to a large pool that's surrounded by the centuries-old pillars. "The hot mineral water rose through the limestone beneath the city," Zane explains. Even in that single sentence he manages twists and turns to rival a sax solo. I crossed an ocean to hear it in person. So why is there a part of me that just wants to go back outside and sit down on the steps of a courtyard, sip a coffee and listen to someone play music?

With Taj.

"The baths were a huge draw," Zane says. "People came from all over the country to be here. For many, it was their dream come true."

He keeps walking and talking, but I don't register anything else he's saying. Until I hear my name. When I refocus, he's staring at me. "Gigi? You're always daydreaming."

"Sorry," I say, embarrassed, then recover. "I think I forgot something outside."

.

It's almost sunset when I join the line that snakes around the modern building for the thermal baths you can actually soak in. I pull out *The Unlikely Pilgrimage of Harold Fry*. I've read it before, but I brought it on the trip because it felt thematic, Harold's trek through England. I flip to the scene in Bath and read the passage, which is less about the description of the town, and more about his mental state. He'd been walking for weeks at that point, but in Bath he realizes that in some ways, his journey has just begun. The words blur as my mind wanders, considering my own trip, and how different it's been from anything I could've ever expected. The line inches forward, and I make it inside the glass doors and up the shiny steep steps to the second floor. In the changerooms, I slip into my black bikini, then wrap my towel around me and bring my book with me. Steam rises from the water, the twinkle of the lights on the limestone buildings below dotting the dark sky. I pause, and look around the pool. But of course Taj isn't here. And I tell myself that's not why I came anyway.

I dip my toe into the steaming water. It feels heavenly. I slide into a spot in the far corner of the pool, taking care to keep my pages dry. My back against the smooth, small tiles, I lean back and look up at the sky. The sun is low. I can't imagine that it's always this way—but Taj is right. Nothing beats this view.

Eventually, I open my book again.

"You're supposed to be looking at the view," a voice says and I look up, knowing instantly it's him. Taj stands before me, the water to his waist, exposing his very toned, very bare chest. I almost drop my book. Oh, who cares about the book?

"I saw it," I say. "Really." I can't feel the water on my skin, as though it's turned to air and I'm floating in place.

"Oh yeah?" he says. "Then tell me what color the sky is." I snap my book closed and put it on the edge, then slink down under the surface of the water. I'm suddenly self-conscious in my bikini. It's not skimpy, but it's still the most amount of skin I've shown to Taj. "Blue," I say confidently, then smile and feel comfortable.

He sits beside me. "Not even close."

I look up at the sky. It looks like it's been painted with watercolors. "Oh, wow," I say. The sun is close to the horizon.

"Golden hour," he says. He shakes his head. "Oh my god, would you listen to me? What a fucking cliché. Everyone knows it's the golden hour."

"Doesn't make it any less beautiful."

"In . . . medicine," he starts, looking out into the distance, "there's a golden hour. It's the first hour, or hours, after a really traumatic injury—an accident, a cardiac arrest. It's this critical period that determines whether the emergency treatment will be successful or not. Everything sort of slows down, like suspended animation, if that makes sense."

I pause for a moment before speaking. "How do you . . . how do you know that?"

His face clouds. "Dad's a doctor."

"And they didn't pressure you to follow in his footsteps?"

Taj cups his hands together, then splashes water on his face.

"Sure, they had a whole plan, of course—coming here from Turkey, wanting the best for my sister and me. But I need to figure out my life myself, you know?"

"Mm," I say. "But you said driving the bus is only temporary so . . . what's next? Whittler?" I tease, remembering the way he was carving the stick in the forest.

"Exactly," he jokes. "Did you see how pointy I made that stick? That's raw talent." His mouth twitches. "I've always loved the feel of wood in my hands. Making it smooth, watching it come together. But alas . . ."

"Alas . . . ?"

"Not exactly the plan for me. I'll get back to things. Just need the break, much to my parents' disappointment."

"If it's just a break, driving the bus, what's the big deal?" I say, realizing that he's avoiding answering my real question about what it is he *was* doing before he started driving the bus.

"My father doesn't believe in breaks. He's not speaking to me."

"What about your mom?" I say.

"My mum sees me when Dad's not around. I don't love that—I don't love that she's lying to him, keeping me a secret. I wish she'd stand up to him, I wish she'd be honest with him. That's not how I want my relationships to be." He's frustrated.

"But you saw her in Rochester, right?"

He nods. "I gave her that book you bought in Cambridge. The cozy mystery. She liked that."

"I thought that book was for a girl," I say, hoping it will lighten the mood. But my face flushes, giving me away.

"You were thinking about what I was doing with that book?" he says, his voice low. He turns his body toward mine, ever so slightly, his knee touching mine. It feels intentional. I press my knee closer to his. The water might be warm, but his touch heats my body to the boiling point. Which helps to mask the sweat seeping out of my pores.

"Maybe," I admit.

His face is inches from mine. His breath is hot.

"Why didn't you kiss me in Brighton?" I challenge him boldly.

"Guess I didn't want the risk," he says. My heart sinks. "Getting hurt stinks."

"Sure," I agree. "Except, isn't living a life where you don't let yourself ever get hurt—isn't that even worse?" I realize that this moment right now isn't just a single moment; it's a culmination of all the moments we've spent together. I may not have envisioned any of this before meeting Taj, but now I don't want to be anywhere else than right here with him.

"Good point," he says. His dark eyes glint and his lip curls.

"You know," I whisper, my lips inches from his. "Carpenters in romance novels are always good kissers."

"And what about in real life?" Taj moves one hand to my waist and pulls me toward him. Now there's no space between us. He puts his other hand on the side of my face, wet and warm on my cheek.

"This is what I wanted to do in Brighton," he whispers.

And then his lips are on mine, and mine on his, and this is not some sort of hesitant, should-we-do-this? kiss. We're both hungry for each other, kissing like we never want it to end. He runs his fingers through the hair at the back of my neck, then pulls me in even closer to him, my back arching as I lean into him.

"Excuse me," says a small voice. My eyes open, I turn, and a child in a bright-green life vest, eyes in goggles, gestures to the other side of the pool, which we're preventing him from getting to. "I'm trying to swim across the pool."

I look at Taj and we both burst out laughing.

"Let's get out of here," he says.

I pull his head down to mine, twisting it to whisper in his ear. "Are people staring?" He tilts his head to mine and whispers back: "I don't care." Then his lips are on mine again. Our bodies pressed close.

"Yes," I say when we've finally broken apart, "I think we should go."

My legs are like jelly, and it takes all my focus to walk like a normal person into the changeroom.

I somehow manage to strip off my wet suit despite my jittery hands and pull on my clothes, then run a hand through my wet hair, only quickly glancing in the mirror at my reflection because there's not much I can do about it anyway. Down the steps, and back out the front door to the street, I look around and see him. Taj is across the pedestrian road, in the shadows of a stone wall, one foot up. I inhale, wanting to savor every second of walking toward him. When I'm inches away, he reaches out for my hand, interlacing my fingers in his, and pulling me into the shadows of the streetlamp. He moves a strand of wet hair from my face, then grabs my hand and holds it. Our fingers interlaced, my chest presses against him. Then he kisses my earlobe, and my neck, his hot breath warming me in the cool night. I tilt my face toward his, running a finger down to his jaw until I get to his chin. He opens his mouth, and nips at my fingertip. I can feel my heartbeat in that finger. I pull it out and then lean in, biting his bottom lip. He lets out a low growl, and bites my lip back, and then wraps his arms around me, and presses his lips to mine. My breath quickens as he moves even closer to me and I feel how hard he is against my stomach.

Then he slips an arm around me, and we take only a few steps before he bends to kiss my ear, then a few more steps, and his hand grazes the top of my jeans. A few more steps, I lace my fingers in his. A few more steps, and his lips are on mine again. Like this, slowly, we make it back to the hotel. The dark lobby is empty, the chandelier lights low.

"I share a room with Angus," he reminds me.

"I don't share with anyone."

He runs a finger down my arm. "Is that an invitation?" he says. I nod.

"Definitely. Room 205," I tell him, then hold up a finger. "Wait—I think." I pull my key card out of my pocket to check the envelope it's in, then nod. "Yep. 205."

"I'll meet you there in five," he says as we pass the bar. "I just want to go dump this"—he holds up his bag—"off in my room and powder my nose." He nuzzles my ear. "I'll be quick." He doesn't seem to care what anyone thinks, if they're looking at us. I let go of his touch, then turn. Out of the corner of my eye, I catch sight of Zane in the bar to the right. He's sitting alone, sipping from a low ball glass, but I turn before there's a chance to make eye contact and head up the stairs, feeling like I'm still floating in the pool.

I race around my room, whipping off my clothes, then pulling a brush through my wet hair, finding my best matching underwear set, coral lace, my fingers trembling with nervous excitement. I pull on a long silky turquoise sundress over my head and brush my hair, then blow-dry it on low so I won't miss Taj's knock on the door.

When it's been five minutes, I turn off the hairdryer, just in case.

I haul my suitcase over to the closet and give it a kick to get it in.

Five more minutes pass.

I connect my phone to the Bluetooth speaker.

Ten more minutes pass. I check my phone, but it's not as though Taj has my number.

Fifteen minutes pass and I open my book, but the words look like they're in Spanish or Italian or German.

Twenty minutes: I text Dory for her take. *Maybe he forgot which room you're in. Message him on the XO app?*

Twenty-five minutes: I open the app. Close it. Open it again. Send him a message. *Hey. In 205. Pretty sure whoever's in 502 isn't wearing coral lace right now.*

Thirty: Wish I could delete that message.

The mattress engulfs me as I flop back down on the bed and stare up at the ceiling, trying to figure out what went wrong.

Chapter Twenty-Four

Day 8, Sunday, 8 a.m.

Bath

The next morning I'm still wearing the sundress and lacy under-wear, and the evening replays in my head. My stream of consciousness amounts to many different variations of *WTF*? Did Taj fall asleep? What sober person falls asleep in that situation? Didn't he say five minutes? Did I misunderstand? I'm hurt and disappointed and confused and embarrassed that maybe I said or did something that made him rethink his actions—and I can't decide which emotion I'm going to let take precedence. Everything seemed so good, everything felt so right. I know I didn't read the signs wrong. And screw those emotions. I'm angry. And in pain from where the zipper of my dress dug into my side while I was sleeping.

I fumble around in the room for two matching shoes, pull them on then head down the slate stairs, into the modern lobby bar, with its tall glass windows and low-back chairs.

The air smells like bacon and butter. Francis and Roshi are sitting together, a chessboard between them. They study the board and take small sips from their mugs.

Coffee. I need coffee. And a plan. And a GPS for Taj. Is he at the bus? Should I look for him outside? What if I go outside and he comes down the stairs?

"Hi, Gigi," Roshi says as I take a seat at the table beside him.

"How's the match going?" I ask to fill the air.

"Very well for Francis." Roshi smiles, as Francis takes his knight.

Charlotte and Angus walk into the lobby bar. They're holding hands. I watch as Angus looks around, then points to a chair a few feet to the left of Charlotte, near the bar, and says something to her. Her face immediately pales and she leads him to the chair. Angus sets a hand on the chairback and then, instead of sitting down, he crumples to the floor.

Charlotte screams. "Gigi! Roshi!"

I run to them and drop to my knees next to Angus, who's in an awkward, half-seated, half-lying-down heap. Tiny beads of sweat cover his face. He stares at the back of the chair before him. "Somehow missed that," he says, and tips slowly to the floor.

I spin around. "Help! Someone call 911." Is there 911 in England? Will anyone know what I mean? Angus's skin is gray like the carpet. His teeth begin to chatter.

And out of nowhere, Taj materializes next to me, kneels beside Angus, and presses two fingers to his neck.

"Everyone take two big steps back!" he shouts. "Now!" He looks around, points at a woman in a white top and black slacks behind the bar. "Call 999. When you get them on the phone bring it here and put it on speakerphone."

I leap up and shuffle back, pulling Charlotte with me. Jenny and Francis and Roshi stand behind us. Roshi puts a hand on my shoulder. "What happened?"

"I'm not sure," I whisper.

"Angus, can you hear me?" Taj says. He rolls Angus on to his right side.

Angus moans.

"Is it his heart?" Charlotte says.

Taj pulls something out of his back pocket. We all watch as he unfolds his penknife and begins slicing through Angus's jacket. "Sorry, mate," he says. "Gotta be done." He makes a cut straight down the back, then the shoulder seam. He pulls at the pieces until he's down to Angus's collared shirt, and begins slicing some more. Charlotte gasps.

Angus's arms and chest are gray, too, just like his face. There's a bandage on Angus's left arm, and the area around it is red and swollen.

"What's this? When did this happen?" Taj looks at Charlotte.

Charlotte looks stricken. "In Cambridge, the first day. He caught it on a fence post, remember?"

"Fuck," Taj says. He tugs at the edge of the bandage. It resists. He places another hand on Angus's arm and tugs. This time the bandage comes off, revealing the skin underneath. It looks like raw steak.

The bartender leans over Taj, a cordless phone extended. "I have a Caucasian male, 74," Taj barks into the phone. "Diaphoretic. Heart rate elevated. He's presenting as myocardial infarction but could be sepsis. Wound on upper arm is red, inflamed."

Diaphoretic? What does that mean? And how does Taj know the term? Charlotte and I exchange a worried glance.

The next few minutes feel like they're happening in warp speed. Taj looks at the bartender. "What's the address of the hotel?" And seconds later he's saying it into the phone. He turns his attention back to Angus, whose eyes are now closed. Is that a good sign or a bad sign?

None of us have moved an inch.

"Help is coming soon," Taj says to him before looking up and registering for the first time that the others from the tour are in the bar. He nods at me and his gaze slides to Charlotte. "Do you want to hold Angus's hand?" Charlotte steps forward, crouches down to Taj and takes Angus's palm. She looks at Taj. "He's so hot," she says.

Please let him be OK. I cross my fingers.

Sirens blare and a moment later a man and woman, both dressed in navy uniforms, appear at the door, pushing a stretcher. They hurry into the room, place the stretcher on the ground. Within a minute or two, Angus is on the stretcher and the paramedics are rolling it back out through the doors to the lobby. They disappear around the corner, Taj following close behind.

Charlotte takes my arm. "What are we going to do?" she asks. "Is Angus going to be OK?" She looks terrified.

I wrap my arms around her. I don't know. I don't want to lie. So I just hug her tight.

·

The lobby bar is quiet, the only sound coming from the whoosh of the tap as the bartender rinses a glass, wipes it dry, then slides it into the rack overhead. Two tables have been pushed together, and we're all sitting around them. All of us except Taj and Angus, and Zane, who took a taxi to the Royal United Hospital when he heard the news.

"I feel like we've lost a collective limb," Sindhi says.

"Our funny bone," Roshi says. Charlotte lets out a whimper. I put my hand on hers.

The door to the back room swings back and forth as the bartender emerges, carrying two big platters. "In times of distress I find it's best to just eat," he announces.

He places the plates of food on the table before us. Eggs, toast, thick sausages sliced on an angle, beans, oranges. We all stare at it. No one touches it.

"What are we going to do without Angus?" Nelle asks. "What if he's not better by tomorrow? Or the day after? Or the day after that?" She wipes her eyes, and Violet puts her arm around her.

"The tour will go on," Violet says. "I'm sure they have support staff."

"I feel like the tour is the least of our worries," Jenny says.

"I don't want to leave Angus behind," Charlotte says.

"He's going to be OK," I say, but it's more to convince myself.

"I think he had a heart attack," Charlotte whimpers.

I wrap my arms around her. "Lots of people have heart attacks and they're fine afterward."

"It might not have been. Could've been heart failure. Or an arrythmia. Or a stroke," Jenny says. All heads swivel toward her. She throws her hands up. "What? There's a lot of medical jargon in murder cases. I pay attention."

"Eighty-five percent of patients with heart failure live for at least another five years," Francis says. And I think: That's fifteen percent that don't.

"I think we should go," I say.

"Go where?" Roshi asks. "To see him?"

A moment later Francis looks up from his iPad. "It's 1.5 miles to the hospital," he says.

"Do you think they'll let us in?" Sindhi asks.

"I'm not sure, but it's better than sitting around here, wondering what's going on." I turn to Charlotte and reach for her hand. It's cold. "Do you want to go?"

She nods, then stands. "Let's go."

"Yes." Nelle agrees. "Let's go to the hospital. Gigi's right. We can't just sit here doing nothing. Let's be with Angus."

"But what if they don't let us see him?" Sindhi says. "If he's in an intensive care unit, they won't allow anyone in, especially not a bunch of strangers."

"We're not strangers, we're his *friends*," Charlotte says, her voice cracking.

"Let's do it," Violet says, nodding, standing with Nelle.

Suddenly our listless group comes alive with purpose. I ask the concierge to call us two taxis, but after twenty minutes, when neither has arrived, I turn to Francis. "How long does it take to walk a mile and a half?"

"Thirty-five minutes at a steady pace, provided it's flat terrain," he says without hesitation. I turn to the others. "Let's walk?" Miraculously, no one protests.

A few blocks on, it starts to rain. Not the usual English mist you see in movies (which we really haven't experienced anyway) but huge drops that feel like pennies falling from the sky. Our pace quickens.

"We can do this," I say, and Charlotte grabs my hand, ducking her head as we walk faster. Charlotte swipes at her bangs, which are matted to her forehead thanks to the rain.

"Thank you," she whispers.

The route to the hospital is straight through the middle of town, over cobblestone we've treaded numerous times, past the Roman baths and the Abbey and all the famous sites. The town is quiet, the streets mostly vacant.

"We haven't had much rain the entire trip," Charlotte remarks, looking up at the sky.

Francis doesn't share a stat. Instead, he asks, "Where are we going again?" Which makes me wonder if I've led us in the wrong direction, but I pull out my phone just to be sure, cupping a hand over the screen to keep it from getting wet. "We're going the right way," I say.

"Oh, good, good," Francis says.

A car passes on our left, splashing through a puddle and sending a wave into the air. We all scatter to stay out of its way.

"Are you alright?" Roshi says to Sindhi, concerned. She reaches out for his hand.

"Once you're soaked to the skin, you can't get *more* soaked," she laughs, washing away tension.

We cut through the park to head north, passing the limestone façade of a grand hotel, a fountain sending water into the already-wet air. The colors in the botanical gardens look even more vibrant against the gray of the sky. I focus on the steady beat of the raindrops, not letting my mind think about what terrible things might be happening with Angus at this very minute.

At some point the buildings transition from quarried stone to more concrete and glass. A row of willow trees leads to a set of office buildings, clean white brick with dark windows. No people. Only a smattering of cars in the lot.

"Here we are," Charlotte says.

"I didn't actually think we'd make it," Jenny says.

"It took exactly as long as it was supposed to," Francis confirms. "Thirty-five minutes."

We march up the path, which leads us behind the trees up to a set of sliding doors, Francis and Jenny and Nelle to my right, Violet and Sindhi and Roshi to my left. Charlotte's still holding my hand. No one's making the first move even though surely every one of us wants to get out of the rain. We walked here in denial, prolonging the inevitable, but now we can't pretend that everything's going to be OK. We'll have only the facts to face. I squeeze Charlotte's hand. "Let's go."

The glass doors slide open. I'm expecting a whirr of activity but inside feels like the set of a zombie movie. A TV crackles from its perch near the ceiling, and the only other person in view is a nurse behind the plexiglass. The halls are empty. I wonder where Taj is—is he in the room with Angus, or another waiting room with Zane? A Black woman sits at the nursing station, typing on a computer. She looks up.

"We're here to see Angus McAllister."

The keys clack.

She looks up and nods. "He's here. But I don't have any news." Her tone is capable and reassuring, like a worn wool blanket that's softened with time. "You can wait over there." She points to our right, to an area of blue vinyl chairs, all empty. Where's Taj? Where's Zane? "I'll let you know when I have an update."

Each of us chooses a chair, like the music has stopped and none of us wants to be removed from the children's game. Violet says she'd rather pace the halls.

"I'm worried for Charlotte," Francis says. "Angus is her lobster." He catches my eye and shrugs. "It's a *Friends* reference."

"I got it," I say.

"My what?" Charlotte says.

"You two are so perfect for each other," Violet says, coming back into the room.

"There's no such thing as 'perfect for each other,'" Sindhi says. Then she seems to reconsider: "But I agree, they are very compatible." Roshi pats her hand.

Jenny finds a remote for the TV and flicks through the channels.

"I wish I had my knitting," Charlotte says to me. "Something to distract me." I nod sympathetically, then look in my purse. I don't even have a book to offer her.

Roshi pulls his crossword puzzle book out from under his coat. Somehow it's stayed dry. He flips it open and reads out a clue: "*Mr. Mom* actress. Second letter is A." For a moment no one answers.

"Garr," Violet says.

When I wake up, the sun is streaming through the window, drying the raindrops on the panes of glass. Things are otherwise pretty much the same as they were before I fell asleep. Jenny watches TV. Roshi, Nelle and Sindhi play cards in the corner of the room. Francis is flipping through a magazine.

"How are you doing?" I ask Charlotte, who's staring out the window.

"I wish I had my knitting," she says again. I think about going back to the bus to get it for her, but if we get any news, I want to be here for her. A moment later, Violet returns with a tray.

"Tea and toasted cakes from the ladies with the cart down the hall," she announces, and goes around the room, lowering the tray when she reaches each of us.

"This was really nice of you, Violet," I say, taking a teacake from a small china plate and placing it in my lap.

A doctor in a white lab coat over royal blue scrubs, stethoscope around his neck and clipboard tucked under his arm, approaches us. He has dark circles under his eyes. Zane follows behind him. "You're the gang here to see Angus McAllister?"

"Yes," Charlotte says, standing. She clasps her hands and looks like she might cry. Everyone else turns to the doctor.

"Good news," the doctor says. "Your friend is going to be just fine." The air is instantly lighter, and we all exhale in relief.

"Was it a heart attack?" Charlotte asks.

The doctor shakes his head. "Presented as such, because he had shortness of breath, elevated heart rate and pain in his left side. But your friend, the one who called 999, he knows his stuff. Recognized the symptoms that pointed to sepsis. That wound he endured on his arm was badly infected."

"Forty percent of people with sepsis die," Francis says.

I whip around. "Francis!"

"We caught it in time," the doctor says. "He's going to be OK. But it's a good thing he got here when he did, and that we had the clue not to run the tests on his heart first. Could've wasted valuable time."

Taj figured this all out? How could Taj recognize sepsis?

"Your friend's going to make a fine doctor."

"What does he mean?" Sindhi whispers to Roshi. Jenny, Nelle and Violet look at one another, confused.

"Did you have any idea?" Charlotte whispers to me. I shake my head, thinking about what Taj told me about his family, and how his father is a doctor.

"Anyway," the doctor continues, "we'll be keeping Angus for a few days while we keep him on antibiotics. He can have visitors. One at a time. Who would like to be first?"

Charlotte steps forward immediately. "Y'all mind?"

No one objects. She looks to the doctor. "Just let me put on my lips," she says, rummaging around in her purse, then stopping. "Oh, for heaven's sake, he's not going to care one bit what color my lips are."

I laugh and reach out to squeeze her hand. Charlotte follows the doctor through the arch into the hall.

Everyone else has a visit with Angus, and when it's finally my turn, I walk down the hall, the sound of laughter coming from the nurses' station. The lights are bright, the floors shiny, the smell of rubber and alcohol in the air.

The door to Angus's room is twice as wide as a regular door, and sage green. One bed juts from the left-hand side of the room, a sheer curtain pulled partway around. Behind it Angus is reclined in the bed, his head propped up with pillows. His skin remains the color of porridge, the areas under his eyes green, but he manages to smile softly and lift an arm. I see a clear tube affixed to the back of his hand with tape.

"You must be tired," I say, realizing now that he could probably do without one more visitor.

"Finally got my own room," he says brightly, and it takes me a minute to get it. I smile. "I had to give up my Harris Tweed for it, though." He shakes his head. "I've had that jacket since I was thirty-nine—so, since last year." He winks.

"At least they didn't take your funny bone."

"Didn't take anything, and looks like I'm going to be good as new. Nothing to worry about, so you can start being yourself again—no need to look so worried."

I lean over and squeeze his shoulder gently, then stand, looking him in his glassy eyes.

"I know you wished this tour started with a different guide," he says. "But I'm really glad I got to meet you."

"Me, too," I say and wipe a tear.

He grins. "I want to hear how it all works out for you." I wonder what he means—if he means with Zane. He couldn't possibly know about Taj—not that there's anything to report anyway. I want to ask him where Taj is, if he's seen him, but I can't bring myself to make this about me any more than I already have.

I smile and nod, then turn toward the door. "Bye, Angus."

Charlotte's standing outside the room, waiting for me, wringing her hands. "Can I talk to you?" she asks.

For a split second the thought crosses my mind that Angus *isn't* going to be OK, that he was lying to me, and that only Charlotte knows the truth.

She takes my hands in hers. "I can't go with y'all. I've got to stay here with Angus," she says.

"What do you mean?" I ask, my eyes wide. "He's not OK?"

She laughs lightly and pats my hand. "Angus? Oh, he's going to be fine. But if I leave with all of you now, that's it. I'll never see him again. He'll go home and that'll be that. And the thought of that?" She bites her lip, which is now coated in velvety dark pink. "Well, I've given it a lot of consideration, and I'd rather not."

My heart swells with happiness for Charlotte—she knows what she wants and she's going for it. "Of course," I say. I give her a hug. "Is there anything I can do?"

She points at my chest. "Keep in touch with me?" She must see the disappointment on my face—I can't hide it—because she gives me a sympathetic smile. "This isn't how I wanted to say goodbye to you, but, well, sometimes life doesn't work out the way you thought it would, does it?"

"Mishaps make memories," I say with a smile, remembering what she said to me in her little cottage in Hythe.

She opens her purse and pulls out a pad of paper, then writes on it and hands it to me. "That's my phone number and my address, in case you ever want to send me a note."

"I'll send you a book, with a note tucked inside," I say. Then she reaches in her bag again, and pulls out a small rectangular box. "I was saving this to give to you at the end of the tour. I guess this *is* the end of the tour for us."

I take the box and open it, then slide out a gold tube into my hand. I realize what she's given me. The lid clicks as I pull it off, and I peek into the end, at the bright-pink lipstick.

"So you can put on your lips," she explains. I shake my head and laugh.

I give her one more hug and leave her to return to Angus. When I turn the corner, Taj stands at the vending machine near the entrance. I freeze in place, as though the door to the vending machine is open, filling the hall with cold air. My breath catches, as though it's frozen, too, and I try to slowly inhale to thaw it. I walk toward him as he bends low, pushing his hand through the black metal slot and retrieving a yellow Flake bar. I stop a step away. Standing so close to him makes my body feel numb. I want to hug him, to hold him, to ask him what happened last night. To know if he's OK, to find out how he's feeling after everything that's happened with Angus. To know what's going on between us.

"Angus was lucky you were there," I say softly.

He turns, and looks at me, his dark eyes impassive.

"A doctor . . . that's the plan your parents had for you?" I ask.

He clears his throat. "I've called a couple of taxis to take all of you back to the hotel."

"Won't you come with us?" I ask quietly. "With me?"

He shakes his head. His jaw is hard. "Nah. I want to stay a bit longer with Angus."

My stomach sinks. A feeling of wrongness settles over me. "Taj, what happened last night?" I say. "You said you were coming, and then . . . ? Did I do something?"

I trail off, hoping he'll jump in to fill in the blanks. He just watches me. Oh, what the hell. "I really like you," I say.

"Gigi, I don't think your story ends with the *bus driver*." His voice is flat, his eyes dull. "Good luck with the tour guide." I feel dizzy. He brushes past me and I want to turn, to call out to him, but the room is spinning and I have no control over my limbs. And it probably doesn't matter anyway, because there's no way he's going to turn around. Not if he knows about Zane. And that seems like the only explanation.

Chapter Twenty-Five

Day 9, Monday, 7 a.m.

Bath

I force myself to go to the botanical gardens early, coffee in hand, to stop obsessing over Taj. No one saw him last night, and no one's seen him this morning.

Charlotte called to say Angus is doing much better. She also said Taj left a few hours after us, last night. For where?

The botanical gardens are beautiful. Lush, full of color, full of plants, paths, and likely many other things besides that, but I don't register any of it. I can't stop replaying the details of Saturday night in the lobby. What could possibly have changed from the time Taj and I got back to the hotel, and I went up to my room, him only a few minutes behind me? What made him decide not to come to my room? And what's upset him so badly that he doesn't even want to talk about it and is willing to never see me again? As many times as I go over it in my mind, there's only one possibility. Zane must have seen him that night, seen *us* together, and told him I came here for him. But why would he do that, when it didn't seem like he particularly cared that I'd stood him up anyway? I can't figure it out.

Eventually I head back to the hotel. I'm almost there when Jenny crosses the street in front of me.

"There you are," she exclaims. "I was looking for you."

"Me? Why?" I'm confused—is the bus leaving? Zane told us we'd be in Bath 'til early afternoon, while he worked out the modified itinerary for the final leg of the trip.

"Come with me," she says.

"Where?"

"Heart-opening sound bath," she says, as though it's as common as a trip to the grocery store.

"I don't know what that is," I say.

"It's a spiritual experience," Jenny says. "You'll see." The courtyard outside the hotel is packed with people. A juggler manages five orange balls. She turns to me. "It's all over social media. A YouTuber I like is really into it."

This is all frustratingly vague. On the other hand, what else do I have to do?

Our destination is a house tucked away on the outskirts of the city. To get to it we have to walk into the woods through an overgrown path, down a dozen makeshift steps—flat rocks nestled into the dirt next to a river. At one point I realize that we haven't seen another human for a while.

"Should we have told someone we were coming here?" I say, but Jenny shushes me, her camera to her face. "It's fine. Plus, I gave my mom the address. She was my first choice but she hates this kind of spiritual stuff. She's so practical. Anyway, if we aren't back at the hotel in three hours, she knows where to find us."

Jenny steps onto a rickety wood bridge first, then follows the path through a bed of white teardrops. Our destination sits atop a small hill—a low stone house with a roof of wooden shingles.

The door is painted lilac, with a small handwoven mat. "Ready?" Jenny says, turning to me. Butterflies flutter in my stomach. I nod. Jenny knocks on the door. A moment later it opens, and out comes a woman a little older than me wearing a long floral dress, her strawberry-blond hair pulled back in a loose braid. She introduces herself as Zinnia; she has a kind smile and a soft, smooth voice. She leads us into the house, asks us to remove our shoes and then closes the door behind us.

The walls are a soft shade of white, and the smell of sage fills the air. Candles flicker on a corner shelf. Brightly colored blankets and round boho poufs are artfully arranged on thick mats on the floor. The circumference of the room is decorated with curved bronze plates—gongs, I think, suspended by cords from wooden frames. On the floor, a series of hammered metal bowls of sequentially decreasing sizes are lined up in the corner, near a selection of soft-headed mallets. Zinnia sits down on a mat, crossing her legs in front of her, twisting her feet onto her thighs. She stretches out her arms, palms up, and invites us to find a comfortable place to sit while she explains the experience. I take one of the poufs. Jenny looks around the room, then plunks herself down on a mat, her camera on her lap, the bag at her side.

Zinnia inhales, her gaze moving back and forth between us. "My role is to lead you through the experience of total immersion into sound," she says, her voice soft and melodic.

"Your role is to remove all expectation. Instead, set an intention, and let yourself be bathed in the sound waves. You might feel overwhelmed or stressed or emotional." At this, I swallow the lump in my throat. I've run the gamut of emotions in the past day. I'm not sure how much more I've got in me to give.

"Whatever you feel, whatever emotions make their way in or

out of you, encourage and accept them, as much as you can." Zinnia's gaze lingers on me, her eyes meeting mine. She inhales, closes her eyes, then exhales forcefully.

Jenny pushes her bag and camera aside, looks at me, and then rearranges the cushions around her.

Zinnia makes her way around the room, her bare feet producing only the slightest sound. She selects one of the metal bowls, fills it with water and sets it down in front of her perch. "Watch the water," she says to us. With a mallet held between thumb and forefinger, she strikes one of the gongs.

The water ripples in the bowl and settles back to still.

"Your body is 70 percent water," Zinnia says. "If the sound of the gong can produce that effect in a bowl, imagine what it will do to your body. Your *soul*." Jenny raises her eyebrows and gives me a quick nod, as if to say, *see?*

Zinnia tells us to lie down and make ourselves comfortable. I put a pouf behind my head, another under my knees. A moment later Zinnia covers me in a blanket from neck to toes. A sand-filled pouch presses across my eyes. The weight is comforting.

"Inhale," she says softly in my ear, and I breathe in through my nose and slowly out through my mouth.

"Again," she says softly. "This time, when you exhale, I want you to let it out as loud as you can, to really expel any fears you may have. Tell yourself that they are not welcome here."

I let out a massive sigh. So does Jenny, and hers lasts twice as long as mine, which makes me feel self-conscious, as though I'm not doing this right. But I tell myself to stop worrying what Zinnia or Jenny think. They're not thinking about me. That's not the point. Zinnia tells us to let our bodies sink into our mats, to let our eyes roll back, to let our feet turn outward. "Let go of everything," she says. "And just be free to welcome any new thoughts, any new emotions into your body." She begins to hum, a deep, low tone that seems to come from the back of her throat. She chants words too low to discern. The gong fills the room. It sounds distant from my ear, and yet, it feels as though it's resonating deep within my body at the same time. I shift on the mat to a more comfortable position.

Why did I really come? The question fills my head. Not here, to the sound bath. Here, to this country. It wasn't as simple as my friends buying me a present for my thirtieth birthday. On a deeper level, I needed this. Sure, maybe I was curious about a voice—about the person I thought could be my soulmate. But that feels like I'm just skimming the surface of the water for this answer. The truth is deeper.

I inhale, then exhale, inhale, then exhale. The humming grows louder. The gongs, more intense. The result is a harmony of sounds. One that, for whatever reason, unlocks a door inside me. *Escape* is a big reason I came. Escaping the sadness of my story—of never again having my mom and dad in my life. Of knowing that anything that happened in the future would never be something I'd get to share with them. Dad will never walk me down the aisle on my wedding day. Mom will never meet her grandchildren. I fell in love with the idea of Zane because he felt like a tie to my parents. The fact that Zane was narrating the story that helped bring my parents together felt like it was keeping them alive, in the same way that their voicemail was, or the way I stayed with David way too long, because he knew my parents, and my parents liked him so much. With Zane, his family story was so similar to mine, too. I'd envisioned discarding the sadness of my own family's end and adopting his parents instead.

I thought Zane was the missing page I needed to keep my story going. But it turns out, it wasn't about finding the pages to complete a story. The story of my family is finished. Now, whatever family I make, that's a new story. One I can't write entirely on my own. It's one that has to write itself, organically.

I consider all that's happened on this trip. Impossibly beautiful weeds growing in walls, Sindhi and Roshi finding their way back to each other after years of growing apart, a desert reminder of a long fight between land and sea, Nelle and Jenny carving out a new relationship, churches reminding us of the history of humankind, of generations of lives lived and lost, Charlotte finding new love, and coming so close to losing it.

And Taj. Right in front of my eyes the whole time, only I was too blind to see the story that was writing itself.

"Let go of expectation," Zinnia says, her voice melodic, swirling with the reverberation of the spoons in the bowls. "Hear yourself. Listen to your heart. Focus on the present. Cut the ties that are keeping you bound in place. That are pulling you along, forcing you to make sense of it all. Every thought is unique. Every emotion stands on its own. Your entire being is comprised of contradictions. Hold the pieces that feel right, reject the pieces that feel wrong. Embrace yourself as you are. In this moment. Not yesterday, not tomorrow. But now."

A minute later the bowls quiet, and a bell chimes like the door to the bookshop opening and closing again. "Our session has come to an end," Zinnia says. I reach up, my arms heavy, to remove the sandbag and slowly open my eyes, adjusting to the soft flicker and glow from the candles. "Take a moment to breathe slowly, to be kind to your body. You may not feel anything right now, you may feel at ease or you may feel discomfort. Allow whatever you're feeling to stay with you, welcome it if you can into your soul, give it permission to stay with you for as long as your body needs it." I sit up. My face feels damp. I touch my cheeks, and confirm that my face is wet with tears.

.

Back outside, I slide my sunglasses on and sling my bag over my shoulder. Jenny and I walk in silence. Eventually, I turn to her as we make our way back through the forest to the road. Her camera's slung around her neck. "Thank you for asking me to go with you," I say.

"Wasn't it incredible?"

"It really was," I say slowly, still processing it all. "It was such a surreal experience. I wasn't sure what to expect—or whether I'd just fall asleep. Now I feel so rested, and yet I was so aware of everything. And it didn't feel quick or long, but sort of like time was standing still."

She sighs. "I'm so glad I did it."

She runs her fingers through her long shiny hair, then pulls it high into a ponytail. We make our way back over the bridge and through the forested trail. "I was kind of disappointed my mom didn't want to come, but I think maybe it was better that she didn't. A lot has happened that I just sort of shut away, and I think if she had been there, I might have been too aware of her presence and not let myself process it all in the way I did." She shrugs. "Or maybe it would've been a bonding experience. I guess it's whatever I want to tell myself," she adds, sounding for the first time on the trip so much older than her twenty-one years.

As we reach the road, we turn left, and Jenny looks over at me. "You want to keep walking for a bit?"

I nod. "Sure." I pause. "Are you guys better now? You and Nelle?"

Jenny exhales. "I guess. We haven't really talked about any of it," she says. "That's part of the problem. It wasn't so much that she came out—even though I was surprised, I really did *not* see it coming—but it's, like, she just acted like it was all going to be great now that she was gay and had found love." Jenny shakes her head and lets out a bitter laugh. "Like, you ruined your marriage and you divided your family, but everything's great because you found the person you love? Maybe that would have been fine if she was this free spirit and everything she did was like, 'Oh, it'll all work out!' but the woman is worried about *every little thing*. You get a splinter and she worries there might be metal in it and you'll die of tetanus. But then she upends our entire lives and she isn't worried about the ramifications one bit?" Jenny throws her hands in the air and sighs loudly.

A woman walks by with a small fluffy dog, and I move out of the way to give her space, then walk closer to Jenny again.

"I think, as her daughter, I should have been allowed to be upset for a bit. But she just wouldn't let me. She kept trying to make it seem like everything was OK," Jenny continues. "That's how she always was with me—'Don't be sad that you're adopted and have never met your real parents because they didn't want you anyway!'" Jenny uses a fake-happy voice, throwing her arms in the air, her fists pumping like she's a cheerleader. "Be happy that you have us." Her tone changes. "I know that sounds ungrateful, but it's hard, feeling like you've been abandoned. All I ever wanted was for her to acknowledge that. And with this whole thing with Violet, I don't have a problem with Violet and of course I'm going to be fine with all of it, but why couldn't she just give me time to be upset or sad or *any* emotion at all? Why couldn't she be worried for once how this might affect all of *us*, and just let us *be* for a bit? I just wanted to be sad. Why couldn't she just let me be sad about the end of our family?" Jenny looks up at the sky.

The road forks at a cemetery and I scan both roads, then lead us to the left. "Of course you're sad," I say softly.

The town comes into view. "Or hurt?" I suggest. Jenny's mouth tightens into a straight line, and she stares straight ahead, but doesn't say anything. "Maybe it's too big," I say. "The little stuff that she worries about—that's manageable. But maybe with this, she couldn't let herself worry. Maybe your mom thought if she let you be unhappy you might not have a reason to stay," I say. "You're old enough to move out on your own, obviously. And maybe she thought your love for her is conditional—that she's not your biological mother and that you don't really have to stay with her."

Jenny looks over at me, and her expression softens. "Well then I wish she would say that. It's ridiculous and she would never *not* be my mom. But I wish, if she felt that way, that she could just be real. Even if that means one of us being mad or sad or whatever. I'd rather that than make believe."

The sun peeks out from behind a large stone church. I take off my sunglasses and look at Jenny. "Have you . . . have you told her *that*?"

She shakes her head, her hair falling over her shoulder. "No. But I think I will." She looks like she wants to say something else, then reconsiders. "I wanted to thank you."

"For what? Coming with you? I'm glad I did."

She shakes her head. "For that day in the forest."

"You already did," I remind her.

"Not just for checking on me, or being nice. You gave me a hug," she whispers. "I really needed it. I wanted to thank you on the boat, but I was too proud." Her eyes well up with tears, and my own nose tingles.

"Oh, Jenny." I wrap my arms around her.

When we get back to the hotel, the bus is out front. "Shoot, I didn't know we were leaving this soon. Did you?" I say to Jenny, but she looks just as confused.

Zane loads suitcases under the bus. "I've reworked the route," he announces, looking at Jenny rather than me. "We'll try to get us somewhat back on schedule. We still have time for a drive through the Cotswolds and Oxford today before getting back to London tomorrow on schedule." He's talking logistics but all I care about is Taj.

"Where's Taj?" I ask.

"Gone back to London," he says, then picks up a large brown soft-sided suitcase.

"What do you mean, he's gone back to London?"

Someone calls Zane's name, and he turns toward the entrance to the hotel. "Coach leaves in twenty minutes. Gather your things, you two."

Jenny hurries inside. I follow.

Gone back to London? What am I going to do?

.

The bus feels empty without Angus or Charlotte. Or Taj. Zane's behind the wheel and I head straight to the back of the bus, sliding into the empty seat across the aisle from Francis, who's also sitting alone. Charlotte's knitting is in the seat pocket in front of me. Francis fiddles with the recorder in his hands. He looks over at me nervously.

"Are you OK?" he asks, leaning toward the aisle.

I shrug, then look out the window. The bus rumbles across a bridge. The river below is muddy and barren.

I take the needles and knitting out of the pocket. The needles are cold. How did she loop the yarn—over, or under? I begin looping one needle through the other, weaving the yarn overtop of the end.

"It never looks like anything at first. You just have to trust the process," I hear Charlotte saying.

There's a click, and out of the corner of my eye, I see Francis leaning close to his recorder. "Gigi is knitting Charlotte's . . ." he pauses. "What's that supposed to be?"

I glance over to Francis, then back down at the soft yarn in my hands. "I'm not sure. There's no real plan, I don't think."

He presses Stop on his recorder.

"How many tapes have you gone through in that thing?" I ask. The analog cassette tape recorder makes me nostalgic for my parents' version of the bookshop, back when people still had cassette players in their car. My parents had a whole section of audiobooks on cassette. Dad always said they were an easy sell in summer— people heading through Ann Arbor on road trips, looking for something to pass the long hours on the I-94.

"This is my seventh," he says. "I brought ten, one per day. Wasn't sure how many I'd need."

Need for what?

"Why do you—" I pause. "Why do you record everything?"

Francis looks out the window. The river tucks in and out of view. He's quiet for a few moments. When he turns back, he doesn't say anything, but I nod toward the seat beside him, and he knows what I mean. He nods back and I slide out of the seats, across the aisle and into the seat beside him, bringing the knitting with me.

He doesn't say anything, and I ask the question again.

"I have early-onset Alzheimer's," he finally says, his voice barely above a whisper.

My fingers dig into the deconstructed security blanket in my lap. "I'm so sorry," I say.

"Me too." He shrugs. "I found out a few months ago. It's supposed to be gradual, and so far it's only been the occasional lapse here and there. One time I couldn't figure out how to get into my house, even though I was staring at my keys. And then you caught me the other day, in Dungeness."

I nod. "That must have been scary," I say, remembering that moment, wishing I'd taken the time to ask him then what was going on.

"Is it—" I falter. "Do you know how quickly it will progress?"

"The doctor said it can start any day. And . . . he gave me this list of things to do. Post-it notes and wipe boards to remember short-term things, egg timers to remind myself to eat lunch or take my medication. I tried doing it at home, but here . . ." He pauses. "It's harder to keep track. The days sort of blend together . . . this could be the last trip I can take on my own." He looks over at me and smiles sadly. "I realized I might not remember it, so I got the idea to record it. At first I was going to use a video camera, but I didn't want everyone to think I was recording them. This was just for me, so that when I can no longer remember, I can listen. Hear the things that were going on with the group. The people I've met. That's the real stuff. The facts—they're sort of a tic, when I'm feeling nervous. It grounds me. But I like that I'll have those, too."

My nose tingles and my eyes sting. I look at Francis, but he's blurry. I cross my arms over my chest and blink, and the tears start to flow. "You don't have to say anything," Francis says, patting my hand. "It's going to be OK, Gigi." But the thing is, I know it won't be. My cheeks are wet. I flip my hand over, and he lets me take his hands in mine. For a moment neither of us says anything.

"You know, I'm really glad you came on this trip." I smile at him through my tears.

His lips turn up at the edges and then he smiles broadly. "Me too."

Then I nod to the recorder. "May I?" I ask.

He scratches his head, his fingers disappearing into his puff of hair, then nods and picks up the recorder from his lap. He presses the Record button. I hold it close to my mouth. "There is a 100 percent chance that I am going to really miss you, Francis. I learned a lot of facts that I didn't know—and many I'd forgotten. But I'm not going to forget you. And if you ever want to know who I was, or remember the details of this trip that you didn't record, you can call me." Then I leave my phone number. I'm about to press the Stop button, but don't, my thumb hovering over it. "Oh, by the way, this is Gigi." I push the Stop button and then hand it back.

"Thank you," Francis says, sniffling. "Now I just hope I don't forget how to turn this recorder on." We laugh, and I wipe away my tears, my face damp and clammy.

"Gigi?" Francis says.

"Yeah?"

"There's something you should hear," he says.

"OK." What could it be?

He fiddles with the recorder, pushing Rewind, then Stop, then Play, then Rewind again, watching the timecode change on the tiny dial. After several attempts, he says, "OK, this is it."

He presses the red button. The sounds are muffled at first, and then Zane's voice comes in clearly. "Taj." My heart pounds. What am I listening to? Except, I know. This is the answer. This is what I suspected but didn't want to admit had happened.

"What's up?" Taj says coolly, in the recording.

"I could ask you the same thing."

"Zane, your point?"

"Oh, I have many. But I think I'll save the best for last."

"Can't wait," Taj says. There's a muffled sound. "A glass of sauvignon blanc and a Coke," Taj says.

"Was this on Thursday night?" I ask Francis, hoping I'm wrong, but knowing I'm not. He nods. Taj must have gone into the bar to order drinks for us, while I was in my room, waiting for him to come up.

"You and Gigi look like you're getting pretty intimate."

"Were you *watching* us?" Taj says, bored amusement in his voice.

"Pretty hard to miss."

Clinking of glasses, muffled voices eats up the next few seconds.

"What's your point, Zane?"

"I think you should know that Gigi came here for a special reason," Zane says. I look around, sure that all eyes will be turned back to me, wondering how they're hearing Zane's voice at the back of the bus, but it's all backs of heads in front of me. And yet, I feel zero comfort. I reach out to touch the recorder, to stop Zane from saying whatever he's about to say. I can't hear this. But I pause, my fingers inches away from the black box. I shouldn't touch it. I try to meet Francis's eye, but he's looking down, at the recorder. I close my eyes, wishing I could disappear as Taj's voice comes on the recorder instead of Zane's.

"I don't think it's your business to tell anyone why Gigi's here, and I certainly don't want to hear about it from you," Taj says and I feel a second of relief, like maybe Taj will get up and walk away, or somehow convince Zane not to say whatever he was going to say. My nose is still stuffed up from crying and I can't breathe through it, so I open my mouth slightly, avoiding making a sound. *Please don't say it, Zane.*

But Zane wastes no time. "She came for me."

"Really." Taj's voice hardens, but there's interest there, too. My eyes are still closed, my full attention on their words, their tone, trying to picture how this conversation even happened, and what they're going to say next.

"Yep," Zane says. "She listened to this audiobook I did and fell in love with my voice. Listened to it hundreds of times. Thinks I'm her soulmate." He chuckles. "That's why she's here. That's what she said, anyway. It's a bit ridiculous, of course. But who am I to argue with destiny?"

I feel like I'm standing between two bookshelves, and they're closing in on me, squeezing all of the air out of me. I double over, my hands catching my head before it hits the seat in front of me.

Don't believe him, Taj. But why wouldn't he, when it's true? At least, some of it. Yes, I came for Zane, but that's not the whole story. Anything Zane says is probably the truth, however, mortifying it sounds, and I don't want to lie, I don't want to hide who I am, and yet I don't want Taj to hear about it this way.

"You're full of shit, Zane." It doesn't make me feel any better to hear that Taj doesn't believe him.

"Meh, doesn't bother me one bit what you think. If I were you, though, I'd ask to check out her collection of audiobooks. See for yourself. Doesn't really make much difference anyway."

"And why's that?"

"Because she'd never be with you. You're the coach driver. Pretty sure that's exactly what she said." Black spots float in front of my eyes. *"I'd never be into our bus driver."* Zane puts on a falsetto American accent. "When we were in Lyme Regis," he continues. "That's when she said it. That was in the afternoon, 'course, when we were alone on the beach. There wasn't much talk of you in the evening. If you know what I mean."

There's a ringing in my ears and black spots in front of my eyes. I'm not sure if there's silence for a few beats or I've missed something Taj has said, but the next bit is Zane again.

"Oh, and Taj?" He doesn't wait for a response. "We have a strict no-hooking-up-with-guests policy. For staff, of course. I'm sure you read that when you signed the contract. And I know that wine isn't for you. Either way, you're fired. Figure out your own route back to London in the morning."

There's tape hiss, then Francis's voice: "Zane and Taj are fighting over Gigi, the beautiful single woman who is so kind, and so strange. Zane just told Taj he's lost his job. Everyone will be so disappointed. Especially Gigi."

Tears soak my cheeks. How could Zane do that? *Why* would he do that? But of course I know why.

Francis looks at me, scratches his curls. "I'm sorry, Gigi. But I thought you should know what he said. He may be a fine tour guide, but saying those things about you—he's not a kind person."

I want to scream. I want to throttle Zane. I also want to curl up and hide from the world. My head hits the seat in front of me. None of this would've happened if I hadn't come on this trip. If I'd just kept the whole thing a fantasy, never allowing myself to take action, I wouldn't be feeling any of this right now.

I reach down into my bag for my phone. I hit the entry for the shop's voicemail, listen to my own voice and then press the # button to listen to the saved messages.

The robotic voice announces, *You have no saved messages.*

I pull the phone away from my ear and stare at the screen. "What?" I say aloud, looking for a mistake—that I've called the wrong number.

"Gigi?" Francis says, sounding concerned.

I slide back to my original seat across the aisle. End the call, then try again, going through the prompts, pushing the buttons I memorized years ago. But when I enter the password, it's the same thing. *No new messages.*

It doesn't make any sense. Where are the messages? Where is *their* message?

And then realization comes. The most plausible answer. I hang up and call Lars. I barely wait for him to say Hello.

"Did you"—and I stop. I try to catch my breath, but all I can get is a shallow gasp of air. "Did you erase the saved messages on the shop voicemail?"

Please say no. Please say no. I hold my breath, waiting for his answer.

"What? Sorry, what's going on, Gigi? You sound weird."

"Did you erase the saved messages? Did you?" My voice is high and panicked. I'm rocking back and forth, shaking. "I need you to think it through. Lars, the voicemail for the shop. Did you check the messages?" My fingers are shaking so badly I can barely hold on to the phone.

"I-I," he stutters, sounding rattled. "I definitely *checked* the messages. It was on the pad you left, right? I was supposed to." He sounds confused. "Is this about an order? Because if it's that woman—I can't recall her name—Bette, maybe?—she placed an order by voicemail, but she came in because I hadn't filled it. She was upset but I dealt with it. Did she complain to you?" He's talking it out, and I keep trying to interrupt him, but no sound is coming out of my mouth.

"Did you erase them?" I croak out.

"Yeah?" he says, still sounding confused, but there's a tinge of nervousness to his voice now. "I don't know. Geeg, what's the matter? There were like five new messages, and they were all people asking if the store was open, and they felt pointless to save, then that woman and so I figured I'd heard them all, so yeah, I guess I erased them. But like I said, I filled that order, so . . . What's the big deal?"

The air is slowly being squeezed out of my body. Their voicemail—the last tie to their voices—is gone. I will never hear them talk to me again.

My stomach heaves as though I can't get the tears out fast enough.

Lars keeps saying my name, like it's a question. Gigi? *Gigi?* He has no clue what's going on—and that's part of the problem.

Finally, I choke out the words.

"I did everything for you, Lars," I say into the phone. "I've run the shop for eight years. You haven't helped at all since they died—just like you never helped when they were alive. And all I asked was for you to run the shop for me so I didn't have to think about it for ten days, and you ruined everything. They're gone now and it's all your fault, Lars!" I shout with frustration.

"Gigi, what are you talking about?" Lars says, his voice full of concern. "What do you mean I ruined everything?" Then his voice changes and he sounds angry. "I've been here every day, running the shop, just like you asked. I'm not going to be bitter about that because I said yes, but you haven't been grateful, you've just nit-picked at every little thing I didn't do your way. I don't know what you're talking about, this whole message thing, and I don't even care." Now he's shouting at me. "But let's get something straight. If I never ran the shop before it's because I didn't want to. Big deal. You chose to keep the shop, and that was your choice, Gigi."

I think back to those first days, how nervous I was to manage the store without Mom and Dad. "No one made you do that," Lars says, lowering his voice, though it's still full of anger. "Not me, not them. You kept the shop because you *wanted* to keep the shop. Don't put that on me. *You* turned it into a romance book-shop because *you* love romance novels." If Lars were in front of me now, I know he would be pointing his finger, jabbing it into my chest. "So whatever grudge you're holding, you should first get your own story straight."

My heart pounds in my ears. I want to speak, but I can't hear my voice. He's right, all of it. I wanted the shop. And sure, I wanted

Lars to run it with me, but he didn't want to. He had other ideas. His prerogative. I changed the story—to be mad at him for not helping out. Because it was easier to be angry with him than to feel hurt by him.

Lars's voice softens. "What was the voicemail?" When I'm silent, he tries again. "Breathe, Gigi. Come on. Just take a deep breath."

Eventually I get the words out. "It was Mom and Dad. They left me a message, the night they died. On the shop's voicemail."

Lars doesn't say anything for a minute. Then he speaks. "I remember that message. You played that for me. You played that over and over again—for days after. Oh, Geeg, you kept that? All this time? Is that healthy?"

"Lars, who cares whether it's healthy?" I hiss. It was the only *real* thing I had of Mom and Dad. Their voices, keeping them alive. And now I have nothing and Lars is focused on whether it's *healthy* to keep a voicemail for a few years?

"Geeg, calm down," he says, which makes me even more infuriated with him.

"Ugh, Lars. Don't tell me to calm down. That's so irritating."

Lars exhales loudly. "You keep shit like this."

"Like what?" I say, because as much as I want to end this conversation, I'm curious, about what he means.

"You hang on to things, people, places, ideas, *voicemails*. You can't bring them back. Nothing will bring them back. Not even staying with David simply because Mom and Dad knew him."

"*David?*" Where did *that* come from? "I'm not with David. I'm not getting back together with David. I broke up with David," I remind him.

"But it took you five years," he says loudly. "You never should've gotten together with David in the first place. Everyone could see he was wrong for you. And you had to know it, too. But you kept thinking you could make your relationship something it wasn't. You can't preplan life, Gigi. It's never going to work out the way you think it should because life isn't like that. If you want a life, you've got to fucking live it. It's that easy. So yeah, I guess I deleted your voicemails. Because it never crossed my mind that you were holding on to something like that for all these years, Gigi."

He says "all these years" as though it's a bad thing, but it only highlights how long I was able to keep the most special thing I had left of Mom and Dad. Eight years I protected that voicemail. And then in eight days without me at the shop, it's gone.

"I hate you." My voice is low. "I hate you so much right now."

"Great. Hate me. At least it's a real emotion rooted in something that happened in the present. In real life."

I throw my phone, and it lands on the floor of the bus with an unsatisfactory thud. I pick it up.

"Gigi," Francis says softly. I look up. Everyone's looking at me with concern in their eyes.

I need to get off this bus. I grip the armrests, my hands turning white.

"Stop the bus," I say softly, my breath catching, like the words are stuck in my throat.

I stand. "Stop the bus," I say again, finding my voice. Zane's face, in the rearview mirror, turns to me.

"STOP THE BUS!"

Zane holds up a finger. The bus turns into a parking lot and lurches to a stop.

I fly forward, grabbing the tops of the seatbacks to steady myself, then make my way to the front. "I'm getting off," I say to Zane.

"*Everyone's* getting off," he says drily. "We're in Bristol."

He pulls the lever to open the passenger door. I rush down the stairs and look around. The sky's dark, like my mood. Jenny's off the bus next. "What's going on with you?" she asks. I shake my head and focus on the doors, waiting for Zane to emerge. He's last. Everyone else seems to skitter away, as though I might blow at any second. They're not wrong. I march over to him.

"How could you?" I say, trying to keep my voice calm.

He stares at me blankly. "Hmm?"

I cross my arms over my chest, my heart pounding in them.

"Could what?" His voice has an edge.

"How could you say those things to Taj?"

He raises his eyebrows. "What? That you came here for me?" His eyes are locked on mine. *Don't look away, Gigi.*

"I thought he deserved to know. Wouldn't *you* want to know?"

My eyes sting, and yet, I refuse to break his gaze.

"But it wasn't your place, Zane," I say quietly, aware that everyone else, who's now filed off the bus and is standing around, presumably waiting for Zane to lead the tour, can probably hear our conversation.

"When did you decide you liked Taj?" Zane asks. The edge is still there. Now, Zane looks away. "Before you kissed me, or after?"

His voice is as smooth as ever, but the edge has been replaced by what I think is hurt. I open my mouth but the words don't come.

He looks back at me, and his eyes narrow. "You crossed an ocean for me, Gigi. That's what you said."

He's right. That's exactly what I said.

I feel like I've been trying to hold up a bookcase that's leaning forward. It's too heavy, it's too much. The books are—one by one—falling to the ground around me. I can't keep the bookcase and the books together any longer. The only thing left is to let the bookcase fall, too.

"You're right, Zane. I did." Maybe it's OK to let the bookcase fall. Maybe the way out isn't by holding the bookcase up, but by letting it fall and stepping over it. So that's what I do. "I guess some things don't go according to plan."

I turn and walk away, past one other tour bus in the parking lot. Then I realize I need my bag. So much for my grand exit.

While Zane opens up the luggage compartment, I turn to Jenny, who's closest. "I'm leaving. But I'm really glad I met you." Her eyes widen.

"What do you mean, you're leaving? You can't just leave."

Everyone gathers around me, firing questions at me, but there's no time, or need, to get into it all. I turn to Francis, who's appeared at my side. "Thank you. You didn't have to do what you did, and I'm glad." I throw my arms around him. He looks alarmed but hugs me back anyway. "I'm going to miss you," I whisper. "If you ever want to remember anything about this trip, make sure you do call me, OK?" He pats my back and pulls out his recorder. "Gigi's leaving. She just hugged me goodbye. I'm going to miss her, too."

Then I say goodbye to Violet and Nelle. "You're a good mom," I tell Nelle. "Jenny is lucky to have you." I turn to Violet. "You too."

To Sindhi, I say I'm going to call her one day, if I'm ever married with kids and things aren't going well.

"I'm not sure I'll have very good advice for you," she says. "Except this: things change. Don't hold on to the way they used to be." Roshi rips out a page from his crossword book and hands it to me.

"For posterity," he says. I slip it in my bag, then hug him, too. Jenny whistles to get everyone's attention. "Come on, come on." She holds up her camera. "One for the street. Don't look at the camera. And don't smile too much. Just act natural." We all look at each other, then laugh because she's just made this moment anything but natural.

"OK, OK, that's enough," she says, once she's taken her photo. I look around one more time, wave goodbye and then lead my rolling suitcase out past the tourist parking lot. I have no idea where I'm going, and I've never felt more sure of my decision.

Chapter Twenty-Six

Day 9, Monday, 3:30 p.m.

London

The train trip from Bristol to London takes two hours, and I use them to think, to consider what Lars said. Was he right—did I think that if I found a story similar to my parents', I'd somehow bring them back? They met each other accidentally, in the real world, not matched together by an algorithm. And then they worked really hard at their relationship to keep it strong. There were times when Mom wanted to give up the shop, wanted Dad to get a different job. There were times she wanted to stay home and take care of Lars and me, without the distraction and stress of book sales. There were fights and there were tears and there was laughter and there was love. There were times they hated their life together and times they loved it. And that was their life together—not mine. I understand that now, I think.

The high arched-glass ceiling of Paddington Station allows natural light into the cavernous space. People bustle past along the platform in both directions. The floors are shiny and the speakers blast arrivals and departures. The pace of the place is mesmerizing. But there's no time for mesmerizing.

I stow my luggage in a metal locker, then follow the crowds through the main atrium and out onto Praed Street. Red double-decker buses line the street. Tourists carry maps and hold out phones to take pics. They pack the sidewalks, wandering this way and that, while locals walk quickly in straight lines.

A red hop-on hop-off bus passes. I run to catch it at the next stop. The entrance steps are steep. At the top, in the open air, I find a seat alone. It's a warm day but the wind is cool. As the bus ambles past a commons, a guide appears at the top of the stairs. He's young—maybe twenty—and full of energy. He's trying, cracking jokes, waving his arms—but he's no Angus. As the bus makes its way down Oxford Street, I study the pedestrians, the shoppers, the tourists and locals on the sidewalk below. I'm searching for Taj's mess of brown hair. As we wind our way through Soho and Mayfair to Marylebone and Regent's Park, apartment building after apartment building taunts me. Is he inside one of those apartments—er, flats, I should say—right now?

Mishaps might make memories. I made a mistake, not telling him the truth. But I don't just want memories. I want the present.

That's easier said than done. I call Charlotte, hoping she can get Taj's number from Angus's phone, but it rings and rings. I try the Wilkenson Tour Company general line, hoping there's a directory to their cellphones that hasn't yet been disconnected for Taj, but no luck.

"This is one of the best places to get great street food in the city," the guide says, and something about that gives me pause. Taj mentioned something about some sort of street food he loved—butter chicken, fried chicken, what was it? An acronym. Chicken Fingers Fried in Fat? There was a B, definitely a B in there. He would get it while he washed his clothes at the laundrette. *It's the first thing I do when I get home from a tour.* In Chelsea. My hand shoots up.

"Ah, we have a question from the lovely lady in blue."

"Are we going to Chelsea?"

"Ah, sadly, we are not. Fancy a football game, do you?" The bus stops and over the edge I see a line of new passengers waiting to get on.

I stand and hurry to the front of the bus, down the steps and out the doors, pushing my way through the people to the sidewalk.

FCB. CBD. It was definitely chicken, a fried chicken sandwich. FCS. No, not a sandwich. A wrap? And there were four letters. To my right I pass a salad shop and I scan the menu looking for clues, but there's nothing and I keep moving, past an electronics repair shop, then a shawarma stand. Shawarma. That's it! Butter Fried Chicken Shawarma. But not here, in Chelsea. Near a laundrette. How hard could it be? I spin around. Cars are bumper to bumper, crawling an inch a minute, and there are people going in every direction on the sidewalk. I walk, then run and weave through the crowd. At the next intersection a cyclist cuts me off, and I look around for a bike-share stand. Two blocks away, three bikes are lined up at one of those automated bike dispensers. I push my credit card into the machine and tap the screen, waiting impatiently for the page to load. With the slip of paper I race over to the first bike. The light is red. The second bike's light is red, too. The third is green. I punch in the number and the bike releases. I type *Chelsea* into my maps app, then slap my phone into the holster on the handlebars, throw my leg over the seat and start riding.

The bike is clunky and the gears won't shift, so I have to pedal as hard as I can to make it go. Where's an e-bike when I need it? A round of pedal-mashing follows, through Hyde Park, past the Victoria and Albert Museum, through South Kensington to Fulham Road, following the directions to get to Stamford Bridge, the stadium where the football team plays, as legendary in its own way as the Big House. Taj said that some nights he'd fall asleep to the roar of the teams when they were playing.

Larger-than-life images of Chelsea FC players line the road. Every bit of my body is covered in sweat. Plenty of food stands line the streets but none that look anything like what Taj described, and I don't see any laundrettes. I turn my bike around and head back in the direction I came, veering to the right, onto King's Road. Up ahead is a small block of grass dotted with people basking in the summer sun. As I stop at a light, I try to imagine Taj walking through the park. I look up at the three-story buildings surrounding the green. Trying to guess which one might be his feels pointless. I put my foot down on the curb and then turn, and there it is. Right beside me. A Middle Eastern joint with a green sign that's flashing the words I'm looking for: *Butter Fried Chicken Shawarma*. I haul my bike onto the curb and lean it against a lamppost, then rush into the small storefront. It's empty, except for a guy behind the counter, wearing a backwards baseball cap.

He grins at me. "Are you alright?"

"Hi," I say, realizing I'm out of breath both from riding so hard and nerves. "I'm looking for Taj," I say, realizing I don't even know his last name. I don't know his last name? I'm ashamed of myself. But there's no time for that now. "He's about this tall," I put my hand up six inches above my head. "With hair to here," I move my hand to the middle of my neck. "He has intense dark eyes and broad shoulders, he's really sarcastic and funny and . . ."

"Oh yeah, of course," he says, nodding. "And he's got those adorable twin daughters."

My body goes cold. "W-what?"

The guy laughs and points at me. "Sorry, that was cruel. You should've seen your face."

"You're kidding?" *He's taking the piss.*

"Yeah." I exhale and he belly laughs. "Gotcha good there."

"Gerry," I say, suddenly remembering his name.

"That's me! And *that* is why I always say Taj is one of my best customers," Gerry says. "Actually, that's not true. My best customers not only talk up this place but visit daily. Taj comes in once every ten days and thinks he's doing me a favor, the bastard," he grumbles, but there's a gleam in his eye. I lean forward against the counter.

"I will buy every single one of your sandwiches if you just tell me where he is."

"Well, you can't really buy every single sandwich. The supply is endless. And I haven't got a clue where he lives. Somewhere close by, of course, but"—he ducks and points out toward the street. I follow his gaze. Building upon building, story upon story— "your guess is as good as mine."

"What about when he leaves? Does he go left or right?"

"Yeah," Gerry says. "Sometimes he goes left. Sometimes he goes right." He gives me a sympathetic smile.

I turn to leave. Then turn back toward Gerry.

"Do you know how far it is to St. Paul's Cathedral?"

•

You should check out St. Paul's Cathedral, Taj had said, on that bike ride in Hythe, when he showed me the Sound Mirror. I pull out my phone. No one has sent me Taj's number. Darn it. The BFCS was my best lead, and it didn't work out. I look up at the sky. It's hot and sticky, and I'm thirsty and discouraged, but something tells me I have to go, to experience this audible wonder. An end to this trip, this story. And then I'll go home.

There is zero chance I'll remember Gerry's impressively detailed list of turns and merges to get to the cathedral, so I plug it into the maps app and get onto my bike. It'll take just over a half hour.

I pedal through Chelsea, along the edge of Hyde Park, down to the path that runs alongside the Thames. I have to pedal fast to keep my position in the bike lane among the steady stream of cyclists. Pedestrians color the sidewalk on one side, cars zip by on the other. Every bump in the road gives me a jolt, but I don't slow down. My legs burn, but after a week of cycling and walking and climbing, I'm fit enough to power through.

Up ahead, the massive dome of St. Paul's takes its place on the skyline, the single spire shooting straight up from the center. There's a bike station in the courtyard, and I crash the bike into the nearest available slot. I take the set of fifteen steps two at a time to the landing, and pause. Am I really going to do this—after avoiding a dozen churches in the past ten days? After avoiding dozens of churches these past eight years?

Taking a deep breath, I pass between the ridged Baroque columns, through the open double doors of the cathedral. The floor is glossy. The air smells like incense.

To the right is an oak counter. A soft woman with gray-and-black streaked hair separates the tangled headphone cords from the black audio devices. She looks up. "May I help you?"

"I'd like to . . . listen," I say, realizing it makes no sense. What am I listening to, if no one's actually talking? Think, Gigi.

"Listen? To the choir, or the organist—or a mass?" The skin around her eyes crinkles. "Oh, or do you mean the audio tour?"

I shake my head. "I forget what it's called. It's in the dome. You can hear others whispering." And then I remember. "The Whispering Gallery."

"Of course," she says, and points. "Take the stairs," she says. "There are a lot of them." She leans over the counter and looks down. Nods at my white leather sneakers. "Some people come in here in heels. But you look like you can manage."

I pay for the ticket, and she hands me a headset. I slip it into my bag and then look around, taking in the enormity of the cathedral.

The floor is a checkerboard of white and black squares, the aisles wide between rows of wooden chairs set up on either side toward the altar. Glowing chandeliers descend from the ceiling. As I approach the altar, I tilt my head back and stare up into the belly of the dome. That's where I'm headed.

To my right, something flickers, catching my eye. A row of red and white votives glimmer in the corner. I pause, then make my way over.

I slide a long match from the canister and tuck it into one of the votives to catch the flame. Then I tilt the match into one of the other votives. One for Mom. Beside that votive, I light another flame, for Dad.

I blow on the match and look down at the tiny flames, and I realize that there's nothing I want to say out loud to Mom and Dad that I haven't already said in my mind.

There's always so much to say to them, to tell them. But I don't actually need to be in a church to be with them—I talk to them all the time. They're there for it all.

So I say the one thing I can never say enough: "I miss you," I whisper.

Then I continue past the quire, the long rows of pews on either side, to a little doorway, guarded by a man in a black vest.

I show him my ticket and he scans it before saying, "Whispering Gallery closes in ten minutes. Golden Gallery stays open an extra half hour. Good luck."

Ten minutes? But I don't argue—I have another obstacle ahead of me: a steep spiral staircase. I focus on my breath to block out my thoughts—the most rational of which says *turn back*—and I climb.

A couple minutes later, I pass a sign that tells me I've made it up 52 steps so far. Only 475 left to go.

Fifty more steps. A hundred. *You did Glastonbury Tor and you can do this, too.* If only Taj were here to tell a story, to distract me from the pain. These steps weren't meant to be taken two at a time.

And then, another sign, telling me I'm halfway to the Whispering Gallery. Inhale. Exhale. Inhale. Exhale. I keep climbing.

Finally, I'm at the top. The stairs open up for just a moment, and then there's a small green door. There's a latch, but no lock. I look around for a clue, then listen to hear if there's anyone coming behind me. I pull at the door, not expecting it to budge, but it opens.

A man stands on the other side. He looks surprised. "Miss, we're closed."

Think quickly. "I left something when I was here earlier. Would you mind . . ." I point off to the other side, past him, into the distance. At what? I'm not sure. "I could just look for it?" I say vaguely. "I'll be very quick."

He clucks his tongue. "Be very quick."

The room is empty and the tiny flicker of hope I'd held out, that Taj might be here, is gone. I've been so busy looking for him, turning it into a game—find Chelsea, find the laundrette, find the BFCS shop, find St. Paul's Cathedral, find the Whispering Gallery—that there was no time to worry about the end. And now, the end is here. And Taj isn't.

The walls of the gallery are smooth concrete and curve around the entire circle. There's nothing spectacular to the walls, and yet knowing their power and heritage makes them fascinating. Saints and angels observe my progress from the ceiling of the dome. Two rows of benches line the circumference of the curved wall, the top one close enough that you can either stand and lean into the wall or sit. I run my hand along the even wall, walking to the other side of the dome, as far away from the security guard as possible. I wanted to come here, to listen, but there's nothing to listen to if I'm here all alone. The whole point is to hear the whispers of someone else. I lean against the wall. Close my eyes to listen to my own thoughts instead. I say goodbye. To Mom, to Dad. To England. To Taj.

And then I hear it: A voice that, in song, is every bit as complex as the one that brought me to this country.

"*Alas, my love, you do me wrong . . .*"

At first I don't think I've heard it right. That I've imagined it. "*. . . to cast me off discourteously . . .*" The melody rushes over me like a wave, sweeping me up, rolling me into its embrace, taking away my control. I'm powerless. And I'm OK with it. Eventually I open my eyes, find my footing. And turn around.

There he is. On the opposite side of the dome, leaning against the cream concrete wall. Blue shirt, dark jeans, his hair tucked behind his ears. He shaved. Our eyes lock, and a smile spreads across his face. I want to freeze this moment in time, because though I don't know what it means, I know that I will think back to this scene for a very long time.

I did Taj wrong. And he's here anyway.

"*And I have loved you oh so long,*" he sings softly, but it's clear as day to my ears. "*Delighting in your company.*"

I hurry toward him.

"You delight in my company?" I say when only a few feet separate us.

Taj's eyes crinkle into a smile and he pulls me into an embrace. He puts a finger to my lips, making them tingle and sending a ripple through my body. His eyes are locked on mine. My lips part, ever so slightly, and my tongue touches his fingertip. He sighs. His finger trails down my lips to my chin, and then down my neck, tracing my collarbone. Every inch he touches catches fire. When his finger finally reaches my shoulder, he slides his hand down the side of my body, both hands grasping my hips. A strand of hair has fallen into his face, brushing his cheek. I reach out, tuck it behind his ear, then cup his jaw. My other hand moves to his face and he dips his head so it's inches from mine.

"I've wanted to do this for so long," I say.

"Is ten days oh so long?" he teases.

And then our lips meet. Softly at first, then with increasing intensity. I tilt my head and press my lips into his, hungry to feel the warmth of his mouth on mine. I slide my hands to the back of his head, running my fingers through his thick, soft hair and pulling his face closer. His face is so smooth against mine. His hands squeeze my hips and he pulls me closer to him, so there's no space between us. Not between our bodies, not between our lips.

We're just accessories to the kiss. Eventually, we break for air, and I pull away from him enough to look him in the eye.

"I did do you wrong," I manage after a breath. "Taj, I'm so sorry."

"I'm more interested in the fact that you went all the way to my favorite sandwich shop in the world and you didn't even *buy* a BFCS?" His voice is low, his breath hot in my ear.

"How did you know?" I run my hands up his arms, my fingers wrapping around his firm biceps. His skin is smooth and warm. I pull him closer.

"I must have missed you by ten minutes. Gerry told me you'd been by. Well, he didn't say you specifically, but I thought, some girl came by, asking about me and asking about how to get to St. Paul's, and I thought, why not see if she's hot?"

I punch his arm. "Promise me you've never told anyone else about this place."

"I've never told anyone else about one of the most famous landmarks in the world," he says solemnly.

"You're taking the piss," I say.

His brow furrows. "Why are you here?"

"Why do you think?"

He slides his hands down to my waist, running his fingers along the waistband of my jeans in the small of my back. "I'm surprised you remembered me telling you about this place, to be honest," Taj says. "I didn't forget, but I didn't know you were really listening."

"I was listening."

He runs his hands up my back, and then down again. I never want him to stop touching me. "Remind me again why we never exchanged phone numbers?" he rasps, bringing his head close to mine, resting his forehead on mine. "It would've made this all a whole lot easier."

"Tell me about it," I say. "But would it have been as romantic?" My eyes lock on his.

The creak of the door startles us both, and we pull apart. I catch the security guard out of the corner of my eye. "Sir, Miss," he says. "The gallery is closed. You must leave." I look at Taj again.

"We have to go," I say. "We're in so much trouble."

"Then we better do this quickly, one more time," he says, and pulls me close to him, so that our bodies are pressed together. I move my hands up to his face, and then pull him in toward me. I press my lips to his, and everything else, all the sounds around us, they all disappear.

Chapter Twenty-Seven

Day 10, Tuesday, 8 a.m.

London

"What do you want to do today?" Taj says, kissing my ear. The sun streams through the sheer curtains into his second-floor apartment in Chelsea. The walls in the two-bedroom apartment are painted a light cream, and bookshelves line the wall above his bed. He made them himself. His bedding is gray and soft, though only a sheet drapes over our naked bodies. Our clothes are spread across the floor. He props his head up on his hand. I touch his bare, warm chest and think about last night, late last night, early this morning, and smile.

"We only have six hours 'til my flight leaves," I say.

"Do you really have to go?" he asks.

My heart swells. In romance novels, they'd figure out a way to be together. But I have a flight. And the bookshop. And several texts from Lars reminding me that he has plans on Thursday and I need to be home tomorrow.

So, for now, Taj and I have six hours.

"I know how I want to spend them," Taj says. He nuzzles his face into my hair and it feels so good, so easy, so exciting.

"Me too," I say, but I still feel wistful.

"We're not saying goodbye," Taj says, touching my nose. "I know that's what you're thinking. But we'll figure it out. I've never been to Michigan. And I've got to see the source of the yellow M for myself."

"*Maize*," I correct him.

"We'll see about that." He rolls on top of me and touches his lips to mine, ever so lightly. "I have one other condition, though," he says between kisses.

"Oh really?"

"Mm-hmm," he says. "And it's very important, so I want you to listen." He pulls away from me and looks me in the eye. My stomach flip-flops. Not because I'm worried, but because I can't believe that we're here, the two of us, together, in his bed. And yet, it feels completely natural, like we've been together forever.

"I'm listening," I say, putting my hands behind my head.

"From now on, whenever we drive anywhere, you're not allowed to sit two rows behind me. I want you right beside me, where I can see you and hear you and reach out and touch you." He runs a finger along my hairline. My head tingles right to the roots.

"Deal," I say, wrapping my arms around his back and running my fingers up his spine. "But I have a condition, too."

"Oh yeah? What's that?" he says.

"*I* get to drive. At least some of the time."

He laughs, then nods, then presses his lips to mine, and I wrap my arms around his back, and we stay that way—for what seems like forever, and also, just a tiny blip in time.

Will we ever be in a bus together again? Or even a car? Or train? Or plane? It's not the way real life works. I'm not giving up, but I'm also not letting myself have expectations. Taj says he'll come visit in six weeks, at the end of summer. He wants some time to figure out what he needs to do to continue medical school. And I'll come back at Thanksgiving. After that, we'll just see. And for now, we have six hours. Which is a lot of time.

I lace a leg between his and he nuzzles my neck. I run my fingers down his chest. Then lower, and lower.

"Oh yeah?" He raises an eyebrow. "Another round? How many would that be?"

"I've lost count."

"Good," he says, his voice low. "Because at the rate we're going, there's no way we'll be able to keep track."

"Let's stay this way forever," I say.

"Deal," he says, placing his lips on mine, soft at first, then with more intensity. I exhale as he pulls away and looks into my eyes. And then I lift my head up to his, and kiss him again and again and again.

Chapter Twenty-Eight

One Week Later

Ann Arbor

It's almost eight o'clock and I've just returned from a run through the Arb. It's warmer here than it was in England, and I've started getting up earlier to run, before it gets too hot. Summer in Ann Arbor is always quiet, so I'm looking forward to fall, when the town gets busy again. Now is that lull between the July tourists and the return of students, their parents in tow.

I take a long shower using the lavender soap I picked up in West Bay, then slip into a white skirt and tank top that look great against my skin, so tanned from all the time spent outside in England. I laugh, thinking of how upset Nelle was that I was wearing a white skirt to bike in in Hythe. In my bathroom, I dab on just a bit of mascara and blush, then I swipe on the lipstick Charlotte gave me, smiling at myself in the mirror. My phone dings, letting me know there's a new video posted to Murder 'n' Makeup Jenny. The tour is still with me, little reminders every-where. I wonder how long this will last, before things go back to the way they were. But the truth is, I don't think they'll ever truly return to the way they were before.

Down the stairs onto Fourth I go, around the corner, past the front of the bookshop to the coffee shop in the Nickels Arcade. The tiny shop is bustling, the air thick with the smell of the fresh croissants they bake every morning. I order two coffees, then make my way down the shaded alley, pausing in front of the travel agency. Photos of a creamy sand beach in Seychelles, rugged mountains in Portugal, and a thatched hut jutting out into cerulean waters in Cambodia flood the window. I can practically feel the warm sun on my skin. How incredible would a warm weather vacation feel, just as a chill fills the Midwest air. Dory's birthday's in the fall—maybe I'll suggest it to the girls, as a group gift idea. I tuck into the flower shop and pick up a bunch of fresh flowers to replace the gorgeous bouquet the book club girls had waiting for me in the shop when I returned home from my trip. As if they needed to do anything more for me after everything they'd already done. I close my eyes for a moment and inhale the sweet aroma of the bleeding hearts that arch out between the ranunculas, and it takes me back to that first day in Cambridge. It's hard to believe it's already been a week since I've been back— sometimes the whole trip feels like a novel, and I get that urge to grab the book from my bag, flip it open to the dogeared page, and see what the next scene will bring.

It's almost ten when I return to the shop. The door's unlocked, but Lars doesn't answer when I call out to him. Footfalls sound near the back. I drop the flowers off on the cash desk, then head down the runnered aisle. Lars is at the end of the historical romance aisle, balanced on a metal folding chair, his arms above his head, his shirt tucked into his pants. He's hanging the kite I brought him back from Brighton.

He turns. "Looks good, right?" The kite hangs between the

Millennium Falcon and the TIE Fighter. "I was gonna put it up in my new apartment, but I thought it might look better here—and then I'd see it. Since I'm going to be spending so much time here."

He climbs down from the chair and folds it, then walks to the back of the shop, and tucks it behind one of the bookshelves.

"Does this mean you found an apartment?"

"Don't look so surprised. And no, not yet, but I have a lead on a place that I'm going to see at noon. On my *lunch break*."

"Back in Ypsi?" I take a sip of coffee and look around the shop, still admiring some of the changes Lars made.

"Are you kidding? I don't want to commute from Ypsi every day. No, State Street Lofts. So close, yet so far away."

"Not *that* far away," I tease. "Want a second opinion?"

"And close the shop?" He raises his eyebrows. "Plot twist."

I laugh. "You're probably right. There's always a little surge at lunch. I should be here. Oh, this one's for you," I say, holding out the coffee cup.

He shakes his head. "I've already had three cups. I should probably pause or I'm going to need to take this kite for a test run just to burn off my energy." He walks to the front of the store. "I put on another pot, too. I got a carafe that keeps the coffee hot for eighteen hours. Made in Denmark. I don't know why we'd need the coffee hot for that long, but if we ever do, we're set."

"Great," I say, following him.

Lars suddenly turns around and pulls on the edges of his blue shirt. "What do you think?" I laugh when I read it. There's a picture of a book with the phrase: *You turn me on*. And underneath: *Love Interest*. "Merch came in ahead of schedule. You've got to see everything, actually. I'm just starting to unpack it but wanted to run my idea by you for where it could all go."

He walks back down the aisle between Westerns and Regency romances. I follow.

"How much is this all going to set me back?" I say.

"Nothing. You handle the books, I handle the merch, remember?"

I take another sip of coffee. At the record player, I place the extra coffee down, then flip through the records with my free hand. The stack has doubled in size.

"Oh yeah," Lars calls from the front of the shop. "I brought my records in. Don't have a player at home anyway, so I figured we might as well have more options here."

I pull out an album at random, and pop it on the player, then walk over to the cash desk. A stack of mail sits in a metal tray. I sift through the bills and flyers. A glossy picture of Big Ben on a 4x6 card catches my eye. The flipside features loopy cursive.

Dear Gigi,

Oh how I miss you! Angus is on the mend and chipper as ever. We're back at his home in Oxford. It's a lovely little spot with three bedrooms and a back garden in full bloom that we sit in for hours. I never want to leave. Though Angus has discovered I don't cook, so we'll see how much longer I'm welcome. When I'm back in Charlotte, you'll have to come visit.

Love, Charlotte

Under the shelf, I pull out Charlotte's knitting and turn over the completed square—or as complete as it's likely to get. I was going to pop it in the mail to her later today, but now I reconsider. Maybe I should hand-deliver it. Just to make sure it gets to her.

At the front of the shop, by the fairy lights which look even better in person than in the picture Lars sent me, Lars pulls the T-shirts, mugs, beanies, baseball caps, pens and notebooks out of the box, showing me each one as he does. "What do you think?"

"Love."

"And this?"

"All of it." It's the truth, but he could also be showing me iguanas and I might feel the same way. I like having Lars around. It's fun.

He beams, that big Rutherford smile he used to give me when we were kids and I'd praise him for building an impressive Lego tower or drawing a funny cartoon.

"But you don't need my approval. You know this stuff looks great."

"Yeah, I do. So I was thinking about getting a shelf for the window," he says, and a flash of Taj pops into my mind, lying in bed, the bookshelves he built himself on the wall overheard. If Taj were here, maybe he'd build me a shelf. But Taj isn't here. I tried calling him last night, but it went straight through to voicemail, and for the first time in a week he didn't call me back. I know it should mean nothing, but of course the thought has crossed my mind that this might be how it will go. At first we would talk every day, but then life would start to get in the way. We'd miss one night, and then I'd call back but he'd be out with friends. When he called I'd be busy with a customer, and by the time I could call him back it would be too late and he'd be asleep. Before we knew it, one day would turn to two, two would turn to an entire week, only a few texts exchanged. He'd meet someone else and . . .

"Yo, are you listening?" Lars is waving a new bookmark in front of my face.

"I'm listening, I'm listening." I'm trying not to write a story that hasn't happened, or that isn't true. There are no guarantees with Taj, but for now I'm challenging myself to just enjoy the present. As soon as Lars is finished, I'll call Taj. Maybe I'll reach him, maybe I won't.

"What were you saying?" I say to Lars. He walks over to the window on Fourth. "I designed a little price sheet; I thought we could put it in the window, let people see it as they walk by. They don't have to ask, they don't have to wonder."

"I like that."

"Great, then if you don't mind watching the front, I'll just duck out to pick up the price list at the copy shop." He gives me a sheepish grin. "You know, the one I whipped up without consulting you. Should be ready and I deserve a break right about now anyway."

I groan and he laughs as he walks toward the front door.

The bells clang as Lars leaves. I finish my coffee and then arrange the flowers I bought in an orange blown-glass vase. The bells clang again.

"What did you forget?" I call out.

"A few things," the voice says, but it's not Lars's. I know it well, that soft yet assertive tone. Blood drains from my head, as though my body is only allowing the sound of his voice, and nothing else can occupy that space. I drop the stem I'm holding, and move around the side of the cash desk. He's not there. I crane my neck. Still no luck.

"I'm looking for a book," the voice says, and I feel dizzy with the confirmation that it's him.

"We've got books," I say, peeking over the top of the row of paperbacks in front of me. Not there.

"I noticed," he says, still out of sight.

"What are you doing here?" I whisper, walking down the aisle, but I've lost all feeling in my feet now, too. I'm floating.

"You said that when you least expect it," he says, "someone can walk through the door of your bookshop and trigger the start of your story—and your lives—together." His words are like puffs of air, boosting me higher.

"I know," I whisper, wanting to slow this moment down.

"This isn't the start," he says, and I deflate, just a little. But then he says, "but what if the start is overrated?"

I float around the end of the shelf and Taj comes into view. He's wearing a light-blue shirt and jeans, white sneakers. His eyes are lighter, his lashes longer, his cheekbones higher. He got a haircut and his hair now sits just below his ears. He looks more tanned than I remember. I reach out to him, wanting to feel his skin touch mine, to bring me back down to the ground, to him.

"You're here," I say, trying to catch my breath. His fingers graze mine and tiny sparks of electricity run up my hand.

"I kept hearing about this bookshop that had *all* the books . . ."

"We don't have all the books." I take a step closer.

"Right, that's right," he says. "Just the happy endings. Isn't that right?"

I nod and throw my arms around his neck. He smells like soap and sandalwood, just like I remember. His hands grab my hips. Our lips meet. It's the best feeling in the world.

"What are you doing here?" I say when we break apart. "I thought you wanted to figure out what's next?"

"I did. Turns out without the bus tour and certain *distractions*, I can get a lot done in a short amount of time. Including setting up a meeting at the U of M's medical school next week."

My jaw drops. "You're gonna need to learn the word *maize*."

"Are you offering instruction?" His voice is low.

"Maybe I am."

"Interesting," he says, then leans back and meets my eye. "So listen," he says. "I know you think the start of the story is the most important part. That it means everything to what happens next. But I've been thinking."

"Oh yeah?" I look up at him. "And what exactly have you been thinking?"

His hands run up the back of my dress, sending tiny sparks everywhere. "What I've been thinking, is this: what if it's the middle that's the important part?"

And then his hands work their way across my shoulders, and up my neck to the back of my head, his fingers running through my hair. The soft scratch of the record player plays in the background. I wrap my hands around his waist, pulling him close again. My face tilts up. His tilts down. Our lips meet and our bodies melt into one.

"I think the middle might be the best part of all," I say when we finally come up for air.

Wishing there was a list of the books and stories Gigi mentioned in *Gigi, Listening*? Well here it is!

Anne of Green Gables by L. M. Montgomery
Bridgerton Collection by Julia Quinn
Bridget Jones's Diary by Helen Fielding
Brokeback Mountain by Annie Proulx
David Copperfield by Charles Dickens
Falling by Jane Green
Float Plan by Trish Doller
Great Expectations by Charles Dickens
The Guernsey Literary and Potato Peel Pie Society
    by Mary Ann Shaffer and Annie Barrows
I See London, I See France by Sarah Mlynowski
Lady Susan by Jane Austen
Love in the Time of Cholera by Gabriel García Márquez
Mating for Life by Marissa Stapley
"The Monkey's Paw" by W. W. Jacobs
The Mystery of Edwin Drood by Charles Dickens
Northanger Abbey by Jane Austen
The Notebook by Nicholas Sparks
One Day in December by Josie Silver
Our Darkest Night by Jennifer Robson

Persuasion by Jane Austen
Pride and Prejudice by Jane Austen
The Road Trip by Beth O'Leary
The Rose Code by Kate Quinn
Safe Haven by Nicholas Sparks
Sea Swept by Nora Roberts
Something Borrowed by Emily Giffin
The Sweet Hereafter by Russell Banks
Tess of the d'Urbervilles by Thomas Hardy
The Unhoneymooners by Christina Lauren
The Unlikely Pilgrimage of Harold Fry by Rachel Joyce
The Weather in the Streets by Rosamond Lehmann

Acknowledgments

I pitched the idea of this story to my two incredible editors, Bhavna Chauhan at Doubleday Canada and Esi Sogah at Kensington, back when we were all stuck at home, dreaming of travel: to somewhere exotic or maybe just the non-essential aisles at Walmart or Target. They, like I, loved the idea of a woman on a journey, both literally and metaphorically, and it felt fitting to be on a coach tour through the gorgeous English countryside. But as I began to write this book, I realized that to really tell the story I wanted to tell, I couldn't rely solely on old photos from past trips, and VR videos on YouTube don't provide the scent of gardenia in the air. But travel during the pandemic? Impossible! And yet, I managed to make it happen thanks to my husband, Chris, who gave me the push I needed by telling me there was no other way and by taking care of everything back home so that I could go. I don't know how you did it, and I am forever grateful. This book has my name on it, but it wouldn't have been possible without you. Or our kids—Myron, Penny, and Fitz— for understanding that writing books takes time and effort and space (and trips away to write and research). You're the best kids a mom and stepmom could ask for.

Bhavna, you came back from mat leave (thank you for coming back from mat leave!) and threw yourself into this story as though it were your own. I know how tiring work can be when you're a new mom (not to mention having to deal with foggy brain). This makes your thoughtful edits even more meaningful to me. Thank you also to editor Melanie Tutino, and to everyone at Doubleday Canada/Penguin Random House Canada including Kristin Cochrane, Amy Black, Val Gow, Kaitlin Smith, Emma Dolan, Maria Golikova, and copy editor Melanie Little.

Esi, I loved working with you, so it was bittersweet that you moved on from Kensington before this book came out in the world. I am so happy for you, but sad not to have your guidance through to the end. But I'm thankful I got to experience your wise insight, editorial direction, and wit. Elizabeth Trout, you have been a pure joy to work with—what luck to get your skilled set of fresh eyes on a later draft. Thank you to everyone else at Kensington, especially Jane Nutter for all your brilliant marketing ideas, Jackie Dinas for the audiobook details, and Lauren Jernigan and Kait Johnson for social media savviness, plus Steve Zacharius, Adam Zacharius, Lynn Cully, Kristine Mills, Carly Sommerstein, and Alex Nicolajsen.

Samantha Haywood, you are one in a million. I am so lucky to have you as my agent. Also to Megan Philipp and the rest of the Transatlantic Agency team.

To my dad, for instilling a love of travel in me. Thank you for all the planning, time and generosity it took to take us on incredible experiences around the world. And to the rest of my family—including my sister, Danielle, who once found love on a solo trip (swoon!), and the three nurses in my family who offered medical advice: my stepmom Susan, mother-in-law Nancy, and sister-in-law Julie. My mom isn't with me anymore, but her spirit lives on in Gigi's story.

To Janis LeBlanc, as always, for being there to text, talk, email, brainstorm, read, re-read, re-re-read, and edit. Plus laughs. So many laughs. And to early readers Melanie Dulos, Sarah Hartley, and Rachel Naud. Sophie Keegan and Anna

Macdiarmid read the book for its Britishness. It's better because of you, and any mistakes are my own.

To my author-friends, including the Coven, but particularly, Jennifer Robson, who helped with naming the Spires, Shires and Shores tour, suggested some logical tour routes (which I may or may not have followed), and offered other useful British advice; Marissa Stapley, who has always been there for me in publishing and friendship, and who came up with the Canadian title, *Two for the Road*; and Kerry Clare, who inspired Gigi's enviable ability to read books very quickly, and is, in general, someone I would highly recommend knowing if you ever get the opportunity (or at least, reading her books!).

To all the romance readers and book clubs on Facebook, who were a welcome community while writing, including Ronny Wilson of the Romance by the Book Facebook group, who answered my pressing romance novel question with lightning speed!

Finally, to all the romance-loving booksellers out there, thank you for loving *love* and supporting this genre (aka the best genre). I always wanted to own a bookstore. Gigi is probably the closest I will get—and I hope you will welcome her into your inner circle. What would this world be without your passion for books? I wanted to shoutout some particular people and stores that do wonders to champion this genre and send my sincere thanks.

To all the amazing staffs at: The Astoria Bookshop, Queens, NY, Belmont Books, Belmont, MA, Bethany Beach Books, Bethany Beach, DE, Black Bond Books, locations all over British Columbia, Bolen Books, Victoria, BC, Book City, Toronto, ON, Bookie's Bookstores, Chicago, IL & Homewood, IL, Bookmark, Halifax, NS & Charlottetown, PEI, Books Are Magic, Brooklyn, NY, The Bookworm Box, Sulphur Springs, TX, Creating Conversations, Redondo Beach, CA, Cupboard Maker Books, Enola, PA, East City Bookshop, Washington, D.C., Fountain Bookstore, Richmond, VA, Happily Ever After Books, Toronto, ON, Katy Budget Books, Houston, TX, Love's Sweet Arrow, Tinley Park, IL (especially Roseann & Marissa Backlin), Loyalty Books, Washington, D.C., McNally Robinson, Winnipeg, MB, & Saskatoon, SK, Meet Cute Romance Bookshop, San Diego, CA, Mosaic Books, Kelowna, BC, Munro's Books, Victoria, BC, Novel., Memphis, TN, A Novel Spot Bookshop, Etobicoke, ON, Page 2 Books, Burien, WA, The Ripped Bodice, Culver City, CA, (especially Lea and Bea Koch), Third Street Books, McMinnville, OR, Turn the Page Bookstore, Boonsboro, MD, and Word Bookstore, Brooklyn, NY & Jersey City, NJ.

One of my first jobs was at Indigo, dreaming of a day when I might see my own book on a table, so to the Indigo booksellers who have ever recommended one of my books to a customer, thank you—it means more than you probably know. And a big booklover's hug to the special Indigo booksellers who gave their valuable input on the cover of *Two for the Road*. Many people *do* judge books by their covers (and so do I!) and you made this cover even better.

And to the biggest romance lover of them all, Billie Bloebaum, mastermind behind Bookstore Romance Day, as well as her kick-ass associates Maryelizabeth Yturralde and Ryan Quinn: you would truly make Gigi proud.

If you find yourself close to one of these shops while on a summer road trip, pop in and show your support by buying a book.